BLOOD
LANCE

The Crispin Guest Novels by Jeri Westerson

Veil of Lies

Serpent in the Thorns

The Demon's Parchment

Troubled Bones

BLOOD LANCE

A Crispin Guest Medieval Noir

Jeri Westerson

MINOTAUR BOOKS ✠ NEW YORK

BLOOD LANCE. Copyright © 2012 by Jeri Westerson. All rights reserved. Printed in the United States of America. For information, address St. Martin's Press, 175 Fifth Avenue, New York, NY 10010.

www.minotaurbooks.com

ISBN 978-1-250-00018-7 (hardcover)
ISBN 978-1-250-01585-3 (e-book)

First Edition: October 2012

10 9 8 7 6 5 4 3 2 1

To Craig, my true knight

Acknowledgments

As always, none of this happens without the careful work and mentoring from my agent, Joshua Bilmes, my editor, Keith Kahla, the proofreading and fact-checking team at St. Martin's Press, my Vicious Circle, Ana Brazil and Bobbie Gosnell, and my husband—my first reader—Craig. But I would also like to acknowledge the loyal following of my mystery Readers who go out of their way to get my books, to come to my events, to send me notes and e-mails, who support me by reading my blogs, sign up for my newsletter, show up on Facebook, Twitter, and Goodreads, and who just generally send out their love and encouragement from afar. To all of you, a very heartfelt Thank You!

BLOOD LANCE

I

London, 1386

CRISPIN GUEST SNEEZED AGAIN and wiped his reddened nose on the grayed scrap of cloth he kept tucked in his belt. As he trudged over the mist-slickened lane, his tired eyes rose to a bright full moon riding on a froth of night clouds. The light's reflection shimmered off the black Thames as it churned past the piers of London Bridge. A few windows of the shops and houses lining the bridge's span still glowed from candle flames, but most were dark. It was late. Sensible citizens were already abed. Crispin shivered. Pity he was no longer one of the "sensible citizens."

He gripped his cloak tighter. Illness was miserable in any season, but this October night seemed particularly icy. He did not recall Octobers being as cold as this but perhaps the winds were changing. Summers were colder, winters longer. First it was plague and now this. Why was God so angry? Was not his anointed on the throne of England?

He coughed, trying to quiet it with his palm.

Crispin thought about the throne, about King Richard. Times had changed since the boy came to the throne and Crispin was cast from court. The king was nearing his majority. Soon he would be twenty-one and his handlers would have to step aside.

Crispin's boot slipped on the slimy paving. He swore and righted himself. Yes, Richard might still be a young man, but Crispin was nearing thirty-two and sometimes he felt far older. He'd just finished a particularly rough job with a difficult client. It had been quite a puzzle finding that stolen necklace. Were all families so greedy and calculating, forging lies and deceptions behind masks of fawning compliments and false loyalties? He was glad to be orphaned, then, if that was what it meant to belong to a dynasty, even if it was a dynasty of wealthy grocers.

A half-smile formed on his chapped lips. It had been a good puzzle, though, and well-deserved coins clanked in the money pouch at his side. If he could avoid the Watch he could get home with a decent purse for a change. He hoped Jack had something warm on the fire, though he felt almost too weary to eat. Perhaps some warmed wine. That would fill the cold hollow in him.

The Shambles seemed farther than ever but he could not make his weary limbs hasten. Thirty-two. He couldn't be an old man yet! He had many good years ahead of him, surely. Look at Lancaster. He was ten years older than Crispin and there he was, off on a campaign to Spain. If Crispin still possessed his title, he would most likely have been on the road with Lancaster, one of the many thousands of valiant knights he had taken with him to the continent. Crispin would have been armed and ready for battle with the others, not weary and sick.

He stopped and turned toward the Thames, watching the lights from the bridge play on the rippling waters. Certainly he was just as fit as before, but how could that be true when exhaustion plagued him from so short a walk across Westminster to London? There had been a time when he had practiced with his sword all afternoon.

Battles would go on for hours with few breaks. His muscles used to revel in the exertion.

Of course, that had been almost a decade ago . . .

"God's blood," he whispered. "A *decade*? How can that be?"

Nearly ten years since he picked up a sword in battle? Ten years? He supposed he was fit enough for a man whose limbs had forgotten how to balance a blade. Fit enough to recover the jewelry of vain women and protect the households of undeserving men.

He sneezed again and snuffled.

He should be the one at Lancaster's side in Spain. It *would* have been him if only . . .

No. No sense going down that deadly path in his thoughts. There was enough to worry over now. All of London feared the imminent threat of a French invasion and there was no lack of soldiers on the streets trying to keep order. Four months ago the king had declared that all London's citizens were to stockpile a three-month's supply of food, and prices had risen, fostering panic. King Richard and his minions were little better than street vendors when it came to controlling the populace. And where was Lancaster when you needed him? In Spain! Of all the foolish enterprises. Mustering all the chivalry of England to invade Spain while France watched and calculated, awaiting the moment to strike. How much more ransom did Lancaster need? How many more titles? For the first time, Crispin grumbled at his former mentor, perhaps begrudging too much the man's endless ambitions.

Disgusted, Crispin turned away from the placid Thames, determined to hurry home . . . and ran right into the Watch for his trouble.

The three men were just as surprised to come across Crispin as he was to find himself face-to-face with them.

The first man held aloft a burning cage of coals hanging from a staff. He stepped forward, showering light and embers on all their faces. "The evening bell has been rung," he said. He was young, face barely flecked with traces of a blond beard. "What are you doing abroad?"

"I—"

"Harken," said his dark-haired companion, a poleax resting upon his shoulder. "Don't you know who this is?"

Crispin waited, tensing. Three against one and they were far better armed. He was damned if he was going to give up any of his hard-earned coins for fines or bribes.

"This here's the *Tracker*." He spit the word. "Heard of him? He's the man the sheriffs are always nattering on about." Lazily, he switched the poleax to the other shoulder. "He's a man who *finds* things. Even finds criminals, they say. Brings them to the hangman."

The others looked at Crispin anew, eyes bright under their kettle helms. Crispin realized they were all quite young, perhaps only as old as the king. But it wasn't admiration in their gaze.

"So," said the one with the poleax. His grip tightened over the staff and he set the butt of it into the mud. "'Tracking' tonight, are we?"

"Aye," said the one with the light. "What poor innocent have you swindled good coin from?"

"I assure you," Crispin answered with gritted teeth, "that they were no innocents. And I do not swindle. I earn my coin with hard work. Not by harrying men on the streets."

The one with the poleax frowned. "'Harrying' you? Are we harrying him, lads?"

The one with the cresset grinned. The flames from the burning cage made his teeth gleam. "Not yet, we haven't."

"He's definitely breaking the law," said the other. "All good citizens know well enough to be indoors after the bell and in such a time as this."

The third man, silent till now, drew his sword and pointed it in Crispin's direction. "That's true enough."

Crispin's hand inched toward his dagger. "Is this how London's Watch conducts itself? Like ruffians?"

"I think he's up to no good," said the torchbearer. "And I further think he needs to be taught a lesson for his sharp tongue."

The poleax lowered toward him. Crispin grabbed it and swung both man and ax into the torchbearer. He tumbled to the ground on all fours, gasping for breath. The flaming cresset rolled into a puddle and extinguished with a hissing cloud of smoke.

The long-haired swordsman made his move. Crispin swung toward him, hands closing over the blade as if it were a quarterstaff. As the surprised man tried to pull away, Crispin leaned back with all his weight, and curled into a roll. The swordsman was vaulted into the air as Crispin braced his feet against the man's chest and tossed him, sword and all, over his head. The guard landed behind him with a hard crunch and a groan.

The torchbearer recovered and staggered to his feet, proffering his sword. The only light now was from the moon. The blade gleamed then faded with the passing whim of a cloud. He and his poleax-wielding companion flanked Crispin on either side. Crispin let instinct guide him as the men slowly closed in. Each moved his weapon, trying to decide who should strike first.

Crispin glanced back. With the discarded sword too far away, the blade currently pointed at him would have to do.

The man began a chopping stroke toward Crispin's head, but Crispin ducked under the blade and elbowed the man's sword arm up, blocking the stroke. Using the curve of his shoulder to upend him, Crispin forcefully rolled him into the poleax man. Together, they tumbled to the ground in a heap, swearing and grunting.

Now there was time to scramble for the other discarded blade . . . but it was no longer discarded. The third man had recovered and with sword held high, advanced.

Crispin pulled his knife and caught the blade's downward descent with the cross guard of his dagger. With brute strength he forced the sword up and away.

Taken by surprise, the man left himself open. Crispin sneezed suddenly into his face and they both froze. Smiling apologetically, Crispin said, "Sorry," and then punched his fist squarely into the man's nose.

Down he went just as the others behind him had gained their feet.

I'm getting too old for this. Crispin huffed a rattling breath and spun, clamping his armpit over the swordsman's arm. Using that leverage, he launched his leg outward and kicked the poleax man in the chest. He went down. By Crispin's reckoning, he would not be up again.

Still clutching the swordsman with one hand, Crispin's other fist found the man's face, and with a sickening crunch and a gush of blood, he knew that man, too, was down.

The other swordsman, spitting blood, uneasily climbed to his knees when Crispin swung out, delivering his boot to the man's head. So much for him.

Panting, he felt the hot blood that had kept him fighting slowly drain away. Crispin surveyed the carnage with aches and pains slowly creeping upon him, including a bruised jaw from when his face had hit the ground. The men at his feet groaned and writhed but made no move to rise. He sheathed his knife, shook out his dagger hand, and slowly straightened. Wincing as pain shot through his shoulders, he grabbed his arm. His foot hurt from kicking and all his muscles rebelled.

Definitely not in fighting form. He groaned.

He leaned over, trying to catch his breath. He'd still have to make a run for it should they recover sooner than expected. Of course they knew where he lived so he'd still most likely have to spend the night in the sheriffs' company, but if he was very lucky and very clever, he might yet escape a fine.

He raised his head, ready to flee. Then he saw it. The moon spread the clouds and shone a bright face, shining dazzling silver over London Bridge and the Thames below. And just when the moon was at its brightest, a man—clearly a man from all his spread limbs—fell out of an upper-story window from one of the bridge's houses and plummeted into the depths of the Thames.

Crispin hesitated only a heartbeat before sprinting for the shore. "Alarm!" he yelled. "Alarm!" He slid down the stony embankment, pebbles flying in all directions. He stumbled and rolled, then righted himself and made it to the water's edge. The tide was out, and the muddy shoreline stretched wide in both directions.

He caught the movement of shutters opening but had no time to ponder it. He leaped and plunged headlong into the icy water.

2

DARK WATER CLOSED OVER him. Crispin's scream was swallowed by the cold river. His head breached the surface, and he whipped his wet, black hair out of his eyes. It stuck to the side of his head as he swam forward, eyes searching the waves for the man.

"I'm here!" Crispin cried. "Where are you?"

Each rise and lowering of waves deceived, but Crispin recalled the trajectory of the man as he arced toward the water. He followed his instincts and swam toward the second pier with its wide pointed barrage. The water was so cold around him and the air so icy against his skin, he could no longer feel his own limbs, but he swam on. Vaguely, he heard more shutters opening, and shouts. He searched desperately for a flailing man, for surely he would be trying to save himself.

Ahead, a clump of seaweed lolled against the barrier but as Crispin neared he knew it was not seaweed. He swam quickly and grabbed the man, turning him over, but the face he saw was not that of an unconscious man. The eyes were wide open and the mouth full of water. He would not draw breath again.

A rope hit the water beside him and he looked up at lanterns being lowered over the side as he bobbed in the shadows under the bridge. Men were shouting at him to take the rope. With numbed fingers he tied it around the man and then looped the rest around himself and let them haul both of them up.

They rose heavily from the water. The Thames seemed reluctant to surrender them, but cascades of river water fell away as they rose slowly into the night. Crispin shivered uncontrollably now, wondering if he hadn't drowned, too. He tried to grip the rope to keep himself from spinning, but his hands were more like claws than fingers and he could not grip it. He hung like a sack, the rope clenching his chest uncomfortably, while within the embrace of the dead man.

Higher they went, the wind tracing frosty fingers over his cheeks and raking through his hair like icicles. The bright stars in the black night sky spun as he drew nearer to them.

Finally, hands took hold of him, lifted, dragged. Like some big fish, he was deposited onto the bridge and untied from his grim burden. Someone wrapped him in a blanket and he dug his face deeply into the rough wool, cheeks burning from cold. Someone else thrust a beaker of hot wine under his nose. He took it gratefully and with shaking hands, pressed it to his lips and swallowed, not caring that the hot libation seared his tongue and throat. It invigorated, and he was able to sit up without help and finally take in his surroundings.

He was on the bridge surrounded by the bridge dwellers. Men were scrambling. Some carried cressets and others proffered jugs and beakers of ale. The dead man was laid out on the ground and someone had covered him with a sheet.

"What happened?" people were asking him.

"I saw him," Crispin said, teeth chattering. He pointed to the strand. "I was there when I saw him fall from a window into the water. I went in after him."

"Poor Master Grey," said someone over his shoulder. He turned and the man looked down on Crispin kindly. "That was a gallant deed, sir. But all for naught."

"I was in the water so quickly," he protested. "I should have gotten to him in time."

"Do not blame yourself, sir. No one could have saved Master Grey. He was doomed before he hit the water."

Crispin held the steaming wine to his lips to warm them. "What is your meaning?"

"Bless me, but he said he was leaving London. Could any of us have guessed it was this way?"

"No, it was an accident, surely. I saw him fall."

"Alas, good sir. Would that it were true. But some men are weak and allow demons into their hearts."

"You can't be serious."

"Indeed, sir, I am." His voice dropped to a whisper and he angled close to Crispin's ear. "I fear that he has taken his own life."

CRISPIN WAS HELPED INTO a nearby shop and bundled before a fire. He knew he would never be warm again until he could get home to strip off his wet clothes, but he also knew he had to await the sheriffs. And now, surely, the Watch would be after him, too. Well, one problem at a time.

The sound of spurred boots clanged against the steps and Crispin braced himself. He turned, just as Sheriff William Staundon stepped over the threshold followed by his associate, Sheriff William More.

"By God's Holy Name," said Staundon. "Master Guest, what is here?"

"A dead man, my Lord Sheriff. Drowned."

"Yes," More interjected. The slight, dark-haired sheriff stood farther back than Staundon, who hovered in the doorway. "Why is it, Master Guest, that dead bodies always seem to be at your very door?"

Crispin coughed for a moment before laying a hand on his breast. "That, my Lord Sheriff, is known only to God and His angels."

More moved closer and peered from behind Staundon's shoulder. "What do you make of it, Master Guest?"

Both sheriffs were garbed in rich finery. Both were slight men, though Staundon was somewhat taller than More. They had pleasant enough faces, he supposed, for aldermen. Staundon's hair was a dull barley color and his beard and mustache seemed like an afterthought of a whitewasher's brush, swathed across his chin with little care, while More's face sported a neat, dark line of beard. Both men were ordinary in the extreme.

"One man suggests it is a suicide," said Crispin. "That the man jumped. Of this I have no knowledge. I only saw him fall from the window and plunge into the Thames. He must have struck his head upon a pier."

Both sheriffs "oohed."

For the last month, Crispin had had to endure these two men in what could only be described as a parade of tedious sheriffs. At least they were not cruel like Wynchecombe, or indifferent like Wynchecombe's nearly invisible partner, John More. Nor like the last pair of sheriffs, John Organ and John Chyrchman. No, these two seemed inordinately interested in Crispin's doings, looking upon him as if he were a character from some epic poem. Always, they seemed to loiter on the Shambles waiting to see what he would be involved in next. He almost longed for the days of Simon Wynchecombe.

"The coroner will arrive anon," said More. He inclined his head toward Staundon and they both made for the door.

"My lords," said Crispin. They stopped and glanced back at him. "Er . . . is that all? You will leave this now for the coroner?"

"There is little left for us, Master Guest. Unless . . ." Staundon leaned toward Crispin, and More did likewise. There was a mischievous gleam in both their eyes. "You have information you are keeping from us."

"I for one would be most interested in what you may wish to offer," More interjected excitedly.

"I have nothing more to offer, my lords. If the man took his own life then that is that."

Staundon smiled and ticked his head. "You *know* something." He turned to More. "Care to wager? That Guest will be on the prowl within the next few hours?"

"I shan't take that bet," said More, making merry over it as if a dead man weren't lying only a few feet away. "For I know it is just as likely. Ah, Master Crispin. I wish I could take a peek into your mind. It is all cogwheels and pulleys rather than bone and tissue."

Crispin struggled not to roll his eyes. For God's sake! There was a dead man here and these men were making of it a mummery. God save him from disciple sheriffs!

"It is a suicide!" he said far louder than he meant to.

Staundon huffed a sigh of disappointment. "Very well, Guest. We shall leave you to the coroner. Such a pity. Er . . . about the man's soul, that is."

"Yes, a pity," sneered Crispin at their retreating backs. He rubbed his dripping nose on the blanket and struggled to his feet. How long did he have to endure waiting for the coroner? Certainly the others, those from the bridge who knew the man, were better equipped to give their testimony. After all, one man who knew him thought it was a suicide. Crispin crossed himself. To give up one's life. He couldn't fathom it. Hadn't Crispin been in dire straits himself? But he had never given up, never given in to the melancholy that threatened to drown him. But this man took his own life. Surely it was a demon that inhabited his soul to make him fling himself from his own window to drown in the Thames.

Wrapping the borrowed blanket tighter about himself, he staggered to the doorway and leaned against it, gazing at the body that was lying in the street surrounded by wary onlookers.

The image of the man in the moonlight was seared on his eyes. He saw it again, the body falling from the upper story and arcing into the Thames. When the image played a second time in his mind, he straightened. If the man were leaping to his death, shouldn't he have . . . well, flailed a bit? Dived away from the window? But, clearly, as he saw it again, the silhouette against the bright moon showed the man, limbs limp, simply . . . falling . . . from the window.

His head snapped up as a dim figure tore from the night and skittered to a halt before him, kicking up mud. "Master!"

"Jack?" But it *was* the boy, freckled cheeks red from running. His ginger fringe was plastered with sweat to his forehead under his hood. "What are you doing here?"

"I heard that the sheriffs were off to see to a man who drowned in the Thames . . . and that there was some fool who jumped in to save him. I was mortally afraid that fool might be you." He stared at Crispin's wet coat and stockings. "I see that I was right."

Crispin grumbled a sound in answer before a deep shiver overtook him.

Jack was at his side in an instant, gripping him with strong, long-fingered hands. "Are you hurt, Master?"

"No. Only frozen to the bone."

"And you with a head cold already. Come to the fire." He dragged Crispin back inside and sat him down again by the glowing log. He grabbed another chunk of wood that was sitting beside the hearth and tucked it into the coals. "A proper fire," he muttered, gazing in envy at the stacked logs. Then he cocked an eye at Crispin. "Why'd you go and do a fool thing like jump in the Thames? Haven't you got any sense?"

Crispin squinted up at his apprentice as the boy began to pace, arms flailing.

"It's mad what you do sometimes," Jack went on, his tirade becoming louder and more desperate. "And then I've got to pick up the pieces. It's not right, sir. Not right at all."

"Are you *chastising* me? I'll have you know that I've been doing even more dangerous deeds since before you were in swaddling! Don't lecture *me,* Tucker!"

Jack stopped and looked down at Crispin with a sorrowful expression.

Oh. The boy had been worried. Crispin suddenly felt very foolish and ducked his head into the blanket.

"Well . . . I'm not drowned, as you see."

"Where did you get the bruises, sir?" He gestured. "To your face."

"A run-in with the Watch. I won, by the way. Until all this happened. Now I suppose I'll be fined."

"Here. Give over the money pouch, then."

Without a second thought, Crispin reached his hand into the blanket and untied the sodden pouch from his belt. He handed it to the former cutpurse. Faster than he could tell what happened

Jack had secreted the pouch somewhere on his person. At least those coins would be safe. For now.

A clatter of horses outside took Crispin to his feet, and he was in the doorway again. The coroner, John Charneye, had arrived with his retinue. He swept the crowd but when his eyes lighted on Crispin, he frowned and dismounted. Instead of approaching the dead man, he went straight for Crispin.

Jack bowed and backed away, finding a place behind his master.

"Guest," said the coroner. "Should I ask what you are doing here?"

"I saw him fall, my lord. They say—" And he gestured at the crowd. "They say it was a suicide."

"God have mercy. And you. What do you say?"

Crispin shrugged. "These men knew him better than I."

Charneye turned to a man standing nearby and pointed a gloved hand at him. "You! Did you know the dead man?" The coroner's clerk hurried to his side, quill poised over his waxed slate.

The man's face was mostly hidden by his hood, but his eyes widened. He bowed to the coroner and nodded. "Aye, my lord. He was Roger Grey, an armorer. A sorrowful man. God's mercy."

"Do you say it was a suicide?"

"Oh aye, my lord. Funny, him speaking of leaving London. I would have wagered good money he meant to do it the usual way. No accounting for it, is there?"

"Married? Children?"

"Neither, my lord."

Charneye pursed his lips and looked back at the dead man. "I suppose summoning a priest is out of the question, under the circumstances," he muttered.

Crispin squirmed. This was abominable. The man was dead and therefore calling a priest was moot, but still. In all decency, a priest should be called. Though a suicide's fate was known to all. They could not have a funeral mass, they could not be buried in hallowed ground. Excommunicated even from the dead.

"My lord," Crispin said slowly, "I . . . am of the mind that this was not a suicide."

Charneye whipped his head toward him. "What? Would you naysay this good man, Guest? You just said you did not know him. How can you say this now?"

Crispin shook his head. "I know all that, my lord. But I saw him fall. He did not leap, at least not of his own free will. And if I had to think about it, I believe it possible that he was already dead when he was tossed from the window."

The coroner stared, his jaw hanging open wordlessly. *Well, that's done it.* Crispin shivered and sneezed, clutching the blanket over his shoulders.

3

———✒———

THE BRIDGE DWELLERS CHATTERED all at once and the
coroner's clerk scrambled from man to man collecting his notes.
Jack shook his head, grimacing into the shadow of his hood.

Crispin *could* have left it alone. He could have made himself
believe the man was a suicide and left it at that. Escaped to his own
lodgings to warm himself and maybe get some much-needed sleep.
But he well knew what he saw, and he feared there was murder
afoot. Just as those two miserable sheriffs predicted he'd say.

Charneye was still glaring at him. Well, Crispin was not a man
to hide from the truth. Everyone knew that. Unpleasant truths,
especially. By Jack's cringing and moaning, it was obvious that the
boy agreed that it was rather inconvenient at times.

"Perhaps we should look at the body," Crispin offered.

The coroner only grunted his reply, but he didn't stop Crispin
as he headed toward the shrouded figure lying on the ground with
a wide circle of curious onlookers around it.

Kneeling, Crispin pulled back the sheet from the dead man's
head. Still, pale, and wet, the man had a dark beard and his closed
eyes sat in smudged hollows. Someone was holding a torch and

Crispin beckoned to him to come closer. The torch was lowered and Crispin probed the man's head through his wet hair. A dent. A good-sized one in the skull. He supposed he could have hit his head on a pier. His nose, also, appeared to be broken and there were bruises around his neck. Crispin was certain there would be others on his person, but this was not the place to look. He rose and stared down at the still, waxy face, crossed himself, and tossed the sheet back over him.

"Well?" Charneye asked.

Crispin scanned the loitering crowd. If murder it was, then the guilty party might still be present.

Before he had a chance to speak, a figure in a cloak was pushing its way through the gathering and finally reached the coroner. He turned his vexing scrutiny away from Crispin and directed it toward the figure, talking earnestly. Crispin could not hear the exchange but the coroner looked just as pleased by that as he had by Crispin.

Perhaps this is my cue to leave. Tomorrow will be time enough to tell the coroner what I know. "Jack, let us go. I am weary and cold and need my bed."

Jack lent Crispin an arm when the coroner and the cloaked figure both turned toward him.

Dammit.

They approached and the mysterious figure tossed back the hood, revealing a woman's face.

Crispin eyed her lustrous dark hair and haunted eyes. She was nineteen, perhaps younger. A sister of the dead man?

Without preamble she said, "Master Grey committed suicide. But you insist he did not. Why? Do you know him?"

Crispin stood and bowed. She did not acknowledge it. He could tell by her garb that she was a merchant or craftsman. The cut of her gown was fine but not that fine, and the material a bit coarser than that of a rich merchant. The hands clutching her cloak at her chin were red and raw, meaning she did the work. His eyes kept tracing the thickness of her lips, chapped, but sensual in their plumpness.

"I saw him fall, damosel. He did not seem to me to have gone out the window under his own power. I would venture to say that he was dead before leaving the bridge. Upon my examination of the . . . of him, I would say definitively that he was murdered."

"That is mere speculation," said the coroner.

"It is based on years of experience on the battlefield, my lord," Crispin countered. "I know a murdered man when I see one."

Charneye smiled grimly. "And yet you jumped into the water to save him. If you knew he was dead before he hit the water, why then did you risk your own life?"

Jack snorted beside him in agreement.

"It . . . happened so quickly. I moved on instinct. It wasn't until I saw his face and gave it some thought that I realized the truth of it. And the witness of my eyes." He gestured toward the shrouded figure. "Though he may have gotten his bruises if he hit one of the piers, there were marks on his neck. He could not have gotten *them* from the river."

The woman grabbed Crispin's arm and pulled him back into the room with the hearth. "No! That cannot be. He was a . . . a man of sorrows. I know he took his own life."

"One man claims that the dead man said he was leaving London, and that he meant in this way."

She shook her head. The hearth flames gleamed darkly in her thick tresses. "He never said he was leaving London. That is a lie!"

The coroner had followed them inside. He rested his thumbs in his thick belt. "Who are you to Master Grey? A relative?"

She ducked her head, hiding her reddened cheeks in her hair. "No. We were . . . we were betrothed."

Charneye expelled his breath and rolled his eyes. "It is for a jury to decide." He waved to his clerk and the both of them ambled toward their horses.

She followed them only a few steps and stood stiffly in the doorway, staring after them with hands clenched white and taut at her sides. After a moment she swung back toward Crispin, eyes wide and angry. "And you! Do you dismiss me as readily?"

Crispin sighed and stared at his feet. He spared a glance at Jack, who was discreetly picking at his nails, eyes downcast.

"I see," she said. She turned to depart when Crispin spoke.

"I do not believe as the others do, damosel. That Master Grey killed himself. I think that he was murdered, and if you have further information on that, then I should like to hear it."

"He took his own life, I tell you!" She grabbed her cloak and bunched it tight over her breast. "Why would you meddle in this?"

"Here now," said Jack, stepping forward. He gestured back at Crispin. "You don't know who you are talking to. This is the Tracker. Maybe you've heard of him. Unless you've been living under a rock."

Her eyes perused Crispin, from his soggy boots to his black hair hanging in wet locks to his shoulders; to his, no doubt, reddened nose. He sneezed again, his whole body wracked.

"You're Crispin Guest. Yes, I've heard of you. What business is this of yours?"

"You might have noticed the state of my clothes. I jumped into the Thames to save him."

"Oh." She nodded and moved back into the room. "I thank you for that. It was a kindness and most brave."

"I was not looking for compliments. What do you know about the man? What could make him so melancholy?"

She raised her chin. "Roger was a quiet man. Who can tell what lies deep in a man's heart?"

"What was his vocation?"

"He was an armorer. He made fine armor for many knights of the court."

"Any idea who'd want to kill him? Did he lack for funds? Was he over his head in debts?"

"No. He was well situated with no debts, praise God. Yet he took his own life." Teeth tugging at her lower lip, she shook her head. Those plump lips pressed together, and her dark eyes studied him silently.

His betrothed, was she? She seemed not so much distraught but distracted. What else was here?

A shiver wracked his body and he pulled the blanket tighter. "I'm no good to anyone in this state," he grumbled, snuffling. "I'll be back in the morning after a change of clothes and a good night's sleep. At least what's left of it." He rose and Jack walked with him to the door. The dead man was at last loaded into a cart and slowly wheeled toward the bridge's gate. The crowd still lingered and Crispin gave it one more sweep when he saw a familiar face.

He strode toward the man. Wide-eyed and frightened, he ducked back into the crowd. Crispin dove after him.

"Master?" cried Jack.

"It's Lenny. You go that way. I'll head him off at the gate."

Crispin ran, satisfied that Jack would cut off Lenny's escape toward the Southwark side. Wherever that man appeared, no good ever came of it. And to be so near a murdered man? Well, he couldn't quite believe it of the old thief, but one never knew. The man was getting bolder since Crispin had made a solemn promise not to turn him in for his sins. He was regretting that offer daily.

His soaking clothes did not help the pursuit. The cold, the heaviness of it, seemed to drag him down, but he pushed his way through the crowd and searched the shadows for signs of the misshapen thief.

The moon, though not as high as before, slipped past the protection of clouds for only a moment, revealing the lean path along the bridge, only some twelve feet wide. It was framed on either side by encroaching shopfronts and houses. There! A shadow streaked across the face of a darkened tavern and disappeared again when the moon hid beneath its sheath of cloud.

Crispin could see nothing but he followed his instincts and felt the heavy footfalls ahead. Lenny was guilty of something, else he would have remained to take whatever bribe he could get from Crispin. Even as he ran heavy-limbed in pursuit, Crispin was loath to discover what the thief had done this time.

The pursuit led inevitably to the gate, shut up tight at night and only opened to collect tolls in the daytime. But because the sheriffs and the coroner had passed through, it had remained opened. A single guard at the portcullis watched from the shadowing arch as the cart with the dead man creaked through. Crispin saw the guard get shoved by a dark figure before righting himself and brandishing his spear. The guard took a few steps past the gate but stopped, head swiveling from side to side.

Too late. Damn the man!

Crispin reached the gate and gulped in a breath before addressing the wary guard. "Did you see which way he went?" gasped Crispin.

The guard, a stumpy-nosed fellow, stared at Crispin with mouth agape. "Who?"

"The man who pushed you aside."

"Him? A demon must have taken him, for he flew like the wind. That way, toward Thames Street."

Crispin rushed forward only to stand still at the end of the bridge, listening. He could hear no steps over the rattling of the dead man's cart. Damn Lenny! "I'll catch up with you yet, you scoundrel."

He shivered again and looked back over his shoulder toward the bridge and the lighted square windows of its shops. He'd make everything right in the morning. The coroner would see eventually. Jack would make his way home, Crispin had no doubt of that. And if he didn't get home himself in short order he might freeze to death on the street. He remembered his encounter with the Watch and what might come of it and he did not relish dealing with that. But home called and he trotted along the lane, trying to keep warm. It was still a long way back to the Shambles and to a dry bed.

ALMOST HALF AN HOUR passed before Crispin reached the steps to his now dark lodgings above a tinker's shop. He climbed the outer stairs, each step becoming harder than the last. He fumbled for his key, hands frozen into claws, and managed to open his door. It wasn't much warmer than the street, but the coals were banked nicely under the ashes in the hearth. He took a poker and jammed it in, throwing on another square of peat to urge the fire into meager warmth. He dropped the borrowed blanket to his feet and unbuttoned his icy cotehardie with stiff fingers. Peeling it away from his shoulders he dumped it, too, on the floor with a splat. The shirt was next, then boots, braies, and stockings. Standing naked before the fire, he wrung out his soggy garments into a pail of wash water before arranging them as best he could before the smoky hearth. He scrubbed his skin with the discarded blanket until his pale arms and legs pinked and then he wrapped himself in it again, rubbing his damp hair as well.

He turned at the sound of the door opening, and Jack entered, shaking out his cloak before he hung it on a peg by the door. "Did you catch him?" the boy asked.

"No. But I will. He ran, Jack. That can't mean anything good."

The lad stood beside him, stretching his reddened hands toward the weak flames. Crispin turned his head and Jack did, too. Eye to eye they looked at each other, and Crispin had a chance to peruse the boy's clothing. He was lanky, all elbows and knees like a newborn colt. The young plumpness of boyhood had left his face, replaced with defined cheekbones and a sturdy chin with only a few spots competing with the freckles. "God's blood, Tucker. You've grown out of another coat. Just look at those arms."

Jack glanced down to his wrists, jutting a good handspan from the cuffs of his sleeves. "I can't help it, sir. The good Lord wants me to be tall, I reckon."

"And so you are. You will be taller than me in a fortnight, I'll wager. Fourteen are you now, Jack?"

"Aye, sir." He seemed to be wearing Crispin's crooked smile. "I'm a man, right enough."

"Not yet," said Crispin softly. "Take some coins from my purse—wherever it is you've hidden it—and get yourself some new clothes. Not too dear, mind."

Jack's freckled face blushed and his eyes drifted toward the flames. "I can get by with what I have, Master."

"Nonsense." He glanced pointedly at the hem of the boy's coat creeping up his stocking-clad thighs. "You are about to embarrass yourself."

Jack tugged down the hem that barely covered his braies but to no avail. "Well . . ."

"Just take the coin, Jack. I owe you back wages as it is. Take that, too."

Unbuttoning his coat, Jack pulled the money pouch free and opened it up. He whistled at it. "You *did* make a goodly sum."

"Yes, and we both know it won't last, so take your share now."

Jack hesitated before he upended the pouch into his hand. He squinted at the sums and counted carefully and slowly before returning six coins back into the pouch and handing it to Crispin. Crispin tossed it carelessly on the table and turned around, rubbing his backside before the fire.

Jack moved away from the hearth to fetch the wine jug from the back windowsill, poured some into a pan, and placed it over the trivet in the fire, crouching beside it. He grinned up at Crispin, chuckling. "You jumped into the Thames."

Crispin rolled his eyes. "Yes, if a foolish thing has been done, no doubt it was me doing it."

"I knew it was you. I would have laid down coin on it."

"Perhaps you *should* wager next time."

"Perhaps I will." He rolled the wine in the pan, watching the steam feathering upward. Rising, he grabbed two bowls from the pantry shelf and poured the warmed wine into them; the larger steaming bowl he handed to Crispin.

"To your good health, sir," said Jack, eyes crinkled in mirth as he raised his bowl.

"The devil take you," he murmured good-naturedly before pressing his lips to the bowl's rim. It warmed all the way down his throat to his belly. He sighed, sniffed, and pulled up a chair, tucking the blanket under him before he sat.

Jack sat cross-legged at his feet. "Do you truly think that man was murdered?"

Crispin rested the bowl on his thigh. "True, if a man was determined to kill himself, he might be lackluster in his leap, but he flailed not at all. And he might have struck his head on a pier, but his nose, too? His neck bore bruises. I have a mind the man was in a fight. Jack, I believe he was dead or dying before he ever reached the Thames."

"But the Lord Coroner does not mean to investigate. At least unless a jury charges him so. He said as much."

Crispin gave his own lopsided grin. "You know what that means."

Jack sighed deeply. "But Master Crispin, there's no money in it. Unless the sheriffs will pay."

"I very much doubt that."

"Then why, sir? We can't govern the whole city on our own, for no wages."

"Being the Tracker comes with its own weight of responsibility, Jack. As a knight I was raised with a set of rules. I believe in them to the letter. And I will not allow a lack of funds to dissuade me. I thought you knew me better."

"Aye, sir, I do. I'm just trying to manage our funds as best I can. I didn't mean naught by it."

He patted Jack's shoulder. "And I am not chastising you. Merely pointing out that calling oneself a Tracker means more than earning coin. It . . . it speaks of honor and integrity. I expect when you take the reins someday that it will come to mean the same to you."

Jack's eyes were wide and honest. "It does, sir! I swear by the Holy Virgin it does. I'll not disappoint you, Master."

Crispin smiled. "I know you won't. And so because we are our brother's keeper, I cannot let this lie. I saw the man for myself, after all. I'd see it through to the last, till he receives justice under the eyes of God. And besides," he said, watching Jack sip his wine, "the man's betrothed might be willing to pay, if she can be convinced."

A WET COUGH KEPT Crispin awake most of the night. He dragged himself from his bed when the false dawn seeped through the shutters. His nose was still red and stuffed like a winter goose.

Dressed and dry, he and Jack made their way back toward London Bridge by first light. The bells of the local parish churches were ringing Prime by the time they arrived to the gate. They paid their fee to enter and walked up the avenue. Industrious shopkeepers scrubbed down the plaster walls of their houses while some in upper stories hung garlands of dried flowers and greenery. *A festive place,* thought Crispin absently. The sounds of hammering, too, plagued the air. Something was always being built or fixed in London. He supposed its bridge was no different, though he was damned if he could envision anything more being constructed on the already overcrowded and overhanging bridge. Would they raise their houses up *four* stories?

After inquiring of a shopkeeper just opening his doors which shop it was, they arrived at last to the dead armorer's. It was wedged between a haberdasher's shop and a tailor's and extended up one more story.

The door lay ajar. Reaching for his dagger and pushing Jack aside out of habit, Crispin cautiously peered in.

The woman from the night before was there, standing in the middle of what looked like the detritus of a terrible fight.

Crispin pulled the door open, and the woman looked up. "Master Guest! You returned."

"As I said I would, damosel. Er . . . I apologize, but I was out of sorts and did not get your name last night."

"Anabel Coterel." She curtseyed.

Jack popped in behind him and swore. "Blind me! What a mess is here."

"Yes," she said warily. "I found it this way this morning."

Crispin walked in and glanced around. He cursed himself for not looking last night.

Tools of the trade hung on pegs above worktables. But the numerous armor pieces—greaves, breastplates, poleyns, cuisses—were strewn about. Such careful armorer's art, now dented and scratched. A chunk of unfinished mail hung from a splintered table edge, and even the ashes from the forge were spilled out and made a gray matting over the floor. The window overlooking the Thames still had its shutters wide open and Crispin examined the floor up to it. In the widely scattered ash, two long streaks showed the floor beneath. The streaks climbed the wall toward the window and then widened to an uneven gray swipe across the sill.

He looked to the side and the ash was a hatching of swirls in all directions, suggesting a struggle. Darker spots mixed with it here and there. More blood. In other spots, gray footprints scattered and dispersed. He crouched and examined and swore that there were two sets of footprints, possibly more. Some were smaller than the others. A woman's? Rising, Crispin rounded a table and found the ash had collected in neat ninety-degree angles, leaving a clean spot in the midst of it.

Striding to the window, he looked out. The Thames, just catching the morning sun through the clouds and casting it in shades of gold and green, churned onward below. Jack came up beside him and looked over the sill.

"That's a long way down," he said.

"Indeed," said Crispin.

"Did all this happen this morning?" asked Jack, gesturing all around him. He tilted his head toward the woman.

She shook her head. "I do not know. My father and I were out most of the evening. We hadn't yet returned when the night bell was rung. Roger often worked late, and he frequently clattered and made loud noises in his work. But last night I lay next door without a wink of sleep. I would know if there had been a sound this morning."

"Are you convinced now, damosel?"

She looked around. "It proves nothing. He was an untidy man. Only God can know what transpired here."

"Master," said Jack, turning to Crispin. "She's right. How can we know?"

Crispin fit his thumbs in his belt. "What do you observe in the room, Jack?"

His apprentice swiveled his head again and took in the scene. His eyes followed the same view, the same swirl of ash, the two long streaks across the floor and up to the window.

He pointed to the floor before the forge. "Looks like a fight here."

"Yes. And blood."

"Oh aye. I see it now, mixed with the ash. It's darker in color. Not too much, though."

"No. Not there, at any rate. Perhaps a bloodied nose. What else?"

"The struggling stopped, for these are the marks of two feet or heels dragged to the window." He looked up at Crispin for confirmation.

"Very good, Jack. And the sill. See how the ash was stirred up enough to leave traces of something large going over."

✳

"Aye, I do. That's horrible, sir."

"What does this tell you, then?"

"It tells me that whatever happened here, a man did not go willingly out that window."

4

ANABEL WINCED. HER FACE, pale and beautiful, betrayed the emotion she seemed so keen to hide. "You have proved nothing to me," she said stonily.

Stubborn woman. Why does she insist? "You said you came this morning and found it thus?"

She nodded.

"Why did you not venture here last night?"

"What would be the point? Roger was dead."

A thin veneer of fine ash lay on the worktable nearest him and he ran a finger over it. "Was the door locked?"

"No."

"No?"

"As I said," she answered with agitation.

"Did you touch anything?"

"No."

He stared at her a long time before speaking to Jack, though he did not turn his gaze from hers. "Jack, is anything missing from this room?"

"Sir, how is a body to know? I knew him not and there's all this chaos strewn about."

"Observe, Jack."

Jack screwed up his face and looked around again, stepping cautiously over the gray spots on the floor. When he got to the end of the worktable he made a noise of exclamation. "Master Crispin! Look here."

But Crispin didn't move. He continued to match glares with the woman. "What do you see, Jack? Describe it."

"Something's missing from here, right enough. Something rectangular. Perhaps a box?" He cast about again and saw what Crispin did: There was nothing there resembling anything that could have made that mark. "Whatever it was, it was taken away after the fracas, for the floor is not covered in ash but has left an outline of it."

"Very good, Jack. Mistress Coterel, are you certain that you removed nothing from this room?"

"Of course I am!" Her cheeks reddened prettily.

"And what of his apprentices? Might they have removed it?"

"Apprentices?" Her fingers found the edge of her lips and white teeth suddenly bit down on her nails. "Master Crispin, his apprentices! They are not here."

It took him a moment to follow her logic. Too long. "Indeed. They would be here, before the cock crowed. And if they found the place thus they would have gone to the law. But they are not here."

"Those boys. Surely . . . surely . . . no mischief has befallen them—"

Crispin walked to the window and looked out, wondering. Did more than one murder occur here last night? He glanced at the smaller footprints again.

What, by God's blood, did this killer want?

"That's a dreadful speculation!" cried Jack, looking desperately at Crispin. "Sir? Are they, too, dead?"

"Were they young boys, damosel?"

She joined him at the window. "One was fifteen, the other ten. Brothers." She gestured to the cots in the corner, both overturned, their bolsters tossed upon the floor.

"Their parents?"

"I know them. Only down the way in Southwark. I shall . . . I shall go there anon." They all fell silent, Jack with his mouth hanging open.

Would the sheriffs wish to investigate now, he wondered. Two boys, two apprentices missing, possibly dead? He squeezed the bridge of his nose, shutting his eyes.

"Mistress Coterel, never fear. I will not rest until the killer is put to the king's justice . . . or mine."

Taking a steadying breath he swept the room again with a probing gaze. "Can you speculate, damosel, as to what that missing object"—and he waved toward the rectangle of clean floor again—"might have been? I must assume you know this place well."

Her hair was mostly caged by a linen kerchief but she tossed the long, looped plaits back with a recalcitrant shoulder. "And why do you assume that?"

"You told me plainly that you were the man's betrothed."

"I had my work and he had his. I did not have the time to dawdle watching him swing a hammer all day."

He nodded and scuffed his boot in the ash. "How long have you been betrothed?"

Her stony veneer cracked slightly and she turned away. She took a step toward the window but stopped suddenly—the ash marks showed so plainly what had happened. She appeared to think better of it and turned toward the worktable instead. A pair of snips had avoided the carnage and her fingers touched the instrument, running down its dark surface. Her jaw clenched. "Not long. But we knew each other a long time."

"Damosel, forgive me." He stood behind her now, trapping her between the table and escape. "I have observed much in this room, but I have also observed that you do not seem as saddened by these events as a woman in your position might be. Care to explain?"

She made an agitated sound. "He was a singular man, Master Guest. Can you understand that? He did not judge . . . people . . . the way other men did. He was going to marry me. He was going to see that I was well cared for." She turned to him and the loss on her face was no invention. Her large eyes ensnared him with their sincerity. The lips she wetted with a pink tongue distracted. "I am saddened at that loss and worried for his mortal soul. But . . . I did not love him, if that is what you are implying . . . and I know well that it is." She hugged herself and glanced toward the window. "His time came early. But perhaps not by his own devising as . . . as I had wrongly supposed."

She whirled and faced Crispin so suddenly that he stepped back. "I know now that Roger was murdered even if that lout of a coroner will do nothing about it. If that is the will of the king's men, then so be it. But I hoped you'd come back for another reason if not for justice for poor Roger. But for me and my father. We need you. We . . . we need to hire you."

"Oh? For what?"

She sighed. "Someone has stolen money from us. Our rent money. And if we don't come forth with it soon, our landlord will turn us out. He threatened the law."

"And?" He sensed there was more to it and could tell by the frown of her brows he was right.

"I came this morning to look for the money Roger said he'd lend me. But it's not here."

"That box—"

She shook her head vigorously. "No. I know nothing of that."

Crispin took the damp rag he had stuffed in his belt and wiped his runny nose, coughing down into his chest. He replaced the rag when it had done all it could. "Very well. Your shop? Show me."

"Come see."

She did not wait for him to follow but darted swiftly out the door. Jack gave Crispin the eye. Crispin nodded at his servant. "What do you think?"

"I think she's lying."

"So do I. Let us see what is next in her poke of tales." Crispin passed through the doorway and spotted the impatient woman gesturing to him from the entry to his right. He followed her to the tailor shop he had noted earlier, his eyes scanning quickly over bolts of cloth on neat shelves and several sizes of shears hanging from hooks above a worktable.

A man was waiting for him by the hearth. Lank hair streaked with gray hung to shoulders slightly bent. His face, riven with lines, drew down to a sharp chin. There was no mistaking their resemblance. His lips and eyes were very like his daughter's.

"Master Coterel," said Crispin with a slight bow.

The man bowed in return. "Robert Coterel. And you are Crispin Guest. My daughter spoke of nothing but you. She seemed to think you could help us."

"This is the sort of thing I do, Master Coterel. For a fee."

He raised his face to his daughter, who was clutching his arm.

"But fees are our problem, Master Guest. We owe our landlord, but our coins have been stolen. He is not an amenable man and will surely turn us out without so much as a by your leave. I expect him here at any moment, I am afraid."

"Have you no way to secure temporary funds? No friends, no kin?"

"If only we did, Master Guest."

"What of a client whose work you can quickly complete?"

He shook his head, face red with mortification. "With the threat of invasion, no one seems to wish a new cotehardie or gown. They are ready to flee with the clothes on their backs rather than be burdened with new things."

The woman was stoic but he could well see the fear in her eyes. He knew that look. There was nothing as fearsome as the threat of losing the roof over one's head. And with winter coming on . . .

Crispin sighed deeply. "What amount did you owe?"

"Five pence," said the man. "We had just spent our last cache on new cloth from Italy. We were counting on a new Flemish clientele when the borders were closed. Our funds have dried up. And the rent, which was in a pouch hidden in a wall niche, was stolen."

"What else was taken?"

"Nothing."

Crispin eyed him curiously. "*Nothing* else was taken?"

"No, good sir. Just the coin pouch."

"The *hidden* coin pouch." He looked once at Jack. The boy's eyes were alight with ideas. Sharp lad, was Jack.

Crispin was about to comment when the door slammed open. A red-faced man with a bald pate and long gray whiskers stomped forth. He clearly only expected to find Robert Coterel and his daughter and sputtered upon encountering Crispin and Jack. He recovered and with a hand on the hilt of his sword he pushed his way in and stood toe to toe with Coterel.

"The time has come for you and your daughter to pack and leave, for I will not tolerate vagrants on my property."

"This must be the exacting landlord," said Crispin. He folded his arms over his chest.

The man turned, still keeping a hand on the hilt of his weapon. "This is a private affair between me and my tenant."

"Your tenant has hired me to find his stolen rent money."

The man sneered. "Stolen, eh? Is that what he told you? More likely it was spent on wine, for he dallies more in a tavern than in his shop."

Anabel released her father's arm and grabbed the landlord's, spinning him. "That is a lie!"

"Master Coterel," he said, grabbing her wrist tightly and tossing it away. "Try to control your daughter. It is rumored she is not easily controlled and goes about most freely."

She raised a hand to slap his face but Crispin grabbed it in time. He ticked his head at her before letting her go. "I don't think you want to be doing that," he told her, backing her away by stepping forward. He faced the landlord and his perpetual sneer. "Sir, you speak too harshly to these people. Insults are not necessary."

"I have drunks and whores under my roof. I would rather they were gone."

Coterel staggered back and sat heavily in a chair. He seemed a bit wobbly to Crispin. He could not tell if he smelled of wine because of his damnable cold, but perhaps the landlord was right on that score. Still, these people had come to him. There was murder no one wished to contemplate let alone solve, and there was the intense gaze Anabel Coterel directed his way. Her obvious charms were affecting him. The sight of a beautiful woman often did. He swore at himself for what he was about to do.

Crispin snatched the money pouch from his belt and counted out five pence. Clenching them in his fist he thrust his hand toward the landlord. "Here is your rent money. Take it, you churl."

He sputtered again. "What? What are you doing?"

"I am paying Master Coterel's rent. Take it before I fling it into your face."

The man reddened even further, and he looked first to Coterel and then at Crispin. "This is absurd! You can't mean to lend this man money. You will lose your funds, for he will never return them."

Hadn't Crispin been in similar straits for years and years? What a pleasure it was to finally be on the other end of it for a change. His lips pulled back in a mockery of a smile. "I said take it or I shall shove it down your throat." Crispin took a step forward and the man held up his hands in defense. Crispin grabbed one of them and slapped the coins into his palm, closing his fingers over it and shoving his hand away. "You've been paid. Now get out."

He merely stared but Crispin made a false leap at him and the man turned so swiftly he almost tripped on his cloak. He stumbled once as he made for the door. Safely outside he turned and shook the fist with the coins in it. "Threats! I will see the law on you."

"Begone, you tiresome man," said Crispin, and slammed the door. Very satisfying. He even smiled at Jack, who was looking back at him with an exasperated expression.

Robert Coterel got unsteadily to his feet, shaking his head. "He is a foul man. But in this instance, at least, he speaks the truth. I am a drunkard."

"Father," said the girl. But she did not contradict him.

"You know it is true, my dear. But I did not spend our rent on drink. I swear by the Rood I did not." His glossy eyes looked up at Crispin. "I cannot pay your fee nor return your five pence, sir. You have done a noble thing, but a foolish one, I fear."

"Nonsense. You will make it up to me." He grabbed Jack by the shoulders and thrust him toward the man. "You will make a fine cotehardie, two shirts, and a pair of stockings for this young knave. And use the best material a shilling will buy. That will cover the five pence and my fee."

"Master Crispin," Jack muttered, struggling to pull away.

"Take your measurements, sir," he said to the tailor. "In the meantime, I have some investigating to do."

Jack was still arguing when Crispin opened the door and stepped out onto the bridge's street. He didn't get very far before Anabel accosted him, pulling her cloak about her. The wind caught the hem of it and billowed it up until she captured it with a wind-chapped hand. "That was a fine thing you did, sir. My father and I are grateful for your honorable deed."

"It is more that I hate greedy landlords. Were you much in arrears?"

"No, Master Guest. In fact, he had never been so impatient before. We were only two days late and he threatened to turn us out. Well, you saw for yourself. He has never been so insistent before."

"Yes, he did seem anxious." The street was busy now with carts and drovers, tapping at the heels of sheep with sticks to move them along toward Southwark. Young girls were weighted down with heavy bougets of water from the cisterns in London proper and they hurried up the street as fast as their heavy burdens would allow. The smells of cooking meats rolled down the avenue as sellers with carts with songbirds on sticks called out to buyers. Shopkeepers and apprentices hustled along the single avenue, setting up their folding shopfronts and laying out their wares, though few were buying in these uncertain times.

"Is it true about your father? Does he overindulge?" Even as he asked it he felt a twinge of guilt. He was one to talk, for he overindulged plenty. And he had the overdue bills at the Boar's Tusk to prove it.

She swiped at the air and rubbed her elbow distractedly. "Perhaps he does. What of it? It doesn't affect us. He gets the job done. There is always food on the table."

"And what of you?"

Her bright eyes caught his. "What *of* me?"

He wanted to ask if what the landlord said of her was also true, but her steady gaze and squared shoulders gave him pause. He offered a crooked smile instead. "Never mind. I . . . God's blood." His eye caught a spectacle he had no desire to see. Down the street on their fine horses dressed in silky trappers, simply waiting in the shadows, were the sheriffs. When they saw Crispin their faces broke into large grins and they trotted their mounts forward.

"You see," said William Staundon. Their horses suddenly flanked Crispin, hemming him in. "I *told* you he would be here."

"I told *you* that!" said William More indignantly.

Good Christ. Crispin sighed and gave an apologetic shoulder lift to Anabel. "And so you find me, my lords. What do London's sheriffs need with me?"

"Oh, nothing," said Sheriff Staundon airily. "Nothing at all." He gave a conspiratorial smile to Sheriff More. "But we seldom find you at your leisure, especially out of the Shambles, Master Guest. Might you be doing a share of . . . investigating?"

No use trying to hide it. "Just as you suspected. There is murder here."

Their squeals of delight turned his stomach.

Staundon leaned down from the saddle. "Pray, Master Guest. Can you tell us?"

"Do you intend to inform the coroner's jury so that justice will be served, for I could not convince Charneye even though the evidence was there."

He exchanged a look with Sheriff More and sighed. "Alas. It is the jury that will decide if it was not an accident."

"Even given new evidence?"

"And what new evidence is there?"

Jack had just come out of the tailor's buttoning his coat when Crispin called him over. The boy bowed curtly to each sheriff. "Master Tucker will show you. Be so kind as to take the sheriffs into the armorer's and explain it, Jack."

"What? Me?"

Out of the side of his mouth Crispin said, "You're the apprentice Tracker. Go ahead and track."

"God blind me," Jack murmured before turning a stern expression toward the far too jubilant sheriffs. "Right this way, my lords," he said solemnly. "If you will follow."

They dismounted and tied their horses to posts before gleefully following the lad into the shop.

"Bloodthirsty devils," Crispin muttered. He took Anabel's arm and hastily pulled her away. She made only a small noise in protest as he held fast and pulled her under the shadow of an eave. The shop had not yet opened and he pushed her against the shuttered window. "And now. I would speak plainly with you. If you would have me find your betrothed's killer and discover who stole your money then I ask you, Is there something you are not telling me?"

She turned her face away but Crispin tightened his grip. It must have been painful, for she winced, but would not face him.

"Damosel, I know you are lying to me. About what, I am uncertain. And why."

She bit her lower lip, causing its already rosy color to blush to red. Her wide eyes fastened on him, searching his face. There were no tears there. Only questions. Her beauty gave him pause. She was like a stone statue, skin so smooth and white. It was far too distracting. Her eyes seemed to look deeper into his, sensing his interest. "I . . . have nothing to tell you," she said at last, and finally cast those eyes downward.

With a frown he released her arm. Though he knew she wanted to, she did not rub the soreness. "Very well. I can't force you. Much as I want to." He stepped away from her and walked in a circle before coming to a stop. "But I warn you, if either Master Tucker or I are in danger because of your reticence, there will be hell to pay."

She raised her chin in answer. He gave up. He took the rag from his belt and blew his runny nose and coughed up a ball of phlegm, spitting it into the street. In the old days he could take to his bed with servants attending him with hot broth and warmed wine. Not now. Oh how he wished he could.

They returned to the armorer's in time to greet the sheriffs coming out the door. They seemed impressed by Jack's demonstration. "Well?" said Crispin without preamble. "Are you convinced?"

"Your boy here is very precise. You have taught him well, Master Guest."

Jack's face was almost as red as his hair.

"That wasn't the question, my lord. Have we convinced you that murders have been committed?"

Sheriff More pinched his lip with long fingers. If they conceded the point then they would have to go to the coroner's jury to plead the case, and it only meant more work for all of them. But there might be fines to exact where there were none before, and he knew that this was also going through their greedy little minds.

Sheriff Staundon put his arm over Sheriff More's shoulder. "I believe there is more to think about, certainly." Diplomatic. They were going that route to hedge their bets. He couldn't blame them. "In the meantime . . ." The sheriff adjusted his coat and then his bejeweled sword hilt. "I think we should talk to the families of these apprentices. What do *you* plan to do now, Master Guest?"

Both sets of excited eyes were on him. *For the love of . . .* "I plan to go back to my bed and mend this illness. My lords."

They were disappointed, damn them. He wanted nothing more than to thwart their voracious curiosity that was mostly in the way. He stood fast, doing nothing but glare at them. Finally they got the hint. He told them that Anabel could direct them to the family of the missing apprentices, and they listened to her explain it. Finally, untying their horses, they mounted and turned the beasts away. "We will do our best with the coroner, Master Guest," said More over his shoulder. Crispin knew those were empty words. He doubted they intended to do much. They'd rather wait to see what *he* would do . . . and likely follow him around like lapdogs, frustrating his every move.

He was happy to see them ride away back toward London and little noticed anything else. "Jack, I am weary and need to rest. This illness will be the death of me."

But before he could quit himself of Anabel Coterel and of the bridge, a knight, in surcote and greaves, dismounted near the armorer and strode into the ransacked shop before they could call out to him.

"What, by God, has happened?" they heard him cry. He came running out again, stopped on the threshold and looked right, then left . . . and spotted Crispin. Crispin startled upon seeing his face and the knight did likewise.

"Holy Virgin! *Crispin Guest?*"

5

HIS FACE WAS WINDBLOWN, lined, and tanned. He looked older than his thirty or so years. There was even gray at his temples, but he was still as trim as Crispin remembered him. His clothes were as fine, too, and his horse, a sturdy chestnut stallion. He wore his surcote over his clothes, the green and white colors bright, even with mud speckling it. And though the greaves covering his shins were mud-spattered and dented, parts of them still had a silvery gleam. It looked as if the man's fortunes had not changed as severely as Crispin's. And why should they have?

"Thomas," said Crispin without thinking. When his mind caught up, he found, to his shame, that he was obliged to bow. Bow to a man who had sometimes been his equal on the lists and in battle. But a man who had not been his equal in social standing. If anything, he had been lower than Crispin. Yet now it was Crispin who bowed, and not Sir Thomas.

Sir Thomas's face showed that he recognized the irony, too. He simply stood, staring at his onetime friend, unable to say anything for his surprise.

Jack and Anabel stood off to the side, silent.

Crispin cleared his throat. "Jack, may I present Sir Thomas Saunfayl." Jack bowed low and remained quiet. He seemed to sense Crispin's mood. He was good at that after three years of knowing him.

The knight made a cursory glance at Jack but fixed his eyes again on Crispin, scouring him with his gaze. Slowly he approached, lifted his arms, and grasped Crispin tightly at his shoulders. "Crispin, Crispin. My God. I thought you were dead."

He barked a laugh, enduring the grasp. "Not dead. Not yet."

"But . . ." Sir Thomas looked him over from head to foot. At least his coat was only a year old now, not the beaten and patched cotehardie he had worn for years. But his stockings had seen better days and the soles of his shoes were loose and flapping. He wore only a dagger at his side, not a sword, not as Sir Thomas sported, hanging from its frog at the stout leather belt.

Crispin was starkly aware of his only ornament, the signet ring upon his finger, a bauble he had denied himself for too many years. But the Guest arms belonged to him and, now more than ever, he felt the need to display them, if not on a surcote then at least on his family ring.

Thomas shook his head. "I thought . . . when we'd heard you were convicted of treason . . ."

He offered a smile he did not feel. "His grace the duke spoke for me. He saved my life but little else."

Thomas whistled low. He could not seem to tear his eyes away from Crispin's face. But his stare was becoming uncomfortable and Crispin moved out of his grasp and toward the armorer's shop to redirect the conversation if not the man's gaze. "Were you a patron of Roger Grey's?"

That seemed to snap him out of it and he straightened his surcote. "I . . . yes. But . . . there seems to be some devilry here."

"Indeed." Crispin's eyes caught on Anabel, who had not moved and looked on with a tight expression. "Master Grey was murdered last night."

"No! No, that can't be!" He rushed into the shop again. Crispin and Jack followed.

Thomas tore about the room, tossing blankets and benches aside. "Where is it?"

Anabel entered, still silent. She merely blinked at Crispin and accepted the knight's intrusion without comment.

Folding his arms across his chest, Crispin watched the further destruction of the room for a few moments more before asking, "Where is what, Sir Thomas?"

Bending over a box of kindling the man suddenly froze. He straightened and squared his shoulders. "I am brokenhearted over these tidings of Master Grey."

I can see that, mused Crispin.

Flustered, Thomas faced him, caught again by the specter of Crispin with his head firmly on his shoulders. His hands twitched over his sword hilt, but not because he wished to draw it. Instead, they seemed to twitch from some other irritation that Crispin could not see. He was sweaty and breathing in a quickened rate, like a rabbit or a bird. His eyes would not light on any one thing, but ticked to this and that about the room, an aimless amble that made Crispin nervous.

"I am surprised to see you, too, Sir Thomas," Crispin said stiffly. They had been friends and he hated this formality that now they were forced into. "Not only for the years that have passed but because . . . well, because I expected a knight such as yourself to be in the company of the duke in Spain."

The man's eyes widened, and he took a staggering step back. He whirled away with unnecessary vigor and stalked toward the window. His gloved hand found the topmost sill and grasped it. He stared down into the churning water of the Thames.

"Have a care," said Crispin. "Master Grey met his doom out that selfsame window."

"Did he?" came the soft reply. Thomas did not move but continued to stare down, enchanted by the sight of water and foam surging past the piers and arches, of the boats doing their best to navigate those treacherous waters, for few dared shoot through the bridge when the tide was high.

Crispin cautiously approached and stood behind him only a few feet away. "Yes. They said it was suicide but I have since discovered it was murder."

Thomas's spine stiffened to hear Crispin's words so close to him. Still, he did not turn. "And what are you now? The sheriff?"

"No. They call me the Tracker. I sometimes get called upon to solve the occasional murder."

"By God. *You're* the Tracker? That wily fellow one hears no end about? Well, I should say I am not surprised. You were always a clever man, Crispin. A clever man. You even slipped the noose. How clever must a man be to escape death when he has committed treason?" The last was said with a bit more fire than his other words, and Crispin could tell the man's body was tense and winding tighter. "So clever. You're laughing at them all, I suppose. So many other knights, good men, were executed. How is it you were spared?"

Crispin felt a sharp spasm of remorse wash through him. Yes, many had died, and he often asked himself why Lancaster chose to spare him alone. Of course he knew the answer. The duke was like a father to him, and he a surrogate son. If any were to be spared it would have been him. But it didn't lessen the guilt.

Thomas answered his own query. "How like Lancaster to spare

you. How many times had he pulled your hide from the nettles, eh? Isn't this just once more?"

The irate tone and the sneer on his face were peculiar for the man Crispin had known. But nine years had passed since Crispin's disgrace and he realized he didn't truly know Thomas Saunfayl any longer.

He lowered his head. "You may be right. I certainly didn't deserve it. But each day I pay my penance in my way." He stepped closer and said in a quiet voice, "I should have listened to you. You told me not to follow the conspirators. You tried to warn me. I owe you for that, my lord."

Thomas began to laugh, a high-pitched, raw sound that had little to do with humor. "'My lord,' you call me. Ah, Crispin, I remember well my calling *you* by that title. How many times?"

There was nothing to say. Crispin felt the words scrape over him like nails over naked flesh.

They both stood immobile for too long before Thomas surged away again, marching through the room, looking again for . . . something.

"What can I help you with, Sir Thomas?"

"It's none of your affair, Guest."

"Forgive me, my lord, but it is very much my affair. I have been charged with discovering the murderer and this is the scene of that crime." It wasn't strictly true that he was "charged" with finding the murderer, but the sheriffs would be amused that he should try, and when pressed they would agree, he was certain. Partially certain.

Thomas grimaced over his shoulder at him, one canine tooth digging into his lip. "You are the devil, Guest. You were always getting into affairs that were none of your business. So you make a living at it now, eh? Well."

"Yes. A living. I get paid my fee for discovering that which is secret and unknown. Being hired makes it my business. Sometimes unpleasant truths are uncovered. Sometimes secrets must be revealed. For instance. You are here in England when the rest of the chivalry are with my lord of Gaunt. I wonder why."

A hit. The knight's face darkened. He strode up to Crispin and sunk a fist into his coat, hauling him forward an inch from his face. Harsh breath rasped over his cheek. "Who do you think you are talking to? Some lackey? I am a knight of the realm! And what are you?"

"At your mercy," said Crispin simply.

All at once the man deflated. He released Crispin and stepped back. Passing a hand over his face he breathed in short, halting breaths. "I don't know why I did that. F-forgive me, Crispin." When he looked up again his gaze swept once over the woman and a feral expression overtook his face again. "What do *you* want?"

"I . . . I have hired Master Guest."

He threw back his head and howled a laugh. "Indeed. Wenches hire you now, do they?"

"I earn my coin where I may. Honestly."

"Honestly? A traitor's honesty." The remorseful expression was gone and he took on the cloak of a demon again. Crispin found it difficult to keep pace.

Thomas gestured toward the woman. "I don't want her here, Guest. Send her away."

Crispin hesitated. After all, he needed the woman in order to do his investigating. But looking at the man's face and the struggle within him, he did not think he could argue. Before he had a chance to say anything, Thomas lunged at her.

She let out a yelp as he closed his hands over her arm and thrust her toward the door. "Get out, wench! Out!" He kicked at her, and she sobbed on her way through the entry, hurt eyes meeting Crispin's once before she was gone.

Thomas slammed the door and stared at it, breathing hard before his shoulders sagged again. He scrubbed at his face. "I never meant to do that."

Crispin glanced once at Jack cringing against the wall. "For God's sake, Thomas! What ails you? I have never seen you behave so. What has happened to you?"

He bobbed his head in what Crispin took for a nod. "Very well. I . . . I must tell you, then. I must."

6

SIR THOMAS LOWERED TO a stool, clutching his hands together over his thighs. Crispin made a gesture to Jack which the boy miraculously understood, and he fetched ale from a jug and poured it into a metal goblet he found on the floor. He handed it to Crispin and Crispin handed it to Thomas.

The man didn't even look at it before he drank, swallowing with long rolls of his throat and spilling some down his cheek and whiskered chin. He wiped at it with his hand and heaved a sigh.

"You were right. I was in Spain. With the duke's army."

Crispin watched him. His fingers traced over the florid patterns etched into the goblet until he let his hand drop between his legs. The cup was empty and he swung it dazedly from his fingers.

"You should sit, too. God's eyes, I'm sorry for my words, Crispin."

Crispin waited a moment before he grasped another stool overturned on the floor, set it upright, and sat. One hand rested on the hilt of his dagger.

"And so. I was with Lancaster's army. Of course I was! I am a knight of the realm, am I not? All the valiant knights have marched to war in Spain. All of us." His sneer was hidden by the lifted goblet, but he seemed surprised to find it empty.

Jack scrambled forward and poured more in. Thomas smiled at him briefly.

"This your boy?"

"This is Jack Tucker, my apprentice."

"Apprentice? Oh, for this tracking you do. Very good, very good." He took a long quaff and smacked his lips.

Crispin was losing patience. "Thomas, you said you'd explain . . ."

"Yes." He would not look at Crispin. In fact his gaze would not rest anywhere. "We were in Spain. There were some skirmishes when we disembarked at the harbor. We hacked our way forward and Spaniards dropped before us, the dirty dogs. We were barely scratched."

A tremor began in the man's hands and he cast the goblet aside. It skidded across the floor and slammed into a discarded sabaton. He gripped his hand to hide the tremor. The muscles at his jaw tightened. "They fell like threshing in our path. And at one point, I found myself in the thick of it, unhorsed, and surrounded. But I acquitted myself well. Many Spaniards fell from my sword, I assure you."

"I'm certain they did. I remember well fighting alongside you, Thomas. I look back on those days fondly."

"I, too," he said quietly. "But those were long-ago days." He jolted to his feet so suddenly Crispin startled back. He paced, kicking up the fallen ashes. "I . . . was sent back to England. There was something I needed to do. And while I was here, I came to this armorer. I paid a great deal of money for something special that would make me unbeatable in battle and on the lists. I paid that whoreson a king's ransom for this object and now you tell me he is *dead*?" He kicked a piece of armor—a besague—and watched it spin away. "I *need* that object!"

He whipped around so quickly his surcote spun around his legs before settling. "Crispin. *You* must find it. You are this Tracker. Surely you can find this for me." His face suddenly brightened. "I'll hire you!"

God's blood. When it rains it pours. "Thomas . . ."

"No. This is perfect. You can find it for me. Perhaps it is here? But no. He would not have left it here in the open."

"Well, what is it, for God's sake?"

His hollowed eyes drooped. "A relic."

Crispin's gut twisted. "A relic, you say. What sort of relic?"

"A relic suitable for a knight. Find it, Crispin. I'll pay you." Thomas fumbled at his scrip, untying laces, and plunged his hand within. He drew out a pouch and began counting out coins. "How much? What is your fee?"

Fisting a flush of humiliation, Crispin leaned forward, closing his hand over Thomas's. "Hold, Sir Thomas. Let us first discuss that which you would have me find. Then we can discuss fees."

"There's no time. Here. Take it!"

Crispin had no choice but to catch the falling coins. Far too many.

"It's too much, Thomas."

"I don't care. Take it and find that relic. Promise me you will. Swear to me."

"You must tell me what it is and I shall."

"What difference does it make? It is a relic, suitable for a knight."

"How can I even begin to look for it if I don't know what it is?"

"You'll know it when you see it, I assure you." He jolted to his feet. Though his movements were still hasty, he seemed much calmer. "I have faith in you, Crispin. Swear to me. I will believe your oath."

He shook his head. "Thomas . . ."

"Crispin."

Sighing, he nodded. "Very well, Thomas. I so swear. As you looked out for me so I shall look out for you. But—"

"Good! When you discover something, meet me at the Falconer's Inn on Knightrider Street. I am taking accommodations there."

"Thomas." Crispin strode with him to the door. "I need more than that to do you justice. Why can you not tell me?"

"I've told you what I could. Grey explained what it was, what it looked like. But I don't see anything like it here now."

"Thomas! I must insist."

He shook his head. "I cannot say. I can only trust you so much, Crispin. I fear . . . if you know all, you might . . . but no." His eyes were a glittering pool of confusion. "If anyone can find it, it will be you. In two days, come to me at the Falconer."

"But Thomas—" Too late. The man was gone. Crispin followed him outside, watched him mount. He turned once, waving gravely at Crispin, before he kicked in his spurs and galloped his beast toward London.

He felt Jack come up beside him. "How, by God's breath, are we to find a relic where we have no inkling of what it is?"

Crispin sighed, coughed, and sighed again. "I was wondering that myself."

THEY RETURNED TO THE Shambles with a full pouch but also with lots of questions. When Jack had stoked the fire and did his best to brew some Flemish broth, Crispin settled in his bed, boots and belt discarded on the floor, and his cloak and blanket wrapped about him. His back lay against the cold plaster and he drowsily watched the single candle flame flickering from its dish on the table.

"This is a puzzle right enough," muttered Jack. He stirred the eggs into the broth with a wooden spoon and allowed it to bubble into thickness. He stuck a finger in to see if it was hot enough. Satisfied, he sucked his finger, took the pot off the trivet, and poured the broth into a bowl in which he had crumbled some old bread. He put the wooden spoon in the bowl and handed it to Crispin. "There you are, sir. That will have you feeling your old self in no time."

"Much thanks, Jack." He dipped the spoon in the bowl and brought up the soggy bread, slurping it into his mouth. The heat soothed his aching throat and sinuses, and he sat back against the wall with a sigh, eyes closed. He brought the steaming bowl close to his face and inhaled as best he could, scooping the liquid and sops into his mouth with the spoon. He ate until the bowl was empty. Jack offered him more, but he declined and set the bowl aside, closing his eyes.

The mattress settled beside him and he cracked open an eye to spy Jack making himself comfortable on Crispin's bed. He sat cross-legged facing him. "So the problems, as I see it," he began, "are threefold. One, there is the matter of Roger Grey's murderer." He stuck up a thumb and counted them down on his fingers. "And two, the matter of the stolen rent money, though I doubt we shall be able to find so obscure a culprit. A pouch of coins is such a wayward thing—"

"This from the expertise of a cutpurse?"

Jack did not seem discomfited in the least discussing his erstwhile profession. "Aye, Master, that is the truth. A purse of coins is scattered quickly with meat being bought here and ale bought there. It disperses like smoke."

"Indeed. And three?"

"Three is this business of a relic." He shook his head. "Blind me, Master Crispin. How they *do* follow you."

"It is perplexing and maddening. But I think perhaps that we have two problems, not three."

"Eh? Which then?"

Crispin lay back again and closed his eyes. "Do you recall the missing object from the armorer's? A box, perhaps?"

"Aye. Wait. You don't mean to say—"

"That is merely a guess, Jack. And I don't like guessing."

"The relic, then. Stolen from Master Grey."

"And not easily. He died for it."

"Good Christ." He crossed himself. "Then what do we concentrate on first?"

"A murderer, of course. He must not be allowed to take another life. He'd already taken three in his pursuit of this object, something that he wanted badly. Well, he seems to have it now. Perhaps he will be easier to find because of it."

"Or she," said Jack.

"What?"

"She. You keep saying 'he' when you talk of the murderer. But haven't we been acquainted enough with women who are devilish enough to do the deed?"

He recognized Jack's solemn expression but made no comment on it. "I see your point. I am always loath to first believe that a maiden is so capable of dealing death, but that is merely hope over experience. Very well, *whosoever* killed Master Grey has the object we seek. Find them and we find both relic and murderer."

"Aye, Master."

"But for now, a little sleep." He eased down the wall to settle on his bed properly and Jack took the bowl away and pulled the blanket over him.

Crispin drifted for a while, listening to the fire crackle and to Jack moving about the small room, splashing water into a pot, breaking sticks over his knee to add to the small fire, and humming tunelessly to himself.

Crispin had just reached a state where he could easily fall asleep when all hell broke loose outside.

He sat up, blinking. The woolliness in his head kept him immobile for a moment before he leaned over and opened the shutters. The blast of cold air took his breath away and caused his nose to run, but he wiped at it with his blanket and leaned out.

The street erupted with men shouting. Men on horses trapped between the hordes tried to rein in their crazed mounts. Fistfights broke out in their midst and there was a general shoving and disorderliness that rankled Crispin's senses.

"Jack, go out and see what the problem is."

"Aye, sir." He rushed for the door and grabbed his cloak from the peg.

"Be careful, Jack."

Jack nodded, lifted the latch, and disappeared out the door. Crispin listened for the thud of his feet down the stairs and saw him join the melee a moment later. Jack was jumping to see over the heads of the rabble but he was soon being swept up in the tide, all heading toward Newgate. Crispin leaned farther out but Jack quickly disappeared. He hoped the boy would be all right.

He lay back. He tried to relax, tried to sleep, but the noise and his worry over Jack would not allow it.

"God's blood!" Whipping the blanket away he threw his legs over the side of the bed, looking for his boots. He grabbed his belt with the dagger sheath still attached and secured it around his waist as he headed toward the door. He fastened the last few buttons on his cloak and grabbed the door latch when it suddenly swung open.

Jack was breathing hard and was startled upon seeing Crispin in the doorway.

"Master! Get back to bed at once." Before Crispin could speak, the boy had grabbed him and was ushering him back to the bed. He twisted him around, unloosed his belt, and shoved him back. He fell onto his lumpy mattress.

"Tucker! I am not a child!"

"Who said you were." He grasped Crispin's ankle, nearly upending him, and yanked off one boot and then the other. "Now lie down."

"Tucker!" Crispin scrambled up onto his elbows. "What is going on?"

Jack went to the door, peeled off his cloak, and hung it again on its peg. He shuffled to the fire and poked at it with an iron. "Well, it's a right mess, that is certain. The king has sent out a proclamation that there is to be no French invasion after all, that all is well. So now the merchants are upset as no one is stockpiling anymore and the people are upset for spending money they did not have to. And then the talk fell, as it always does, on taxes. And when taxes are brought up, fights break out. Men have been shouting of the days of old King John and mayhap the barons need to tell the king what for as they did in the olden days." He shook his head. "There's some talk of the king's chancellor, Michael de la Pole as well as Robert de Vere, but I do not know the nature of it. Did you know them, Master Crispin?"

Crispin sat up, draping his wrists over his knees. "Yes, I knew them."

"Thought you did. What is all the talk of them for?"

"I'm uncertain. I know that the chancellor has been responsible for raising taxes and de Vere for . . . well. For being a burden on the royal income. They are favorites of the king and as favorites, not well liked."

"Well, the talk out there is rough, sir. Talk of hanging, even."

"As much as I would like to gloat, there is much to concern me."

"Why? These men are nothing but favorites to the king, pushing in where they don't belong, receiving rewards they don't deserve. No wonder the people are unhappy."

Jack had obviously absorbed the talk that Crispin and Gilbert Langton often shared while dousing their sorrows at Gilbert's tavern, the Boar's Tusk. It gave him the idea that perhaps he should go there to get more of the news. As good an excuse as any. He scooted to the edge of the bed again. But Jack aimed the poker at him.

"Where do you think you're going?"

"I am going to the Boar's Tusk."

"It's mad out there."

"I cannot sit here idly while this is going on. I must know more news. With Lancaster out of the country we are in great peril."

"Blind me," Jack muttered, lowering the iron.

Crispin donned his boots again and strode toward the door. "Come along, Jack."

When they reached the bottom of the stairwell, Crispin measured the crowd. The king's horsemen were trying to disperse them, but the lane was so narrow it was difficult to move that many people out of the way. Crispin grabbed Jack's cloak and they allowed themselves to be swept toward East Cheap and when they reached Gutter Lane, they took to the left, stumbling away from the melee. Crispin watched the men pass for a moment before he turned away and headed up the lane to the square building with the ale stake leaning into the street. A curled boar's tusk hung from a rickety sign, and by that as well as the ale stake passersby knew that the Boar's Tusk was open for business.

They entered the dark interior full of smoky smells and spilled stale beer. Crispin moved quickly to his favorite spot—back to the wall, eyes on the door—and waited for Gilbert or his wife Eleanor to bring a jug of wine.

It was Gilbert with the jug, and he hurried over, no doubt anxious to exchange news with Crispin.

"Greetings, Gilbert."

He set the jug and bowls down, pouring wine into each of them. Crispin noticed—and so did a sour-looking Jack—that Gilbert still refused to bring a bowl for the apprentice. "How you managed to get here in one piece, I'll never know," said Gilbert, wiping the sweat from his wide brow. He took a quaff and set the bowl down, leaning in earnestly. "I was hoping you'd come."

"Jack tells me the barons are restless."

"Aye, that they are. I have it from a steward who frequents the Tusk, that thirteen lords have been appointed as a special council." Crispin sat up at that. This was indeed serious. Michael de la Pole, Suffolk, though loyal to the duke of Lancaster, was swiftly becoming a liability at court. He, like Richard himself, would seldom take the advice of his colleagues. Did he think that having the ear of the king was enough? Why was history so easily forgotten at court? The place where history was made.

"They have just arrived in London," Gilbert went on. "And riding in on the news that the king does not expect an invasion. Well.

I do not know what to think of that. Was it all a ruse to redirect our attention away from his own troubles?"

"I think if the French did not strike when Lancaster's army was well away to Spain earlier in the year, they had not the funds or the vitality to do so. I think the king is correct in this, yet it does serve as a good distraction."

A swell of noise rushed just outside the doors of the Boar's Tusk, and the men in the tavern lifted their heads momentarily before it passed on again to another street.

"Although not distracting enough," Crispin amended.

"And the joust," offered Jack. "Don't forget that."

"The joust?" asked Crispin.

"I heard it a day or two ago. There's to be a joust on London Bridge. For the knights who were left behind to guard the city, so they say."

Crispin snorted. "Beguilements in a time of war? Yes, more distractions indeed." So that was why the bridge folk were washing their walls and hanging garlands. The constant noise of hammering made sense, too, for viewing stands needed to be constructed.

Gilbert slammed his hand to the table. "Then all those stores he bid us buy? Useless!"

"Not so, Gilbert. You will make use of it. Eventually."

"Pfft. I could have spared the expense. Now the prices are high due to lack of supply. I have as little patience for these games as does this new council."

Crispin sipped the wine, easing the tension in his limbs. "Did you by any chance hear who is on this council?"

"I have heard that the Archbishop of Canterbury is in the retinue."

Jack gasped and Crispin silenced him with a gesture. Gilbert looked from Jack to Crispin. "Oi Crispin. You were in Canterbury last year. Did you . . . acquaint yourself with the archbishop, by any chance?"

Jack snorted loudly but that was all Gilbert needed.

"Not the archbishop!" he rasped. "Crispin, have you not enough enemies?"

"Then what's one more?" He smiled and took a drink, licking his lips.

Gilbert shook his head and rubbed nervously at his brown beard. "Crispin, I wish you'd have a better care. This tracking has made you hasty, foolhardy even. You cannot afford to offend the Archbishop of Canterbury."

"I think that ship has sailed, Gilbert. But what more have you heard? With Lancaster out of the way, I am concerned as to what might transpire in the government when he is not here to crush dissenters."

Gilbert scooted closer. "Dissenters? Crispin, what do you think this council means to do?"

"Who else is on the council?"

"I only heard a few names. The king's uncles, the duke of Gloucester and the duke of York. Richard, earl of Arundel. Oh, and Richard, Lord Scrope. He was Lord Chancellor before, was he not? He would know if anything was amiss."

"Indeed. An august body. Well, knowing what I do about the players, they mean to punish Suffolk by impeachment."

Gilbert gasped.

"The king must be reminded of his limits and responsibilities and that he is obliged to consult with Parliament," Crispin went on, "especially when excessive household funds have been spent. They can't punish the king so they diminish his favorite. From what I know of Richard, he believes himself to be an infallible judge, like the early kings of Briton. He has never learned that those days are long gone."

"But he is the king. The anointed of God."

"Yes, that is true. But the barons imposed limits centuries ago to prevent the indulgence of favors over the well-being of the country. Has he forgotten so soon the sins of his great-grandfather, Edward II?"

"Hush, Crispin!" Gilbert looked around and crouched his bulky frame low over the table. "Talk of the late King Edward could be considered treason in these worrisome days."

Crispin raised a brow. But he made a hasty scan of the room nonetheless. Edward II was deposed and murdered for his ignorance of his responsibilities. He, too, favored men who did not earn their station. He supposed throwing the name around at this juncture might be too bold, but he was past caring what the nobility thought of him. "I am too well acquainted with treason, as you know, to worry over it now."

A hand clutched his arm. "Master Crispin, Gilbert's right," said Jack. "There's no need to bring unwanted attention to you, sir."

Crispin drank down the bowl of wine, but Jack filled it again. "There will be discord until this is resolved. Perhaps it is a good thing that you bought extra stores, Gilbert."

"If it's not high prices it's high taxes. What the devil is Lancaster doing leaving the country at a time like this?"

Crispin kept silent. He brooded over his cup of wine while covertly surveying the room. Seeing Sir Thomas had awakened in Crispin something he had thought long dormant. The very idea of battle and encounters the knight must have had made Crispin's sword arm itch. *He* should have been there with Lancaster! Nothing would have made him leave his lord's side when the smell of battle was in the air. Thomas said he was sent back to England, but Crispin would have found any excuse to stay. Dammit, he would have stayed to the last stroke!

He pushed his wine bowl away and stood up. Perhaps a bit too fast, for the wine made him dizzy. Or perhaps it was that persistent fever and wooly head. He took a moment to feel the ground under him settle and stepped away from the bench. Jack stood, too, trying to anticipate his mood.

"Thank you, Gilbert, for opening an ear." He reached for his pouch and was glad to have money for once to pay for the drink. "Here," he said, offering more coins than that single jug cost. "I owe you more than this, I know. But you are too kind a friend to keep a roll of my debts. Please take this, at least, while I am flush." He laid the coins on the table since Gilbert seemed loath to take them in his hand.

He walked out the door without looking back, knowing Jack would follow. At some point, Crispin would pay a call on Abbot Nicholas. The abbot of Westminster Abbey was bound to know all the more intimate details of what might be happening around the throne. But he supposed his presence in Westminster would not be welcomed, especially now.

He stomped through the mud churned by the rabble. He could hear shouting in the distance but the king's men, no doubt, were doing their job.

"Master! Master Crispin!"

He did not stop but glanced over his shoulder at Jack trotting to keep up with his furious pace.

"Wait, Master Crispin. You are stirring yourself up."

That boy knew him too well. "Go on, Jack. Go on to whatever devilry you do all day."

"I don't do no devilry, sir."

"Go on, Jack. I would be alone."

"Now Master Crispin, don't go doing that, sir. You'll only upset your fever."

"My fever is no business of yours. Go on!"

"Bless me. You'll be the death of me," he muttered, hanging back.

The death of *him?* The nerve. That boy was getting too big for his station.

Crispin returned to the Shambles and trudged up his stairs. He opened the door and looked around, scowling. This room, this single room above a tinker's shop, seemed as barren as his soul. A simple table with a chair and a stool. A coffer, a bed, a bucket. He didn't own any of it. Only the meager things stored in the coffer and perhaps a few of the clay pots and iron pans hanging by the tiny hearth. His scowl deepened and he kicked the stool closest to him. It clattered along the floor. He was lucky it hadn't shattered, but what of it if it had? He'd just owe his landlord one more coin, one more day's wage. Paltry wage. Sixpence. That was the wage of an archer, but at least *they* were clothed and fed along with their regular sixpence.

He slammed the door shut behind him and stalked to the hearth, leaning his arm on the wall over it, glaring at the smoky embers glowing under their mantle of ash. Sir Thomas sneered at the very idea of the knights who had gone to Spain. Sneered! What would Crispin have given if *he* could have gone?

Nine years ago, he had no idea how much he was throwing away. Oh, but he had learned just how much in the intervening years. How he had learned.

He sat hard on his bed, tallying the list. He knew it wasn't healthy, always put him in a fouler mood and encouraged him to seek out a wine bowl in which to drown the memories, but he indulged anyway, couldn't stop himself. All that he had lost. And then some.

And then the woman, Anabel. Her face rose up in his mind. A beautiful face. How a beautiful face could turn his head. She had a face any man would be pleased to wake beside. She had been betrothed to Roger Grey. There was a hint of desperation in her talk of him. She was quick to pronounce him a suicide. But why would she want that?

Round bold eyes, luscious mouth. He certainly didn't mind picturing her. She was below Crispin's station, though . . . at least the place he used to occupy. She seemed quick and spirited, traits he valued in women, but he knew he shouldn't get too close. Only close enough to solve this riddle.

He always got too close and where did it get him?

He swore he wouldn't do it, made oath after oath that he would never look at it again. But now that his humor was completely black, he got up, knelt by his bed, and reached under the straw-stuffed mattress. His heart gave a lurch as his fingers closed on the object and pulled it forth.

It lay in his palm, the small portrait. Framed in twisted golden wire, the figure on the painted surface looked up at him with seductive eyes and he slowly lowered to the bed, staring. How long had it been since he'd seen her in the flesh? How long had it been since he'd touched her, held her in his arms?

Her face was pale, lips small. Red-gold hair. And those eyes. Even as paint and ink those eyes seemed to know him. Lids beguilingly heavy as they were in truth, they seemed to say they had a secret. And indeed, she had many secrets.

He choked out a whispered "Philippa," running a calloused finger down the painted face. Philippa Walcote was married, more than two years now by his reckoning. She had nothing to do with him any more than he had with her. That case had long ago been closed. He certainly had not laid eyes on her since she parted from these very walls. Yet the sound of her name and the face looking back at him still stirred something in him he did not wish to name. So long ago and there had been other women in between, perfunctory couplings, to be sure, but he could not escape that unmistakable feeling in his heart when thinking of her.

He clutched the portrait. Why did he keep the damned thing? Was it loneliness that made him covet it like a dragon over its treasure?

The fire in his hearth was low and glowed a dull red. *Just toss it in!* He'd only told himself that a thousand times, and a thousand times he had hesitated.

Standing, he moved toward the fire, alternating glaring at the flames and the portrait. He leaned an arm again on the wall above the hearth and stared hard at those slanted eyes looking mildly back at him. Regrets were for the grave. Philippa was lost to him. There was no going back. And no use in feeling sorry for himself.

After all, *he* was the one who had turned *her* away.

Unbidden, his mind filled with the face of Anabel Coterel again. He shook his head with a disgusted snort. "Don't be more of a fool than you already are, Crispin." Love was for poetry and courtly pursuits. Men on the Shambles were lucky to find a wench to wife. A sturdy maid to keep the house and bear the children, children to help the business, to leave one's worldly goods to. It was a business proposition, and rightly so. Life was too hard on the Shambles to gamble on love. And it wasn't just the Shambles. A lord married off his daughters to other wealthy and noble lords to propagate the line. If they found love later they were lucky. After all, Lancaster had married twice, yet he still kept a mistress on the side. Was that love?

The portrait weighed heavy in his hand. His fingers rubbed over the surface, loosening as he held it poised over the fire.

A knock at the door startled him and, instinctively, he clutched the little frame. Hastily he stuffed it back under the mattress, went to the door, and opened it.

Crispin took a staggering step back.

In the doorway stood his old friend, Geoffrey Chaucer.

7

"G-GEOFFREY!"

Chaucer smiled. His eyes danced with the old fire of their schemes and folly. "May I come in?"

The flashing moment of recognition and happiness on seeing his friend again vanished instantly. Geoffrey was to see for himself how Crispin now lived. But there was nothing for it. He gritted his teeth and stepped aside.

To his credit, Geoffrey did not flinch, said nothing. No cutting remark as he was wont to make. He knew Crispin's situation, had met him again only last year after almost eight years of exile. Crispin reminded himself that it was *good* to see the man again when by all rights he was not truly allowed to associate with him for fear of bringing down the wrath of the crown upon him.

Chaucer righted the stool and sat in it, resting his hands on his thighs. He wore a long gown with a few ornaments, a necklace, some rings, his jeweled dagger, the one Crispin had gifted to him over a decade ago. His eyes caught the glint of the family ring on Crispin's finger.

"Surprised?" he said, mustache curled in a grin.

"Geoffrey!" Crispin was breathing hard. "You shouldn't be here. It's dangerous for you."

He waved Crispin's fears away with the careless flick of his hand. "Don't vex yourself over it, Cris. I'll be fine. I was in the parish so I thought I'd visit."

Crispin frowned and slowly lowered to the chair opposite his friend. "Oh? I can't imagine that this is the first time you've ever been to the Shambles. And you have never graced my door before this."

Chaucer picked at invisible lint on the fur trim of his gown. "I have never had occasion to 'grace your door.'"

"What are you up to, Geoffrey?"

"Now why do you suggest I am 'up to' anything?"

"Your presence here. Don't try to lie to me," he said, cutting off Chaucer's reply. "What are you *truly* doing here, Geoffrey? Does it have anything to do with these councilors come to censure de la Pole?"

The grin faded. "You are clever, aren't you?"

"I am often paid to be so. Tell me."

"Good God, Cris! No 'how have you faired in the year since I've seen you, Geoffrey?' No other words of greeting?"

"Geoffrey, you *know* why. Why are you playing games with me? You know I have no patience for them."

"Indeed, not. You are the most impatient man I have ever met. Say," he said, glancing around. "Do you have any wine?"

"No!" He slammed his hand on the table. "Tell me what you are doing here!"

"Very well. If you insist. I understand you have been talking with Sir Thomas Saunfayl."

Crispin's senses went on alert. He was unprepared for the convergence of such diverse incidents. "I . . . yes. He hired me to find . . . something."

"Did he? Well never mind that for now. Where is he? Do you know?"

"Why do you ask?"

"Why do you hesitate to tell me?"

"Because it is you who wants to know."

"Cris! I'm appalled. That I should garner such mistrust in you."

"Your patron name is Deception. I've known you a long time, remember?"

Chaucer frowned. "This is most upsetting. Here I come to you in perfect friendship—"

"Spare me, Chaucer!"

"*Perfect* friendship. Expecting to be treated as a favored guest. And there is no wine and no hospitality whatsoever."

"Things are different on the Shambles," he growled.

"Indeed they are. It is like another country."

"Are you going to tell me what you are doing here or do I toss you out on your ear?"

"That temper of yours," muttered Chaucer. "Very well, then. If you are going to growl at me I might as well tell you. I am in search of Sir Thomas to aid him. He is in very grave peril."

Chaucer's words were finally making sense. Thomas had been nervous and ill-tempered about something. Crispin was finally going to get to the bottom of it. "I am sorry to hear that. I have not seen Thomas in some years but I did notice he did not seem . . . himself."

"No, indeed. I am here to defend him in court."

"What has he done to need your defense?"

"What has he done? Why, he is a coward. He has deserted his

post amongst Lancaster's army. I will do the best I can but there is little to be done if he continues to hide from me."

"Wait, wait." His words made no sense. Cowardice? Sir Thomas? "There must be some mistake. Sir Thomas is no coward. He is a brave and formidable fighter. He always has been."

"Perhaps. But he has deserted, and he is being brought up on charges. There are those who will testify that he ran from the enemy."

"No! That is not possible. Sir Thomas is incapable of such fear. I know of no knight who is braver."

Chaucer straightened the liripipe artfully draped from his hat over his chest. "All I know is what I have been told. His grace, the duke, has asked me to intervene where I can. And my sources say that he was seen talking to you not more than a few hours ago."

"Your sources?"

"Yes. I'm certain you have *your* sources."

Crispin suddenly thought of Lenny. More often than not, the thief served as his spy. And the man was running away from the bridge last night. What mischief had he been up to? Up until this moment, he had forgotten about Lenny.

"What did he want with you, Cris?"

Crispin sneezed, and he pulled that dreadful rag from his belt again to wipe his nose. He prayed for the day this damned cold would disperse.

Chaucer watched him with a faintly disgusted expression.

Replacing the rag once again in his belt, Crispin cleared his throat. "He . . . that's between him and me, I'm afraid."

"Oh come now. I told you what *you* wanted to know."

"Hardly the same thing, Geoffrey."

"Then where is he so I may speak with him? He must report to the court."

Crispin sat back. "How do I know you aren't on the other side?"

Chaucer narrowed his eyes. "Because I am telling you."

"Oh yes. I can surely believe that."

Chaucer jumped to his feet. "Absurd! I thought in Canterbury we came to an understanding."

"You lied to me over and over again. You kept secrets from me. Am I to believe you now that you appear at my door out of the blue?"

"We're friends, Cris. I expect you to believe me."

Crispin leaned forward. "Then believe this. I don't know what sort of foolishness this is, but I know Thomas Saunfayl. He is no coward."

"Is that your last word on it? You won't help me?"

"Yes. My last word. And no. I won't help you."

A shadow passed over his eyes but he shrugged and turned toward the door. "I see. You don't trust me. We've been friends a long time, Cris."

"Then you should know that I would be loyal to my oath to him."

"You forget that I am a knight as well."

"I haven't forgotten."

Chaucer's eyes widened but just as quickly his expression fell to a blank one. "I see. I am a member of Parliament, you know. I can make you tell me."

Crispin raised his brows at this information but sent a cool expression toward his friend. "You could *try*."

Chaucer glared for several more heartbeats and Crispin gave back as good as he got. Finally, Chaucer headed toward the door. "Well. Farewell, then, Master Guest."

Guilt niggled at the edges of his conscience. He hadn't seen

Geoffrey since their disastrous trip to Canterbury over a year ago and now he was letting him go again. He rose, staring at the table. "Geoffrey, I—"

Chaucer held up a hand. "Don't trouble yourself, Crispin. I shall make my way. But mark me. Don't stand in the way of the court, or of Parliament."

"Is that a threat, Geoffrey?"

Chaucer set his jaw. "It very well may be." With that, he grasped the door latch and was gone.

Crispin stood a moment, listening to the silence. Quickly he made for the door and trotted down the stairs. He looked down the Shambles toward East Cheap and thought he caught a glimpse of Chaucer's blue gown. He pulled his hood up over his head and went in pursuit. Geoffrey thought he was clever, did he? Well, it was time to see what the man was truly up to. Member of Parliament, indeed! Bah! Threaten him, would he? *We'll see about that!* And then this business about Sir Thomas. He couldn't quite believe it, but there was definitely something wrong with the man. Whatever it was, it had to do with Chaucer.

He followed, staying several yards behind him. He dodged carts and riders threading their horses down the narrow lane. The occasional shout rang throughout the alleys and streets where some of the rabble met at crossroads, but for the most part, commerce had tried to return to normal.

Crispin kept his head down when Chaucer turned to look behind him. But his eyes swept unseeing over Crispin, pressed against a wall and standing behind a shopfront awning. He waited for the poet to turn again before continuing his pursuit, and wondered where the man would lead him.

They were leaving the city, making their way along the Strand toward Westminster. It would be harder to follow him unseen. Just as Crispin was wondering if he shouldn't drop back, Chaucer turned and entered a tavern.

Crispin waited a good long time before he cautiously approached the door and gently pushed it open.

The place was dark except for the tallow candles he could just smell flickering on the tables and for the wide hearth, flinging licking flames over the logs. Head down, he made his way to a dim corner and spied Chaucer meeting with someone at a table near the back. They were flanked by armed men. They wore no livery but it was obvious they were guards. Crispin couldn't quite see the hooded man Chaucer was talking to, but the poet was gesturing and talking quickly, wiping the ale from his curled beard when he drank.

The hooded man nodded, intent as he listened. Though he held a horn, he never drank from it. After a while, Chaucer looked as if he were done talking. He settled in and drank his cup before setting it down again. He rose, bowed low to the man, and turned toward the exit.

Crispin hunkered down in the shadows, only lifting his head enough to see past the hood. He waited until Chaucer was out the door, then looked back at the hooded man, who stayed for some time, drinking slowly and deliberately from the horn. His guards were motionless but for their eyes constantly scanning the room.

At last he rose, and with the sweep of his cloak behind him, headed for the door. *Now,* Crispin murmured to himself.

Careful to keep his face shadowed by his own hood, Crispin made his way forward, strategically colliding with the man. "Oaf," the man grunted, and shoved Crispin into a set of stools surrounding a small table.

His quarry lifted his hood, giving Crispin a momentary look. Stunned, Crispin staggered back and barely recovered before the guards shoved him with such force he clattered to the floor, knocking over a stool. On his knees, he stared after them as the three guards followed the man out.

Crispin pushed himself slowly to his feet. There was no mistaking the face under that hood. Chaucer's clandestine meeting was with the earl of Suffolk, Michael de la Pole, chancellor to the King of England.

8

LOST IN HIS OWN thoughts, Crispin walked, heedless of the direction the meandering lanes took him.

Chaucer, Lancaster's man, conspiring with Michael de la Pole? This was madness. If Suffolk's ouster was imminent, then all those associated with him were in grave danger. His dismissal—possibly even execution—would be a great insult to the king and leave Richard on very thin ice. He wondered if Richard could even appreciate the extent of the damage being done, if he understood what he was in danger of losing.

And now Chaucer was involved. Crispin walked slowly down the muddy streets and tried to make sense of it. Geoffrey and Crispin had both served Lancaster and had become the best of friends and confidants. Though Geoffrey was older—the same age as Lancaster, ironically—they treated each other more like brothers. It hadn't made a difference to their jests and pranks.

The man had a family, for God's sake. How could he throw them into jeopardy? At least Crispin had sacrificed no one but himself when he stepped into the role of traitor nine years ago.

That settled it. He'd have to go to see Abbot Nicholas and beg answers. But should he not first go back to the bridge? He had craved rest before but now his blood was up, and he knew he had more questions to find answers to before this day was out. Bridge or Westminster? They were at opposite points of town.

He took a step forward and stopped. A crouching figure dashed across the avenue. Looking back at Crispin, the man winced and darted into an alley.

Goddammit! Lenny!

Off he ran, but the cursed man was slippery. Crispin reached the alley but no one was there. He halted and cocked an ear. Silence. How could he have lost him twice in so many days? The man wasn't that clever. But he was surely that scared. What had he done that he feared Crispin so desperately? "Lenny, Lenny. I don't like this feeling in my gut."

He made more halfhearted attempts to search for him, but gave it up.

Thoughts of whether to go to Westminster Abbey or London Bridge disappeared.

He turned toward Knightrider Street.

THE FALCONER WAS A fine inn with bright, lime-washed walls and a formidable door. Crispin swept in and called for the innkeeper. He was an ordinary man with bland, sandy hair. When Crispin asked for Sir Thomas, the innkeeper eyed Crispin with suspicion. A coin pressed into the man's hand soon allayed his fears.

Crispin waited by the fire, warming himself until his thighs were toasted through.

A step behind him. Sir Thomas, still clad in his surcote as if reluctant to relinquish it, wore a face twisted into an angry scowl. "What are you doing here?"

"I have come to ask you questions, my lord."

"I told you. I only want to hear from you when you've found the . . . the object. Have you?"

"No. But I—"

"Then there is nothing to say, Guest." He spun and pushed his way none too gently past some traveling men bundled in cloaks and with bulging scrips.

"Why didn't you tell me of the charges against you?" said Crispin.

Thomas's step faltered to a halt. He turned his face only half-way back. Shadows hid his features but not the tightening of his shoulders. "What are you talking about?"

"It seems I had a visit from your defender, Geoffrey Chaucer."

Thomas stalked up to Crispin and grasped him by the upper arms. "What did you tell him?"

Crispin glanced down at those whitening hands with disdain. Quietly, he said, "Do you truly wish to discuss this here?"

Thomas looked around wildly. His lips curled downward, and he released Crispin. He stomped toward the stairs and hissed over his shoulder, "Come with me!"

Crispin straightened his cloak and with as much dignity as he could muster, followed the man up to his room.

It was spare but in better order than his own back on the Shambles. The fire was larger, for one, and the two chairs both had high backs and arms. Thomas paced, running his hand over his beard. "What did he say?"

Crispin edged toward the fire and stood before it. "He said . . . he said you were charged with cowardice and desertion. Did you desert?"

There was a long silence, broken only by the faint sound of a whimper. Crispin grimaced. God's blood! Could Geoffrey possibly be right?

Thomas felt around for the chair, grabbed it, and pooled into it. His shoulders sank, head drooping. "So now you know. My disgrace. You can't begin to imagine, Crispin. You can't know . . . I think . . . I think it was the noise of it. The cries of the men and the clash of steel. My heart thumped so hard I feared it would bolt from my chest. And never would it rest during the heat of battle and even afterwards. Christ Jesus help me! I . . . I tried, Crispin. I tried to ignore it, thinking it merely a momentary befuddlement. But when it would not abate, even in our pavilions at night, I truly feared for my sanity. Even the sound of marching men, of armor clattering around me, caused my skin to crawl. I . . . just couldn't take it any longer." He raised his face and long silvery trails of tears marred his cheeks. "Crispin, you know me. I was never a coward. Could I have been bewitched?"

Crispin stared. He'd never seen the like. This man was the most courageous he had ever known. What could it be other than witchcraft to have turned him to this sniveling coward before him. He swallowed his revulsion.

"I know nothing of such things, Thomas. But Chaucer is looking for you."

The man looked afraid. "You didn't tell him where I am, did you?"

"No. I held my tongue. Is he here to defend you, as he said?"

"Yes, I suppose."

Crispin couldn't stand it anymore and kicked at a basket of kindling, sending it tumbling over. "I don't understand this, Thomas! You have served Lancaster almost as long as I have. How could you desert him? How could you *ever* leave the field without consent?"

"I know, I *know*. Trouble me not, Crispin. I have flogged myself enough over it."

"Not enough, obviously." He took a deep, calming breath. "What are you up against?"

"What am I up against? Death, of course. They will condemn me to die for my sins. And I cannot blame them."

"And you can just sit there—"

"No!" He jolted to his feet. "No. I came to England to that damned armorer to save myself. I'd be invincible. I would not lose and in so arming myself, I would not f-fear to face an opponent on the lists."

"Trial by combat?"

"Most likely."

This was damnable. "You must face it sooner than later."

"I know. Find that relic, Crispin, and I can."

"I can only hold off Chaucer for so long."

He offered a weak smile, the first Crispin had seen on him. "You are a good friend."

"I made an oath to you. I do not forswear myself lightly."

Thomas studied him. "No. Not even when they put you on trial for treason. There is not a shred of cowardice in you, Crispin Guest. You can be proud of that."

"Yes, well. That was a long time ago." He shuffled uncomfortably before settling in front of the fire again. "Can you tell me anything of Richard's chancellor?"

Thomas seemed bewildered by the question. "Suffolk? What has he to do with me?"

"I wondered."

Thomas shook his head. "There is nothing. Lancaster used to speak well of him but lately he only says the name 'Suffolk' in disparaging tones. And so I keep my association with him at a minimum. But this is foolish talk. There is nothing to discuss but the relic. Find it, Crispin."

"It would help to know what the *hell* it is!"

The knight shook his head and turned away toward the fire. "You should go."

"Thomas . . . I . . . it would truly help me to know. Can't you give me some sort of . . . hint? Why keep it such a secret?"

"A soldier. A proper soldier would have such a thing. Such a great thing." His eyes were on Crispin again, gazes locked. "No one else must know. But you'll find it. God help me if you do not."

Crispin stared at the man for several heartbeats, willing him to capitulate. He said he didn't quite trust Crispin. Why? What was this relic that caused such distrust? But Thomas was adamant. He had turned away, dismissing him, and Crispin supposed that was that. Exasperated, Crispin muttered, "God keep you, then," and strode quickly toward the door. *He is the only one who shall.*

9

WESTMINSTER SEEMED FARTHER TODAY. His cold throbbed his head into something like a swollen melon and his nose was frozen shut. He hurried his steps along the Strand if only to keep warm. Armed men patrolled the waterfront and there were clusters of them to his right where the roads drifted into pastureland. Though the king had declared that there was no danger from France, the soldiers were still on alert.

Westminster Abbey rose from the mist. Crispin made his way through the old arch and strode purposefully down the nave, avoiding the milling clerks and scribes looking for work. He made it to the south transept and stopped a monk who was polishing a statue in a niche. "Pardon me, Brother," said Crispin. "But might I be taken in to see Abbot Nicholas?"

The young monk's pimpled face looked up. Though his tonsure was bone white, his brown hair around it was bountiful and hung almost to his eyes. He gripped his rag and straightened. "And who might you be, sir?"

"Tell him Crispin Guest would like to see him."

The boy's eyes widened. "Oh! Yes. I . . . I will tell his chaplain."

Rag still clutched in his hand, he ran out the door to the cloister, feet slapping hard on the tiled floor.

Crispin shivered and pulled his cloak tighter about him. He looked back at the clerks haranguing others wandering in the nave. Positions were scarce, what with the threats from outside the borders. It was doubtful these anxious clerks would find employment from the merchants who made their prayers beneath Westminster's arches.

Presently, the young monk returned. "You are to follow me, Master Guest." He bowed awkwardly, and Crispin smiled. This boy reminded him of when he first met Jack Tucker. Jack had been just as awkward, but in three years' time had learned some aplomb. No doubt he acquired it by mimicking Crispin. Young Jack was a perfect chameleon, to be sure.

Crispin walked the familiar arcades and shadowed arches of the cloister and reached the abbot's lodgings, where he was greeted at the top of the stairs by Brother Eric. The usually jovial monk wore a face of concern.

"Brother Eric."

"Master Crispin," he said sternly in a voice that seemed to say, "I wish you had not come."

Crispin acknowledged the sentiment with a nod. "May I see him?"

The monk turned toward the closed door before looking back at Crispin. Without another word, he opened the door and announced him.

The old abbot was lifting a hauberk by its shoulders and thrusting it toward his companion, Brother John Canterbery. Neither seemed to notice Crispin's arrival, even after the announcement. Crispin moved into the familiar warm room. Light from arched reticulated windows shone bright on the wall and tiled floor. The hauberk sparkled from shafts of sunlight. He had only a moment to wonder at their industrious conversation before Abbot Nicholas turned at the sound of his step.

"Crispin!" He seemed happy at first and then he frowned, his white brows curling over his eyes. "Crispin," he said more soberly. "What are you doing here?"

"I know my presence is less than welcome at such a volatile time, Lord Abbot, but it is because of these times I come to speak with you. But if I may ask, what are you and this good brother here doing with armor?"

"He wishes to don it and protect the city," said Brother John, ticking his head at his abbot.

Crispin stepped forward and fingered the fine rings of the hauberk. "Is that so?"

"Yes," said Nicholas, pulling the shirt away. Beside it upon the bed lay a breastplate and cuisses. "I am fully prepared to march with the king to do my duty and protect the realm."

Crispin gazed fondly at the aged man, his pale, wrinkled skin, and faintly pink nose. White hair fell from his tonsured scalp to his ears, curling around the shell. "Don't be a fool, Nicholas." He took the hauberk from the abbot's hand and laid it aside.

"I am not being a fool, Crispin Guest. And fie upon you for such talk to your elders. These are troubling times."

"And well I know it. And I would have more news from you, if you are willing to give it."

Nicholas fussed a few moments more until Brother John sighed and with an exasperated, "Bah!" Nicholas turned away. He shuffled very slowly and deliberately to his chair by the fire. The usually robust old monk seemed to have diminished in strength in the last few months. Crispin quickly moved forward and took him by the arm.

"Are you well, my lord?"

He waved Crispin off but sat in his chair by falling into it with an exhausted huff. "I'm tired. These days are vexing. My archdeacon is out of the country again, and I fear for his safety." His hand gestured vaguely. "Now all of this."

"How is Brother William?" Crispin appreciated the intellect and expertise of the abbot's archdeacon, William of Colchester, who kept the business of the abbey running smoothly both at home and abroad in Rome and Avignon. The old abbot needed someone with a good head on his shoulders, but the man was rarely present, always on a mission to do some papal business or other.

"By all accounts he is well, but it is dangerous traveling abroad. Rome has its eye fixed on Spain at the moment, as do we all. But France must not be neglected."

"The king has decreed—"

"I know well what the king has decreed. It is his way to pacify the people in hopes that they would not notice his household is under siege. But they have noticed nonetheless."

"Yes, there was a rabble on the Shambles just today."

"On the Shambles? Bless me. Well, the people are angry, to be sure."

"At what, exactly? Taxes, of course, and fear of invasion have everyone on tenterhooks."

"Taxes. Oh yes. The Lord Chancellor has angered everyone where taxes are concerned, but more than that, the barons are angry at his presumption of authority. He was never well liked and to have the king put him in such an exalted position . . . well. Blood will be spilled."

"But whose?"

"Well," said the said abbot, nodding his thanks as Brother John handed him warmed wine. He poured a second goblet for Crispin. "If the counselors have their way, it shall be Suffolk's."

"They mean to impeach him?"

"Some say it will be far more than that. And it is all designed to embarrass the king and bring him into conformity. And the *duke* of Ireland," he added with some disdain, shaking his head. "Robert de Vere, indeed. It was bad enough when King Richard created him the Marquess of Ireland but did he have to spit in the eye of his counselors and create him *duke*? Is he the king's brother? Uncle? It is not well to grant a . . . a *friend* a dukedom. That along with the household expenditures, so they say, would seem to show that Richard is uncontrollable. The closer the king comes to his majority, the more highly of himself and his office he seems to think. Too highly."

Crispin leaned back but said nothing.

Nicholas squinted at him and then glanced once at Brother John, busily storing away the armor in a coffer. "It doesn't matter how right you might have been nine years ago," he said quietly to Crispin. "The fact remains that he is the king."

"And I shall defend the crown as I have always sworn to do." He sipped the mellow Spanish wine.

"You obfuscate with words, Crispin," said Nicholas.

"'He who is to be a good ruler must have first been ruled.' These words are not obfuscation."

"Your Aristotle also said, 'It is unbecoming for young men to utter maxims.' I tell you, Crispin, do *not* involve yourself again. Lancaster is far from England's shores."

"I need no reminding of that, my lord. Nor of the need to keep myself out of court politics. But sometimes it is unavoidable."

"Crispin, harken to me. You *must* not involve yourself. Richard will soon find he is cornered, whether he realizes it or not. And a cornered beast is most dangerous."

"'A bad man can do a million times more harm than a beast.'"

"Stop that! You will not quote your pagan philosopher at me."

Crispin swallowed his grin. "What can you tell me of these counselors, then?"

Nicholas narrowed his eyes. He was not fooled by the change of subject. "Alexander Neville, the archbishop of York; Nicholas, abbot of Waltham; William de Courtenay, the archbishop of Canterbury—" He paused and studied Crispin's face. Crispin continued to sip at his wine. "Richard, Lord Scrope; Thomas of Woodstock, the duke of Gloucester; Thomas Arundel, bishop of Ely; Richard, earl of Arundel; Edmund Langely, duke of York; John Lord Cobham; and Sir John Devereux. Have I missed anyone, Brother John?"

"William of Wykeham, bishop of Winchester; Thomas Brantingham, bishop of Exeter; and John Gilbert, bishop of Hereford," he said from the back of the room.

"Oh yes, yes. A horde of bishops. An uneven chessboard. But the king must be made to see."

"Will he?"

Nicholas shook his head. "It is difficult to say. It is no coincidence that this move was made while Lancaster is out of the country."

No, Crispin didn't think it was either. "What's to be done?"

"For you, nothing. In fact, I advise staying out of Westminster altogether. But I doubt you will take that advice."

"But what would I do without your council?" Crispin smiled at the old man's frown but soon enough he was frowning himself. "Do you also know about . . . have you heard anything about the convening of a trial for cowardice and desertion?"

Abbot Nicholas rubbed tiredly at his eyes. "It is no secret that the Earl Marshal's court is condemning a knight for cowardice."

Crispin took a deep breath. "Sir Thomas Saunfayl."

"Yes." The abbot raised his yellowed eyes. The blue of his irises was pale, like thin ice. "And Geoffrey Chaucer has been charged with defending him. But it is said there is little expectation of a positive outcome. Trial by combat is his only hope. You knew him, I take it?"

"Yes. I thought I did."

"If he is a coward then is he not best left to God's mercy?"

If a man could not take his rightful place on the battlefield then he was a detriment to those around him. A man who could not defend his lands let alone the king's was a liability the realm could ill afford. Crispin bowed to the sense of it, but he could not separate the man he had known from this new disgrace. Even so, he had made a vow to Thomas, and he would see it through.

"I don't have an answer to that," he said after a long pause. "I leave such discussions to theologians. Like yourself."

Nicholas nodded and seemed to sink into the furs on his chair. The greyhound lying before the hearth raised its head, tail thumping, before he lowered it again and blew a huff of breath along the stone tiles.

Brother John was suddenly at Crispin's side. "My Lord Abbot is weary, Master Crispin. Perhaps we should leave him to his rest."

Nicholas was already dozing. Crispin rose and handed the younger monk his goblet. "Thank you, Brother," he said quietly. "I forget that Abbot Nicholas is an old man. We have had so many robust arguments."

"Yes, I know. But of late, he has slowed down considerably. It is the way of things. The old must make way for the new."

"I would not be so quick to dismiss the old, Brother John. I have known Abbot Nicholas to be full of surprises." He walked with the monk to the door, bowed to him, and saw his way out through the cloister.

When he passed through the south transept and out onto the

street at last, Crispin's thoughts were a jumble. But one thing was certain. Knights and politics aside, he had a murderer to apprehend, and he could not do it in Westminster. He had to return to London Bridge.

10

IT WAS WELL PAST None by the time Crispin reached the bridge. Where had the day gone? Between traveling to Westminster and back to the bridge, he had walked across London more times than he could count. He paid his toll again and passed through the bridge's gate, then made his way down the avenue. A brisk wind from off the Thames whipped his hood about his face but the tight position of the buildings afforded some shelter from the river's wind and spray. The late afternoon sun gave bleak light behind a shade of clouds, laying a pale yellow sheen over the bold faces of the shopfronts.

The hammering continued, and now the narrow stands were forming along the avenue. They'd block some of the shops and houses, and the shop owners looked none too keen on that, but everyone loved a joust, especially if it meant that a man was fighting for his very life.

Crispin scowled and turned away from the beams and carpenters.

Among the background noise of shopkeepers, lowing beasts, and hammering, the susurration of the river passing beneath and clashing against the piers hummed in his ears. He supposed it could have a lulling effect when all were quiet in their beds, but it could also drive a man mad with the constant hiss at his senses.

He reached the armorer's and slowed to a stroll. Two men in the livery of the city of London were boarding up the door. The sheriffs' men were keeping all secure, he supposed. He stood behind them as one hammered—badly—and placed one board atop another while the other man picked through a handful of nails.

"What is this?" asked Crispin, and got grim satisfaction as the man hit his thumb instead of the nail. He howled while the other laughed, but the other was soon howling, too, when the board fell and landed on his foot. They were both hopping around until they turned twin scowls on Crispin. "I beg your pardon," he said with a bow to hide his smirk. "By whose order are you securing this shop?"

"By order of the Lord Sheriff," grumbled the one with the swollen thumb. "And if you don't want to find yourself in Newgate this night, you'll move along."

He watched them for a moment more before he quit them and went next door to the haberdasher, who was yet to be talked to. If there was much ado in the armorer's, surely *they* would have heard.

He passed through the archway. A wire-thin man was bent over a bench with a wooden form. Wool batting stuck through the loose seams of dark blue material wound about the form, and the man was carefully stitching a long liripipe tail to what would become a roundel hat.

"I beg your pardon, good master," said Crispin with a bow.

The man continued on without acknowledgement of Crispin's presence.

Crispin cleared his throat. "I beg your pardon," he said a bit louder.

Still, the man worked on.

Either the haberdasher was being insulting or . . .

Crispin reached out and touched the man's shoulder. He jumped so abruptly he fell off his stool. Crispin knelt to help him up.

"Why by God's teeth are you creeping up on a man like that!" he accused.

Crispin brushed the dust off the man's gown and bowed. "I beg your pardon."

"Eh?"

"I said, I beg your pardon?"

"What? Speak up. I can't countenance mumbling."

"I SAID, I BEG YOUR PARDON."

"No need to shout, young man."

Crispin sighed.

It took a great deal more shouting before Crispin discovered from the nearly deaf craftsman that not only had he heard nothing the night of the murder but he did not even know the armorer was dead.

"How did he die?"

"I BELIEVE HE WAS MURDERED."

"Murdered? By Saint Agatha, bless us all."

"HAD YOU ANY REASON TO BELIEVE HE TOOK HIS OWN LIFE?"

"Eh? I thought you said he was murdered. I don't hear well, you know."

"Yes, I know. BUT THERE WERE SOME WHO THOUGHT AT FIRST HE MIGHT HAVE DONE IT HIM-SELF."

The man shook his head. "No. Not Roger Grey. He was a ro-bust man. A man of ambition. He would never do such a thing. I was under the impression he expected a windfall and had planned to leave London."

The third time someone had said as much, yet his betrothed said it was not so.

Crispin thanked the man, walked out of the shop, and headed for the tailor only two doors away.

Master Coterel was at his bench, carefully sewing a sleeve for a blue and as yet sleeveless cotehardie hanging from a straw-stuffed mannequin. The coat was still in a raw stage with seams open and chalk marks where pleats would be added. Crispin realized this was to be Jack's new coat. He looked it over, running his hands along the shoulders. A fine coat. The man was a decent tailor, at least. "Master Coterel," he said softly, not wishing for a repeat of the scene at the haberdasher's.

The man glanced up and put his sewing aside. "Master Guest. You're back. What may I do for you?"

Anabel peeked down the stairs and soon she trotted down the treads to stand on the bottom step. She patted her hair under its kerchief. Those large eyes looked him up and down again.

He noticed a window overlooking the Thames, similar to the one in the armorer's shop. "I had hoped to look again in Master Grey's shop for more clues, but the sheriffs' men are locking it up tight."

"Yes," she said, approaching him. "I saw that. I begged them not to but they refused. What will you do?"

In answer, he walked to the window and opened the shutters. The Thames rushed briskly below. It wouldn't be low tide until Compline.

He looked to his right, and not too far away—about five feet, by his reckoning—was the armorer's window. The shops cantilevered out over the Thames. He could not see the base of the bridge below him except for the piers in the midst of the water, but there were corbels jutting out from the shop foundation beams running every two feet. It would have to do.

He leapt onto the sill and climbed down to the first corbel. Anabel screamed, as did her father, and they both dashed to the window
and leaned over. She reached out with her arms. "Sir! What are you
doing? Come back inside!"

"I must get into the shop next door. Short of climbing down
his chimney—which I do not think a wise choice—this is my only
way in."

"But . . . but—" Her eyes were wide in fear, taking in the white-
caps of the Thames below.

"Master Crispin!" cried Robert Coterel. "Don't be a fool, sir.
Return to the safety of our shop."

Crispin held on to the half-timbering of the outer walls. The
mud and plaster that swathed the wattle beneath had been worn
away by the weather and by the harsh water, and there were plenty
of handholds. He dug his fingers into the threaded sticks and carefully stepped to the next corbel. It didn't take him long to reach the
armorer's window. But as he suspected, it was barred. He took his
knife from its sheath and slipped it between the crease of the shutter
and lifted it as high as he could. Fortunately, the bar was a handy
height and he slipped it up and off. He sheathed his knife and easily
pulled the shutter open. With a toe in the wattle he lifted himself
up onto the sill, and dropped nimbly onto the floor.

"No! Anabel!"

Crispin stuck his head out to see what the tailor was yelling
about and saw the woman making her way as he had done over the
corbels. She had rucked up her skirts, exposing blue stockings gar-
tered just below the knee, with a bit of pale leg visible above. "What
the hell do you think you are doing?" he cried.

She spared him one swift glance before she turned back to the
wall, concentrating on where to put her hands and feet as she care-

fully but deftly made her way closer to him. "I will go with you," she said breathlessly. "I want to help you find Roger's slayer."

He was about to chastise her again, forbid her to come along, but she was already past the halfway point. Damn the woman! Frustrated but admiring her at the same time, he held out his hand until she was able to grab hold of it.

He yanked her up and hauled her unsteadily over the side, depositing her none too gently onto the floor.

He helped her up and scowled. "That was an extremely foolish thing to do."

She pulled her skirt into order again, hiding her legs. "Foolish for you, or foolish for me?"

He did not answer, but turned instead to the room. At least the sheriffs' men did not seem to have disturbed the room's contents. "You say you searched here for the money he said he was to loan you?"

"Below, yes, but I never made it upstairs. You arrived first."

"The bedroom is a likely place."

"True, but he was a most unusual man. He kept his strongbox down below."

"Do you see it anywhere here?"

"It would be hidden."

"But you don't know where."

She cast her gaze down for a moment. "I did not know if I could trust you before. I know where it is hidden."

He clenched his jaw. Women. Duplicitous at the very least. And to think he had paid her rent. "Show me."

She picked her way over the pieces of discarded armor, trying not to disturb them. Moving back toward the large window overlooking the Thames, she faced the wall beside it instead and stood before the only item left hanging on the wall: a small round shield, a buckler, made of leather with a shiny metal central boss. He wondered why it hadn't been touched, but as he watched her he reasoned out why. The buckler was somehow attached to the wall in such a way as to prevent anyone from simply tearing it free. Reaching forward, her hands closed over its opposing edges and with a quick jerk, she turned it in place. A click and it swung away, revealing a small door—no bigger than a rabbit's hole—situated in the wall. In the center of the door sat a brass lock.

She gave Crispin a smile that made him realize why Roger Grey had cast his eye toward her. But her smile of triumph was short-lived. "I don't have the key," she said.

Crispin gently nudged her aside. "We won't need one." He un-buttoned his coat and pulled out the lace to his chemise. He raised the long, metal point at the end of the lace along with the tip of his knife, and slipped them both into the keyhole. Closing his eyes, he manipulated them in the lock until he could feel the lock pins fall-ing into place. The lock clicked and the door whispered open.

She looked at him in shock. "You're a slippery fellow, Crispin Guest."

He raised a brow, but said nothing. He opened the door wider, half-expecting to find the relic—whatever it might be. But the space was empty. Not even a money pouch.

Strange. There should at least be some coins inside, for, no doubt, the man did good business and the wares were expensive.

"Nothing." He gauged her perplexed expression.

Crispin headed toward the stairs. "His chamber was up here?"

She nodded again, following him.

"Damosel, perhaps, under the circumstances, you should stay here."

They both were thinking of the missing apprentices, but she raised her chin. "No. I shall go with you."

"Very well. But stay behind me." Crispin drew his dagger again and carefully crept up the stairs. Once his head cleared the floor he scanned the darkened room but saw no one lurking.

Nor any bodies. If Grey's apprentices never showed again, he suspected that their bodies had been carried far down the river with no chance of recovery.

He hastened up the stairs. Strangely, the room looked relatively untouched. Not sacked as the room downstairs, but there was still some disarray. The mattress was rolled back, the bedhead flipped to the side. Clothes seemed to flow from the coffer. Though they were not thrown about, someone had definitely searched through them.

"Light a candle," he told her, and she quickly ran to comply.

A moment later she was back, but instead of handing the candle to him, she held it just over the floor and made a circle, examining. "No blood," she declared.

He stared at her anew. "Just what I was thinking." He opened his hand to her. Reluctantly, she gave him the candle.

A crash below.

Crispin pushed her behind him and blew out the candle. His dagger was ready when he slowly made for the stairs. But before he could get down, a ginger head popped up.

"Master Crispin? What, by the devil's own bollocks, are you doing?"

"Language, Jack. Mistress Anabel is present."

"Oh!" He spied Anabel in the dark, smirking at him. "Beg pardon, damosel."

"How did you get in?"

"The same way you did, Master. The foolhardy way." Jack grinned and climbed up the stairs to join them. He took the candle from Crispin's hand and found the tinderbox. The wick fizzled and the room was framed again by the small candle's nimbus of light. "Blind me! Aye, they were looking for something."

Crispin's boot turned over a chemise lying on the floor. "The question is, did they find it?" He turned to Anabel. "Did Roger Grey tell you of a relic he had obtained for his client?"

"You seek a relic? Roger never said anything of it to me, but he did say that he expected a windfall. That through careful plotting he would soon see great rewards." She looked about the room, rather sadly, he thought.

"But you say he made no mention of leaving London?"

"He never said such to me."

"Mmm." Crispin stared into the rafters. "What relic would suit a knight, I wonder? Any idea, damosel?"

She shook her head. "A relic of St. George, perhaps?"

"Possibly. But I know of none that would make a man invincible. Sir Thomas seemed to hold great store by it."

"He was your friend?" she asked.

Crispin hesitated. It wasn't something he wished to dwell on. "Yes. Years ago."

"I hope, for your sake, you find this thing he desires. But I wish to know whether you intend to find Roger's killer."

She was undaunted and faced him squarely.

"So now you believe he was murdered?" She shrugged. "I assure you, damosel, that this thief is foremost in my mind. For I believe it is he—or she," he said with a nod toward Jack, "who killed him."

"For a relic? God save us all." She becrossed herself.

"Believe, me, damosel, I have seen worse associated with relics."

Jack poked through the coffer. "What else could it be, Master? Blood? Hair of a saint?"

"Sir Thomas said it was something suited to a knight. What is associated with a knight?"

"A sword," said Jack.

"A helm," said Anabel.

Crispin sniffed his runny nose. "Let us look to the armor below."

They tromped down the stairs and began collecting all the loose pieces of armor. There were several breastplates, even more greaves, and various other pieces that would make up the full harness for a knight.

Jack found a splendid spear handle of wood covered with silver that was decorated with bas-relief designs of knights on horseback. It had yet to be fitted with its sharpened point. He held it up for his master but Crispin shook his head.

A pair of sabatons, armor for the feet, were fashioned with expertise and elegance, articulated so the foot could move easily. Crispin held them for a moment, wistful, before setting them gently aside.

One breastplate lying on its side caught his attention. On it was incised the delicate pattern of a blazon, the arms of Thomas Saunfayl. He picked it up and ran his fingers along the raised design.

"This would appear to belong to Sir Thomas, my friend. Did you know anything of this work?" he asked her.

"Roger was in the business of making armor. I would not have known these arms from any other."

The breastplate was still shiny and was shaped so that a lance or arrow would glance easily off its planed surface. Clean lines, understated styling. Crispin would be proud to wear such a thing . . . were he allowed to, that is.

"I must inform Sir Thomas that his armor, at least, is here." He laid it carefully on the worktable.

"If a man were to kill another to steal something he possessed," Anabel began, taking care stacking like pieces of armor together as she had, no doubt, seen her betrothed do, "What would he do with the stolen object? Sell it? Keep it for himself?"

Crispin examined a carved and bejeweled metal dagger sheath. "Both are possibilities. But in my experience, a coveted object like a relic is often stolen to keep."

"Yet the relic might also be sold?"

He looked at her steadily. "Perhaps. We have yet to determine the nature of this thief."

"Why won't your friend tell you what it is?"

"I do not know. Perhaps because he does not trust me. He seems to be overly . . . cautious." Crispin fingered a gauntlet before setting it aside.

"You seem troubled," she said quietly, tossing her head to look up at him. Her hair was in twin looped plaits wound over her ears. A short veil just covered them. Her eyes were kind but in them he could see her own troubles. How long had Master Coterel been without a wife? How long had Anabel had to shoulder the burdens of a household where a father was enamored of drink? And now their funds were stolen and her betrothed was dead.

"I have had . . . distractions. It is nothing important."

"Distractions, yes. I think that there are a great deal of distractions plaguing us all. Do you know what I did yesterday after you left? I went to the home of Roger's apprentices. When they heard the news that their sons were missing, they wailed in fright. It was a sore thing." She lowered her head and clasped her arms under her cloak as if cold. "The sheriffs arrived not long thereafter and I slipped away. How can this evil be, Master Crispin? How could there be such suffering in the world?"

"I have no answer for you. It is best asked of a priest."

"Yes. But I was not anxious to talk to a priest. Instead, I went about the bridge, talking to my neighbors, trying to ascertain if anyone had heard anything. The haberdasher, though a kind man, is deaf as a post."

"Yes," said Crispin. "I have already made his acquaintance."

"Oh? Well, I further inquired and there had been men hereabouts that were unknown on the bridge, though our craftsmen do cater to those in London's many parishes."

"Anyone in particular?"

"The presence of a triad of knights was repeated more than once."

"Three knights?"

"Yes. Not particularly identifiable except for one. He was blond and sported a scar just here." She motioned from the top of her left eye down to her chin. "This was news to me. And though I am not well versed as you are in this sort of inquiry, I did find it . . . interesting." She smiled, briefly. "I see why a clever man could immerse himself in such a vocation."

He was still caught by that flash of smile before he shook her gaze loose. He cleared his throat. "Yes. Well."

"You investigate by asking questions, by using your wits, by observation. I would help you in this. I find the prospect of doing so . . . intriguing."

He leaned toward her but Jack insinuated himself between them, scowling at them both. "So what does that mean, then, eh? Three knights? The man was an armorer, after all."

She glared at him. "So, too, did I speculate. When I questioned the bridge folk they cast their eyes downward. They would not look at me. When I probed further, they became agitated."

"Interesting," said Crispin, easing the boy back. "How many did you query?"

"Five told me of seeing these knights."

"Wait! I recall them, too," said Jack eagerly. "The night the armorer died. Three knights together."

"I would help you if I may," she said. "Investigating as you do . . . it is invigorating to the blood."

Crispin shrugged. He supposed that was one reason he liked his vocation. He wasn't burdened by the whims of a master or at what hour of the day he could do his task. It was almost the same sort of freedom he had enjoyed as a lord. Without the benefits.

"Master Crispin don't need no help, especially from the likes of you." Jack had moved forward again. He postured before her, standing with his back to Crispin.

What is that boy on about? If he didn't know better . . .

"He's already got an apprentice," Jack sneered.

Crispin burst out with a laugh. "By the Rood, Jack. You're jealous."

"What? I never! I'm not jealous. W-what would make you say such a thing, Master?"

Crispin slapped the boy on the shoulder. "Jealous! Of Mistress Coterel. Jack." He shook his head.

The boy's face flushed. He frowned and curled his hands into fists. "I'm not!"

"Now Jack," said Crispin, chuckling at the boy's deepening frown. "You do not have to worry. Your position is safe, I assure you."

Jack pushed away from Crispin and stomped toward the door. With a sigh, Crispin went after him. "Jack . . ."

"I'll show you who's an apprentice and who is not," he muttered.

"Jack, stop that this instant."

Jack pulled at the front door but it would not budge. He flushed even more when he realized the door had been nailed shut. He cast about and reached for the window shutters. Remarkably, the sheriffs' men had neglected to secure them. Jack threw them open and climbed onto the sill.

"Jack! Stop this foolishness."

The lad looked at his master once more and with a scowl jumped to the ground. When Crispin reached the window the boy was already halfway down the bridge. "God's blood," he swore under his breath. God save him from moody apprentices!

"He's a hotheaded lad," Anabel remarked, suddenly standing beside him.

"Yes. And disobedient. I suppose I should have beaten some sense into him more often."

"He's growing into a man. He does not know his own mind. All he knows is that he is different and that you see him differently."

How did she get so wise? "Have you a brother?"

"No, but I have seen many an apprentice and journeyman. Boys are all the same, whether they are fourteen or two score." That gamine smile again. Crispin wasn't as charmed this time. He shuffled and looked about the room again.

"I seem to be shy an assistant. And I wanted to question the bridge folk."

"Come with me, then. I will be your assistant. I want to. Besides, they may not talk to you. I do not know the way of it in other parishes, but those on the bridge seem especially closemouthed to strangers."

"Have you lived here all your life?"

"Yes." She began to climb over the sill, but with a huff of exasperation, Crispin lent her a hand. He closed the shutters once he climbed through. Shoppers were staring at them but he ignored it. "I was born on the bridge," Anabel went on. "My mother, too."

"Where is your mother?"

"Died. Three years ago. That's when Father began to drink."

"Forgive me, damosel, but you seem to have a blithe manner when it comes to your family's troubles . . . and to death."

"Do I?" She tilted her face up toward his. A bit of sun caught the curve of her cheek and kissed it with a blush. "I have always been a practical woman. One cannot wallow in sadness. We haven't the luxury."

"But your betrothed was killed only yestereve."

"What's done is done."

They walked, Crispin following her. They talked to various shopkeepers and apprentices and it was as Anabel said: Some had made mention of three knights who kept to themselves. Three knights were sometimes seen near the armorer's shop.

Anabel's arms pumped as she walked. Her hands were clenched into fists and she kicked her skirts with each bold stride. Crispin caught a glimpse of blue stockings again, thinking only of the pale thighs above them. She swiveled her head once to make sure he was still behind her. Her cheeks were flushed and her eyes seemed to glitter with the challenge ahead. It made him wonder all the more about Roger Grey and what manner of man he was. And what of these schemes he was involved in? The relic, certainly. He did not know how much Thomas had paid the man, but it sounded like a great deal. Enough to purchase a house somewhere off the bridge? Did he aspire so? Anabel did not think so but she was more and more a puzzle to him.

He glanced her way again. She was close-lipped on the matter, at any rate. Was it any of his business? *You've become quite the spy, Crispin, meddling in matters that are beside the point.* Still, he was finding of late that a woman of Anabel's status was becoming more interesting to him. No doubt it started with Philippa Walcote—but he must not think of her. No! No more.

Anabel Coterel. She had secrets, too. How women liked their secrets.

He looked up into the sky. Church bells began ringing for Vespers and indeed, the bleary sun was setting over the city beyond the bridge. Shadows stretched, lengthening across his path. He escorted her back home.

"It is late . . . Anabel. I will continue tomorrow." He bowed and turned away, but stopped. He bounced on his heels for a moment before reluctantly turning back to her. "You did fine work today. I appreciate the help."

She curtseyed to him and brought up an unexpectedly mischievous smile. "You had best find your apprentice, Master Crispin. For I fear he was not pleased with you today."

With a blush, he realized he hadn't given Jack a thought the whole time. He gave a sheepish grin. "Perhaps I had better." He bowed again and left her.

As he strode toward the gate, he wanted to look back but had no wish to make a fool of himself. *Only a hairsbreadth, Crispin,* he admonished, *between a fool and a martyr.*

JACK TUCKER WAS NEITHER at home on the Shambles nor in any of the usual places Crispin was likely to find him. "Damn that boy." He rubbed his chin, feeling the sharp scratch of stubble. He could wait or he could go to the Boar's Tusk.

He glanced at the wine jug on the back sill and knew it was low. "Boar's Tusk it is."

II

THE NIGHT DREW ON later and later and the candle before him got shorter and shorter, and somewhat blurrier as the wine filled him. Someone slid next to him on the bench and Crispin sluggishly shifted his gaze.

Gilbert looked back at him, his face questioning as usual, his disapproval thick.

"Gilbert, I sense you are about to admonish me." His tongue felt thick and unmanageable. A proper drunk had set in and he liked the feel of it. It was better than the feeling of that damned head cold. "Why don't we pass over this part since I already well know what you are going to say?"

"That you're drunk and you should go home? What makes you think I was going to say that?" He slid a horn beaker into view and took Crispin's jug, pouring himself a dose. He took a drink and smacked his lips.

"Because you always do. Because I always am. Drunk, that is."

"Why so intemperate today, Crispin? Is it that knight you spoke of, your friend?"

He shrugged. It threw him off balance and he had to grab the table to keep from falling backward off the bench. "Maybe. Maybe not. I've encountered plenty of former acquaintances."

"And each time, you drink." He saluted with his cup and drank.

"Why shouldn't I?" Crispin grumbled. "Every one of them is doing far better than I. And little wonder. They have moved on, taken that one step higher on the ladder rung while I wallow where I have been for the last nine years."

"Now Crispin." Gilbert laid an arm on the table and leaned on it. Wine moistened his beard. "That is not true, and you well know it. You did not start on the Shambles as the Tracker. You earned that title and much admiration since."

"Amongst shopkeepers," he sneered.

Gilbert elbowed him hard, eliciting a grunt. "*And* tavern keepers, you wretch. You never rejoice in your achievements, you only compare your failings to those above you. Those of our rank—yours now, too, mind you—never do that. Why should we? We will only achieve so much. But a good day's work and food in our belly is a satisfying thing, Crispin." He shook his head and drank again. He eased the cup down, placing it on the table. "You have an apprentice now. A new cotehardie." He brushed his hand over Crispin's crimson sleeve. "And coins on your person for a change. Things are looking up, are they not?" He took another drink and rubbed his bearded chin. "You and I must not continue to have this conversation. I'd much rather talk to you of festive things, of cheerful things."

"Cheerful things." Crispin made an unsteady perusal of his friend's face, a round and generally merry countenance. Gilbert Langton was a man with much. He had a loving wife in Eleanor and they owned this tavern. And though it wasn't as proud an establishment as some others of its ilk, it was a good and affable place. Their greatest sorrow was in not having children. He knew this vexed them sorely, for what were they to do in old age? Who would care for them? Strangely, Crispin never thought of that for himself. He had assumed a long time ago that he would eventually lose his edge and get involved in one too many altercations. It would take only once to let his guard down and a dagger blade could easily slip between his ribs. Yes, he knew how his days would end. And yet, this did not frighten him or darken his mood. It was not the future that vexed him but his past. He could not let it go. Never would he.

He drank again. His sleeve caught the dribble down his chin. "Gilbert, you are ever my conscience in this. You are always right. And yet I find myself here time and again."

"I'll bring you some food. How about a nice roasted coney, eh? Ned has an extra one on the spit. I'll bring that and share it with you."

He nodded sloppily. "Yes. That would content me."

Gilbert climbed out of the bench and straightened his coat. "Where's that rascal of yours, Jack Tucker? Shouldn't he be here taking you home?"

"I was wondering that myself. It seems he rushed off in a jealous fit."

Gilbert paused by the table. "Eh? Young Jack? Jealous of what?"

Crispin smiled, remembering. "I was with a client who showed exceptional perception when it came to investigating. Jack got it into his wooden head that she was taking his place."

"She?"

Crispin drew patterns on the table with the spilled wine. "She. A beauteous maid. Well, perhaps not so much a maid."

Gilbert sat again. "Older?"

He smirked. "Not older. Merely . . . experienced. At least that is my impression."

Gilbert tsked and shook his head. "You need the company of decent women, Crispin. How will you ever find a woman to wife?"

"I'm not looking for a wife. I've told you that."

"So many have slipped through your fingers, women of worth."

"But not fit for a knight," he muttered.

"Crispin," he said, rising but leaning down to whisper close to his ear. "You are *not* a knight."

Gilbert walked toward the kitchen as Crispin scowled in his direction. "I don't need reminding," he said to the nearly empty room. But when he looked into his wine bowl he saw the face of Philippa Walcote, the woman he had discarded because of his lingering sense of his past. A woman he had loved. A woman he still loved.

He pushed the bowl away, sloshing its red wine on the table like blood. What was it that *truly* vexed him, he wondered, among all other thoughts? *Was* it Philippa? Was it Anabel, who reminded him so of her? Was it Sir Thomas, who was throwing away that which Crispin longed for? "Maybe it is all of it," he muttered. "Perhaps I am a flagellant and these memories are my flail. Only then may I find my peace, when I have done proper penance."

"Are you Crispin Guest?"

A man stood over him, one he did not recognize.

"Who wants to know?"

"Pardon me for interrupting your conversation with your wine bowl." The man snickered. His reddish gold hair was covered by a close-fitting cap. His clothes were those of a middling merchant, no velvets but good cloth, no patches, and a decent dagger hanging from a belt carved with decorative designs. "I am Lucas Stotley, a clerk. You are the one with Jack Tucker as an apprentice, no?"

"What of that scoundrel?"

"Well, I saw that boy being dragged away by some knights who were none too happy with him. Thought you'd want to know."

Crispin staggered up from his seat and leaned shakily on the table. *"What?"*

"I saw them back up the lane. He was talking vigorously with a group of knights. They didn't like his tone or his manner. He did not treat them with the proper respect and they set about to teach the lad a lesson. I would have thought you would have tutored him properly in this yourself, Master Guest, his being your apprentice and all. Well, they are doing the job now."

Crispin grabbed his arm. "When? Where?"

"Not long ago. Just up the lane."

"By God's death, where?" Crispin grabbed clumsily for his coin pouch. He managed to withdraw a coin and tossed it on the table. "WHERE?"

"I'll show you." He grabbed Crispin's arm and led him outside. He pointed up the street to a stable. "See there. Their horses are still tied to the posts. They must be teaching him a lengthy lesson."

Crispin drew his dagger at last and staggered up the lane.

"Wait! Master Guest, you do not intend to rescue him by yourself? In your state?"

Crispin looked down at himself and felt how wooly his head was from a cold and from the wine. "I have no choice."

"Wait there, Master Guest. I will get Master Langton."

Crispin swayed with uncertainty. He knew the man was right, but he did not wish to delay. Jack was in grave danger. Who knew what those knights were doing to him?

It wasn't long before Gilbert was at his side, and the clerk, too.

"What mischief is this, Crispin? Young Jack is in trouble?"

"And so he might be. Master Stotley, this clerk, says so."

Gilbert eyed Stotley. "So he has said. What do you need of me? I am ready."

Crispin heartened at Gilbert's presence. "Draw your daggers, men. I know not what trouble Jack might be in."

Flanked by his companions, Crispin hurried up the road and stopped before the stable, trying to sober himself with deep gulps of fresh air. The roof bowed inward, and bits of plaster had chipped away from the walls, leaving the wattle exposed. The stable looked to be abandoned, but Crispin knew that it was still in use, renting old horses to unwary travelers.

Crispin motioned for the two men to stand behind him while he reached for the door. Carefully, he pulled it open and peered inside. The stable was dark except for a lantern hanging by its chain from a post peg near the center of the straw-covered floor. A shaggy horse in a stall whinnied in agitation. The sharp smell of horse dung twined with the oily smoke from the lantern.

Jack stood under the lantern's light. Two men each had him by an arm and were pulling those arms to their extremes, keeping him secure. Jack's worn coat had been discarded and lay in the dirty straw. His shirt was rucked up over his shoulders, exposing his back. Coming closer, Crispin saw why. Behind him, the third man swung back his arm and delivered another stroke with a switch. From the look of agony on Jack's profile and the sweat on his cheek, this had been going on a while. Yet he bit his lip bloody and made no sound except for a grunt when the switch fell.

Lurching forward, Crispin captured the man's arm before he could swing the lash again. Grabbing the switch from him, Crispin broke it over his knee and cast the pieces to the ground. "What, by God's bones, are you doing to that boy?"

The man glared, and Jack tried to twist around to look. His

back was striped with red welts. But the men held him firm and he could only struggle and flick his head over one shoulder and then the other.

The spare lantern light slipped across the man's face. A scar ran down his cheek from his eye to his chin. Lank blond hair fell to his shoulders in greasy strands. "This boy needs to learn how to speak to his betters. And he appears not to be the only one." His hand slid toward his sword hilt but Crispin was quicker and before he could consider the consequences, his dagger was pressed to the blond man's throat.

"I wouldn't do that if I were you," said Crispin, suddenly sober.

The other two men released Jack. He dropped to the hay-covered floor like a sack full of meal. They unsheathed their swords and Gilbert and the clerk drew back.

The blond man with Crispin's dagger at his throat smiled. "Three swords to three daggers. I wonder who will win?"

"Well, I doubt they can save *you* before I slash a seam in your throat . . . my lord. So that will be one sword down."

The man's smile faded. "You realize what you are doing, knave?"

Crispin felt sweat break out on his face, though the stable was cold. "It's not a very good position I'm in at the moment, is it? But neither is it good for you." And he emphasized that by pressing the blade harder against his throat. The man's Adam's apple bobbed as he swallowed.

Crispin kept the dagger steady and glanced at the other swordsmen, who hesitated at their companion's peril. He was in too deep. There was nothing for it but to get in deeper. "Will you drop your swords, or would you see your companion wear a crimson smile across his neck?"

There was much silent commiserating, but in the end, the swords clanged loudly onto the hard dirt floor.

Crispin studied the man he had captured. Well-bred, surcote, sword. Knights all, but it was too dim to see their arms properly. Each had different blazons. He could see that much. His dagger remained at the man's shaven throat but his other hand grabbed the surcote at the collar. At this point his fuzzy brain was a little uncertain how to proceed.

"Jack, are you all right?"

The boy regained his feet and was easing down his shirt with a hiss between his teeth. He winced upon reaching to the floor to retrieve his soiled coat. "Aye, Master," he said breathlessly. "As well as can be expected."

"Is what this man says true? Did you not treat them with the proper respect?"

He stuck an arm in a coat sleeve and then carefully repeated the action with the other arm, but he left it unbuttoned. "I just done what *you* would have done—"

"Answer the damned question, boy!"

He hung his head. "Aye. I reckon."

"Then what should you do now?"

Slowly, Jack got down on his knees and looked up at the knights surrounding him. "My lords. I beg your mercy. Please forgive me for speaking above my station. I meant naught by it. I only wanted to help my master, who cannot be blamed for my impertinence."

The man held captive by Crispin glared into his eyes with a look that seemed to say otherwise.

Jack knelt for several moments before Crispin told him softly to rise. With a sigh, Crispin turned to the knights.

"My apprentice has apologized. I hope you can forgive him as good Christian knights. He is young and as yet inexperienced. Perhaps he failed to frame his questions with the right tone. And so *I* will attempt it." Though he could well see the irony, as he had a dagger to one of the men's throats. "You and your companions have not, by any chance, been to London Bridge of late, have you?"

The blond knight under Crispin's dagger sneered. "We go to many places in London. Among them, Newgate. Perhaps you would also visit there again, Master Guest."

Crispin paused at the use of his name. "No, thank you. I've seen enough of Newgate."

"Have you? One wonders." His eyes dropped to the knife again.

"There was a murder. A man was killed on the bridge last night. But rumors had it as suicide."

"Maybe it was."

"Oh no. I have seen much evidence to the contrary. The sheriffs are now treating it as a murder." He hoped. "You were seen that night."

"Oh? By whom? We shall visit them and ask them personally."

Crispin did not look at Jack. "That won't be necessary."

The man's expression did not change. "Are we done here, Master Guest?"

He tried one last time to make out their blazons in the dim light, but could see little. The wine also made certain of that.

Reluctantly, Crispin withdrew the dagger and stepped back, bowing deeply, hoping that the man would not now hew off his head while he was so vulnerable. "My sincerest apologies, my lords, and I beg your mercy for my foolish servant. And also I apologize most humbly for my own actions. My only excuse is that I was out of my mind for fear of my servant's safety, for I alone am responsible for him."

Crispin remained with his back bent and his head lowered, not daring to look up. This would either be the end of it . . . or the end of him.

A fist clouted the side of his head and toppled him. He rolled in the hay and righted himself, standing none too steadily. "I should kick you to death, Crispin Guest," said the man he had captured, teeth gritted. He rubbed at his neck where the dagger's blade had been. "But I know you. I should have known that this knave was yours. Have better care. And teach him some manners." He swung a kick at Crispin, catching him in the shin. He went down on that knee as the man strode by him, pushing Gilbert and the clerk out of the way.

The other knights retrieved their swords and looked as if they, too, would clout him, but they merely sneered in his direction and left the stable, shouldering him roughly on their way out.

The shaggy horse seemed relieved and snorted once before its whiskered muzzle reached over the top of the wooden stall and it began chewing on the wood.

Crispin straightened and found Jack beside him, offering to help. The boy looked as chastened as a penitent, but that was not enough for Crispin. Without acknowledging him, he turned to the tavern keeper. "I thank you, Gilbert. And you, Master Lucas."

The clerk bowed to Crispin. "Always willing to help." He held out his hand and Crispin found there the coin he had given the man earlier. Crispin took it with a nod and clenched it in his fist.

"Home, Jack," he rasped. He did not need to look back to know that the boy followed him.

Though it was only a few lanes to the Shambles, tonight it seemed like a much longer walk. Crispin was still in the throes of wine spirits and now the hot blood that had sustained him during the encounter had cooled. Jack followed silently behind and climbed the stairs to their lodgings with light steps.

Once Crispin unlocked the door and moved into their dark

surroundings, Jack slipped past him and knelt at the fire. He immediately set to work churning the coals to a small flame.

Crispin sat on his bed and pulled off his boots.

Jack continued at the fire, breaking off a piece of peat and laying it on the glowing flames, watching it catch. The firelight flickered over his face and glossy eyes. It was only then, in the safety of their lodgings, that Jack's emotions seemed to give way, and big, round tears overflowed his eyes and streaked trails down his cheeks. He stifled a sob and that was when Crispin rose from his bed.

He knelt beside the boy. "Does it hurt much?"

With tears still gliding down his face, Jack turned his amber eyes to his master. He slowly shook his head.

"Come now. That coat must be scratchy."

"But it's cold."

"Here. I'll help you put it on backwards."

Jack allowed Crispin to help him off with his coat and then slip his arms in so the back of the cotehardie covered his chest. "Now turn your back to the fire and you will be warm enough."

Crispin crossed the room to retrieve the wine jug and then a wooden bowl from the pantry shelf. He poured what was left into the bowl and handed it to Jack.

"No, sir. That is all we have."

"In truth, I've had enough this day. Take it."

Jack did and drank it thirstily.

Crispin watched him for a moment more before he sat on the floor next to him. He clasped his legs, rubbing his bruised shin, and positioned himself with his back to the flames as well.

"I think we both learned a lesson today."

Jack wiped at his face, sniffing. "Aye. I learned not to be smart to my betters. I'm not you, after all. What did *you* learn?"

Crispin stared straight ahead at the legs of the table and at the shadows climbing up the door and walls. "I learned that I must remember you are still only fourteen."

"But sir!"

"Do you dare naysay me, you with a raw back? I should have inflicted those wounds myself. I still should."

"Aye. You'd be in the right."

"Of course I would! You've no right going about London behaving as arrogant as . . . as . . ."

"As you?"

He backhanded Jack on the ear, but out of the corner of his eye he could see the boy smiling. "As a lord. What the devil did you think you were doing?"

"I was questioning them. And they didn't like it."

"Of course they didn't. All they saw was a scrawny apprentice harassing them."

"I'm not scrawny," he muttered.

"So you saw that lot on the bridge?"

"Aye. They was—*were*—standing in the back of the crowd, looking pleased about something."

Crispin rocked on his haunches, thinking. "Did they tell you anything of worth?"

"No, Master. When I pressed them they did look surprised but then they got cross, as lordly men are like to do with my ilk." He peeked at Crispin under the curled fringe at his brow. "Some get angrier than most."

Crispin hid his smile by laying his cheek upon his upraised knees. "No doubt. Though I wonder at their mercy. I was surprised to get off with a bruised shin and nothing more. They were well within their right to kill me or have me arrested."

"Perhaps they did not wish your attention, Master. The one man knew you."

He lifted his head. "From that night or by my reputation?"

"Dunno. Either way, it is a good thing. But you are right in that they wish to be rid of you, which means they bear more scrutiny. Though . . . from a distance." He studied Crispin's profile. "I know why I suspected them, but why did you?"

"For one, I trust your judgment . . . mostly." Jack's cheeks reddened. "And for another, Anabel's witnesses said as much."

Jack sniffed and lowered his head. "So she *is* a better apprentice than me."

"Don't be a fool."

Jack blinked, staring into the shadows until he slowly turned his face back to Crispin. His eyes were dark pits with the merest hint of a glittering reflection. Softly, he said, "I'm sorry, Master Crispin, for getting you into trouble."

"I certainly don't need help to get into trouble. I do it very well on my own, thank you."

"Still." Jack pulled fretfully at the frayed sleeve cuffs of his cotehardie. "I'm a terrible apprentice. I can't even question people properly." The hitch in his voice shouldn't have disturbed Crispin since he was angry at the boy, but he suddenly realized that his anger had abated a while ago and now he was only relieved that Jack was alive with only a striped back. It could have gone much worse for him.

"You'll learn. Take your time. And always, *always* show respect, especially to your betters. Do not be schooled by my actions for I have a long history with men of that station. Do as I tell you and not as I do."

"Yes, Master Crispin."

Fourteen. He recalled quite well what he was like himself at that age. Always ready to go fiercely forward to some dangerous enterprise. But he had had arms training to cool his blood and keep his itchy limbs occupied. He had even gone to war with Lancaster when he was only fifteen, but he was already well accomplished on a horse and with arms. Lancaster had made him glow with pride when he told him what a quick study he was, how well versed on battlefield tactics and how quick with a sword.

Jack was like a colt tied in a stable. He longed to stretch his legs and run wild.

"Let us both eat and then get some rest, Jack. We'll have a busy day tomorrow."

IN THE MORNING, JACK seemed to have recovered and was in fact whistling while preparing the hot water for Crispin's morning ablutions.

Crispin, on the other hand, was nursing a headache from the previous night's drinking. "Must you do that?" he grumbled.

"You look none too steady this morning, Master. How about I shave you?"

Crispin eyed him warily but decided the boy wanted to make up for yesterday. He nodded and let Jack assemble the basin, towel, soap, and razor on their table. Crispin sat with the basin in his hands while Jack soaped his face. Crispin sat very still as Jack, with face screwed up in concentration and teeth biting his overhanging tongue, carefully dragged the iron razor over Crispin's cheek. It took longer than Crispin might have done, but both master and servant were pleased with the results.

Jack wrung the wet towel in the basin and dumped the water out the back garden window. "How come you don't favor a beard, Master?"

Crispin wiped the remaining soap from his face with the back of his fingers and shrugged into a clean chemise. "I never cared for the look on me, Jack. Simple vanity."

"You have a good strong face, sir. You don't need no beard."

"Flattery, Jack?" He pulled on his cotehardie and began buttoning. "I already forgave you for yesterday."

Jack, face red as he put the razor back on its shelf, turned away from Crispin. "I know, sir. I just . . . want to make it up to you."

"And you will. You will comport yourself better, will you not? You represent me when you conduct my business, Jack. I expect better."

"Y-yes, sir."

"Very well. That is done. I will work you hard today. We have a stop at the bridge and then to Islington."

"What's in Islington?"

"You'll see."

JACK REMAINED QUIET BUT alert. A little stiff from his beating, but he seemed to have recovered well, as the young often did. He strode alongside Crispin down the Shambles where it became East Cheap, swinging his long arms and darting his eyes to this and that, even turning his head and then his whole body to watch a pretty maid carrying a baby goat over her shoulders with a dog at her feet, urging her small braying herd of goats ahead of her. He walked backward and grinned at her. The girl noticed him, too, and turned to look back, offering a dimpled smile.

"Stop thinking with your cod, Tucker," said Crispin out of the side of his mouth.

Jack turned a beaming smile toward him. "I can think with me brain at the same time, sir."

He chuckled. "I've never met a man who could."

A drizzle began, graying the streets before them. Some ran for the eaves of the shops and chatted with shopkeepers within. Others, like Crispin and Jack, lowered their faces, letting their hoods cover them as they trudged on.

After the bells of the churches rang Terce, they reached the bridge, paid their toll, and passed through the gatehouse. The rain was steady now, and they trod the rain-slickened lane to the armorer's once again. The door was still boarded and there was a parchment with the seal of the sheriffs nailed to the door. Crispin didn't bother to read it. He opened the window shutter, climbed up onto the sill, and jumped inside. Jack followed and they stood in the dark and musty shop side by side. Crispin strode immediately to a rack that held swords and lifted two of them free. He handed them both to Jack without a word.

They clattered in Jack's clumsy embrace. "Er . . . sir? Are we . . . *stealing* these?"

"Of course not," said Crispin, searching the room for what he sought. "We are only borrowing them. Ah!" He found a flail and a wooden shield sheathed with leather and handed those, too, to Jack. Jack fumbled with the new additions and cursed under his breath, trying to balance it all.

"That's enough for now. Let's go."

Crispin, unencumbered, climbed out the window easily and waited on the street for Jack.

The shield made an appearance first on the window sill and then the arms clattered behind it, with only a tuft of ginger hair in the rear. "Master! I cannot climb with this burden."

"Give it here." Crispin snatched shield and swords and leaned them against the shop wall as Jack made his way over the window and down. He closed the shutter and picked up his burdens again.

"Where to now?" Jack looked around anxiously, and a few bridge folk did look at them with peculiar frowns.

"To Islington. To practice."

"To practice what, sir?"

"Arms. You are sorely lacking in instruction, Jack. It is well past time I teach you to fight properly."

IT WAS STILL RAINING when they reached the fields outside of London. The archery butts stood alone and unmolested at the far end of the field but there were soldiers lingering under the trees, watching them warily.

As soon as Jack understood what Crispin meant to do with the weapons, he had a spring in his step and never complained at his ungainly burden. But once they reached the place, he dumped the weapons to the ground with an apologetic expression. He shook out his hands and stood silently, waiting for instruction.

Crispin smiled. The boy liked learning things. He had taken to reading and writing readily enough. But he could see now that the lad was more than ready for this particular tutelage.

"I want you to realize, Jack, that never should you raise a weapon to one of your betters. I am a different case, as you know. I did so with those knights last evening . . . and it was a mistake. I never should have done that. I was . . . perhaps a little in my cups." It was embarrassing admitting it, but he knew that Jack knew it well. "And so this is only to teach you to defend yourself. Never should you challenge a man for a point of honor. That does not suit your status. Neither will you likely be carrying a sword . . . but one never knows. You can learn to fight with it at any rate, and use any other weapon like it to your advantage. So. Pick them up and give one to me. I will show you the basics."

"Do I not need a shield, sir?" he said, eyeing the shield on the ground while he picked up both swords and handed one to Crispin.

"No. A good fighter does not need a shield. Indeed, it can sometimes get in the way."

"Of one's flesh, you mean," he muttered.

"I wish Master Grey had had wooden practice blades but we will do our best not to injure each other, eh, Jack?"

"Aye, sir." Jack clutched the hilt, blade down.

Crispin curled his hands around the grip of his weapon and felt the heft of it. It was a good sword. Good weight, good balance. He held it aloft and gave some practice swings, cutting the air with a whistle. Rain pattered off its shiny surface and he couldn't help but smile to feel it in his hand. It almost made him feel like himself . . . yet that was all so long ago, and with an alarming pang in his heart, he realized that he didn't know if he could quite recall anymore who he had been.

"Now Jack, observe. The blade, an edge on both sides. The guard." He ran his other hand along the cross guard. "It protects your hand, gives you balance, and can be used in a manner of ways which I will show you anon. Here the pommel. Feel how heavy, how solid it is. It can also be used as a weapon."

Jack followed his lead, holding the sword as Crispin did and running his hand over each part as Crispin enumerated them.

"Jack, you face your opponent, knees bent, ready for anything." Jack did likewise, bouncing on his knees.

"And then—"

Crispin lunged, sword raised over his head to chop down.

With a shout, Jack raised his sword to block it. But metal did not touch metal.

Crispin slowly lowered the blade and laughed. "Excellent, Jack.

You have superb instincts. We'll do bladework first before I show you what your body should be doing."

Crispin instructed him on using the sword, not only for chopping, but for swinging like a club, using as a hook with the cross guard, like a hammer with the pommel end, and then how to disarm with feet, dagger, and hands. Despite the rain, they were both in a sweat.

The boy never complained of growing tired, wet, or sore from his striped back. Jack's eyes told Crispin all he needed to know. The lad gloried in arms training just as much as Crispin had. Such a pity that they had so little time with these weapons.

A crash in the underbrush. Crispin pivoted, brandishing his sword.

But it was only Ned, the scullion at the Boar's Tusk, stumbling upon the wet grass with an exhausted breath. "Master Crispin," he huffed as Crispin helped him to his feet. "I've been looking all over London for you!"

"For me?" His heart gave a shudder. "Gilbert and Eleanor? Are they in danger?"

"No, no, Master. Nothing like that." His eyes took in the swords and then raked over Jack with a tinge of envy. "Your landlord, Master Kemp, came looking for you and Master Gilbert sent me to find you."

"How did you know to come here?" asked Jack.

"I'd exhausted everywhere else and your master has been known to practice with the bow on the butts." He turned to Crispin. "Your landlord, sir, says you are to come home at once. The sheriffs are awaiting you and will not leave until you make yourself known to them."

Crispin exchanged looks with Jack before he handed his sword to Ned. "Ned, make sure these are returned to their owner. Er . . .

give them to Master Coterel the tailor on London Bridge. And here. Two coins; one for your passage and one for your trouble."

He dug into his pouch for the coins and left the weaponry behind as he ushered Jack quickly across the field to the road back to London.

12

CRISPIN ENTERED HIS LODGINGS, catching the sheriffs going through his things. There wasn't much to go through, but an uncomfortable feeling still slithered up his spine. He shut the door harder than he meant to do.

"My lords," he said, and Sheriff More, startled, dropped Crispin's wax slate back into the coffer. He turned with an apologetic smile on his face, which quickly transformed to a somber expression when he noted Sheriff Staundon's carefully schooled demeanor.

"Ah, Master Guest," said Staundon in funereal tones. His usually cheerful face conveyed an unaccustomed expression of solemnity, as if he were addressing a great crowd. "We came to tell you that last night a young lad was found washed ashore from the Thames, upstream, and I regret to say that he has been identified as one of Master Grey's apprentices."

"The younger one," put in Sheriff More, closing the lid of the coffer. "God have mercy."

Crispin crossed himself and set his jaw. "And so now you believe me."

Staundon looked to More and nodded. "Indeed. There is no sign of the other one, but the inquest jury was quick to declare the deaths murder. All three. We . . ." He gestured to More. "We wanted you to know, Master Crispin."

"I thank you, my lords."

They all fell silent. Crispin thought by their grave expressions that that would be the end of it and they would leave him to it, but no such luck.

Both sheriffs hesitated before leaning forward, rolling on the balls of their feet. Staundon's somber façade dissolved. "Well? Have you discovered anything more of any consequence, Master Crispin?"

"Yes," said More. "We are most anxious to help. For it is most definitely murder now."

Crispin curled his fingers around his dagger hilt. "I have no further information to share." They frowned and Crispin tried again. "That is to say, there are no further tidings."

Disappointed, the sheriffs commiserated silently before moving toward the door. "I see," said Staundon. He glanced back at the coffer, at the wine jug on the sill. "You will let us know how the investigation progresses, will you not, Master Crispin? You have promised."

He bowed. "I give you my solemn word, Lord Sheriff."

"Hm," he snorted before grabbing the latch.

More gestured toward the coffer from the doorway. "I used to read a little Greek. When I was a boy, I had a foreign tutor. But it has been a while. Pray, what does the wax slate say?"

Crispin had written it for Jack to copy out. He set his features to a blank expression. "'Righteous indignation is a mean between envy and spite; the man who is characterized by righteous indignation is pained at undeserved good fortune, the envious man is pained at *all* good fortune, and the spiteful man falls so far short that he even rejoices.'"

More paused. His brows lowered over his eyes. "Oh. Well. An interesting philosophy, I suppose."

"I am fond of the wisdom of Aristotle."

"So I have heard. But 'envy and spite'?" He reddened. "Surely there is room in between for true righteous indignation. For those, er . . . interested in seeing justice served. I daresay, these are strong words and from a pagan, no less. How can his opinion hold such store today?"

"Truth is truth, no matter the messenger." He bowed.

More took the hint at last. He narrowed his eyes at Crispin before escaping out the door. Crispin listened to their footfalls gratefully before he rested against the closed door. "I grow weary of those two."

"And not one word of paying your fee, Master. They've got their nerve."

Jack suddenly clamped his lips shut. Someone was returning up the steps. Crispin didn't hesitate to open the door, expecting one of the sheriffs.

Instead, Sir Thomas pushed his way through and all but pounced on him. "Crispin! Where, by the saints, have you been? I waited an eternity for those sheriffs to depart."

"I've been out." He bolted the door after him.

Jack removed his wet cloak, hung it by the door, and then went immediately to the fire to stoke it.

Thomas tore his gaze away from Crispin as he, too, removed his sodden cloak and draped it over the chair by the fire. Steam rose from the dank wool. The knight paced, wringing his hands. "I am being followed," he said, striding back and forth across the tiny room.

"Are you certain?"

"Yes . . . NO! I . . . do not know." He stopped before Crispin's chair and clutched the back of it. "I *think* there were those following me."

"More than one man, you mean?"

"Yes. But sometimes . . . sometimes my mind conjures these injuries where there is none. Now it is worse than ever."

"And so . . . no one may be following you?"

"I tell you I don't know!"

Crispin breathed a long breath. "Sit down, Sir Thomas." Jack was already beside him with a bowl of ale. "Drink, Thomas. And tell me what you would have me know." He handed the man the bowl and he took it, slowly sinking to the chair.

"My mind is besieged. I fear every shadow, every creak of wood. There *were* men following me. I *know* it." The hand not holding the bowl clenched to a tight fist. "What am I to do?"

"Have . . . have you surrendered yourself to the judges yet?"

He shook his head, scrubbed his face, and shakily drank from the bowl.

"You know you must. These shades that haunt you may very well be your conscience."

"I know, I know." Shoulders slumping, his breath was harsh and irregular in the quiet room.

"At least I found the armor that Master Grey made for you."

"Eh?" Thomas's eyes were dulled and stared into a dim corner when he lifted his face.

"Master Grey made you a fine new breastplate with your arms scrolled upon it. It will surely help with your trials to come."

"Yes. My trials. He is—*was*—a fine craftsman. Where is it?"

"Back at his shop. I will go with you to fetch it, if you like."

"That is good of you, Crispin. You have been kind and patient with me. More than I deserve."

Crispin sat on the stool and scooted it closer to the man. "What has happened to you, Thomas?"

He shook his head. Stubble peppered his chin. He had not combed his hair nor shaved. His whole appearance was that of a disheveled beggar. "I do not know. Would that I did. But I must face my judges and win my trials. Did you know the joust is to be on the bridge?"

"I had heard that. I did not know it was to be for your trials."

"Why not? Sport and humiliation go hand in hand."

"You will be triumphant."

"You are so certain. I am not."

"Thomas—"

"I am under no delusion, Crispin. I am as good as a dead man."

"No. NO! I refuse to believe it. And *you* must not. The battle is won in the mind first, you know this as well as I."

Thomas shot to his feet. "That is why I need that relic! Crispin, are you any nearer to finding it?"

Guiltily, Crispin rose, too. "No, Sir Thomas, I am not. But—"

"There shall be no more secrets between us, Crispin. I feared that you would somehow let it slip, that others would know and then they would seek it out and grasp it for themselves. And I could not allow that. But now I see the folly in this. I must tell you what it is. Then, sweet Jesu, you may find it for me and save my life."

Crispin waited, unwittingly grasping his dagger hilt with tightening fingers.

"This armorer, this Master Grey," said Thomas slowly. "He was a most ingenious fellow. He obtained this precious relic through means I know not of. Legal? I didn't care. He had it and I wanted it. He wrote me letters, keeping me apprised of his dealings, and when he had it in his possession, he begged me to return to London to receive it along with my new armor."

"God's death, Thomas. Tell me! What *is* it?"

Softly, he said, "It is the Spear of Longinus, the Holy Lance; the spear that pierced the side of our Lord while he hung dying on the cross." His red-rimmed eyes stared distantly with a glassy haze. "That very relic was to be in *my* hands, on the end of *my* lance. I would be victorious every time. He wrote me of its provenance. It was the true relic, Crispin, and it was to be mine. And now it is gone."

Crispin hadn't realized that his mouth was hanging open until he shut it. He spared a glance at Jack, who was pressed against the wall beside the fireplace. He wore that same fishlike expression.

"The . . . Holy Lance? Good Christ. What . . . where . . ." Crispin sat. "God's blood, I never expected *that*."

"But you will search for it, will you not, Crispin? You made an oath to me."

"Yes, I know, but . . ." The man wasn't even looking at him anymore. His thoughts were far away, and so were Crispin's. On impossible tasks. But he *had* made an oath . . .

Crispin gazed up into his rafters; dark, smoky, cobwebbed. "Thomas, at least go retrieve your armor. Talk to Master Coterel, the tailor next door. His daughter will get you inside."

Thomas said nothing more, didn't even ask what Crispin meant. He simply rose and dragged his feet to the door.

"One thing more," said Crispin, stopping the knight. "The letters from Master Grey. Where are they? May I see them?"

"I burnt them. I did not want anyone to know."

Crispin closed his eyes briefly, mourning the loss of a valuable clue. "Of course not. Regrettable."

Sir Thomas glanced at Jack, then Crispin, and nodded solemnly, before unbolting the door.

When they could hear the tread of his feet on the steps no more, Crispin sat and stared into the fire. Jack came up beside him. "You don't think that Master Grey *really* got the Spear, do you, Master?"

"Anything is possible."

"What do you know of this relic, sir?"

"Nothing. Only as much as anyone might."

"Then we'd best go to the Abbot of Westminster, eh? He knows all about relics and such. How else are we to find it?"

"That is a very good suggestion, Jack. Let us go now."

WESTMINSTER WAS BUSTLING AT midday, even through the rain. Though shopkeepers seemed to have empty shops, people were on the streets, moving from place to place or talking furtively in front of braziers.

Crispin stopped a meat pie seller pushing his cart through the mud and bought a small hand-size pie each for Jack and himself. Remarkably, his was still warm when he bit into it, the flavors of clove and cinnamon awakening his tongue. The exertion of earlier seemed to have burned the illness out of him and he inhaled appreciatively, simply because he could. He could taste the pie, too, and he chewed enthusiastically, even though there was more gristle in it than meat.

When he finished, he rubbed his hands together, divesting them of crumbs and grease. By then the abbey stood before them and Crispin led Jack through the ancient church to the south transept and asked a monk to allow him in to see the abbot.

But instead of the young cleric hurrying him through as Crispin was used to, the monk apologized with a sorrowful expression. "Forgive me, Master Crispin. But the abbot is not here."

"Not here? Where is he, then?"

He becrossed himself and with a hitch in his voice declared, "He has taken ill, sir. Very ill. His chaplain, Brother John, has taken him to the abbot estates at La Neyte."

"His estates? But I saw him here only yesterday." Crispin's mind had suddenly stopped working. The abbot had always been at Westminster, seldom at his estates. He had known Nicholas a long time. He *was* Westminster Abbey. He was the architect of all the renewal and renovation the abbey had undergone, commissioning the Purbeck marble for the pillars, enlarging the abbey cloisters, and so many other innovations that Crispin had lost count. He did not want to contemplate the abbey without him, and, selfishly, he did not want to lose a friend and ally.

"May I go to see him there?"

"He is at his ease for the moment," said the monk, sniffing and rubbing his nose. His eyes were red and ready to tear. "I think he would be pleased to see a friend."

"Then I will go. Thank you, Brother." He bowed and Jack did likewise before following Crispin out.

He walked dazedly away from Westminster, north toward Tothill Fields. Houses were few as they left the city behind.

Jack had been quiet but he wiped the rain from his face, looked up at the darkly mottled sky, and sighed. "You've known the Lord Abbot a long time, sir?"

Crispin's thoughts had been on that. "Yes. All my life, in truth. But I did not know him well until I became a young man. At eighteen or so."

Jack said nothing more and followed Crispin down the muddy lane into the meadow and past small clusters of woodland at the slow rise of the land.

They entered a wood—little more than a stand of sweet-scented laurels—and when they emerged again they came to the lane of a manor house surrounded by a low stone wall. There was no one at the gatehouse, and so they proceeded up the pathway to the front entrance. Crispin pulled the bell chain and waited. Presently, Brother John came to the door and bowed to him. "Master Guest," he said. "Please come in. He will be cheered to see you."

They entered into a great hall and stood on straw, their cloaks dripping. Crispin discreetly shook out his heavy mantle and peeled back his hood. He moved forward at the urging of Brother John and entered into a room under an arched doorway just off the hall.

A canopy hung over a bed, where the pale abbot lay propped up against a bedhead. He was not in his cassock as Crispin was used to seeing him, but instead in a chemise and a fur-trimmed bed gown. Crispin approached. The abbot appeared asleep, but when a floorboard creaked under Crispin's boot, his eyes snapped open, focusing on him.

"Crispin. So soon I see you again."

Crispin knelt by the bed. "My Lord Abbot. I heard that you had taken ill. It is not usual for you to retreat to La Neyte to take your ease."

"Ah, Crispin. Does not a dog at the end of his day return to the hearth? And so, too, do I. For I know I am at the end of my day."

"No, Nicholas. You are robust yet. It was only yesterday that Brother John was laying out your armor."

"No more battles for me. Please get up, Crispin. Here. Young Jack? Fetch a chair for your master and bring it here beside my bed."

Jack scrambled and found a folding chair in a corner by a window, grasped it by its arms, and hustled it back to the side of the abbot's bed. Crispin swept his cloak aside and sat.

"Though I am not a wagering man," said the abbot, "I am willing to venture that you did not come to wish me well." He held up his hand to Crispin's protests. "I merely mean, Master Tracker, that you most likely went to the abbey to query me on some matter and discovered I was here."

Caught. Crispin shook his head. "It does not matter now, Nicholas."

"Oh come. My eyes are too weary to read and my ears too taxed to listen to Brother John." He smiled, his wrinkled mouth furrowing. "So tell me, Master Guest. Use me, while there is light left in this soul."

Crispin glanced at Jack, and the boy, as usual, was standing behind his chair. "You know me too well, Father Abbot. Very well. This will pique your interest. I came to learn of the Holy Lance."

Nicholas's eyes widened. "The Spear of Longinus? Crispin, I . . . it frightens me when you ask these questions."

"Frightens, my lord? I merely ask out of curiosity—"

"It is not appropriate that you should lie to me, Crispin. We have known each other far too long. You have come to me for years asking about this relic and that. Haven't you ever wondered? Haven't you ever pondered why the Almighty has graced you with their care?"

Crispin shifted on his seat. "I try *not* to think of that, Nicholas."

"But why? Crispin, I have contemplated God's wishes for the many decades that I have been a brother in the Church, trying as best as a man can do to fulfill my vocation. I have prayed, I have built up His mighty church, an edifice of faith at Westminster. I have followed the dictates of my king, the anointed of God.

Without the sin of pride, I can heartily say that I have done more than is required in sacrifice and suffering." He touched his heart and bowed his head, his ermine hair swaying with the movement. "I have made a great study of the relics of his Holy Ones throughout Christendom. But Crispin, I have never experienced what you have undergone when guarding or returning His most holy relics back to their proper places. And yet you tell me you do not believe in their power."

Crispin drummed his fingers on the arm of the chair and stopped when he realized what he was doing. "My lord, I haven't your strength of faith. I see them as objects of greed and envy, something to be bartered in the marketplaces. Something to be stolen. To kill for. I cannot see that they are a benefit to man when such ill-doings are associated with them. I'd rather they never existed."

Nicholas gasped and Crispin cursed himself for his wayward tongue. He was used to being honest with the monk, used to arguing with him. It did not occur to him that this was not the appropriate moment for such stark candor.

"Forgive me, Nicholas. You know me. I give no quarter when my opinion is asked."

"Indeed not, Master Guest. Your frankness has always been valuable to me. But I see that you wear a blindfold when it comes to God's relics."

"We mustn't continue to have this argument," he said kindly.

Nicholas chuckled. "You are a most stubborn pupil." He raised his eyes to Jack, still standing stoically behind Crispin's chair. "Is it so, young man? Do you find your master to be a stubborn man?"

Jack, startled to be addressed, paused. Finally, when Crispin twisted around to look at him, he lowered his eyes. "I must not say so, my lord."

Both Nicholas and Crispin laughed. "And perhaps a stubborn apprentice, as well," said the old monk.

"It's what I deserve," admitted Crispin.

The abbot's chuckle became a hum and he smoothed the crisp sheets with a quivering hand. "But we distract ourselves. We were speaking of a most holy relic, no? I take it you know what it is."

Crispin nodded. "It is the spear that a centurion used to pierce the side of Christ on the cross."

This time it was Jack's turn to gasp. Over his shoulder, he heard his apprentice mutter a prayer.

"When it pierced the side of our Lord, blood and water poured forth, the blood of our sins and the waters of baptism. *Lancea Longini,*" said Nicholas. "From the apocryphal gospel of Nicodemus. The spear head, at least, was said to be passed from the family of this centurion, Longinus, to other holy men, who kept it in safekeeping for many years." He licked his lips and coughed. "Please. A little wine."

Crispin rose but Jack was faster. He poured wine from a silver flagon into two silver-rimmed horn cups sitting on a sideboard. With a bow, he gave the first to the abbot and the second to Crispin.

Nicholas smiled at Jack. "A fine apprentice," he muttered before taking a sip, clearing his throat, and then sipping again. "As I was saying, the spear made many journeys to many places. Eventually, the spear tip was broken off and sent to France where, as you know, it is housed in the Sainte Chapelle in Paris."

"Along with the Crown of Thorns," said Crispin, drinking the pale Spanish wine.

Jack leaned forward. "But Master! The Crown—"

"Is back in Paris, Jack, where it belongs." *Minus a thorn or two,* he mused to himself.

The monk raised his hand. "However, the other piece of the spearhead disappeared. At one time, pilgrims have said to have seen it at the Church of the Holy Sepulcher in Jerusalem, but when Jerusalem was sacked by the Persian infidels, it made its way to Constantinople."

"Jack," said Crispin out of the side of his mouth. "You're breathing down my neck!"

"Oh! Sorry, sir."

"And from thence," the abbot went on, "it made its way to various churches, after which it seems to have disappeared. Though I greatly fear that you, Master Guest, are about to tell me where it is now and in what peril."

Crispin choked on his wine and Jack thumped his back until he turned to give the boy an evil eye.

Setting his wine aside, Crispin straightened his coat. "I merely wished to discover its provenance, good abbot. It has not yet crossed my path, though . . . as you have guessed, I am charged with finding it."

"Bless me!" Agitated, the abbot jerked his hand and the cup spilled a patch of wine onto the sheets. "Oh! Look what I have done!"

Jack pressed forward but it was Brother John who swooped in like a sparrow and with a cloth, blotted the golden wine until the abbot waved him off with an impatient mutter. "Don't fuss, Brother John. You know I cannot abide it."

"My lord," he said with a bow and stepped deftly away from the bed, glancing at Crispin as he passed.

Nicholas wagged a finger at Crispin. "Master Guest, take care. This is a dangerous object. The owner of the Spear is utterly invincible."

"The thorns from the Crown were supposed to have the same influence."

"No. It is much more than the thorns from the Crown of Thorns. The thorns protected the man who was pure of heart. They made him invulnerable to harm. But the Spear is different. It imbues the owner with an invincibility unmatched. Why, he could conquer his enemies, wage war and be the victor, he could—"

"Win a joust?"

The abbot's pale blue eyes scoured Crispin's gray. "More than win it. He could win far more than that. But he need not be pure of heart, as the thorns demanded. *That* is what makes this a most dangerous relic. It wields its own power."

"Master!" whispered Jack.

"Hush, Jack." Crispin handed his cup to the boy, who set it on the sideboard. "Nicholas, I have sworn to turn this relic over to . . . someone. I made an oath."

"And your oaths are worth more than gold. I only hope that this can come to a happy conclusion. You have seen much sorrow, my young friend. I hope, that in the end, you will make the right choice."

Nicholas said no more. He seemed content to merely stare with disconcerting concentration.

"I will do my best as always, my Lord Abbot."

"See that you do. Now Young Master Tucker, convey your master hence so that I can get my rest. This is troublesome business, dying."

"God keep you, good sir," said Jack, bowing and standing beside Crispin, who rose from his seat. The abbot sketched a cross over them both in blessing.

"And no more talk of dying, old man," said Crispin with a brief smile. He took his leave, and with a gesture to Brother John, quit the bedroom.

In the hall, Crispin took Brother John aside. "I know he is ill, but—" Crispin frowned. "I saw him only yesterday! You were helping him with his armor."

The monk shook his head. "He has not eaten in some days now. He takes only small quantities of wine with a little bread. He is an old man and I suppose the body knows . . ." He looked back at the closed door, but it was more to conceal a tear than to worry whether the abbot could hear him. He wiped at his eyes. "I fear the king will be choosing a new abbot soon."

It was like a blade twisting in his heart. Crispin could barely breathe. But the man was seventy-five if a day. He was due his rest in the arms of God. Such a selfish heart to want to keep him here.

He clenched his jaw, nodded to the monk for he did not trust his voice, and led Jack out the door.

He stood on the path and looked back at the manor house, at the vines crawling up its stone face, at the pleasant fields surrounding it. He thought of the man within, whom he had known well for nearly two decades, and at the quiet tragedy unfolding.

He whipped his hood up over his head and strode quickly down the path to the road.

SUBDUED FOR MOST OF the journey back to Westminster, Jack finally spoke when they reached Charing Cross. "He always seemed like a kind old gentleman. Not like a monk at all."

Crispin smiled. "A fine compliment. He would be pleased. I shall tell him when next I see him." And then he wondered when that would be. *If* it would be.

Jack stopped abruptly and threw an arm across Crispin's chest.

About to admonish his servant, Crispin saw his eyes. They were hard gems. "Master Chaucer," he whispered, and gestured with the tilt of his head.

Geoffrey Chaucer rode down the Strand, moving his horse with purpose toward the direction of London. Crispin said nothing to Jack, but they both hurried their pursuit.

13

CHAUCER TURNED OFF THE London road and into an inn yard. He tossed the reins to a waiting groom. Crispin and Jack waited in the shadows across the lane and watched as Chaucer crossed the yard and entered the inn.

"Jack, I can't go inside. I'll be spotted. You must go."

"Right, Master!"

He grabbed the lad's hood and yanked him back. "Make certain you are not seen."

"Aye, sir. I understand." He made to move forward again but Crispin pulled him back a second time.

"Find out who he is meeting."

"I *know*, Master Crispin! I wasn't made no Tracker's apprentice yesterday." In a huff, he stomped toward the inn and disappeared into the shade of its muddy courtyard.

Crispin crossed his arms over his chest and leaned against a gatepost. His hood hung low, nearly blocking his view, but he was glad of it, as the rain had not stopped, though it had eased from before.

He tried not to think about Abbot Nicholas. Instead, he thought of his current situation, threading the many bits and patches through his head: the dead armorer and the missing relic; the stolen rent money; the three knights; Lenny; Sir Thomas. And Chaucer. How did *his* presence slip into these strange and unrelated events? What the hell was he up to in that inn? Oh to be a fly on the wall. But his own little fly was doing his spying for him. Crispin could only hope he did it well enough that Chaucer would not notice him.

He sniffed, feeling with relief the stuffiness finally receding. He didn't suppose standing in the rain would ease his cold, but it couldn't be helped. He glanced down the lane— God's death! Not those damned sheriffs again. Didn't they have the peace to keep? From atop their mounts the pair smiled at him.

He didn't need this right now.

He composed his features before pushing away from the post and sauntering toward them. They all but rubbed their hands together in anticipation. When he came alongside them he bowed. "Lord Sheriffs."

"It's a small world, isn't it, seeing you again so soon, Master Crispin?" said Staundon. "But a fortunate meeting, for I have new tidings. We have looked at the evidence and made the notation that you have done your job well, being the First Finder, Master Crispin."

"Indeed," put in More. "You called the hue and cry as is prescribed and you gave good testimony to the coroner. All in all, we cannot see fit to fine you."

"That's a mercy," he mumbled.

Staundon leaned down. "Did you say something, Master Crispin?"

"No, nothing. Only that I am glad that the jury found Grey's death a murder. It was not fit to bury the man without the blessings of the Church."

"Rightly so," said More, crossing himself. "We hope to find the other apprentice. It does not do well that he should lie at the bottom of the Thames without the proper burial sacraments."

Staundon nodded his head solemnly for the allotted moment before he got right to the point as he leaned an arm across the pommel of his saddle. "Have we caught you in the midst of your investigations, Crispin?"

More looked around with bright eyes. Did he hope to see the murderer come striding up to Crispin, a flag of surrender in his hands?

"Er . . . it is a delicate business, my lords. I am waiting for my apprentice to arrive with information."

"Oh?" Staundon dismounted and grabbed the horse's lead with a gloved fist. "Perhaps we can help."

"Yes, indeed!" More slipped off his horse as well and anxiously surveyed the lane. "From which direction is he bound to come?"

Crispin flicked his eyes across the lane. "He is in yon inn, spying."

"Spying!" cried More with glee. He clapped his hands together and then rested one on Staundon's sleeve. "Did you hear that, William?"

"Indeed I did. Why don't we go in, Master Guest, and help you get your information. The presence of the Lord Sheriffs will surely help you in your cause."

He grabbed their arms as they made to cross the lane. "My lords! Why don't we let my apprentice do his work? Sometimes it is best to keep a low profile in these endeavors."

They stared at him until More broke into a smile. "Low profile. I get your meaning, Master Crispin. And we, being the sheriffs, are the highest profile to be had, eh?"

He nodded vigorously. "Oh indeed, my lords." *You pompous asses.*

Staundon pressed his fists to his hips. "Dear me. And I was so looking forward to helping. Master Guest, you take the fun out of it."

"I apologize, my lord. I did not realize that investigating the murder of three men was somehow . . . fun."

Staundon lowered his arms and shuffled in place. "Ah. Yes. Well, certainly I did not mean that."

"Of course you didn't," said Sheriff More. "That would be most vulgar. But Master Guest must also certainly realize that without our patronage, his job would be much harder. And his fines would be more rigorous."

Crispin set his jaw. "My lords, what would I do without your help? Your full credit for solving this murder will, of course, be heralded throughout London." Again.

Sheriff Staundon smiled. "Of course. Master Guest is a clever fellow. He never misses a clue." He gazed longingly at the inn before turning abruptly on his heel. Mounting his horse, he said, "We can be as patient as the Tracker. We will wait for the conclusion of this until his apprentice returns."

"So be it," said More from atop his horse again. "He is a clever boy. Jack is his name, is it not? Whence did he come to you, Master Crispin? A servant from your *former* days at court?"

There seemed a little too much emphasis on "former," he thought, but he plastered on a faint smile. "Not at all. He used to be a cutpurse."

With swallowed gasps, the sheriffs fell blessedly silent. He stood beside their horses, allowing the flanks of the beasts to warm his back. Still, the drizzle seemed to grow colder the longer he stood. Crispin tilted his head down and crossed his arms under his cloak. Standing like a pillar, he let the rainwater cascade around him. The horses snuffled and chewed their bits with the jangling of bridles.

But the sheriffs were the impatient ones, whispering back and forth to each other, as if Crispin couldn't hear what they were saying.

At last, Jack trotted from around the wall of the inn, and stumbled when he beheld the sheriffs. The look on his face told Crispin that the lad was deciding whether to run in the opposite direction, but since everyone had spotted him, he continued on his course. When he reached Crispin he bowed to all three. "Master. What goes on here?"

"The sheriffs are here to help me, Jack."

Jack gathered the full meaning in one. "'Slud," he rasped.

"Well, Master Tucker," said Sheriff Staundon congenially. "What have you discovered?"

Eyes like bezants, he looked to Crispin for help. Crispin obliged him by turning to face the sheriffs. "My apprentice is used to dealing only with me, especially on delicate topics."

Sheriff More frowned. "Eh? Delicate?"

"At times, my lord, the subjects of our inquiries are persons of . . . grand nature."

The sheriffs exchanged glances. "Oh!" piped Staundon. "Oh, I see. You do not wish to divulge—"

"No, my lords. It is for the best. *You* would not wish to be found at fault should our subjects discover our clandestine activities, would you?"

Even their horses shied. More clutched at the reins and pulled the horse to. "No, indeed, Master Crispin!" He cast a furtive glance toward the inn. "He didn't see you, did he, Master Tucker?"

"N-no, my lords."

"That's a good lad. He's a clever boy, Crispin. Did we not say that, William? Well! Sheriff Staundon and I must be off. Do report your findings to us when you can, Master Guest."

Crispin bowed again, hiding his smile beneath his sodden hood. "In all haste, my lords."

"Good. Good." He turned the horse and, with Staundon beside him, they galloped their beasts away toward London.

"God be praised," Crispin muttered before turning to Jack. "Well?"

"It wasn't easy, Master Crispin," he said. They both began to walk toward London, leaning in toward each other to keep their conversation to themselves and to keep the rain at bay. "It was a small inn. But I kept me hood low and, luckily, Sir Geoffrey had his back to me. He met a man in a dark cloak and they retired up to a room."

Jack pulled Crispin aside and stood in front of him when a cart, going a little too fast, cast up a splatter of muddy water. His cloak took the brunt of it, and he looked back at the cart with a sneer before continuing with his tale. "As soon as they closed the door I crept up the stairs, but I couldn't hear naught through the door. Anyhow, it would have looked suspicious my standing outside it, so I went to the end of the gallery where there was a window and climbed out of it."

"You what?"

"I reckoned I'd have to listen in some other way. So I climbed out the window and went up over the roof. It was powerful slippery, mind you, with the rain and all. But I crawled along the roof and found the room below. There wasn't no balcony—"

"There wasn't *any* balcony," Crispin softly corrected out of habit.

"As I said," he went on, "so I crept as close to the edge of the roof as I dared. Their shutters were open—a good thing, too—and I listened. But because of the rain I didn't hear much. Only that Master Chaucer said he was doing the best he could and that the other man's lord would have to wait. And then the other man spoke but he had a foreign accent, and it was twice as hard to hear what he was about."

"What sort of accent?"

"I'm sorry, Master, I could not recognize it. But then in the midst of their talking, Sir Geoffrey told the man he was a Spanish dog, and by that I reckoned it was a *Spanish* accent."

"*What?*" Crispin pulled him to a stop and they stood on the muddy road on the cusp of Fleet Street. "Geoffrey was talking to a Spaniard?"

"That's what it would seem like, sir."

"But you couldn't make out what they were discussing?"

"No, sir. I swear on the Holy Rood, sir."

"You did well, Jack."

"Master Crispin, if Sir Geoffrey was talking to a Spaniard, and our knights are fighting in Spain, then what *would* Master Chaucer be talking about in secret at an inn?"

Any number of scenarios ran through Crispin's head. "I don't know, Jack. It can't be anything good, that is certain. I may just have to confront Geoffrey."

"But he's your friend, Master Crispin. Surely he will tell you something."

"Something, yes. But will it be the truth?"

It took another quarter of the hour to reach the Shambles, and by then it was nearing sundown. Discouraged merchants and butchers were shuttering their shops. Business had been poor on the street again. But the business of murder seemed to be booming. Crispin sneered at his own cynicism and trudged up the stairs, but pulled up short just shy of the landing.

His door was open. Either his landlord had let in a client, or he had an unwanted visitor.

Jack pushed forward, grumbling at his master's hesitation. But Crispin laid a hand on his shoulder to impede him.

Jack jolted to a stop.

Shadows moved past the crack below the door. Crispin eased his dagger from its sheath. He stepped up the riser to the landing, stretched out his arm, and pushed open the door.

It was almost a relief to see Chaucer standing there.

Crispin sheathed his dagger and walked into the room, heading straight for his chair. He sat, leaving the stool for Geoffrey. "I almost expected you."

Geoffrey scowled, glared at the stool, and finally sat hard. "I'm tired of playing games, Cris."

"So am I. What exactly are you playing, Geoffrey? It seems very dangerous. To all of us."

His lip twitched. "I don't know what you mean."

Crispin hunched forward and folded his hands on the table. The small tallow candle flickered. A ribbon of smoke rose between them, clouding Chaucer's eyes. "I don't like the company you keep."

Geoffrey's eyes narrowed slightly before the shadow passed and he threw his head back with a laugh. "You have been following me."

"What else was I to do?"

"I should have thought of that myself. I should have followed you."

A smirk pulled up one side of Crispin's mouth. "But I was waiting for that."

Chaucer shook his head and scooted the stool closer to the table so that he could rest his hands upon it. Fingers toyed with the clay dish that held the pooled wax of the candle. "So. Cat. Mouse. Which the cat and which the mouse?"

"Depends on the game."

Geoffrey leaned on an elbow and stroked his carefully combed beard. "No game. But many players. Where is Sir Thomas Saunfayl?"

"So bold a strike for your first move? Geoffrey, Geoffrey. Lancaster taught you better chess than that. 'Do not show your opponent your strategy so soon.'"

"I don't want to be your opponent."

Crispin chuckled humorlessly. "Too late for that."

"Oh, you have become hard, haven't you? Although I can't recall you being a particularly merry fellow in days gone by. But this? How can you say you know me and have so little trust?"

"I'm still waiting."

"Very well." He grabbed the edge of the table with whitening fingers. "I needed information on an object. Something of great importance. Something . . . I think you know about."

Now we are getting to it at last! "You jest. An object?"

"Dammit, Cris!" A hand slammed the table. The flat pool of melted wax spilled over into white ghostly fingers, reaching across the wood. "You know what I am talking about. You went to see the abbot about it." A pause. "Oh, very well, I *did* follow you."

Crispin didn't move, didn't speak.

"We both know what we are talking about," said Chaucer.

"Then you go first."

Chaucer's ire seemed to melt away. A smile, and then he closed his eyes, chuckling. "I have so missed you. Bless me." He turned to Jack, standing in the shadows. "Has this God-forsaken hole of a room any wine?"

Jack's gaze slid to his master first before he answered. "No, my lord. Shall I fetch some, Master Crispin?"

"I think you had better. And make haste, Jack. Master Chaucer won't be staying as long as he thinks he will."

Geoffrey laughed at that, but his eyes still followed Jack as he took up the empty jug and hurried out the door.

"Now that we've gotten rid of him," said Crispin, sitting back. "What did you want to say to me that you didn't want him to hear? Mind you, I'll be telling him anyway."

"You see plots in cobwebs."

"I have good reason to. What, Geoffrey? Tell me, then. The only wine I can afford won't be worth the wait."

"The Spear of Longinus."

"Ah. Finally. And what makes you think I am looking for it?"

"Coy? No. I *know* you are looking for it. Just as I know that Sir Thomas Saunfayl paid money to obtain it from the dead armorer on London Bridge. Just as I know it is missing."

"You know a lot. I could have saved my feet from all that walking."

"There is still a great deal I don't know. Who killed the armorer, for instance, though little I care."

"You should care more. It is likely the killer has this relic."

"You think so? I have reason to believe he doesn't."

"And what reasons are those?"

"I have my sources."

Crispin began to rock his chair gently, the soft *creak, creak* soothed him. "What sort of sources?"

"Does it matter? Cris, we don't need to do this. We can join forces to find this thing. It needs to be found."

"And when it is found what will happen next?"

"It will be returned to its rightful place."

"And where is that?"

Suddenly, Chaucer's effusiveness stilled. "Never fear, Cris. It will be a goodly place."

He smirked again. "Why is it when someone tells me 'never fear' I find that I must fear very greatly?"

"Cris—"

"What do I get out of this?"

Chaucer's thoughts seemed to stumble. "Why, the accomplishment of your task."

"I do this work for money. It is my livelihood. I say again, *what* do I get out of it?"

"So it's coins you want. Perhaps I was mistaken about you, Cris."

"Geoffrey, you are a clever man, a sometimes rake, and, God help us, a fine poet. But you have never been a stupid man. Why are you playing stupid now?"

"I seem to have missed a page in this manuscript. You asked about compensation and I was incredulous that you wanted it. And so. If that is our bargaining chip, I will pay." He unbuttoned the flap on his scrip and took out a large pouch, bulging with coins. "What will it take, Master Guest? How many marks? We can pay whatever you like."

"We?"

"Surely you do not imagine I am working alone. If I pay you your fee then you will deliver the Spear to me and me alone. You will also speak of this to no one." He began counting coins onto the table in neat piles. Crispin didn't stop him. He merely watched, counting them out in his head. The fee was climbing higher by the moment.

"I will not take your money."

Hand suspended over another growing column of coins, Chaucer looked up. "You may have little choice in the matter. It would be better, I think, to at least have the coins in hand. You never know what the future will hold."

"I know there is no future in taking your coins, from whatever the source. I will find this object and I will decide then what I do with it."

"You would do well to bargain with me now. I doubt that this offer will come again."

A sudden wave of anger swept over Crispin and he gritted his teeth. "Don't. Don't sound like those cursed dogs I must deal with every day. Twisted men with a vile purpose. For God's sake, Geoffrey! Don't sound like them."

But Chaucer's face was hardened. "Forgive me. I suppose I forgot myself. For I have forgotten you, the man you used to be." Slowly, Chaucer collected the coins from the many piles he had positioned on the table and dropped them back into his pouch.

Jack burst through the door, out of breath and panting, but holding the jug with two hands. His eyes caught the glitter of silver and he was in time to watch the last of the coins disappear into their pouch and scrip.

Jack's eyes looked as if they would bulge from his head, but he controlled himself and fetched the bowls from the shelf and filled them with the wine and set them before each man.

"I'm afraid I can't partake of your wine, Crispin. It appears I must be going." Chaucer rose.

"Oh? So soon?" Crispin stayed where he was.

"Yes. I'm sorry we couldn't do business together. It would have been so much easier if we had."

"Yes. Easier. Though 'All persons ought to endeavor to follow what is right, and not what is established.'"

"Are you still quoting that philosopher? I thought you would have grown out of that by now."

"Not when Aristotle proves so apt time and again."

"But he is dead and gone. He can no longer speak on these topical issues."

"Well, we've all got to die sometime."

Chaucer gave a pained smile before he pulled open the door and left, leaving it open behind him.

Jack slowly closed and bolted it and stared at Crispin. "Was he offering to pay you?"

"You don't truly want to know."

"You're right. I don't." He picked up the bowl. "May I?"

"Why not? Here's to your continued health, Jack."

They both drank quietly.

LYING HERE WASN'T GOING to solve this, thought Crispin. On his bed, hands tucked behind his head, Crispin stretched. Morning light, such as it was behind a layer of gray clouds, filtered in through the partially opened shutters. Roger Grey and his apprentices were dead. For the sake of a relic? That did seem to be the case, but Geoffrey all but told him that the killer didn't have it. How did he know? What more did he know? Had Crispin been a fool to throw that information away? As well as the silver?

Or was Geoffrey merely lying again to get what he wanted?

"Ah, Jack," he sighed.

"Aye, Master? Is there something you wanted? I have hot water for your shave and hot broth to break the morning fast."

"In a moment. I've been thinking. If Chaucer is right—and at the moment we will indulge ourselves that he is speaking the truth—then the relic either didn't exist or is missing by other means."

"So, Master Crispin, Sir Geoffrey claims the murderer does not have it?"

"Correct. And if that were true, then it is in the hands of another."

"How are we ever to know that!"

"We must think it through as we always do."

"Very well, then." Jack sat on the end of Crispin's bed and leaned against the wall beside the window.

Crispin folded his legs, making room for him. "First of all, this business of Lenny running from the scene. I do not like it, Jack. I think he had something to do with it."

"He is a slimy fellow. I don't trust him. He scares me a bit."

"But is he a murderer?"

"Lenny?" Jack scratched his nose thoughtfully. "Well, you would know him better than me."

"I do not see him in that role but it does not mean he is not capable. For what do I truly know of the knave? But I know with certainty that he is a thief. He might have stolen the relic."

"And why would he do that, Master? He wouldn't know what it was. That it was worth anything. Especially with all the fine things in that shop."

"True. Unless he was hired to steal it."

"Ah! Now that is a possibility, sir. But, of course, that still doesn't tell us who is ultimately responsible."

"But if we find Lenny—"

"Aye, Master." He rubbed at his upturned nose. "Of course, it might also be that he didn't do so grand a burglary and is more likely responsible for stealing the Coterels' rent money."

"Yes, about that. Why was it that the rent money and only the rent money was stolen?"

"That has troubled me too, Master."

Crispin scooted up until his back rested against the wall. Jack took this as a signal to bring over a bowl of hot broth. Crispin took it gratefully, for his head cold had not entirely surrendered. He dipped his stale bread in it and chewed on the softened scrap.

Jack sat back on the bed with his own bowl and bread. He clamped his teeth on the crusty edge of the loaf and tore it free, chewing loudly with his mouth open.

"Manners, Jack," Crispin reminded.

"Oh," he said, tongue pushing the bread to the side of a bulging cheek. "Sorry." He closed his mouth and chewed more silently. "And so," he said, still chewing. "Why would a thief ignore all the finery around him—as well as needles and thimbles, which are expensive—and steal only coins in a hidden place? And *would* he know that place? It don't make no sense . . . er, *any* sense."

"No, it does not. Except . . . What is the outcome if the rent is gone?"

"The tenants get booted out on their ears, that's what. Master Kemp has been good to you, sir, and allows you to be late many a time."

"Yes, he does. But other landlords are not as charitable. Though Mistress Anabel said that her landlord has not in the past been so adamant. What would make him suddenly irate about late rent now?"

"It's a good excuse to roust out your tenant."

"But why would one do that? Surely a new tenant would be hard to come by, paying those higher prices on the bridge."

"I dunno, sir. The place would stand empty. And that can't be profitable."

"Indeed not."

"It wouldn't be good for tenants or landlord."

"Just so. Perhaps we are speculating in the wrong quarter."

"It would help to ask Lenny what he was up to."

"Indeed. I should very much like to talk with him but he is more slippery than an eel."

"Shall *I* search for him, sir? We haven't made much of an effort till now. I am more familiar with his haunts, having made them myself."

"You're right." He scrubbed his face, fingers trailing down to his unshaven chin. "Too many distractions. Damn Geoffrey. Why can't he just come out with it? And what the hell is he doing plotting with a Spaniard?"

Jack slurped his broth until Crispin raised his eyes and looked at him. The boy folded his lips and sipped instead. Wiping his mouth with the back of his hand, Jack set the empty bowl aside. "I know this vexes you the most, Master. Sir Geoffrey and Sir Thomas. Friends of yours who are at odds. It doesn't sit well with you, I can see that. And I'm sorry for it."

Crispin shrugged. "It's damnable, to be sure. But I must not let it distract me. And we must be careful, Jack. If Geoffrey is somehow following us, we must make certain he does not know what we are about."

"That's a certainty. Well! He'll never dog *my* steps, sir."

Crispin smiled at the arrogance of the boy and swung his legs over the side of the bed. "See that he doesn't."

WHILE JACK WENT IN search of Lenny, Crispin found himself returning to the bridge. He made a circuitous route to get there, making certain he wasn't followed. *Damn Geoffrey.*

He strode down the main thoroughfare of the bridge, observing the viewing stands rising, the carpenters and their apprentices calling to one another, their workers planing posts into shape over sawhorses. The stands were to be narrow, as there was little enough space for the tilting yard.

When he reached the armorer's shop, a sheriff's guard stood before it. Word must have gotten back to them that some suspicious goings-on were occurring.

Crispin leaned against a post across the way and ran his eyes over the building, its windows shuttered tight now. Beside it to the right was the haberdasher's. And then there was the tailor, Coterel's shop. If Crispin had not paid their quarterly rent money for them, their shop would stand empty. Why did that suddenly trouble him? An empty shop on one side of the armorer's. And there was something in the armorer's that someone wanted. *If I were devious,* he thought, *I would use that empty shop to bore a hole and get myself inside, in secret, to steal what I wanted.* But what of the apprentices? Apprentices were often sent on errands, as Jack was doing. It would be an easy thing when Master Grey was out to tell his apprentices that they were wanted at the other side of London. How long would the place stand empty? Long enough to get through the wall and rummage about at will. But something had gone wrong. The plan had changed. Roger Grey was killed and his apprentices along with him.

A talk with the Coterels' landlord was in order, that was certain.

"Yet they had not gotten the relic," he muttered. But then the memory of that missing box or at least *something* with a rectangular shape came to mind. It seemed likely that a reliquary of some kind had housed the Spear. Suddenly, he recalled the ornamented spear shaft that Grey had fashioned. It had no spear head but was awaiting it. Maybe Grey had lied. Maybe he had not yet received the Spear.

No, some event had triggered all these happenings. Crispin was certain the Spear had been present. But where was it now?

Crispin watched the tailor shop, waiting for Robert Coterel to open the shutters and begin his day as his neighbors were doing. His shop, however, remained quiet and dark. Crispin frowned. He pushed away from the post and strode across the lane, allowing a wagon loaded with long beams to ramble in front of him until it passed, heading for the viewing stands.

He knocked on the door and waited. Nothing. He pushed and the door yielded. The room was dark and smelled of smoldering hearth. He was careful to open the door slowly.

In the dimness, he saw a figure on a chair. But as his eyes adjusted, he could see the man was tied to it with a gag in his mouth and his head slumped on his chest.

Crispin rushed to him, shaking his shoulder as he slipped the gag off. "Master Coterel! Awake! What has happened?"

His eyelids fluttered and he slowly opened them. His lip trembled. "Anabel," he rasped.

"Master Coterel." Crispin quickly took his knife to the tailor's bindings and cut him free. "What has happened to your daughter? Is she here?" He glanced behind him up the darkened stairs.

"No, no! They took her."

"What are you saying?"

"They took her, those men. They kept asking us but we did not know. So they took her. God help us!"

"Asking you what?"

"About some spear. I did not know what they were talking about. But they took her, Master Guest. They *took* her!"

14

HE HAD CALMED COTEREL with wine and busily set about lighting all the candles he could find. Light helped in terrifying circumstances.

After a time he settled opposite the tailor, leaning in. "Who were they, Master Coterel?"

"They were knights. Men in surcotes of different colors. But I do not know their names or houses."

"What did they look like, then?"

"There were three of them. One had blond hair down to his shoulders and a scar crossing his cheek. He was the one who spoke to me, s-slapped me."

Anabel was right and Jack had been right to question them. If only he'd gone about it better.

"I have an idea where they might be. Are you well enough for me to leave you, Master Coterel?"

"I will go with you!" He snapped to his feet, but his legs wobbled and he fell back to his chair again.

"No, you won't. Stay here. I will go."

"But Master Crispin! My daughter . . ."

"Trust me on this, Master Coterel." Crispin bowed and quickly took his leave. When he had stepped outside, he raced down the lane and out the gate before anyone could stop and question him. Gutter Lane. He had to get to Gutter Lane. If the knights favored that particular stable to carry out their illicit proceedings, then he would find her there. *If* they favored it.

And then what? He was still a man alone against three knights. Well, he'd had worse odds.

It took some time to get to Gutter Lane and Crispin slowed to a halt near the crossroads of Gutter Lane and West Cheap, breathing hard. Peering around the corner, he was relieved to see three horses tied to posts outside the stable. The street seemed fairly deserted. Up the lane stood the Boar's Tusk and men were coming and going from the tavern, but no one he knew, no one he could trust. In the end, he didn't want to involve anyone who might get injured. And there wasn't time to get the sheriffs.

He pulled his dagger and headed for the door. Leaning in, he listened. His eyes scanned the dingy walls, their plaster now gray from mud, hay dust, and dirt. Shadows moved, circled. Anabel was tied with her back to a post, standing in a shaft of murky sunlight. A purple bruise puffed her cheek directly below her left eye.

A furious rage suddenly broiled in Crispin's chest, and his senses roared with renewed vitality. He slipped away and carefully circled the stable, looking for another way in. A small door near the back afforded an entrance. He pulled it open soundlessly. Creeping along the walls, he drew as close as he dared.

It was them, the same men who had harassed Jack. The one with the lank blond hair and scar pushed his face close to Anabel's. With lips tight, she turned away, but he grabbed her chin and forced her to face him. He smiled, and then made a slow perusal down her body. There was no mistaking his intent. "Wench, this will go very badly for you unless you tell me now. Where is the Spear?"

"If she won't tell, *I've* a spear for her," said the dark-haired knight, rubbing his groin through his surcote.

She tried to pull her chin away but the scarred knight held fast, his fingers pinching into her flesh so hard it was leaving red marks.

"I told you," she said between gritted teeth, but there was a tremor creeping into the undertone of her voice. "I *don't* know. I do not have any idea what you are talking about!"

Crispin looked around for any advantage. His gaze followed the leaping shadows from the circling knights and rose up the posts to the dim ceiling. A loft jutted just over the stalls below. Squinting, his eyes captured the shapes of ropes and pulleys hanging from rafter beams. He searched again and found a ladder to the loft standing only a few feet away.

Quietly, he moved toward the ladder and tested the bottom rung with his boot. Silent. Up he went, gently putting his weight to each rung for fear it would creak.

Reaching the loft, he looked down. The men encircled Anabel like jackals.

A rustle overhead made him whip his head around. A pair of gray doves squeezed through a hole in the roof. They flapped and settled on a beam, sending feathers and dried bird droppings showering around him. He ducked, peering over the side again. The men concentrated on the girl, not on anything above them.

Crispin smiled grimly.

He turned back to the loft. The rope and pulley hung from a beam over the stable floor, but it was too far out for him to reach it. He cast about and spied a wooden pitchfork thrust into a pile of straw. Being careful to tiptoe along the edge of the loft where the joins were strongest and not liable to squeak, he made his way to the pitchfork and slowly pulled it free. With the pitchfork's handle tight in his grip, he leaned precariously over the edge, and thrust the pitchfork up into the gloom, its tines just touching the rope. Holding his breath, he inched the fork forward until he maneuvered it in front of the rope and coaxed it back toward him, all the while keeping an eye on the knights below as they surrounded Anabel.

Her hands were tied tight and her fingers moved restlessly, wrists squeezed by the rough hemp.

He pulled the rope in and grasped the heavy block and tackle with its iron hook and wrapped one arm around it. He gripped the pitchfork in his other hand like one of Hell's demons. Before he could change his mind, he clutched the rope, backed up as far as he could to the stable wall, and ran like the Devil himself leaping out over the stable floor and swinging in a wide arc.

The rope rolled out of the block and tackle with a whir, sending him downward fast while at the same time arcing him toward the post on which Anabel was secured.

The knights looked up. He slammed into the first one, feet first. Like kayles pins, they crashed into the other, toppling each, shouting with surprise and confusion.

While they were still twisted together on the floor, Crispin landed on solid ground and brandished the pitchfork.

"We seem to meet too frequently for my liking, gentlemen," he said. "Kindly remain on the floor. Except you." He jabbed the blond scarred one with the tines. The knight grunted. "Cut her loose."

"Crispin Guest," he growled. "I think you are not long for this world."

"No? Then best go out fighting." He jabbed a second time. "I won't ask again. Get up and release her."

Without tearing his glare away, the knight rose and staggered toward the girl. Drawing his dagger, he paused.

"Careful, now," said Crispin. "Only the rope. Or your belly shall be wearing this pitchfork."

Reluctantly, the knight sawed slowly on the bindings until they fell away. Anabel moved quickly to scramble behind Crispin.

"Toss it over here," said Crispin, nodding toward the blade. He waited till the knight complied. It skidded along the hard-packed dirt floor and stopped at Crispin's feet amid a hatching of straw. "Back on the ground, then, like the dog you are."

The man trembled with fury. His hands stood away from his body and flexed, looking as if they'd grab the sword, unable to decide to do it or not. Crispin's hands tightened around the pitchfork and he raised it slightly as if ready to jab.

With a second glance at the fork, the knight got down on his knees but he would not lie back.

"If I hear of any more trouble associated with Mistress Coterel or her father, I will have the law upon you."

"Guest, you don't know what you are talking about. And you certainly do not know who you are crossing."

"Oh? Care to enlighten me, then?"

The knight closed his mouth. His chin jutted forward as if clamping down on a misspent breath.

Crispin reached behind and groped for Anabel's hand. Once his fingers closed over her wrist he backed away, holding the pitchfork forward. When he reached the door, he tossed the fork into a rounded pile of fodder. He inclined his head slightly. "I'm sure we shall meet again."

"Yes," said the knight. An unpleasant smile crept across his face. "I am *certain* we will."

Slamming the door, Crispin took off at a run, dragging Anabel behind. He headed for the Boar's Tusk and crashed his shoulder into the door, throwing it open. He ran into another patron who cursed at him, but Crispin did not take the time to stop and apologize. Instead, he plowed his way through the people, kicked aside benches, and made his way to a curtained doorway that led outside. They traveled through a short covered walkway into the back courtyard kitchen.

The warm smells of cooking filled his senses only momentarily. He scanned the small room with its large hearth. Ned, the tavern's servant, snapped his head up, recognizing Crispin but not the woman he dragged behind him. A servant girl stood with a dripping serving spoon in her hand, staring at Crispin.

"Where's Eleanor?" he asked.

Behind him came a gasp and he twisted round to look. Eleanor Langton, the tavern keeper's wife, stood in the doorway. Her plump pink face was framed by a white kerchief carefully pinned in layers over her head and down like a cascade of hair to her shoulders. "Crispin, what are you doing?" But then she must have noticed the bruises on Anabel's face. "My dear child, what has happened?"

Before she could speak, Crispin thrust Anabel's hand into Eleanor's. "Nell, please look after Anabel. I will be back in a moment."

"Crispin!"

But he was already out of the kitchen and back in the Boar's Tusk doorway, looking the room over. He stayed just behind the ragged curtain, staring hard at the door. But no one came in. No knights hell-bent on damage.

He relaxed a little and spied a friendly face. Pushing the curtain aside he headed toward the table where the clerk, Lucas Stotley, sat, drinking with some other men. The man looked up and smiled. "Master Guest!" He lowered his voice and added, "I hope all is well. From the other day."

"Well enough," he admitted. "My apprentice is none the worse for wear. He is, after all, a hearty young lad. But I meant to thank you for intervening on our behalf."

"Tut! It was nothing, sir." He took in the men with him. "Won't you join us, Master Guest? We would hear your brave tales as the Tracker. And of the young lady you brought in."

The others—men he had seen before in the tavern—chuckled and all agreed with cups raised and nodding heads for Crispin to join them. They had entreated many times in the past, but he had never done so.

Crispin saluted them. "I thank you for your kind offer. But at the moment, I have something to attend to." They laughed again, elbowing each other. He bowed and left them, returning to the kitchen, glancing back over his shoulder once more at the door.

He found Anabel being attended to by Eleanor, who had a basin of water in one hand and was dabbing an impatient Anabel's face with a wet cloth in the other.

Crispin crouched beside her and the look of relief on her face made his heart flutter. "Mistress Anabel. Are you well?"

"Yes, God be praised." She rubbed the red welts at her wrists grimly. "Please, madam," she said to Eleanor, moving her face away. "I am well."

Eleanor took the hint and dropped the cloth in the basin and set it aside. "A little wine, then?"

Anabel nodded but kept her gaze on Crispin.

Eleanor motioned to Ned, who scurried to fill a jug from the mews below. Standing aside with her hands plunged into her apron, wiping them in slow strokes, Eleanor looked from Crispin to Anabel and back again.

"Eleanor, this is Mistress Anabel Coterel, from London Bridge. She has had a . . . mishap." He saw Eleanor drop her sharp gaze to

Anabel's wrists but she said nothing. She lifted her face to Crispin again, expression neutral. "I appreciate your care of her, Nell." He was about to depart with her when Ned returned, proffering a wooden goblet of wine. Crispin thought it might be a good idea and took the goblet himself, handing it to Anabel.

If he had not known better, he might have mistaken the glimmer in her eye for amusement. But she ducked her head and drank, all the while pushing at her hair and smoothing the untidy strands that had escaped her careful plaits.

Eleanor returned to ordering her servants, casting a wary glance back at Crispin and his charge. Moving closer, Crispin spoke quietly for Anabel's ears alone among the clattering of pots and the shouts of Eleanor. "Do you know who any of them were? Seen any of them before?"

She shook her head and lowered the goblet to her lap. "No, Master Crispin. Knights have come and gone to Roger's shop. Many of them." She set the cup on the table and sighed. "These are clearly the ones the others spoke of. The other two knights called the blond one by name."

"Indeed. What is it?"

"Sir Osbert. Only that. No surname."

Crispin ran the name through his memory but could come up with nothing. He did not know this knight. Not unusual, being out of court life for over nine years.

"What did they ask you?"

"Only the same question over and over. 'Where is the Spear?' But I do not know what spear they speak of."

"Did not Master Grey discuss his work with you? Of schemes not directly related to his making of armor?"

"No. Roger would never speak of his business. He was a close-lipped man."

Too much so. "And you know nothing of any kind of spear; anything that Grey might have mentioned?"

"No! I told them and I am telling you. I know of nothing like that! What is it, Master Crispin? Why is it so important that they would molest a woman and kill a man and his apprentices?"

"Men desire power and prestige. If they can add to that with a simple object . . ." He considered. Best to keep it to himself. "Never mind, damosel. It is not your concern."

"Not my concern? My entire world has collapsed! My betrothed is dead, my landlord is bent on evicting us, and strange men threaten to kill me over this thing you would hide from me. I demand to know what it is!"

"Leave it, damosel. I think it wise if you and your father stay elsewhere until this is resolved."

"What? We have nowhere to go!"

"Find an inn, then."

"Without money?" Her expression was grim and he could hardly blame her.

The foolish feeling was creeping over him again. When he reached for his scrip she closed her fingers over his hand. "Oh no, Master Crispin. You mustn't."

"You can't go home. Not until this is solved. Go to the Unicorn Inn on Watling Street. I'll send your father after you with your things." He pinched some coins and took up her hand. Placing them in the cup of her palm he closed her fingers over them. "Tell them Crispin Guest sent you. That name holds a little weight with them. I did them a service not too long ago."

She stood with the coins clutched in her hand, staring at him. She had lost her veil somewhere and her hair, parted in the middle and pulled taut for the braids on either side of her temples, gleamed in the failing sunlight from an open window. Her gaze softened.

She reached up with her free hand to balance it on his shoulder and bent over to kiss him on the cheek. The supple lips stayed perhaps longer than was polite, but she withdrew quickly and lowered her eyes. "I thank you, sir, for your generosity. I know you were once a knight. In my eyes, you are still one."

He rose and surveyed the room, hiding a blush with the shuffle of his feet. "Make haste. I do not trust those knights to leave you be. In fact . . . Eleanor!"

The woman must have had half an ear bent in their direction, for she was at his side in an instant. She made no secret of the wary eye she directed at Anabel. "May I borrow Ned from you for about an hour?"

"Here!" perked Ned. "What you want me for?"

"I shall need you to escort Mistress Anabel to the Unicorn and then get a message to her father on the bridge."

Ned rubbed his stumpy nose and turned to Eleanor with an expectant face. The lad knew a coin was in it for him but he also knew he could not go unless his mistress approved of it.

Eleanor knew Crispin well and all she needed to do was to look at his expression to agree. "Very well, Ned. You make haste, now, and don't dawdle. Master Crispin is not a patient man . . . is he?"

Crispin offered her a grin. "No, he is not." He handed Ned several coins and informed him of the message to Robert Coterel and then he sent him off. Anabel looked back at him with a doleful look in her dark eyes and Crispin remembered her lingering kiss to his cheek just as she disappeared through the doorway.

Eleanor ticked her head. "Crispin, need I warn you again or will it fall on deaf ears as it has so many times before?"

He straightened his coat. "I have no idea what you are talking about."

"Crispin—"

"Eleanor," he said with a bow. "I regret I cannot stay to talk. I must take my leave. Give my greetings to Gilbert."

"Very well. We'll be here when you need us."

What was the woman implying, he wondered as he stalked through the covered walkway and entered the nearly empty tavern. Did she think he would need their sympathetic ear, their wine to drown his sorrows in, when his foolishness culminated to its ultimate conclusion?

He pushed open the doors more harshly than intended. *Well, she may have a point.* If he was honest with himself he had been in the same position many times before. He could not seem to help himself when it came to women who found themselves in trouble. He mixed in their lives and when it all went to hell he was left with the broken shards. Why did he continue to do it time after time?

Because you're a fool, was the simple answer. But he knew it was more than that. It was inbred in him as much as his skills with weapons had been, as much as his horsemanship, though both had been too long ago. He had been taught courtly ways, a chivalric code, and some of that included protecting the weak.

But these women who had crossed his path had not been weak in the least. Especially not Philippa Walcote. She had climbed from the lowest position in society to become the wife of a wealthy merchant. But he had been drawn in by her plight nonetheless. Why had it been so? He admired her fortitude, certainly. He would have admired anyone in similar circumstances; at least he had always told himself so. But would he have? Did it also have to be accompanied by a pretty face and a clever wit? Was he doomed to make this mistake over and over? As he pushed his way through the streets, past sellers of roasted sausages, singers singing their tales of far-off places, and the crowds that gathered to listen—some little noticing as their purses were cut and stolen away by dark men—he thought of the little portrait of Philippa he kept in his room. Ridiculously sentimental. Was he to play the lovesick paramour in a romance? Was he to suffer and sigh in the style of court peacocks? He was lonely, dammit! And yes, while it *was* safer to long in silence for a love that could never be his, he could do something about it instead.

He liked Anabel Coterel. She had an innate vivacity that seemed to give her strength. *Sera nimis vita est crastina; vive hodie.* "Living tomorrow is too late; live today." He had to live now. But love? Did that come but once a lifetime?

He huffed a cold breath out to the street. Wasn't he putting the cart before the horse? He had several things to do first. He had a murder to solve, for one, and the location of this damned relic to discover for another. The rest of it could wait.

His head jerked up with the sound of shouting. A man came tearing around the corner in a curious but familiar gait and right after him came Jack Tucker, long limbs swinging, face red but determined, chasing after.

Lenny.

15

THE OLD THIEF RAN as if his life depended on it, and by the look on Jack's face, it might. Londoners stepped aside to watch, leaving a crooked path of escape for the thief. But when Lenny looked back over his shoulder to measure how far back Tucker was, Crispin stepped into the street and stuck out his foot.

Lenny saw too late, struck it, and soared over the road for an instant before careening into a wattled fence.

Crispin was on him instantly. He grabbed his uneven shoulders with a shackling grip and hoisted him to his feet. "Got you at last, you knave." Lenny whimpered. Crispin cast about for a place to take him. The Boar's Tusk was the most convenient and he twisted the man around, stalked back up the street, and shoved him toward the large doors.

They burst through and the remaining men at the tables looked up, glaring.

"Clear the room!" Crispin demanded, but only white surprised faces greeted him. "I said all of you out!"

Crispin slammed Lenny onto a bench. The thief cried out and

tried to get away but Crispin backhanded him hard. He hit the table, knocking over a discarded horn cup and spilling the ale across the wood.

The men jumped to their feet, ready to defend, but Crispin drew his blade. "Who will argue with me?"

The few men in the tavern looked at one another and in a moment of silent agreement, shuffled toward the exit, skirting wide around Crispin's table. They pushed open the door just as a panting Jack Tucker entered, staring at the dispersing men. When the last one left, he lowered the beam over the door.

Gilbert Langton came rushing forward from the kitchen, wide-eyed and furious. "Crispin! What is the meaning of this? This is my business you're disrupting."

"And this is murder." He grabbed Lenny's grayed shirt with a fist and shoved his knife toward his face. "We're going to have a talk. And you are not going to lie to me."

"Mercy, Master Crispin." Lenny raised his hands. The palms were scored with dirt in all the creases. He was nearly toothless and what hair he still had on his head hung in long strings to uneven shoulders. His bald pate was bruised and dirty. "You've always been a reasonable man."

"You've been avoiding me. Why?"

His hands were still raised, protecting his face. He shook his head. "I haven't been avoiding you, good master. Old Lenny just had a lot to do."

Crispin knocked him in the side of the head with his blade, pleased to see a bruise forming. "Tell me another."

"Ow! That hurt! I always avoid you when I can for just this reason."

Crispin did it again and Lenny bent over, keening.

"I saw you on the bridge when that man was killed," rasped Crispin. "You ran away then. What did you do? Answer me, or so help me I will bash your head till it's cracked like an egg."

"Please, Master Crispin! Please! Don't hurt old Lenny. I've done no harm."

"Then tell me, you scoundrel. What have you done?"

"Nothing! Nothing!"

Crispin drew back his hand to deliver another blow when Jack grabbed it and held on. He glared at Jack in amazement and shook him off roughly. "What the hell do you think you are doing, Tucker?"

"Stopping you from making a fool of yourself. Look at him. Miserable piece of dog shit that he is. Don't soil yourself touching him, Master." Jack frowned and with his fist raised, he turned viciously on Lenny, who cringed back. "And you! Answer my master's question. We both seen you on the bridge. We both know you're up to no good. You stole from that tailor, didn't you!"

Lenny's eyes darted from Jack's to Crispin's and the hope of mercy slowly died in their dark depths. "Peace! Don't strike me again, I beg of you. You've got a damnable wallop, you have." He rubbed his mouth where his lip bled. His tongue flicked out and licked at it but only managed to smear the blood. "I was a desperate man, living off of filth in the streets to get me bread. I've nothing to me name and that's God's truth. I was starving."

"And so if I turn out your coat right now I will not find half a dozen purses belonging to other people," said Crispin, gritting his teeth. He felt like slamming the man's head to the table. But Jack was right. It wasn't worth the trouble with the sheriffs.

One hand came up to the neck of his coat in defense, but when Lenny realized what he was doing, that hand dropped away. Lenny lowered his face. "Aye. I was on the bridge that night. But I didn't do naught to that man. It wasn't me."

"Damn you! What *were* you doing?"

"I came for me payment. I done a job for a man."

"What job?"

"I'm getting to that, Master Crispin." His eyes shifted to the barred door. "I was hired by a man to . . . to steal money from the tailor shop next to the armorer's."

Crispin stepped back and looked down at his blade. His reflection was blurry and distorted on its shiny surface. "Tell me everything," he said quietly.

Lenny finally lowered his hands and rubbed his palms against his thighs in their torn and disreputable stockings. "Well, then. A man approached me 'bout a sennight ago. Told me he wanted me to do a job and paid me half then. I waited till the place was empty, when both went off to mass—" He cringed at Crispin's look of disgust. "He told me exactly where to find the funds and told me not to take anything else. I done what I was told and took the money to him. He paid me some of what he owed me but said he'd give me the rest in a few days' time. I asked him why he couldn't just take it from the pouch then and there, but he told me no. So when I come back he doesn't have the money. And I come back again, and again he puts me off. Nobody cheats Lenny, and so I pursued him on the bridge but we were interrupted by your rescuing that dead man. And now that he sees me talking to you he'll kill me for sure."

"And how can he see you? Only a handful of men saw me drag you in here."

But suddenly Lenny became remarkably tight-lipped. His eyes darted to the door again.

"There was someone here."

"I didn't say that."

"But your eyes did." Crispin walked slowly away. He sheathed his dagger and rested his hand on the hilt. "Did the man say why he wanted you to steal the money and nothing else?"

"Said it was a scheme to make the place empty. That was all he would say. What did I care? I did it for the money."

"That don't make sense," said Jack.

"Yes, it does." Crispin raised his hand to silence his apprentice. "And who is the man that hired you?"

"I don't know his name."

"Was he here in this room?"

Lenny said nothing and Crispin swiveled to look at him, hand curled tight. "Well?"

He swallowed loudly, staring at Crispin's fist. "Aye."

Crispin didn't like that at all. Spies everywhere. Even in his favorite tavern. He glanced quickly at Gilbert, who seemed a little shocked by this revelation.

"Describe him."

Lenny sighed and licked at his bleeding lip again. "He's not too tall, what I'd call middling. Not fat and not thin. Darkish hair."

Crispin frowned. "What are you playing at?"

"I'm not playing at naught, Master Crispin! I swear. That is the man. I can't help it if God made him look like every other man. But I do know this," he said, raising a shaking finger. "He mentioned someone in high ranks, someone at court whose orders he was following."

"What? Who?"

"He didn't know he let slip mention of a 'Sir Geoffrey.' How this Sir Geoffrey would be pleased."

Chaucer? Could he be involved—Crispin laughed unpleasantly.

But of course he was involved. Could he have hired this man to hire Lenny? Damn him.

"You shouldn't have run from me, Lenny. You should have come to me."

"It wasn't no murder, Master Crispin. It was just thievery. And you gave me your word that you would leave the sheriffs out of it when I done you that favor two years ago."

"This involved a man's death."

"How was I to know that? And I don't see how, anyway. It happened days before."

"Nevertheless. The bargain I made with you was a contract with the Devil. I wipe my hands of you."

"Ah now, Master Crispin. You mustn't say that. I'm useful to you, I am. Lenny knows things that others don't."

"Tell me the name of the man who hired you, then."

"I can't tell you what I don't know."

"Get out."

"'Slud, good master. Don't be that way about it. I can be useful to you still. Why, a farthing goes a long way with old Lenny."

"I've had enough of you. I said get out."

The thief frowned and staggered to his feet. "You'll be sorry. One day you'll need old Lenny, and where will he be? Out of your reach, that's what."

"Dead, you mean?"

Lenny cringed. "Ah now! Bless me! Don't go laying a curse on me, Master. That isn't sport, is it?"

"There's worse than dead, you know."

Lenny clapped an involuntary hand to his shorn-off ear. The sheriff had cut it off years ago because of his thievery, but he was lucky he'd gotten off with only that and not the noose. And that had been due to Crispin's charity.

Lenny shuffled toward the door, wary that he would be stopped. When he stood before it, he looked back at Crispin. "I'm marked now, like Cain. He'll want to kill me because I told you."

Crispin scowled. "How is that *my* problem?"

"You're hard today," he said, and spit on the floor. Gilbert made an indignant gasp. "So that's it? You would send me away? I've done good work for you in the past, Master Crispin. In truth, I've done my share of thievery over the years. Why now does it vex you?"

"I'm tired of it, Lenny. I'm tired of your lack of conscience. Of your devilry. There is too much of it afoot in London."

Lenny gestured to Jack. "But you don't mind this one cutting a purse or two to keep the wolf from the door, eh?"

Jack shot him a murderous glare. "I never! I don't do that no more, you scum. Master Crispin well knows about my past."

"Past, is it? So you would have him believe."

Jack pounced and the both of them went down. Jack got in a few good punches to the man's gut before Crispin and Gilbert pulled him off. When he pushed Jack aside his face was red and tears brimmed at his eyes.

"See what a devil you are," said Crispin with a sneer. "Throw this rubbish out."

Gilbert grabbed him and pulled him toward the door. He threw aside the beam and opened it.

Lenny grabbed the doorway and turned back to Crispin with fear on his face. "But Master Crispin! I'll be killed for certain!"

Crispin stood impassively as Gilbert thrust Lenny out the door and barred it again. He rested his back against it and stared at Crispin.

But Crispin was looking at Jack. The boy's shoulders heaved and he wiped angrily at his eyes. "Don't believe him, Master Crispin.

It's the Devil's own tongue he's using. I don't do that no more. Not unless you tell me to."

"I know that, Jack. Never fear." He lowered himself to a bench, his back to the table. "Damn Lenny. And damn that man who hired him."

Jack sniffed. "He said he was here in the tavern."

Gilbert sat beside Crispin with a huff of expelled breath. "You know such fine people."

Crispin fell silent and stared into the fire. Lenny *had* been useful over the years, but Crispin had had to turn a blind eye to his mischief. He couldn't any longer. He dropped his head into his hands and raked his fingers through the thick locks of his hair.

"I'll wager anything that the tailor's landlord was in on it," said Jack.

Crispin raised his head. Jack had composed himself and looked more like the stalwart apprentice he was.

"Yes. He'd have to be. But how would he know exactly where the tailor hid his wealth? It's not likely something the tailor would tell him." He ran his hand through his already untidy hair. "I've been sloppy, Jack. Too sloppy. I haven't asked enough questions of the right people. That landlord, for one. And Master Coterel for another."

"You've been ill, Master."

"A dreadful excuse. I must not allow that to continue."

"Very well. We will work together. So as Lenny said, there is a 'Sir Geoffrey.' Why is Master Chaucer involved in it?"

"Because he wants the Spear, Jack. If the Coterels were evicted then the culprits would have time aplenty to break into the armorer's to search for it."

"Blind me!"

Gilbert sat before the fire, wringing his apron. "What spear?"

Jack sat beside Gilbert. "So who was it that was here in the tavern tonight?"

"The usual," said the tavern keeper. "All men you are acquainted with. But what is this spear you're speaking of?"

"Excepting maybe one or two," said Crispin thoughtfully. He smacked his forehead suddenly. "God's blood! They saw Anabel leave with Ned."

"Who's Anabel?" asked Gilbert.

Crispin caught Jack's gaze. "She was captured by those same knights that you encountered."

"God's bones," he muttered.

"They were questioning her about the Spear."

Gilbert edged closer. "What spear? Who's Anabel?"

"I told her to go to the Unicorn Inn on Watling Street. Ned will get the message to her father."

"I'll go after them, Master Crispin, and see that all is well."

Jack got to his feet and hurried out the door, leaving it to fall shut behind him.

Gilbert turned to Crispin and quietly asked, "Who is Anabel and what is this spear?"

"I must go." Crispin headed for the door.

"Crispin!"

He turned back, one hand on the latch. "Yes?"

Gilbert offered a weak smile and a shrug. "God keep you."

Crispin nodded and pulled open the door. He stepped out onto the darkened street and wondered where to begin. The landlord, surely, for he was in it as deep as any other. And Chaucer. It was time to have it out with him and about his Spanish friends. But then there was Sir Thomas getting wound tighter and tighter.

Deciding, he stepped in the direction that would take him toward the bridge. But something heavy collided with the back of his head and all his thoughts dissolved into darkness.

COLD WATER ON HIS face and in his mouth. He struggled to the surface, imagining he was drowning. But he was not underwater.

He opened his eyes and saw a vague light cast by an upper window to the stinking alley below. He was kneeling in the mud and furiously trying to recall how he got there when the boot sunk into his gut. Doubling over, he dry heaved, gasping for air at the same time.

Well, he certainly expected this, just maybe not so soon.

He curled in on himself, trying to protect his gut, when a kick to his side sent him rolling over.

Have to gain my feet. Being on the ground was a distinct disadvantage. He rolled again and hands grasped him, lifting until he was slammed against a wall.

He cracked open his eyes and saw their dark shapes. Three of them. The blond one was closest. His foul breath puffed into his face.

"No stable this time, Sir Osbert?"

The man hesitated. "How do you know my . . . Oh, the girl."

"Are you going to ask *me* where the Spear is, too?"

He pushed his fist into Crispin's neck, grasping his coat collar and grinding his knuckles into his skin. "As a matter of fact, yes."

"I don't know. I was rather hoping you did."

Backhanded. He bit the inside of his cheek, even though he had prepared for it. Dammit. A rush of blood filled his mouth and he spit it in the direction of the man's surcote.

Sir Osbert looked down at the red blotch on his chest. "Whoreson." He grabbed Crispin's hair and slammed his head against the wall.

Stars flickered behind his eyelids. "I don't suppose I can convince you to stop," he grunted.

He got a fist in his gut for an answer, which sent him down again. His knees hit the mud.

"I thought . . . you had . . . the box," Crispin gasped.

Osbert chuckled above him. "It was as empty as your head, apparently. I told you, Guest, you were in over your head. I'm telling you now to forget you ever heard of the Spear."

He coughed and pried open an eye. The other two knights still stood in the shadows, while Osbert smacked his fist into his palm, mouth twisted into a leer.

"Forget the Spear? You must be jesting."

Osbert planted his beefy hands on his thighs and bent over to stare into Crispin's face. "Do I look like I'm jesting?"

Crispin inhaled a shaky breath. "Indeed not. But once I am commissioned to do a job I rarely surrender it."

"You'll surrender like you're told. Though, mark me, I'd rather continue to thrash you."

"I got that impression." Crispin rubbed his sore belly. "Perchance, may I ask why I am being told to disregard my oaths?"

"You're not good at obeying orders, are you?"

"Orders by whom, my lord? You see, I find it difficult to obey random requests by men who snatch women off the streets for nefarious purposes."

He laughed. "Listen to you. 'Nefarious purposes.' As I said, you don't know what you are talking about."

"Then instruct me, my lord. Tell me why I must forswear myself."

"You still think yourself a knight, Guest?"

"True. But just because I am no longer a knight does not mean I am without honor."

They all laughed at that and Crispin scowled. "A traitor?" Osbert chuckled, including his men in the jest. "An honorable traitor! Fantastic, your arrogance."

"Nevertheless. You haven't yet offered me a good reason to abandon my search for the Spear."

Osbert frowned. "Because I'm telling you. That should be good enough for the likes of you!"

Crispin shrugged. "Alas."

With a grimace, Osbert cocked his leg back, ready to deliver another blow, but as it swung forward, Crispin caught it by the sole and shoved the foot upward, hurling the knight onto his backside. The others froze for a heartbeat before they descended on him, feet and fists thrashing.

Ducking his head, Crispin punched and rolled, trying to avoid fists and delivering as many blows as he could curled like a hedgehog. In the end, two against one—and then Osbert joined in—proved too much.

They stepped back, panting and huffing clouds of breath into the night. Crispin landed against the wall. He slid down until he sat with his back to it. His head swam and the shadowy men became that much more obscure.

Osbert jutted a finger at him. "Do what you are told, Guest. Or next time we won't stop with such a friendly request."

Friendly? Exhausted, sore, Crispin slumped. "One thing more, my lords."

The men were already walking away when they stopped and glared at him in amazement. "You want more, Guest?"

"Merely an answer to a burning question. Did you kill Roger Grey and his apprentices?"

Osbert's face changed only slightly. He licked his lips and his chest rumbled with a malevolent chuckle. "If I were you, Guest, I'd keep my mouth firmly shut. Or it will be shut for you."

"Apprentices, my lord? Young boys? I cannot abide a killer of children. I will not rest until I bring such a foul creature to justice."

Osbert sneered and spat. He leaned down again. "I welcome the chance to have at you again, Guest. I truly welcome it." He turned on his heel and the others followed.

But suddenly they stopped. Through the haze of his blurry vision, Crispin saw three men blocking their escape.

"*Buena tarde, mis señores,*" said a deep voice, and then the sound of a sword drawn.

Crispin tried to sit up but his head was too woozy. Osbert and his men drew their swords and six blades suddenly clashed, ringing like church bells in the narrow alley. A shimmer of moonlight breaking through the clouds slipped over the blades in flashes and in a momentary lapse, Crispin grabbed for his own sword and cursed when he remembered that there was none.

No one spoke but each knight found his own opponent. As if by a secret signal, they all began at the same time.

The fight scattered the muddy puddles, kicking up soaring splashes caught by moonlight. Steel clanked against steel, followed by grunts and gasps. Blades slapped shoulders and fists found jaws.

Right above Crispin, two men fought. Their moonlit faces snarled and one had his arms clasped in a bear hug around the other. Crispin could not tell who was which until the one on the right gasped out a string of what Crispin thought might be curses, only they were in a foreign tongue. The English knight suddenly pushed him away and cocked back an arm to strike with his fist, but his opponent ducked and used his shoulder to shove him into a wall.

The English knight gasped out a whoosh of air and dropped his sword. He seemed to recover quickly and nimbly drew his dagger in time to deflect the down-rushing sword blade.

Crispin struggled to rise, to help, but sank down again. In the haziness of his thoughts, he suddenly came to the disturbing acknowledgment that the men who came to the alley to fight Osbert's men were Spanish. He did not know whether he should help them or Osbert.

Osbert came into view again, swinging his sword up at a Spaniard. The foreigner laughed and knocked his sword aside, but then he lost his own when Osbert kicked up with his boot. Their combat devolved into a fistfight. Osbert took a blow to his mouth and despite not knowing who to cheer for, Crispin felt a sense of triumph as blood spattered the knight's chin.

Turning to watch the others, Crispin saw only shadows and silhouettes slashing with blades or punching torsos.

With a grunt, Osbert fell and skidded toward Crispin. Once more Crispin tried to rise but his dizziness would not allow it. Moonlight showered around the combatants when the clouds parted and it was enough to show clearly the blazon on Osbert's right sleeve. Blue with a stripe of yellow and three yellow panther heads.

Osbert dived for his lost sword and closed a bloodied fist around the hilt. He jumped to his feet and shouted to his men.

By now, citizens were leaning out of their windows and yelling down to them. Some were even throwing objects. One emptied his chamber pot. The falling contents spattered Osbert's shoulder and the stench filled the narrow space. He looked up to the window, raised his fist, and cursed the man, who closed his shutter smartly on the scene.

Looking hastily about at the other swordsmen, Osbert gathered his fellows, and with a few more wide strokes of his blade, he turned tail and ran with them out of the alley.

All fell silent. Even the citizens at their windows finally withdrew and shut them. Only the Spaniards remained. Crispin could hear their labored breaths but he could see only their silhouettes against the alley's opening. They came closer but still their faces were lost to shadows. The moon seemed to have deserted the scene again.

Crispin braced for a blow. He'd been bracing for something similar for years. He just didn't like the idea of being cut down in a stinking alley in the mud. He turned his face upward, willing to meet it head on. There was not even a prayer passing his lips. He steadied his gaze on the one closest, who seemed to be leaning down to peer at him.

Slowly, one by one, each man sheathed his blade.

"*¿Está usted bien, Señor Guest?*"

"What? I don't understand you."

"Forgive me," said the man in a heavy Spanish accent. "I asked if you were well." He held out his hand to him.

"Well enough." He did not take the offered hand, and it was a moment longer before the man realized that Crispin would not.

He drew back and huffed a sigh. "By my Lady, but you are a stubborn man. Very well. We will leave you to it. But I would take that *perro's* advice. Stay out of it. Let the others play their game, *señor.* It is too dangerous for you."

"And who the hell are you? Spies?"

The man looked back at the others. One of them made a signal and he nodded. "We must go, *señor.* Try to stay out of trouble. *Dios esté con usted.*" He bowed and then they all turned and flew from the alley, leaving nothing but echoes in their wake.

Crispin leaned against the wall and pushed himself up to his feet. He stood shakily for another few heartbeats before testing his legs on their own.

Well. Now there were a few more problems. These Spaniards seemed to be multiplying. He feared their plots were being hatched in England while Lancaster was away.

But worse. Crispin had recognized the blazon on Osbert's arm. He should have been more shocked that those arms on the shoulder of the knight were that of Michael de la Pole, earl of Suffolk.

16

JACK LET OUT AN oath when he beheld Crispin's face. "Why does this always happen to you?"

The boy was exasperated, but beneath it, Crispin could see his worry. He shuffled to a chair and sat, his head falling back. Jack scurried to fetch cloths and poured the icy water from their bucket into a basin. While Jack ministered to him with the cold wet cloths to ease the swelling, Crispin recounted what had happened.

Jack dabbed gently at Crispin's bruised chin with a folded rag. "Spaniards! And the earl of Suffolk. That's who Chaucer met that first time you followed him."

"Yes, Jack." He pushed the cloth aside and felt his face with cautious fingertips. A little swollen around his left eye and at the right side of his jawline, but no permanent damage. His belly and lower back were sore but there were no broken ribs, praise God.

"Why does the Chancellor of England want the Spear, sir?"

"Why wouldn't he? His days are numbered. He somehow got wind of the Spear's existence and sent his henchmen to do the dirty work."

"Do you think they killed Roger Grey?"

"Unquestionably."

Jack walked across the room to fetch the wine jug and poured some of the amber liquid into a bowl. "And what about them Spanish dogs, sir? What did they want?" He handed Crispin the bowl.

Crispin drank deeply, thirstily. He licked his lips and set the bowl aside. Jack made to refill it but Crispin waved him off. "It seemed that they only wanted to rescue me. And warn me, of course. I seem always to be warned to 'stay out of it' when it is far too late."

"Rescue you? Are they not England's enemies?"

"Not exactly. Not when Lancaster vies for the Spanish throne."

"Are you sure you didn't . . . imagine it? I mean, sir," he retreated, fending off a scowl from Crispin, "you were knocked about quite a bit."

"I know what I saw. He spoke to me. And he knew me."

"Bless you, sir. Doesn't that frighten you?"

"Now that you mention it, yes."

They sat in silence. Jack sat on the stool and rustled about, finding a comfortable spot on the small seat. "I'm just glad they left you alone."

"Likewise. But what of this other matter? The matter of the killer knights?"

"Aye," said Jack. "I wondered, Master, why they'd bother to steal the Coterels' rent money. Why not just kill them? Or for that matter, why did they need to bother with them at all?"

"I don't know, Jack. Something is amiss here. Was it *those* men who hired Lenny? I can't imagine it."

"Was that bastard Lenny lying to you, sir?"

"That is certainly a possibility, but I doubt it. I gave him only a small dose of what I just got. He is not a brave man."

"What do we do now, Master Crispin? If those men killed

Roger Grey and *they* do not have the Spear, then where is it? Them Spaniards?"

Crispin sighed. "Why would they bother to warn me off? No, I have come to the uncomfortable conclusion that I should attempt to talk to the Lord Chancellor."

Jack stepped back, a cloth hanging limply from his hand. "Of England?"

"Yes. All roads seem to lead to him." With a grunt, Crispin gained his feet.

"But Master! You can't go to court."

"I know that!" He shuffled to the bed and sat. He bent over and started to unbuckle his boot. Jack dropped to his knees and pushed Crispin's hands away. Lying back on his elbows and allowing Jack to do it, Crispin contemplated the rafters. "But I must. Tomorrow. After I sleep. God's blood, but I'm weary!"

WEARY OR NO, CRISPIN'S sleep was disturbed more than once that night by dreams of enduring a thrashing. It didn't help that his jaw and gut ached from the real beating he'd received.

Finally, at dawn, he rolled out of bed, the first to be up for a change, and knelt by the fire, rustling the flames from under the banked ashes. Jack yawned loudly from his corner straw pile. "Master Crispin? Is it morn?"

"Yes. Get up, Jack. We're going to court."

JACK GRUMBLED AND COMPLAINED almost all the way to Westminster: He didn't see why Crispin kept opening himself up to risks by showing himself at court; why did he need to prove something that was beyond his control; it wasn't right to put himself in this position and threaten the harmony of their household.

Crispin had looked askance at Jack for that last one, but his apprentice had only rolled his eyes and flapped his arms in a gesture of surrender. "I don't know how to convince you," he said at last.

"Don't try," said Crispin with a scowl. "I'm doing what must be done."

"But sir, how are you ever to get an audience with the chancellor? Hasn't he got his own problems?"

He hated when Jack was right. Jaw tight, he said nothing.

They reached the outer ward at the gate and Crispin narrowed his eyes at the scene of marching men and servants scurrying. Mercifully, Jack kept silent while Crispin ran ideas through his head. He'd snuck in before, pretending to be a servant. Perhaps . . . no. Last time he had worn the livery of the duke of Lancaster and had stupidly thrown it away.

His gaze snagged on a familiar servant, bearing the king's livery. Bill Wodecock, steward of the lower servants, was wagging a finger at a servant boy with sagging stockings. He was speaking low but sternly to the boy, who looked as if he would burst into tears at any moment.

"Master Wodecock!" he called.

The man turned. His round face squinted, brown eyes searching for the voice. When he found it, he looked none too pleased. But he sent the servant boy on and made his way to the gate, standing with fists at his hips. He was a broad fellow, almost as stout as he was tall, but Crispin had seen him hurry throughout the palace. His girth did not seem to impede his pace.

A tight cap on his head made his face all the more round and his upturned nose gave a sniff of impatience. "Master Guest," he said quietly. He tilted his chin down in disapproval. "What is it?"

Crispin bowed. "Good sir. I find I have need to get into the palace today."

"Have you now? And I'd like a good reason to allow it."

"I am . . . tracking."

"I know your vocation, Master Crispin. I also know your history. My head would be in a noose if I let you in."

Pressed against the wall as close as the guards would allow, Crispin spoke quietly. "You must know it is no mere whim that brings me here. I would speak to his grace the earl of Suffolk."

"Ha! A good one, Master Crispin. But I am not in the mood today." He turned on his heel.

"Master Wodecock!" he hissed. But the man would not return. "Dammit!"

"You can't blame him, Master."

"Be still," he growled. Hated, *hated* when Jack was right.

Crispin glanced at the guard, who had never stopped eyeing him, and pushed away from the gate with a muttered oath. De la Pole would never see him, of course, but he had to try. Even if he could somehow get a message to him . . . No, that was foolish. A message could be ignored and at any rate, who would take it in? Maybe he could question one of Suffolk's servants . . . bah! There didn't seem any point in staying. And yet he didn't move.

"Master," said Jack quietly, careful not to touch him. "Master?"

"I know." Yet still he stood, staring at the courtyard mere steps beyond him. It might as well have been the gates of Paradise, equally closed to him. "Perhaps the kitchens, Jack. Onslow Blunt, the head cook, would allow me to—"

"You took a chance at that before. And look where it got you. You were accused of trying to kill the king."

Barred, every way he could think of.

Behind him was the clatter of horses and he reckoned that a lord and his retinue were heading toward court. Reluctantly, he stepped out of the way, pulling Jack with him. He raised his head and saw the bright trappers and lurched in surprise. House of Lancaster? But the duke was in Spain.

On the white horse in the lead of the retinue sat a young man with a pale auburn mustache and beard. He wore the Lancastrian colors and surveyed the crowd with a faintly amused air. Until his eyes fell on Crispin.

He yanked on the reins and startled his horse, which whirled once and nearly reared. The stocky young man pulled hard on the reins again and the horse's head curled downward. The stallion calmed enough for him to slide off the saddle.

"Your grace!" complained his companions, but he didn't heed them as he made straight for Crispin, who sunk down on one knee.

"Crispin Guest! Good Christ! I would know you anywhere though I have not seen you in . . . bless me, how long now?"

Crispin felt Jack sink to the ground beside him. "I know not, your grace. Well over a decade, I imagine."

He took Crispin's shoulders and pulled him to his feet in remarkably strong hands. The young man shook his head slowly, searching his face with softened eyes. "Let me look at you. Crispin, Crispin." He ticked his head at the bruises he saw. "How I've missed you!" Suddenly, Crispin found himself embraced by the duke of Lancaster's son, Henry, earl of Derby.

"I've missed you, too," he said gently into the familiar auburn curls.

Henry pushed him back but kept hold of his upper arms. He scanned Crispin's bruised face. "Still getting into fights? You shouldn't, you know. You're getting old, Crispin." He laughed and turned to encourage his companions to join in his humor. The others, seeming to know well who Crispin was, did not appear to have as positive a reaction as the young lord. Henry was Richard's cousin and only a year older. Crispin wondered if they were still on as good terms as they had been as children.

"Crispin here was something of a companion when I was a child," said Henry in explanation to his mounted friends. "He was my father's protégé and we spent many an hour getting into trouble, didn't we, Crispin?"

"Er . . . yes, my lord. Much to the duke's chagrin."

Henry laughed, throwing his head back. "By my Lady, I remember this one time—"

"Your grace," said one of his knights. "Hadn't we best get to the palace?"

Henry's face fell. He spoke quietly to Crispin but not too quietly that the knights nearest him couldn't hear. He kept his arm slung over Crispin's shoulder. "He is trying to remind me how unwise it is acknowledging your presence in public so close to the palace."

Crispin bowed his head. "It . . . might be best for you to take that advice, my lord."

"Nonsense." He looked back at the retinue of footmen and mounted household knights. "Go on, then," he said, gesturing toward the gate. "I will be in presently."

The knights exchanged glances. "Your grace?"

"I said go on. All will be well. I would speak with this old friend."

The knights were reluctant to leave Derby alone but the young lord stood his ground and his face took on a glower that made him look exactly like the duke.

Finally, they moved their horses forward under the arch of the gate, glancing back as they passed through the shadows.

Henry sighed.

"They are only trying to protect you, your grace."

"Henry, Crispin. You used to call me Henry."

"I do not think it wise that I do so now. Under the circumstances."

Derby scoffed and rested his gloved hand on his sword hilt. And then he noticed Jack. He smiled. "Crispin, you have a son?"

Grinning, Crispin spared a look back at the stunned servant. "No. This is my apprentice, Jack Tucker."

Jack had the presence of mind to bow low. "Y-your grace."

"Apprentice? Oh yes! You have that very provocative moniker, do you not? The *Tracker*!"

"Yes, my lord. It is better than some of the other names I have been called."

Henry laughed again. "Indeed! And so. Is it a mere coincidence finding you here in Westminster, or are you performing your new vocation?"

Unaccountably embarrassed, Crispin looked down and nervously shuffled. "Well, I was attempting it, yes."

"Attempting it?"

"It is nothing, my lord."

"Now come. I know my father helps you from time to time. And while he is out of the country, I suppose, it is up to me. And that's as I would have it, Crispin. Verily, I have missed your presence in my life. And though I cannot sanction what you did all those years ago, I know that your heart was in the right place."

His speech did nothing to sweep away Crispin's embarrassment. In truth, it only made his cheeks warm.

"How can I help you, Crispin? I know that you do not do anything without good cause."

"I fear you will not wish to help after you know my mission."

"Try me."

This was Lancaster as a young man, true enough. He wore the same gleam in his eye when he saw a challenge. But he was the same lad Crispin had known, too, for Henry of Bolingbroke did not seem to fear anything that might spoil his fun.

"Very well," he said with a shake of his head. "I was trying to devise a way into the palace—"

"Ah! I will let you accompany me!"

"To see the Lord Chancellor."

Henry's radiant face fell. "Oh."

"Oh, indeed."

A mischievous smile returned. "I should like to see that. I have been in many talks concerning the earl of Suffolk. Yes, let's go."

"What?"

"Come, Crispin. Don't dally." He threw the reins over his shoulder toward Jack and, even though surprised, Jack deftly caught them.

Henry tugged him along, but Crispin balked. "My lord, this is not a good idea."

"But you wish to talk with him. And I wish to see you talk with him. Come now."

There was no backing out. Crispin allowed the young lord to pull him along. Jack followed, cautiously leading the horse.

"May I know the subject of this talk?" Henry asked as they climbed the steps to the great hall. Jack left the horse with a groom and scrambled to follow close on Crispin's heels.

Crispin weighed the facts. "Murder."

Henry stopped and stared at him. "Murder? Did *he* murder someone?"

"Not by his own hand but perhaps at his urging."

"Interesting."

"And . . . it certainly involves an important relic."

"A relic, eh?" He walked on. "What relic?"

"I . . . am loath to say, my lord."

"Why?"

"The fewer who know of it, the better."

Henry stopped again. "But I should like to know it." At twenty-one years old, Henry was a formidable man. He no longer had the look of a lanky child, nor did his gaze brook obfuscation. He was his father's son.

"An important enough relic to kill for."

A slow smile spread over Henry's lips. "I remember you well, Crispin. You always had your secrets."

"For good reason, my lord."

"Very well," he said, bobbing his head. "I trust you. As I always have."

Crispin reasoned that they were heading for the Lancaster apartments. He was familiar enough with the path they were taking.

But even though he was in Henry's company, he thought it fit to keep his hood up and his head down. People were staring as it was and surely they recognized him, based on their astonished and ill-concealed gasps. Ladies in fur-trimmed cotehardies with ornate brocade surcotes eyed him with fascination. But it was their male companions who, after bowing for Henry, would rest their hands threateningly on their sword hilts.

Tall cressets burning with oak kindling cast warm light upon the walls and vaulted ceilings. The twin sensations of familiarity and discomfort warred within him. To be at court again felt like home, but a home where he was not a guest, but an alien.

"When we get to my chamber," said Henry, speaking in low tones, "we will send for Suffolk. Or perhaps go to him. Will you accuse him to his face about this murder? Whom did he have killed?"

They both came to a sudden halt upon encountering a large entourage coming through a wide arched entry. Henry stood slightly in front of Crispin, blocking him, but Crispin was taller and couldn't help but notice that it was the king in the archway.

And King Richard couldn't help but notice Crispin.

17

RICHARD'S EYES ROUNDED. IT would have been comical in another situation, a situation that did not involve possible imprisonment and death.

The king's mouth turned down in a scowl so black his bearded chin furrowed. "What is *he* doing here?" The royal hand lifted a bejeweled finger and pointed at Crispin.

Crispin dropped to one knee and lowered his head. He said nothing. There was nothing to say. He heard Jack plop on the floor behind him, breath wheezing like a bagpipe.

"Sire," said Henry, rising from his knee. "I encountered my old friend and childhood companion outside the gate—"

"Cousin, you are aware that this man is not allowed within my palace walls, are you not?"

"Oh, but sire, such an old friend. With such an interesting vocation. Did you know—"

"I know all about Crispin Guest. He is a traitor and those who encourage him are considered traitors as well."

Henry sprang forward. "Your grace!"

Richard glared at him. "Well, cousin? Do you track with trai-tors now?"

Henry trembled with suppressed rage. "I am ever loyal, sire. Your grace and I are blood, my lord. To say such a thing to me is the gravest insult to my honor and my house."

The king bounced on the balls of his feet and seemed to calm, raising a softer gaze to his childhood companion. "No, Henry. My tongue spoke before my wits could trap the words. You are ever loyal to me as my closest and dearest cousin." He turned again to Crispin, his scowl renewed. "But this one, on the other hand . . ." He stepped forward until he was standing directly over Crispin. Crispin stared at the long-toed slippers, their points nearly touch-ing his knee pressed to the floor.

"Get up," said the king.

Slowly, Crispin rose, and it was another moment before he dared raise his eyes to Richard. The king's gaze was furious. "How dare you set foot in my palace when I expressly forbade it."

"Sire," Crispin began, but a gesture from the king cut him off.

Henry laid his hand on Crispin's shoulder. "Your grace, it was important that he come. He brings criminals to the crown's jus-tice. I know this. And so do you. He saved your life—"

"I have no need to be reminded of that, Derby." He was breath-ing hard, barely containing his anger. Crispin silently waited for it to explode at him.

"But he has another murder to unravel. For that, he needs to talk to your chancellor."

"Suffolk? Oh, does he?" He stalked up to Crispin and looked him in the eye. "What would you speak with Suffolk about, eh, Guest?"

Crispin gazed mildly into the king's eyes, more mildly than he felt.

"Nothing to say? Only to the earl, then? Well, let's call him here. Better still, let us go to the Painted Chamber and await him. Come, cousin." He glared at Crispin. "Guest. You come, too."

Crispin swallowed the oath on his lips. This was not exactly the audience he craved. He had no choice but to follow. His glance cut to Jack and he could plainly see that the boy was terrified. He closed his hand over his shoulder reassuringly.

But who was to reassure Crispin?

They followed the king and his companions to the chamber, another hall. Richard sat on a chair set on a dais with his men around him. Crispin and Henry faced them. Richard was served wine while they sent for Michael de la Pole.

Crispin felt many eyes on him but kept his face impassive. This was insane! How could he possibly question Suffolk in this . . . this circus?

It wasn't long until the chancellor arrived with his own entourage. *More men. Excellent.* One was another of Richard's close associates, Robert de Vere, earl of Oxford. At first Crispin thought the sneer Oxford wore was for him. But on second glance, he realized the earl was aiming it at Henry.

"Your grace," said Suffolk, sweeping Richard with a bow. "How may I serve you?"

"You see before you a specter, Suffolk. Lo, Crispin Guest."

Suffolk turned and his aristocratic face darkened with a scowl. Without turning from him, he said to the king, "Did you summon him, sire?"

"No indeed. Never would I have done so. And yet here he stands."

"Shall I call for your guards, your grace?"

"No, my lord. He is here by the good grace of our cousin Derby."

The chancellor whipped his head around and beheld Henry,

giving him a slight bow. Henry acknowledged him with the nod of his head. Crispin noted the definite chill between them.

"You have heard, my lords," said Richard to the assembly, waving his goblet, "that Master Guest is a discoverer of criminals and scoundrels. What is that they call you in London, Crispin? Traveler, Trapper . . . ?"

Crispin licked his lips. "*Tracker,* my lord."

"That's right. What a quaint title. Still, I suppose it's better than no title at all." He did not smile and neither did the assembled. He drank his wine and Crispin couldn't help but wonder what Lancaster would make of this; if he would dare admonish Richard with his eyes or leave it alone. Certainly Henry's emotions were worn on his sleeve. He was not happy about the accusation of treason and seemingly less happy about bringing Crispin into the palace than when he first began. What had been a lark was now turning to something more deadly.

"And why do you suppose this *Tracker* has come to court? It appears, my lords, that he is looking for a criminal."

A few nervous titters made their way over the crowd.

"Or at least criminal intent. Is that it, Crispin? Is that what you are looking for?"

"I do not know entirely until I find more answers, my lord."

"But here is where you expect to find them? In my palace? And what crime are you researching, Crispin? Has someone lost a thimble?"

The laughter was a little less nervous.

"No, sire. It involves the murder of a man on London Bridge and the theft of a religious relic."

The laughter came to an abrupt halt. Richard glared at him. He leaned forward. "Murder and thievery? In *my* court?"

"I merely have questions, my lord."

"And you wish to ask them of my chancellor?"

Suffolk stepped back, his hand on his sword hilt. *"What?"*

Richard smiled and sat back, getting comfortable. He glanced at de Vere, whose eyes barely slipped over Crispin but instead trained on Henry. "Yes, my good Suffolk. Master Guest is here to talk to you. And so I have summoned you."

Suffolk's outrage was barely contained. "And you will permit this?"

Richard shrugged. "Why not? Proceed, Crispin. Ask your questions. I'm certain we'd all be fascinated to see how a Tracker performs his vocation."

Suffolk glared. He changed his stance to one of fighting readiness and faced Crispin with a dark scowl.

Crispin couldn't help but cast his gaze about the room, taking in all the disgusted expressions. He was little more than something nasty tracked in on one's boots.

He threw his shoulders back and raised his chin. "My Lord Suffolk, a knight with your colors is known to be looking for this relic, and is suspected of the crime of the murder of Roger Grey, armorer, and his two apprentices. Are you aware of the goings-on by your own men?"

Crispin quickly ticked a glance at King Richard. His eyes showed surprise at Crispin's words but no culpability.

In Suffolk's eyes, on the other hand . . .

"This is absurd!" he sputtered. "Which knight?"

"His name is Sir Osbert. He travels and does his mischief with two others."

Richard turned to Suffolk. *"Do* you have a knight in your employ named Osbert?"

Suffolk cast his hands in the air. "I have many knights, your grace, as do you. Can you name them all?"

Richard did not reply but he was plainly no longer as amused as he had been. "And what else, Master Guest? What is this relic?"

"I . . . do not know what the relic is, sire." He heard Jack make a squeak behind him. "But it is the cause of these murders. Perhaps my Lord Suffolk can enlighten us as to what the relic might be."

"I don't know what this cur is talking about!"

"I happen to know that Geoffrey Chaucer is also searching for it." Richard sat up at this news. "And you were seen talking to him at an inn in London. Were you discussing it with him?"

Suffolk drew his sword and lunged forward, but Richard quickly directed his own men to stop him.

"But sire!" he pleaded. "This man, this *traitor*, has impugned my loyalties and my honor."

"He merely asked a question, the answer of which I, too, would like to know."

Suffolk slammed his blade back in its sheath. "Your grace! I cannot believe I am to stand here and be questioned by the likes of Crispin Guest, a known criminal and plotter. Everything he says must be a lie."

"*Are* you lying, Guest?" asked the king.

"No, your grace. Why would I have cause to do that?"

"To foment rebellion amongst your nobles," said Suffolk, red-faced. "Why else? There is already discord on the streets. This is meat to him."

"To what purpose?" said Crispin. "I have no commerce with you or the king's nobles. I stand to lose more than I gain in such a venture. My only interest is in seeing justice served."

"Answer the man, Suffolk."

"He lies. I was never talking to Chaucer at an inn."

Richard raised his brows, turning to Crispin.

"I know what I saw, my lord."

"And I say again, you are a liar!" Suffolk's hand was on his sword hilt again, but Richard stayed him with a calming gesture.

"Stalemate. You have had your questions, Crispin. Now you may go."

Suffolk's eyes were dark with loathing and Richard looked on with a mild expression. There was nothing more to be gained. In fact, Crispin was happy to be getting off this easy.

He bowed low to the king as he used to do in court and, sweeping his wet cloak aside, moved swiftly for the exit lest Richard change his mind. He signaled to Jack to follow and the lad wasted no time and scurried quickly behind him.

Out of the corner of his eye, he saw Henry take his leave and follow his furious pace toward the great hall. He and Jack nearly made it out the door when Henry stopped them. He looked none too pleased himself and he grabbed Crispin's arm and dragged him to a shadowed corner with Jack in tow.

"Why didn't you tell me all of that? Why didn't you speak of these things before we were made a spectacle of?"

"I did not get a chance to, my lord, as you well know."

Henry shook his head and breathed deeply. "Christ, Crispin. I only recall when you were the carefree companion of my youth. I was only told of your . . . indiscretions . . . much later."

"Now you are a witness. Perhaps you regret befriending me."

Taken aback, Henry measured him. "No! No, I do not. I regret . . . putting you in that situation. Forgive me. I thought it only an amusement to bring you into the palace and face the chancellor. Had I known what would transpire, well—"

Crispin quirked a half-smile. Softly he said, "I forgive you, Henry."

The young lord's face burst into cheer. "Ah! That's the Crispin I knew."

"Well, that was a terribly long time ago."

"I know." He fell silent and only just noticed he still had a grip of Crispin's arm. He released him and stepped back. "Shall I see you again?"

Crispin shrugged. "I do not think it wise, my lord."

"You already said that."

"And I believe I was right."

"You used to be such fun." Henry stood a moment before he reached into his scrip and pulled out a coin pouch. "Here. I want you to take this."

"No, my lord. Absolutely not." Crispin's eyes darted about the large hall; he hoped that no one was paying attention to them. But of course, someone was always watching at court.

Henry grabbed Crispin's hand and shoved it in. "You will take it. My father would insist."

"Your father would have more discretion where he handed over money pouches, my lord."

He laughed. "You're right, of course. This looks terribly suspicious."

"Terribly," rasped Crispin.

"Doesn't matter." Henry spared Jack a glance and raised his hand in greeting to him. "Young squire, guard your knight well."

"It is an honor to do so, your grace."

"Ah, Crispin. You have found a gallant attendant."

"There is none better than Master Tucker, I must admit."

Jack glowed with pride and looked as if he would burst into grateful tears. Crispin cleared his throat. "We must not tarry and vex the king's generosity."

"No, you mustn't. Off with you now, Crispin. I'm sure we will meet again."

"I will do my best to avoid it."

Crispin crossed over the threshold with the tinkle of Henry's laughter on his ears and his coin pouch clutched in his hand.

18

THEY HEADED BACK TOWARD the Shambles. Jack seemed to take a long time to say what he wanted to say. "Er . . . Master?"

"Yes, Jack."

"I think you done well back there. Under the circumstances."

Crispin quirked an eyebrow at his apprentice. "Do you?"

"Aye. That was a mess indeed. Almost shat me braies."

Crispin chuckled. "I'll tell you a secret." Jack leaned closer. "Me, too."

The boy gave a tentative smile.

"But we did learn something."

"We did? Oh, I know. Don't go near the palace *ever* again."

"No. We learned that Richard did not know anything of these doings."

"Oh. I didn't know we cared about that."

"I didn't know it either until I noticed. I was somehow . . . relieved."

"But that earl of Suffolk . . . he had guilt painted all over his face. And he was lying."

"Yes, he was. That makes it all the more dangerous. For one, I have played my hand. Now he knows what I know."

"But he doesn't know where the relic is."

"No."

They ambled down narrow lanes and turned corners where men gathered around smoky braziers burning merrily.

The day was drawing on. The shops were already beginning to close. Crispin bought the last meat pie from a cart and Jack came running up from another street with sausage links held high in the air like a victory garland.

When they reached their lodgings, Jack poked the sausages with a long iron fork and set that leaning against the trivet over the fire. Soon, they were spitting and dripping with juices. Crispin cut the meat pie in half and pushed one of the halves nearest the stool and poured wine in both bowls.

They sat down to the table to feast, each holding a hot sausage in their fingers and chewing thoughtfully into the companionable silence.

After a time, Jack offered, "I think Master Chaucer is lying."

Chewing, Crispin looked up. "Oh? About what exactly?"

"I think he knows where this relic is. He just doesn't want anything to do with it."

"That makes no sense," said Crispin, mouth full. He chewed and swallowed before adding, "I can assure you, if he knew, we'd not see him again." As soon as he said it, his stomach did a small flip. Chaucer was more than an opponent in this instance. He was one of his oldest friends. And he did not want their friendship left in tatters over this.

"What does Chaucer want?" Crispin muttered. "He was seen with Suffolk and he was seen with a Spaniard. What can that mean?"

"So he don't have the Spear?"

"No. He doesn't, and he doesn't know where it is. You can be certain we are being followed all the time now."

"Damn! I forgot to look for him!"

"He's there. Or his minions. They are not far away."

Jack pushed off from the table and went to the window. He flipped the bolt and pulled it open slightly, glancing down at the darkening street. "I don't see no one."

"I don't imagine you would."

He closed and bolted it again. "Blind me. I don't like people watching and following me."

"The shoe is on the other foot now, eh, Tucker?"

Jack smiled and sat again, taking another sizzling sausage from the trivet. He tossed it from one hand to the other until Crispin speared it mid-flight with his knife. He handed it, knife and all, to Jack. The boy took it sheepishly.

"We will have to talk to Mistress Coterel again," said Crispin. "Perhaps there is something she heard Grey say that might indicate where he could have hidden the relic."

"Could he have given it to someone for safekeeping?"

"Perhaps. Anabel might know."

"Anabel, is it?" he muttered.

Crispin glared at the boy as he chewed, juice dripping down his chin. "You have something to say, Tucker?"

Jack sighed. "Sir, it's just that . . . This woman. I think she's trouble. You shouldn't have aught to do with her."

"That opinion is not relevant to the situation. I suggest in future you keep such judgments to yourself."

"Yes, sir," he grumbled.

Crispin continued to eye the lad until Jack rose and cleaned the cooking things, stirring the ashes and adding more peat and a few sticks of wood to the hearth.

Crispin turned his chair to face the fire and Jack settled on his stool to pore over the brief lesson Crispin had written in Greek. With his wax slate in front of him, Jack attempted to copy it out and translate, tongue firmly planted between his lips.

A knock on the door made them raise their heads.

Crispin motioned Jack down and drew his knife. He crept to the door and rested his hand on the latch. "Who is there?"

"It is Anabel Coterel," said the muffled voice. Immediately, he cast the bolt aside and pulled the door open.

"I . . . apologize for arriving here so late in the evening."

Crispin glanced over the landing and poked his head out the door to look down the stairs. Exasperated, he closed the door and sheathed his knife. "You should not be out at all! And alone, damosel? I thought I made it plain—"

"You have every right to be angry. You are taking fine care of me . . . and my father."

Stiffly, Crispin stood over her. What the hell was she doing here?

She offered a bundle of clothes and held it forward a long time until he slowly took it from her. "The coat and shirts for your apprentice, sir. Father only just finished them. I know they are not fitted, but if Master Tucker will return to the inn with them . . ."

Jack was there in an instant and took them from Crispin. His eyes were alight with gratitude and he sat quickly in his corner of straw and carefully laid out each item, whistling softly to himself. Of what Crispin could see, the blue coat was well made and the shirts looked sturdy as well. As long as the boy didn't suddenly sprout up another foot, these clothes would do him justice for at least another few years.

He expected Jack to whip off his old cotehardie but he spent a great deal of time running his hands gently over the fabric of the coat laid out on the straw and toying with the many cloth-covered buttons down the front and at the sleeves.

"I thank you for that," said Crispin softly.

Jack's head popped up. "Oh aye! Thank your father for me, damosel! Please do. It is a beautiful coat."

"I shall," she said. She stood before Crispin for a time until she ducked away from his scrutiny to stand before the fire, raising her curled fingers to the meager flames. "I'm certain they will fit you well for many years, Master Tucker," she said to the hearth.

"That was kind of you to bring them," said Crispin, "but as I said, foolish."

He walked around the table to join her at the hearth and she looked up at him then, suddenly startled at his appearance. "Oh! What has happened to your face?"

He had forgotten the bruises. His jaw still felt tender but he was used to it by now. "An altercation with the same knights who detained you." He raised a finger to the yellowing bruises on her cheek as well, but she turned her face away. Her veil hid it from view.

"Who were they?"

"They killed Roger Grey."

"Christ have mercy," she gasped, blinking.

"As you might have surmised, they do not have the relic that was surely the reason Master Grey was killed. I must ask you to search your thoughts, your memories, damosel. Is there anything that you can tell me—of Grey's associates, of his enemies—that could help us identify what might have happened to this important object? For I fear that the danger to you and to me will remain until this item is found."

She shook her head, her plaits gently swaying with the motion. "Roger had many secrets. He did many favors for rich patrons. I feared that some of the things he did were not quite within the law. He was well paid for them, that I do know, for he did show me once what he made from one of his schemes. There was a lot of gold."

"Yes. That begs the question, too, of what became of his fortune."

"It would have been a great comfort to me and my father had it been found."

"He has no heirs?"

"None that I know of. But as you saw, there was nothing there." She continued to stare into the fire. "Master Crispin, are you any closer to finding the culprit who stole our rent money?"

"I might be."

"Oh? Who, then?" She turned and was closer than Crispin thought.

He cleared his throat and stepped back. "No one you are likely to know. He is a thief, and known to me."

"Then it isn't likely our funds will be returned, is it?"

He shook his head, watching the shape of her mouth as she spoke.

"I fear you must forget this theft, then. It is a waste of your time. And I'd rather you spent that time bringing Roger's killers to justice."

"The crimes may have to do with each other."

She seemed surprised at these tidings. Her lips parted but she said nothing.

"Strange," she said at last. "What would these killers need with our rent money?"

"It seems to me, damosel—"

"Anabel," she corrected softly.

"Anabel," he whispered. "It seems that the killers wanted your eviction to empty your shop."

She kneaded her hands together before the fire. "Very strange," she muttered. "Still, I would forget the thief and concentrate on these knights."

"You have never seen them before?"

"Never," she said.

"Nor have you heard of this relic."

"As I've said. Would that I had!" She spun away from the fire and paced, coming to stop before Crispin. "I wish Roger never had anything to do with relics. What does it matter now that it's gone? If you know who killed him, hadn't you best tell the sheriff? You *do* believe it is these knights? But how can you bring noblemen to justice?"

"True, they are knights, noblemen. I can't just accuse them without further proof. And the relic will supply that proof."

Her veil shadowed her face. "Maybe," she said softly, "maybe it is best . . . to forget . . . all of it."

"I am very much afraid, damosel, that I cannot."

She looked up. Her pliant lips worked gently, trying to form just the right words. "But why? You and I know in the sight of God who did it. Is that not enough?"

"No. It is very much not enough. You must think of someone, somewhere who might have either helped Roger Grey find this relic in the first place or kept it safe for him until he called for it."

She shook her head again and took a step closer. "I can think of no one. He confided very little."

"You were to be wed to him. Could he not trust you?"

"As far as I knew, he trusted no one enough. Not even his apprentices. In your experience, have you found such men to be forth-coming to their wives?"

"Sometimes. But as you say, he was not such a man."

"No. I am sorry for his death." She traced a cross delicately over her face. "But I cannot say," she said, voice falling to a whisper, "that I am sorry I did not marry him."

A throat cleared behind him and Crispin turned, remembering Jack. The boy buttoned his cloak and, slump-shouldered, headed toward the door. "I'll just be on the landing, then," he muttered, his reluctant steps taking him outside. He closed the door and Crispin, astonished, merely stared at it.

She laughed softly, a deep rumble in her throat. "Your appren-tice is a perceptive lad."

When he looked back at her, he knew again why Roger Grey had chosen her. The firelight claimed one cheek, dusting it with gold, while the other lay in shadow. The dark plaits shimmered with glossy amber fire. Her lids slid lower and she looked up at him through lashes that reminded him of another who was fond of gaz-ing at him through sleepy eyes.

Was it fair that the other, that Philippa, was safe and married behind manor walls? Was it fair that Anabel's betrothed, her safe harbor, was taken from her? A rush of emotions, anger laced with something else, swept over his heart and he grabbed her arms, clutching hard.

She gasped, the small puff of breath pelting his chin. He lifted her. "What did you come here for?" he rasped, voice coarse. "What do you want of me?"

She didn't answer.

A heartbeat, and then he pulled her in, mouth devouring hers. She gave another gasp but it was drowned in the onslaught of his mouth. His lips slid over hers until they were raw, tongue hungrily questing. He had her suddenly against the wall beside the hearth, pressing her into the plaster, his body tight against hers, touching from knee to chest. He continued to kiss, thinking that he was the one taking, until her hands slid around his waist and her fingers dug in, pulling him even closer.

He yanked his head away and looked dazedly down at her. His hands loosened on her arms. "Anabel, I . . . we shouldn't."

"No, we shouldn't."

He felt her hands at the small of his back. Instead of pushing him away, they pulled him in until he was crushed against her once more. Her face was tilted upward toward his, breath fast and warm against his moistened mouth. Her plump lips beckoned and he angled his face down. It was softer this time, a lick over her parted lips, a gentle press against them. He drew back again and gazed at her. "My apprentice has left. We seem to be alone."

"I noticed."

They were only steps from the bed. He could not help but shift his eyes to it. Hers twitched in that direction, too.

"Will you . . . stay a while? What of your father?"

Such a question should have thrown cold water on the proceedings, but Anabel's expression did not change. Her smile widened. "All is well. Don't worry."

Crispin pulled the pins from her veil and let it drop away. He took her face in his hands and leaned forward. "Then I won't."

HE SHIMMERED UP FROM the depths of a dream, his body sated. But when he opened his eyes he was alone in the bed. Light filtered in from below the shutters and the rattle of metal pots against clay roused him to lean toward the hearth.

Jack crouched before it in his new blue coat and jabbed angrily at the peat as if by sheer force he could make the flames higher.

Crispin stretched languidly and got out of bed. The room was still cold, even for all the anger Tucker directed at the hearth, and his flesh pimpled from a chill. Naked and shivering, Crispin first grabbed his discarded shirt and slipped it on. He sat, scratched his head through his disheveled hair, and pulled up his braies. A loud yawn failed to redirect Jack's single-minded attention away from the fire and Crispin proceeded to pull up each stocking and tie them to his underwear. "Porridge?" he asked hopefully.

Jack said nothing, but dragged himself up and to the pantry shelf where he grabbed a bowl and returned to the fire, ladling in a gray glob of porridge. He set it harshly before Crispin on the table and returned to the fire.

Crispin eyed him and sat, running his hand over his chin stubble. Dare he ask about shaving water? What was the matter with the boy? "Why so sulky, Tucker?" He dug into the bowl with a wooden spoon and licked the tasteless paste.

"'M not," he grumbled.

"Oh? Then your cheerfulness leaves much to be desired."

"I think there is far too much *desiring* here already."

Crispin rolled his eyes but continued to eat. "Are you, by any chance, referring to the late visit of Mistress Coterel?"

"I told you she was trouble."

"All women are trouble. It needs only be decided what kind. Besides, she is full of good humor. She is sharp. She helped investigate." He glanced sidelong and rubbed his bristly chin again. "You're not still jealous of her, are you?"

Jack tossed the poker down with a reverberating clang. "I'm *not* jealous!"

"Your reaction would seem to say otherwise."

"I'm not 'reacting.' I'm being smarter than you."

"Careful, Tucker. That smacks of rebelliousness and in a tone most unseemly for your place."

"Now who's thinking with his cod!"

Crispin jumped to his feet. "Damn you!"

Jack backed away as Crispin followed him around and around the table. "Master Crispin," he said sternly, "you aren't thinking clearly, sir. I know you're lonely and she seems to be a smart wench and comely, too. But she's too close to this. Why is she here with you when less than a sennight ago her betrothed met with a vile death? Something is amiss, sir. The first moment we met her we thought she was lying about something. Have you forgotten that? Have you got the truth out of her? If it were me with a woman in similar straits you'd tell me the same thing, now wouldn't you?"

Crispin paused. Damn the boy but he might be right. "God's blood!" he hissed. He did question why she was here last night and yet she could not give him a satisfactory answer. She knew it wasn't safe and yet she went abroad unescorted. He admired a certain amount of tenacity but there *was* something amiss here. She had absorbed his fears with her body and did a good job of it, too!

He brought up a sheepish expression. "How did you get so wise?"

"Learned it from you, didn't I."

That made it worse. "I owe you an apology."

Jack finally loosened his shoulders and his face softened. "Not a bit of it." He brought the pot of hot water to the table. "Shave, sir?"

Slowly Crispin sat and allowed Jack to do the ablutions. When he was clean-shaven again, he helped clear the basin and porridge bowl.

"Let us think of this thing logically," he said to the boy. "What was her purpose in coming here last night, barring the obvious?" He could not help the heat crawling up his neck.

"Well, a woman might be good at getting information from a man when he is in such a state."

Crispin gave a crooked smile. "We did very little talking."

Jack rolled his eyes. "Aye. Well then. What else? Did you say anything to her?"

"I told her I was detained by the same men who accosted her. But that only served as a warning that we need to conclude this investigation quickly."

The boy nodded. "But you also told her you did not know where the relic is."

"This she already knows."

"But did she? She was ever anxious to help you find it. Maybe she knows something we don't."

"She was unaware of it previously."

Jack smacked his own head, no doubt wishing he could do the same to Crispin. "And a woman has never lied to you before?"

His fourteen-year-old apprentice was making him look like a complete fool. Crispin sat back. "By my Lady, Tucker. I am not being myself. I have been caught up in my . . . my solitude, I suppose. Thinking of . . . another."

Jack's eyes flicked to the mattress, and by that simple gesture, Crispin knew that Jack was aware of the portrait of Philippa Walcote.

Crispin stared at the table. "She wanted me to forget the robbery. The whole thing."

"Forget the murder, too?"

"It wasn't . . . put in those terms. Not exactly."

"If you were any other man, might you have put it all aside . . . for her?"

He frowned. "I have a need to stroll the bridge, Jack. Care to accompany me?"

THE CARPENTERS HAD WORKED fast, for the viewing stands were already finished by the time Crispin and Jack reached the bridge. Shopkeepers seemed energized by the business they were sure to acquire when the jousts began, which put Crispin in mind of Thomas Saunfayl. He hoped he had turned himself in by now. It was still difficult to believe that a man like him could be a coward, but he had admitted it to Crispin's face. The whole world had truly gone mad.

He reached the armorer's and there was no longer a sheriff's man guarding the shop. He checked the nailed boards. The window remained unbarred and he pushed the shutter open.

"Here now!"

Crispin's foot was on the sill when he stopped and turned. A woman with a basket of turnips tucked under her arm was wagging a finger at him. "Get away from there. That's been barred by the sheriff."

He stepped out of the window and faced her. "I do know that. I am here investigating—"

"There's been too many men going in and out of there. I've a mind to call the king's guards again. That poor Master Grey being murdered and his apprentices, too! It's foul, it is. What's this town coming to?"

"How many men have been coming and going through here?"

"Half a dozen or so. First those three knights and then those other men. It's not right. Looting a poor dead man."

"Were they taking things?"

"Well." She hitched the basket higher on her hip. "I live in yon lodgings." She pointed across the way to a second-story window. "I can see the street well enough during the day and at night. And I could see these men coming and going without so much as a by your leave."

"Did they take anything?"

"And who are you for asking?"

With a hand on his breast he bowed. "I am Crispin Guest. I'm called the Tracker. Perhaps you've heard—"

"By the saints! The Tracker? Wait. Aren't you the one who pulled Master Grey from the Thames?"

"Yes. You were telling me about—"

"Well then." She sidled closer and spoke confidentially, all the while eyeing Jack suspiciously. "People coming and going. But nothing taken. Naught that I could see. Strange, isn't it?"

"Yes. Why have you not reported this to the sheriff?"

"Stranger, that. I saw *her* leading one man in there."

"Her?"

"Her. You know. The tailor's daughter."

"You mean Master Grey's betrothed?"

"Betrothed? Absurd. She was never betrothed to him. What honorable man would want such tainted goods?"

An angry flush warmed Crispin's cheeks and he found he had to clench his fists to keep them from grabbing and shaking the old woman. "I beg your pardon."

"She was his lover, not his betrothed. Everyone on the bridge knows that. And I dare say, he wasn't the only one."

19

"MASTER?"

"Be still, Tucker."

"Master. We best go inside."

He tugged on Crispin's sleeve. Exasperated, Crispin turned his head and Jack gave him a meaningful look.

"Do you mean to say that it is *rumored* that Mistress Coterel was not betrothed?" he said to the woman.

"It is no rumor, sir."

"Forgive me. But there was also a rumor that Roger Grey killed himself. That was found to be false."

"I did hear that rumor but I never believed it. But you can ask any man on the bridge about Anabel Coterel. Even at a young age, barely out of swaddling it seemed, she was sniffing after men. Gets her way, too. Knows how to twist them round her finger. If anything, Grey was jealous of her meandering. She'd deny it, as any woman would. And just as soon as he was twisted good and tight around her wrist again, off she'd go to the next man. A vixen, is Mistress Coterel. She'll never lack, that is a certainty. Never go hungry and never be out in the cold. But mark me, someday she'll coil around the wrong man. It wouldn't surprise me at all to hear that she is found with a knife in her throat. Lord bless her."

Try as he might, Crispin could not utter a sound. He was ready to burst with rage but he swallowed it down.

Stiffly, Crispin bowed. "If you will excuse us, madam." He could do this. He could walk away. Except he still needed to know. Not for himself, but for the investigation, or so he told himself, over and over. "Madam, may I ask? What man did Mistress Coterel lead inside?"

"The knight. The one with the silver and green surcote." Saunfayl. No doubt to retrieve his armor. He felt better about that until she added, "And that other."

"What other?"

"Don't know."

"Can you describe him? Was he a knight?"

"No, not a knight. Just a merchant or some such. Did it after nightfall."

"Was he a stranger, then? No one you have seen before on the bridge?"

"Oh no," she said, with a self-satisfied smile. "I've seen him before right enough."

"Does he dwell here?"

"I don't know. But I have seen him in her company. Many a time. Young, auburn hair. Has a confident way about him."

The first person to come to mind was Lancaster's son Henry, but Crispin dismissed it just as quickly. It was only because the man was in his thoughts of late. What would Henry have to do with this?

"I trust you will allow us to proceed inside?" asked Crispin.

She curtseyed and gave a nervous smile. "Of course, sir."

He slapped his boot on the sill and pulled himself in. Tucker soon followed and closed the shutter behind him.

"I know what you're going to say," said Jack.

"Do you?" he snapped. "Perhaps you don't need me at all in this investigation. Perhaps you should do it all yourself."

"Now Master Crispin, don't be like that. I just saved you from throttling her, is all."

"I would have been very pleased to do it. Except that she gave us some very valuable information."

"Aye. Mistress Coterel *was* lying."

"Indeed," he said tightly. "She could hardly have told the coroner that she was the man's lover. She received little enough respect when she declared she was his betrothed."

"Verily, I can see the reason for the lie in this instance."

But it didn't sit well with Crispin. If she were Grey's lover, then her strange distant attitude to his death seemed even worse. And then last night . . .

"A lover who was not very devoted to her lover. One does not take a lover except for an emotional bond. What could that mean, Jack?"

He shrugged.

"Perhaps not an emotional bond. And if not that, then . . ." That didn't sit well either. He turned toward Jack. "As that woman said . . . for gain?"

"He paid her?"

"Not so much that. But she seemed to think he would lend her money for rent. Perhaps he was more devoted than she."

Jack looked around the dusty room. The shutters were all closed but light did filter in through the seams. "What are we looking for, Master?"

"Something, anything to give us a clue as to where the Spear might be."

"But we already looked."

"Without the knowledge of what we were looking for."

"So it's the point of a spear?"

"No. Remember what the abbot said?" Mention of the abbot caused a spike of discomfort for the fate of the man he cherished. "He said that the tip is in the Sainte Chapelle in Paris. It's the rest of it that seems to be the missing piece."

They both looked at the decorative spear shaft leaning against the wall. Crispin reached it first and hefted it in his hands. "I suppose if the spearhead were attached to this, one might construct a point for it, but I am no swordsmith."

Jack took it in his hands and turned the shaft, examining the bas relief designs. "This is fine work, Master. Then he must truly have had the Spear, otherwise he would not have gone to the trouble and expense. Why did he wait to affix it to this shaft then?"

"It could be he had to construct a way to give it a point without harming it and was interrupted in his task."

"Blind me. We've already got Suffolk who wanted it and Master Chaucer and Sir Thomas. Who else wanted it? And how many people knew about it?"

"It's becoming quite a list, isn't it? I wonder from whom it actually came. Was it gotten illegally as Anabel—that is, Mistress Coterel—implied? And perhaps the seller wanted it back."

"And got it, without these others knowing?"

"Yes. And if that is the case, we will never find it now."

They stood silently, staring at the dim interior. Jack gently laid the spear shaft aside.

"Jack," he said quietly. "If you were still a thief, where might you hide your letters?"

"Letters, sir?"

"Master Grey had a correspondence with Sir Thomas, but he might also have had one with whomever he obtained the Spear from. He had a hidden place in the wall, behind that buckler." Crispin pointed to the round shield on the wall. "But there was nothing there. Either someone had gotten to it beforehand or he had some other secret place."

"It would be in his bedchamber," offered Jack.

Crispin nodded and headed for the stair. Jack followed. When they reached the top the shadowed room seemed to be asleep in its gloom and stillness. There was a bed, a coffer, a sideboard, and two chairs positioned before the cold, dark fireplace. Crispin watched from the doorway as Jack made his way stealthily about the room. He went first to the fireplace and ran his hands over the opening, even to reaching up into the firebox. He dusted his hands together to rid them of soot when he stood again, and made his way around the walls, knocking occasionally at a timbered beam running up to the rafters. With an ear cocked, he listened, paused, then moved on. When he reached the sideboard, he stopped again and opened the doors. Peering inside, he leaned in, trailing his finger along each seam and pressing firmly on the boards, both of the interior walls and the doors themselves.

The boy is thorough, he mused, and then began to wonder at the former career of his apprentice. He knew the boy was an accomplished cutpurse, but by the looks of it, he had learned his trade of thievery a little too well.

After examining the turned legs, Jack continued on until he came to the bed. It had a sturdy frame of dark wood and an overhanging canopy of heavy drapery. Crispin thought the lad would turn over the mattress or perhaps the bedhead, but instead, he ran his careful hands over the frame, his eyes glittering in concentration, until Crispin heard a soft click.

Jack made a sound of pleasure and opened a door on the heavy frame, which swung away from the mattress.

He reached in and pulled out a stack of folded parchment, wrapped with a leather strap. Holding it up, the boy beamed.

Crispin took the bundle and Jack scrambled to find the tinderbox and light a candle. Crispin untied the strap and laid the first document on the table under the candle. The first was a receipt, as was the second. But the third was a letter from a Moor in a place near the Spanish border. The writing was small and tight and the English was poor. Much of the seal was torn away, but when Crispin held the parchment in the light, he could make out some of it.

"Jack," Crispin breathed. "Listen. *The object you seek is rare. Rarer still is the man who can obtain it. He will be of high price but worth it. What shall I tell my brokers? The gold you have sent is insufficient. Twenty marks more is his price.*" His gaze met Jack's over the candle flame. "It is dated earlier in the year." He scanned the next letter, discarded it, scanned the next. He angled it toward the light. "Aha. See here. *Master Grey, your price changes with each missive. My lord is becoming anxious. He will deliver unto you the amount on our last agreement and I beg you not to change your mind again. I will send it to you anon.*"

"There's no signature, nor seal, sir."

"Yes. But I know this writing. It is Geoffrey Chaucer's."

"Blind me. Is the lord he is speaking of the duke, sir?"

"I do not know." Crispin gazed at the tawny parchment a moment longer before setting it aside. He took up the next one and read. "*The plans have changed. And with those changes, more gold I send to you. I shall reach you by the middle of October. I shall take possession as my lord has instructed. The object shall now be in my keeping. See to it that all is made ready for my arrival . . ."*

"That does not look like the same hand, sir."

"That's because it isn't. It is signed Sir Thomas Saunfayl."

"Wait." Jack grabbed Chaucer's letter and read it over, then read in his slow, careful perusal Sir Thomas's letter. "Sir, it looks to me as if . . . as if . . ."

"As if Sir Thomas bypassed Chaucer to make his own move on the relic? It certainly looks that way to me." Crispin scowled at the parchment. That would mean that not only was the man a coward but a cheat as well. For if Chaucer were negotiating the Spear for Lancaster, Sir Thomas was maneuvering to slip it out from under him.

Of course, if Chaucer was trying to obtain it for a Spaniard, then Sir Thomas would be a hero.

Crispin searched through the rest of the documents, but they were either more receipts or matters inconsequential to their present circumstances. He gave them back to Jack. "Return these where you found them. They'll be as safe there as anywhere else."

Jack did as ordered and then jerked up his head. Crispin wondered at it until he heard it, too. It sounded like someone in the place next door. The tailor's.

They hurried downstairs and out the shuttered window. The door to the Coterels' home was ajar and Crispin crept to it, pulling it open. A shadowed figure picked through a small coffer, head bent low in its search.

"I'd stop right there, if I were you," said Crispin.

The pale face of Robert Coterel shot up and stared with wide eyes.

Crispin let out the breath he was holding. "God's blood," he muttered. "Tucker, light a candle."

It took a few moments with some stumbling and scuffling, but soon Jack had one, then two candles lit. Coterel's frightened expression did not change but he turned and groped for a chair. Without a cold clogging his sinuses, Crispin could now tell that the man reeked from wine.

"Master Coterel, did I not give you strict instructions not to leave the inn?"

"Yes, yes, but I needed my needles. I had left some behind in our haste to leave." His fingers moved restlessly over the small ivory cylinder in his hand. But he seemed in no hurry to leave just yet.

Crispin watched him, his uncertain swaying over the chair, his tongue licking sluggishly over his lips, the day-old beard that came in grayer than the hair on his head. He couldn't waste this opportunity, even if it meant taking advantage of the man. "Master Coterel, can you tell me about . . . Master Grey?"

Hesitantly, he jerked his head toward Crispin and blinked, as if only just remembering he was there. "Master Grey? What would you like to know of him?"

"Was it true he was to marry your daughter?"

"Marry Anabel? Oh my, yes." He shook his head sloppily from side to side. "He was devoted to her. Did my heart good to see it. A man worries over his daughter, you know. Do you have children, Master Guest?"

Crispin resisted glancing at Jack. "No. Were the banns posted?"

"No, not as yet. Anabel said he was waiting for something. Some great opportunity was coming his way. In fact, she spoke of the possibility of leaving London. How right he was."

"Leaving London?" And yet Anabel insisted this was a lie. "For where?"

"I don't know. She said he had plans to make. Always plans."

"So he had formally asked for her hand?"

"Let me think. No. No, he never actually asked me. It was Anabel who told me. Told me of all his plans."

A sinking sensation swooped in Crispin's gut. He refused to look at Tucker. "It was Anabel alone who told you these details."

"Yes, yes. Such a good daughter. Whenever we seem on the brink of destruction, it is Anabel who pulls us from the fire. She can always find the funds when they are needed. God be praised for such a wise and thoughtful daughter."

"How does she find the funds?"

"Well, she sells small portions of our cloth."

"Oh? Why then did she not do so when you needed to make the rent?"

He wagged a finger. "Ah, but then she found *you,* did she not?"

Crispin felt his jaw clench. "Indeed. She did." That swoop in his gut was now turning into a ball of anger.

"She is always making friends. Friends who help us when we are in need. I am afraid to say that sometimes . . . well." The tailor crooked a finger to bring Crispin closer and the fumes of wine were strong when he huffed an embarrassed laugh. "Sometimes I drink too much. And then I gamble. And before I am aware of it, our funds are diminished. I have tried to be less of a sinner, but alas. I do penance but then I return to the tavern and the dice games before I ever realize that I have fallen back into sin." His smile faded, his eyes glistened, and soon tears rolled down his cheeks. "I am a poor father indeed!" Dropping his face in his hands, he sobbed.

Crispin stared at the wreck of a man before him. He had been negligent. He should have talked to Coterel much sooner. Instead, he had relied on his heart to lead him, an unpredictable organ at best.

"I'm gladdened that she has such good friends," he whimpered. "Men who watch over her when I cannot."

Crispin tried to keep his voice even. "Are there many such men, Master Coterel?"

"A few. There is the carpenter, Master Mark; the law student, Master Jonathan; the clerk, Master Lucas, the cordwainer, Master—"

"I beg your pardon. Did you say a clerk by the name of Master Lucas?"

"Did I?"

"You did," said Jack, drawing forward.

"Then I did." He nodded vigorously.

"Do you know his surname?"

"Stumpy, Stately . . ."

"Stotley?"

"Of course, it must be."

Crispin curled his hand around his dagger hilt. He did not like the shape of this.

"You cannot remain here, Master Coterel. You must return to the inn. Jack, see that he gets there."

"Yes, Master Crispin." He tugged Coterel to his feet, and the man stood reluctantly. "Come along now, good master, it is time for you to return to your inn. No doubt your daughter is waiting."

"If she is back she might very well be."

Crispin turned as they reached the door. "If she is back?"

"I heard her come in very early this morning, but now she is gone again. She has her many friends to consult. Many places to be. She always returns with a small bit of coins. A good daughter, is my Anabel."

"Yes, perhaps she is back and wondering where her father is." He didn't mean it to come out with such vitriol, and Jack frowned at him for it, but Master Coterel did not notice as Jack led him outside and down the lane.

Crispin closed the door and locked it with the use of his knife in the lock. His hand shook from anger but he kept it in check. He'd save it for later. He'd need it for facing Lucas Stotley, convenient Samaritan from the Boar's Tusk and, if he was not mistaken, also acquaintance of Lenny.

HE TOOK HIS ANGER with him as he stomped through the streets of London. His intention was to return to the Shambles and brood. The multiple levels of deception were an outrage to his sensibilities. But as he turned a corner, his eye caught an ale stake angling into the street. He could do with a cup of wine to cut the edge off his wrath. He veered toward the unfamiliar tavern and pushed open the door.

It was dark inside the raucous interior, but it took only a moment for his eyes to adjust. When they had, he stopped dead. In a darkened corner stood Chaucer, talking furtively to a man. And who should that man be but Lucas Stotley.

He drew his dagger and pointed it. "You!" cried Crispin. Stotley whipped his head toward Crispin. Terror swept over his face and Chaucer quickly pushed him away and gestured for him to escape.

"Oh no you don't!" The crowd was in his way, and Crispin tried to push through, to no avail. He growled his frustration and leapt onto the nearest table, to the outraged cries around him. He jumped to the next, making his way toward Stotley over the tables. Stotley moved furiously through the crowd toward the door, looking back at Crispin with widened eyes.

Men sitting at the tables shouted and fell out of Crispin's way as he strode along the surface, oblivious to their curses. His feet kicked wooden cups and ale spilled out in cockerel tails through the air.

Stotley scrambled toward the exit, pushing men out of the way. Crispin changed direction after him, still bounding from table to table, now knocking over candles and spilling wine jugs, some crashing to the floor in scattering shards.

Crispin leapt and hit the floor. He lunged, nearly reaching the clerk, when hands pulled him back. He lost his footing, slipped, and careened backward, barking his shoulder on a bench.

"Stop him!" he cried, but Stotley was out the door before anyone could react.

Crispin twisted around to see who had had the audacity to hinder him and wasn't surprised to see Chaucer's face. He hauled back a fist and punched him.

Chaucer's head snapped back and he wobbled but was able to whip his head about and shake it off.

"God's blood, Geoffrey! What the hell do you think you are doing?"

Geoffrey moved his jaw back and forth, testing it, before he frowned with a painful squint to his eye. "Damn you, Crispin." He swung but Crispin ducked, coming up with a fist in Chaucer's gut.

Geoffrey doubled over, took a breath, and head-butted Crispin.

Crispin crashed backward into a tray of bowls and jugs. Everything scattered and splintered and he found himself gasping and sitting on his bum surrounded by a pile of broken crockery. He sneered and jumped to his feet.

By then Chaucer was standing upright, balling his hands into fists. He drew one back and swung forward, but Crispin caught it in his hand and twisted. Chaucer yowled and sank to one knee and bit Crispin's leg on the way down.

It was Crispin's turn to yell, and he kicked, not caring where the blow landed.

It landed in Geoffrey's side. The man spun away, clutching his ribs, and glared back over his shoulder. He made a sudden lunge and grabbed Crispin's coat, hauling him close. "Come with me!"

But Crispin fought and grabbed Geoffrey's gown at its furred collar.

"No, you're coming with *me*!"

They struggled for a bit with the sound of ripping cloth before both came to a halt. Glaring got them nowhere until Crispin heaved a disgusted sigh. "Let's have this out." He pointed to the alcove with a curtain and Chaucer silently agreed, though neither one let go of the other's gown.

It was obviously a place for a servant to sleep, nothing more than a space for a mean cot and a niche for an oil lamp, but Chaucer pulled the curtain closed and pushed Crispin hard against the wall. Crispin recovered and shoved Geoffrey into the opposite wall and kept pushing, fists curled around his now torn collar.

"Are you a murderer, Geoffrey?" he rasped, mindful of the thin curtain separating them from the tavern. The scrape of bench and table being righted and men talking loudly about the disruption masked something of their conversation. "Are you aware who that man is?"

"I'm not a murderer, you idiot! Let go of me!"

Crispin shoved harder. "Tell me, dammit, or I swear I'll . . . I'll . . ." With a growl he released his friend's gown and stepped back, running a trembling hand over his mouth. He shook his head and grimaced. "Lancaster put you up to this," he whispered. "Answer me."

Geoffrey didn't fix his clothes. His expression warred between rage and disbelief. He seemed to be deciding, shoulders tensing.

And then he let it go, all of it. His body became fluid and he leaned against the wall, head back, throat rolling as he swallowed. "Cris. Damn you. Why did you have to be involved?"

Crispin flopped against his own wall, needing the plaster and stone to hold him upright. "Answer the question."

"Of course Lancaster charged me! He is my master."

"To kill?"

"No! What do you take me for? I am no assassin."

"And yet you track with them. What of Lucas Stotley?"

He didn't think Chaucer could look more shocked, but his face configured that way. "He is not a murderer, nor did I contract with him to that end."

"But you did hire him. To do what?"

Chaucer sighed and sat on the cot. The straw crunched beneath his weight. "He was to find a thief to steal the Coterels' rent money so that they would be evicted so that the shop would lie empty, allowing us to do our work."

It was everything Crispin suspected, but knowing it was true did not give him pleasure.

"But *you* fouled it up when *you* paid their rent," Geoffrey continued. "I thought you were without your own funds."

"Thanks for your confidence. Yes, that is generally true, but I was flush from a recent venture. How did he know where the money was hidden?"

Chaucer shrugged. "I don't know. I don't care. All I know is that Stotley was accomplished and did his part well. Until you showed up."

"Lancaster wants the Spear."

"Of course he wants it. Wouldn't you?"

"How did Sir Thomas get wind of it, then? Of your transaction with the Moor?"

Chaucer's cheeks flushed. "How the devil did you know that?"

Crispin crossed his arms and simmered.

Geoffrey ran a hand through his hair and only just realized he'd lost his hat somewhere. He looked around for it for a moment and then gave up. "I'm not certain. Possibly he overheard my discussing it with someone. His messenger was faster, his gold heftier. He slipped in right under my nose."

"Is that why you are after him?"

"Among other things. He *is* being tried for cowardice. And you need not hide him any longer, for I have found him. He is in custody now."

Crispin slumped. Not good news.

"So there is no more a reason to hide the Spear either, Cris. You should hand it over to me as soon as possible."

Crispin raised his head and studied his friend, his torn collar, his mussed beard and hair. So fastidious, but not today. Crispin's voice was rough and low when he asked, "Why were you conspiring with the earl of Suffolk?"

Chaucer's lips parted but Crispin interrupted whatever he was about to say. "You need not lie. I saw you with him. At a tavern."

With brows raised the man nodded. "I have forgotten how thorough you can be. Well . . . he, too, wanted the Spear for Lancaster. He has supported the duke in the past, you know. I told him my plans and he agreed."

"Are you certain it was for Lancaster?"

He frowned and would not look Crispin in the eye.

"I think you are over your head in this one, Geoffrey. I think he might have changed loyalties. He either wants it for the king or more likely for himself, for he is in sore need of it."

"So I have heard."

"Nevertheless, no matter how much you must have trusted

him, he did not reciprocate the feeling. He hired his own men to kill Roger Grey and be done with it. Those men also killed his innocent apprentices, brothers, aged fifteen and ten. One of their bodies was recovered by the sheriffs."

Chaucer was suitably horrified and Crispin felt a modicum of satisfaction. His arms tightened across his chest.

"How do you know—but you must be certain. I believe you. All the more reason to surrender the Spear, Cris."

"I might be tempted if only I had it, Geoffrey. I do not. I am still searching for it."

He shot up from the cot. "But you can't be! You must know where it is by now!"

"I am no miracle worker. Chances are it is far from here, perhaps even heading back to where it belongs. Wherever that is."

"But this is ghastly! I thought—" He sat again, his head in his hands. "Ah Cris, I thought you had it. What are we to do now?"

It was tempting. Working *with* Chaucer would certainly be more rewarding than working against him, but a niggling doubt still poked at his senses. After all was said and done, he didn't think he could truly trust Geoffrey. Keeping silent was the best option, and he took it, watching his friend moan and roll his head. At last, Geoffrey finally looked up.

"What are you going to do now, Cris?"

"I'm going to ask you one more question."

He straightened. "Oh? What more could you possibly need to know?"

"Why you were discussing these matters—or any matters at all—with a Spaniard?"

With his hands gripping his knees, Geoffrey huffed a humorless laugh. "Very well. You've earned it. Come with me."

His doubt must have been written on his face, for Chaucer

laughed at Crispin's expression. "I swear on my life. I am not trying to trick you."

"Then lead on." He gestured toward the curtain, which he pulled aside.

The men of the tavern turned to look at them and Crispin felt their resentful glares as he made his way between the rearranged tables. The floor was still wet from spilled wine and ale and there were a few shards still kicked by wayward feet across the floor. He made it to the door, and noticed Chaucer hanging back and paying the tavern keeper for the destruction. He felt a bit guilty until he surmised that Geoffrey could well afford it.

They walked up the avenue and soon left the bridge, where they turned at Thames Street and followed it to Queenhithe. The Swan Inn had a newly painted sign and they passed under it through the door. Crispin followed Geoffrey as they climbed the stairs to the end of the gallery. Chaucer stopped at the door there and knocked with a series of particular taps. They waited. A scratching at the door and a bolt was thrown.

They entered into darkness. The faint glow from the hearth did little to illuminate the shadows but a spark grabbed Crispin's attention. The spark ignited a bit of moss in a man's hand until he lit the candle with the small flame and then tamped out the clump of moss on the candle's dish.

He picked up the candle and held it in his hand close to his face. The bearded man looked familiar.

"*Buenos días, Señor Guest.*"

"God's blood! You are Juan Gutierrez. You're—"

He bowed. "Ah, you remembered that I am my Lord of Gaunt's Castilian secretary."

20

"WHY ARE YOU HERE in England, Bishop Gutierrez? Should you not be at Lancaster's side?"

The man strode to another candle and lit it with the one in his hand. Two other men moved out of the shadows and bowed warily to Crispin.

Gutierrez set both candles on the table and sat, offering places for both Chaucer and Crispin. "There is much to be done, Señor Guest. My Lord of Gaunt—that is, his grace the *King of Spain*—is poised for opposition. As his secretary, it is my duty to protect his interests."

"And so you call him 'king'?"

"Did not your own sovereign declare him so? Did he not crown the duke and his wife, the Lady Costanza, Easter last?"

"So I heard. He sailed to Spain with his family to claim his throne and to find husbands for his daughters. So why are *you* here?"

"As I said. To protect his interests."

The other men stepped into the small circle of light cast by the candles. "May I introduce Don Lope Pérez and Don Gonzaluo de Castilla?"

"You rescued me in the alley."

They bowed. "It was necessary," said Don Lope. "It was I who spoke. Bishop Gutierrez said you would recognize his voice."

"But why come to light now?"

He looked back at Gutierrez, who shrugged. "We should have hired you in the first place," said the bishop, looking sternly at Chaucer.

Geoffrey smiled. "We all could have saved ourselves a great deal of trouble."

"Except for the murders," said Crispin. "They spoiled your plans."

"Indeed."

"It was those men, you realize. They killed the armorer and his apprentices. And they are working for the earl of Suffolk."

"*Madre santa*," said the bishop, becrossing himself. "Are they any closer to finding the Spear?"

Crispin ran his hand over his beard-roughened chin. "I don't know. I don't have any idea where it is or who might have it."

"We must join forces," said Don Lope.

Everyone was nodding, including Chaucer, but Crispin still had misgivings. "Gentlemen." He rose. "I appreciate your sense of urgency. But I am accustomed to working alone."

Chaucer edged closer. "You don't trust us."

He locked gazes with Geoffrey. There was hurt in his eyes but a hard edge, too. It soon smoothed to resignation. Finally, Chaucer looked away and masked his discomfort by toying with the poker. He jammed it into the fireplace, stirring the logs to a flame. "Master Crispin has little cause to trust me or you, Excellency."

Gutierrez nodded. "I suspected as much. His grace the duke— the king—said the same to me. He said that even if he had given his word, it would mean little to Master Guest at this juncture. He also said he hoped that someday—someday soon—that Master

Guest's opinion would change." He moved around the table and stood beside Crispin, studying him. "The two of you were close at one time. I wonder what has caused this rift between you?"

"My Lord of Gaunt is aware of the reasons and that is enough," said Crispin. At least Lancaster didn't expect him to jump to the orders of these Spaniards, no matter how seemingly close they appeared to do the duke's bidding. *The king's,* he reminded himself ruefully. He smiled to himself. Well, he was a king at last, though not of England as Crispin would have had it; as Crispin had tried to achieve, much to his chagrin now. After all, if he had not attempted that very thing nine years ago, his life, his status would not have been forfeit. He would still be a knight and in the personal retinue of Gaunt, wearing his colors and standing beside him while he sat on the throne of Spain.

Crispin turned toward the door. "My search continues," he said over his shoulder.

"Will you keep us apprised, Master Crispin?" asked Gutierrez.

His hand paused over the latch. "I . . . cannot guarantee that, my lords."

"But Master Crispin." Gutierrez rushed to the door, pressing a hand against it, preventing him from leaving. "We have told you of our need. It is for the duke of Lancaster, I assure you."

Crispin surveyed the Bishop of Dax, Lancaster's longtime companion and secretary. The man was at his side when he traveled through Spain and sometimes to other places. "I have known you for years, sir." He admired the man, for though he was a bishop, he was not afraid to pick up a sword, as he had done in the alley to protect Crispin. "But it is plain by your words that you do not know *me.*" He pulled at the door experimentally and Gutierrez slowly released the pressure, dropping his hand away. "The duke and I have a long history," said Crispin. "And I seem to have a history of sorts with relics. Some would say I owe my loyalty to the duke. And some would say I owe my loyalty to God and to what belongs to Him. But in the nine years since my exile, I have learned to serve another master, that of myself and my intellect. If my intellect tells me to surrender the Spear to the duke, then I shall. But if it tells me to discard it down the deepest hole . . . well, gentlemen, then that is what I will do. Good day."

He pulled open the door. Chaucer and Gutierrez rushed after him. "Crispin!" cried Chaucer. "You cannot mean what you say."

"Geoffrey, I always mean what I say."

Gutierrez blocked his path. Crispin stiffened. He did not like to use force on an old friend, and a bishop at that, but he would if necessary. "The relics of God, of His Son, should be in the hands of His clerics who know how to safeguard them and to put them to their proper use," said the bishop. "Have a care, Crispin, in these grave decisions, or you may find yourself in opposition to the might of the Church."

"It won't be the first time, Excellency." He waited. Gutierrez seemed to be deciding, and it was a long time until he slowly moved, stepping out of his way. Crispin didn't look back as he walked stiffly across the gallery, down the stairs, and through the inn to the door.

HE STOOD IN THE street, debating with himself. In truth, he felt a bit lost. Was it a Spanish plot? Or was it what Chaucer would have him believe it was? A scheme to get the Spear's power into the hands of Lancaster? For as much as he had seen, he still did not know if he believed in the power of relics. There were many explanations to cover their seeming miracles. So he told himself. But if it did have great power, then why did he hesitate to surrender it to the duke? He was more than his liege lord. He was far closer than that. At least, at one time this was so.

"God's blood!" he hissed into the bleak sunlight. He started walking, little caring in what direction.

If it were a true relic with power, then he would see it safe away, out of the greedy hands of men. For who was to say that it would stay in the hands of the duke? Others could take it and use it for their own purposes. What if it fell into the hands of the French? No, if he found it—*when* he found it—he couldn't allow it into the hands of just any man.

His mind whirred with all the players laid across his path: There was Thomas Saunfayl, now in custody. Damn, he should have asked Chaucer where that was. But, listening with a tilt to his head, he knew all he had to do was wait, and Chaucer would present himself.

After all, if he didn't know better, he would say those were *his* steps following him on the empty street.

He turned toward a shadowed wall and leaned against it, pulling his cloak about him to stave off the cold sweeping up through the lane. A mist had rolled in, obscuring even the nearest houses.

The soft footfalls slowed to a stop and Crispin smiled a feral grin. "Join me, Geoffrey?"

A pause.

Then out of the mist, "How did you know it was me, damn you?"

A figure stepped out of the gloom and approached and soon joined him against the wall. "You have become a very cautious man."

"Would that I had done the same nine years ago, eh?"

"Yes."

They stood silently, neither looking at the other.

"It occurred to me, Geoffrey, that I do not know where Sir Thomas is being held and I should speak to him before his trial."

"He is in Newgate. The trial is tomorrow."

"That's very . . . soon."

"The king is anxious for a distraction. He wants the joust to commence quickly. Some of the knights left behind by Lancaster's expedition would enjoy the entertainment. They have become restless while awaiting a thwarted French invasion."

"The invasion that never was."

"Indeed. I admit it's been a while since I've seen a joust, though I doubt I shall enjoy this one overmuch. Thomas has been loyal to Lancaster. If he prevails the duke will take him back . . . though he will send him far away back to his estates."

"And if he dies on the lists?"

"Well, that is the way of it, Crispin. No general can countenance a coward."

Kicking at the mud, Crispin nodded. "I know." He gazed at his boot a while longer before lifting his face. "Geoffrey, do you ever get the feeling that events, people, are always in flux? That we are not the masters of our universe as we thought?"

He chuckled. "Oh yes. We are only allowed to play in the garden but for a little while . . . until the storm drives us away. Changes, yes. We grow older, that is a certainty. Politics sweep over the continent with each whimsical breeze and we are caught up in it like autumn leaves. We grasp it for but a moment and then . . . it is loose again, whipping in another direction. We think we are the puppet masters but it is an illusion. We are helpless after all. And I tell you, Cris, with all that I have done and in all my travels and dangerous dealings, with all my confidence either deserved or undeserved, never have I felt so helpless and in need of God's good grace than when my children were born. As simple as that. The master of my house and a man of duty and purpose, but powerless in the lying in."

"So I have heard similar tales from others."

He looked at Crispin steadily. "None of your own?"

He shook his head. "And Lancaster's children are all grown. I sometimes felt like . . . well. An uncle, perhaps. I stumbled upon Henry, Lord Derby, just the other day."

"No! Well, he's quite the man now."

"Yes, he is. I do regret missing his childhood." He was being a fool, he knew it. Wallowing in his morose past? He could use a wine bowl about now.

"But it is God who guides our lives," said Chaucer. "And so it is a vain and foolish thing to imagine we have reign over our destinies. When we sin we ignore His good council. When we thrive it is because we are living holy lives."

Crispin laughed. "Geoffrey. You? A holy life?"

"I resent the implication, Cris. I am a model husband. I am a good citizen and a loyal servant of Lancaster and the Church."

"And a member of Parliament, don't forget that on the accounts, Geoffrey."

Chaucer huffed. "You are making light of me."

Crispin smiled. Geoffrey always was easy to insult. "Not so light. You have done well. You must know something of Heaven that I don't."

"I fear God, Cris. For the life of me, I do not think that you do. You are forever Jacob wrestling with angels."

The smile faded. "Perhaps."

"Why not give Lancaster the Spear?"

"Aren't you putting the cart before the horse? I haven't got it yet."

"But I know you will get it. Since last year I have been following your exploits, looking into your history."

"Oh?" A warm glow settled in his chest. "Are there histories of me?"

"Once your name was whispered in secret corners. People are most anxious to talk of you now in voices that have the sound of admiration. If I were King Richard I'd be worried."

"He has nothing to fear from me. I am entirely repentant and reformed, a devoted champion for the crown."

"So I also hear."

Now his friend's warm scrutiny began to irritate. He pushed away from the wall and started walking. Geoffrey trotted to catch up.

"I will not surrender the Spear to Lancaster. I will give it to the Church where it belongs. *If* I find it."

"You will." Geoffrey halted, letting Crispin walk ahead. "Think, Cris," he called, "what Gaunt could do with it."

"I *am* thinking of it, Geoffrey," he said over his shoulder.

CRISPIN DECIDED TO GO to Newgate that day. It was possible the serjeant would not let him in, but it was also possible he would. And without the interference of the sheriffs. That would be a boon.

Crispin approached the stark exterior of Newgate's damp stone walls. A cresset burned in the archway and he entered under it, rousing the sleepy guard, who blinked at Crispin in surprise. "Master Crispin? What would you be doing here?"

"I have come to visit a prisoner."

"Have you permission of the sheriffs, sir?"

"I am certain the sheriffs would not object. As you know, they are curious about my exploits. They would not want to interfere in them."

The man scratched his head through his leather cap. "We-e-ell, seeing that you have been here before and that it is well known these sheriffs favor you, I suppose I can allow you through. But don't make no mischief, Master Crispin."

"Me? Mischief?"

The guard scowled as he reached for the keys to unlock the gates. He pulled them open with a rusty whine. "Er . . . which prisoner, sir?"

"Sir Thomas Saunfayl. Where are they keeping him?"

The guard gasped. "Curse me, I should have asked you that first. No one is allowed to see that particular prisoner, Master." He gestured for Crispin to go back through the gate, but Crispin had already put a foot on the first step of the stairwell leading up into the tower.

"Oh, don't worry. I'll see that all is accounted for."

"No, Master Crispin, you must come back down, sir. I am not allowed to let you up." His hand twitched near his sword.

Halfway around the curved corner, Crispin peered back at the now perspiring guard. "All is well, good sir. I won't tell anyone you let me up." Crispin didn't wait, but quickly made his way through the shadowed stairwell, the swearing rant of the guard below disappearing into echoes.

Sir Thomas was likely housed in the better cells, more like chambers with a hearth and a cot with a straw mattress. He headed down the gallery toward the nearest cell and peered through the barred window in the door. "Sir Thomas!" he rasped.

A stirring. Someone shuffled toward the door and Crispin could see his face. A faint glow from the hearth behind him lit a forlorn countenance. "Crispin."

"Thomas. Geoffrey told me he had found you."

He nodded listlessly. The knight looked haggard and drawn.

"The trial is on the morrow."

"It is not so much a trial as a hearing. The joust is to be tomorrow afternoon as well. That is my true trial."

"Well, better to get it over with, eh?"

"Yes. Over with." He sighed. "Crispin, I am weary of this world. I shall be glad of my fate."

"Thomas! Don't talk like that. You are a fine warrior and a valiant knight. You will prevail. Pray on it."

"My praying is done. Without the Spear, all is lost."

Crispin gripped the grille and drew himself right to the window. "Dammit, Thomas! You mustn't speak like that. Do not give in to melancholy. You should have seen a barber. You should at least have been bled to restore your humors." The man was exasperating! He had surrendered before the fight was ever fought. No wonder he found himself in peril.

He pushed it aside. There was other business that needed attending to. "Thomas, you must tell me about this relic. How did you hear of it?"

His eyes rose toward Crispin at last and a rueful twitch of lips was the only expression he wore. "Rumor. I was lucky."

"This is no time to lie. I saw the letter you wrote to Roger Grey."

Thomas frowned. "And so. You have discovered all my secrets. Why ask me, then, except to trap me in a lie, another sin?"

"I am not trapping you. I merely need to know. Did you intercept this relic that was meant for the duke?"

"Yes!" he cried suddenly. "I had the greater need. He had already conquered his foes. Many times! What need did he have? I heard Chaucer talking with that Spanish bishop who cleaves to Lancaster's side. I got the name of the man who was retrieving the Spear. My runners were faster. I sent gold, more than what Chaucer was going to send. I got there first! It was mine!" His eyes, wide and wild, searched Crispin's. "Grey was cheating me, is that it? There was no Spear?"

Shaking his head, Crispin released the grille, its cold still permeating his hands. "I am uncertain of that. Chaucer and others seemed to believe Grey had the Spear. If he hid it, then it is hidden well. Who else might have stolen it, Thomas? I know Geoffrey was after it. And Juan Gutierrez."

"He is here?"

"Yes, and with two Spanish knights. Also . . . the earl of Suffolk. He, too, sent men for it. They killed Grey but they were unable to find the Spear. Who else, Thomas? There must be someone else."

He shook his head and finally rested it against the iron grille. "I don't know. Don't you see? There could be any number of people who could have known."

Crispin did see. So many were now implicated. Lucas Stotley, for one. And Lenny for another. Lucas hired Lenny to steal the rent money but he could have told him about the Spear. And maybe even the landlord, for he might also be involved. And then there was Anabel, the one who kept the most secrets. He was certain now that she knew more than she had let on. It was entirely possible she had known of the Spear all along and might even have already sold it to the highest bidder. This certainly warranted more scrutiny.

"You are right, of course," he said vaguely to the knight.

"Crispin," he said quietly. "Will you be there? At the joust?"

"Of course. And I shall be cheering the loudest when you win and prove yourself."

He smiled. "You are a good friend. I have been a poor one to you. I abandoned you with all the others because that is what we were told to do."

"Thomas—"

"But you have never abandoned me, even in my blackest hour. Knowing full well that I am a coward and deserter. You made an oath to me and you have kept it. I release you, then. You owe me nothing more. Nothing more than what you wish to give. It's a shameful thing, what happened to you, Crispin."

"And you tried to talk me out of it, risking your own neck. I owe you more than I can give, Thomas. I was guilty of treason. I should not now be standing before you."

"Your crime was in being faithful to Lancaster, your liege lord. A ten-year-old boy was not fit to be king. Perhaps we all should have looked at that with more care."

"Richard is the rightful heir. Lancaster has been his steward. The kingdom has not crumbled while he reigns. I was mistaken."

"Perhaps. But storm clouds are coming, Crispin. Next year when the king comes into his full majority, what will happen then? With men like Suffolk and Oxford at his side, what will happen then?"

"We will see, Thomas. I will not worry over it now. I worry over you. I will be on hand tomorrow afternoon on the bridge and you will win."

Thomas chuckled low in his chest. He shuffled away from the door and sat on the scraped and chipped chair in front of his meager fire. "We shall see. We shall see."

THE DAY DAWNED COLD but clear. Excitement was in the air, even on the Shambles. Jousts had been rare of late and this one on London Bridge was positioned to be a memorable one. It was rumored that King Richard would be there. Ordinarily, that would have made Crispin think twice about going, but he had promised Sir Thomas, and there was no way around it.

Jack was buzzing with enthusiasm. His brief bout with weapons practice had not sated his appetite for action, only whetted it. Yet even through Jack's excitement, he had the aplomb to try to curb it. After all, he knew that they were going to see Crispin's old friend destroy himself. For Crispin sensed that Thomas had already surrendered.

They were on their way to an execution.

But there was time before it all began. They were early yet, even though most of London was heading in the direction of the bridge. There was time to go to the Unicorn Inn and confront Anabel.

Jack was silent at his side, wearing his new blue coat from Robert Coterel's talented hands. There was much to say but Crispin wanted to speak of it to Anabel, to push her against the wall, not in a passionate embrace, but to strangle the truth out of her.

And the more he brooded on it the more he convinced himself that she had more to do with the disappearance of the Spear than she had let on. She certainly knew Lucas Stotley, and if her loquacious neighbor could be believed, knew him very well. Even her father had corroborated that relationship, though little he understood of it. She was worse than a whore, then, for not only did she receive money for the favors she doled out, but she schemed ever greater. And schemed with Lucas Stotley. He didn't know how and to what extent, but he was damned well going to find out.

They reached the street where the inn lay between a two-story house and an open field with a view of a wharf stretching its wooden piers into the Thames. Muscles tensing, Crispin entered and climbed the stairs as Jack directed. They reached the door, where Crispin knocked. He waited, wondering if he should send Master Coterel on some errand. It seemed the merciful thing to spare him the ugly truth about his daughter.

There was no reply, no shuffling of feet, no movement of furniture. He knocked again and again heard nothing. He grabbed the latch and when it yielded, he pushed open the door.

The room was empty but for the furniture, a cold hearth, and Lucas Stotley lying on the floor in a pool of his own blood.

21

CRISPIN KNELT AND TOUCHED the man's face. He gurgled and fluttered his lids. In his chest was thrust a pair of scissors, a pair that looked like the same type the tailor had used for his trade.

"Jack, go get help!"

The boy scrambled away, and Crispin gently lifted the man, leaning the tailor's back against Crispin's thighs. "Master Lucas. Who did this?"

"She was angry with me," he gasped. "She complied with all of it . . . until the murders. She was . . . frightened."

"Anabel?"

He nodded, licking his bloodstained lips. "We had nothing to do with murders."

"I know. I know the culprits."

The clerk nodded again. "Jesus mercy," he whispered. "She was my lover. She pretended they were betrothed but they were not—"

"I know that, too."

"Oh? I see." His voice thinned to a rasp. "She knew of the bargain I had made with Sir Geoffrey. She told me where the money was. They . . . they . . ."

"Would be evicted," said Crispin. Stotley nodded, struggling to speak. "You would have given them shelter, to keep her close to you," Crispin went on. "Then Geoffrey's men could do their will and break into the armorer's."

"Not to kill," he gasped.

"It was not Geoffrey."

He nodded. "Good. He seems . . . like such a merry fellow. Despite it all, I loved her. I knew about her and Grey. And the others. But I loved her."

"What of the relic? Did you know of that?"

He gulped, nodded. "Later."

"Where is it?"

He gulped again, tried to speak, coughed a spurt of blood. He saw it splatter upon his chest and weakly reached for the scissors. Crispin pushed his hand away. It was a cork to keep him alive, plugging the hole punched in his heart. Once pulled he would be done.

"Do you know where the relic is?"

Stotley's gaze rolled about the room. "Anabel?"

"She is not here. No one is here. They have fled."

"With all the money?" Suddenly he seemed more concerned with that than his life.

"The relic. Did she have it? Did she sell it? Come, man!"

He raised his eyes to Crispin's and opened his mouth, but the red-rimmed lips worked silently. His eyes widened as he expelled a long breath and then his heaving chest moved no more. The light in his eyes dulled and he looked not at Crispin but into the middle distance.

Jack came running with the innkeeper and several other men. They crowded the doorway. "I'm a barber," said one, trying to push his way through from the back of the crowd.

"It matters little," said Crispin, laying him back down. "He's dead."

Crosses were gestured over faces as some of the braver men entered. "Jack," said Crispin. "Best go for the sheriffs."

CRISPIN STOOD NEAR THE back of the room, watching in brooding silence as the sheriffs tutted and made pronouncements and gestured to their clerks and serjeants to do this or that. The body was removed at last and servants waited in the doorway with buckets and rags to begin their grim work. Another life was snuffed out, and once the blood was cleaned from the floor, he would be forgotten.

But not by Crispin. Inside he seethed. Anabel was no longer the beauteous maid, the unfortunate of circumstances. No. She was a conniving, clever wench who would not allow anyone to stand in her way, even if that meant murder. He would bring her down. He would find her. He promised himself this, even as the servants knelt before the pool of congealing blood and swabbed the floor until their buckets ran red.

Someone poked him and when he turned he looked into Jack's concerned eyes. "Come, Master. We've done all we can. The sheriffs are done with you. We have to get to the joust."

"I must go after her."

"I've already questioned everyone at the inn, sir. No one knew where they were off to. You will find her, Master Crispin. Just not today. Today you must go to the joust as you promised Sir Thomas."

Crispin swallowed the vitriol he wanted to express, and followed Jack silently out the door.

It was after Sext by the time they reached the bridge. A rumble of voices threaded over the long lines of people waiting to get through the gatehouse, of sellers of ale and meats calling their wares. Men and ladies on horseback pushed their way through and Jack danced on his toes, looking above the heads of the crowd in front of them, trying to see when they would reach the entrance.

"We should have been here earlier," he grumbled. "We might never get in."

"Yes, so inconvenient of Master Lucas dying like that."

"That's not what I meant, Master Crispin. Bless me but you are in a fine state."

"I've been duped," he growled. "And I have no liking for it."

"Aye, I know it."

"You were correct about your assessment of her. You have every right to mock me."

"I'm not mocking you, sir. Far from it. But aren't you always telling me, Master, to learn from my mistakes? I suggest you do the same and put aside your ire for a time to attend to the business at hand. That of this joust. If we can ever get through the sarding gate!"

The crowd surged forward. It was only another half an hour before they got through, but it was evident to Crispin that they would get nowhere near the viewing stands. People were hanging out of windows along the avenue and some were even sitting on the roofs.

The pavilion tents of the contestants stood on either end of the lists with makeshift corrals for their horses. By the colors of the closest tent, Crispin surmised it belonged to Sir Thomas. He shoved his way forward, tempted to assist with his dagger. He managed to bully his way through and when he reached the tents, he surveyed the area. Young men who looked like squires and pages were milling by the horses, and lances were propped against a stand.

"Master," said Jack, tugging on Crispin's sleeve. "What is going to happen?"

"This is a Wager of Battle, a sort of trial by combat. Ordinarily, the combatants would be the plaintiff and the defendant. They would fight on foot with simple weapons, bare legs, bare arms, and simple sandals on their feet. In this case, because it is a situation of cowardice and desertion, I suppose the Earl Marshal's court chose a joust to prove once and for all Sir Thomas's fitness to serve."

"Who will he joust, then?"

"I don't know. I would have thought it would be one of Lancaster's men since he offended the duke, but it seems more likely that it will be another champion. I'll wager the king chose the competitor. And he will be very good."

"Sir, do you think Sir Thomas will prevail?"

Crispin's glance swept out past the stands to the fluttering pennons whipping in the wind, the striped lances, the horses being paraded in their caparisons, and gave a sigh. The bridge now sported a dirt field with a fence running down the center directly before the viewing stands. The jousters would each stay on their side of the barrier. It was empty now except for a few pages with brooms, clearing it of any debris. The viewing stands in the center were covered and formed a private box. That would be for the king and his retinue when they arrived right before the joust was to begin.

Crispin's heart beat with a conflicted tempo. To see the lists again, the tilting yard, brought back good memories of his own competitions. He missed his old destrier, a dapple gray stallion named Hippocrates. A strong horse with a good heart, who could turn on the spot with just the slightest pressure from Crispin's knee. He often wondered what had happened to that horse. Probably served some other master. The grim thought that he might be dead weighed on his soul.

"Will . . . will he fight to the death, Master?"

Crispin set his jaw. "This is the *Joust á l'Outrance*—the joust to the bitter end. It is finished when one surrenders, becomes wounded, or is killed. The only prize here, Jack, is Life. If Sir Thomas surrenders or is wounded, he will hang on the spot."

"Blind me," he whispered, crossing himself.

"It is a just measure. It is an opportunity to publicly prove himself. There is no other way."

"Master Crispin!" hissed Jack in his ear. "Look, sir. I think that page is beckoning to you."

A young boy in Thomas's colors stood by his tent and was indeed motioning to Crispin. Crispin pushed his way forward again and finally reached the boy.

"You are Crispin Guest?"

"Yes. What is it, boy?"

He shook his head sadly. "Sir Thomas won't let any of his pages or squires attend him. He threatens us and throws things when we try to enter. He won't let his squire arm him. I have heard him talk of you. Can you do something, sir?"

The man had gone mad, there was no other explanation. Crispin said nothing as the page led him to the tent opening. "Have a care, sir, when going in. He throws weapons as well."

Crispin exchanged glances with an anxious Jack before pulling the flap aside and ducking in.

"Get out! I told you to leave me!"

Thomas sat in a folding chair, his legs sprawled and covered with greaves. They were the only armor he wore. He was dressed in his shirtsleeves and hadn't even donned his padded aketon. He sagged over his sword hilt, the point digging into the carpets layered on the tent's floor. The fine breastplate made by Roger Grey lay on a table alongside his pig-faced bascinet and the rest of his armor. On the floor beside the arms table lay broken pottery, a jug, a cup, in a pool of red wine. It reminded Crispin of Lucas Stotley's final breaths.

"It is me; Crispin."

Thomas lifted his head. His eyes were rimmed with red and tear tracks were plain on his face. "Oh. So you've come."

"As I said I would."

Thomas made no move to rise. If anything, he seemed to slump further. He smelled of wine but he did not appear to be drunk. "Well, at least a friend will be on hand to bid me farewell."

"Thomas, get hold of yourself. Be a man, dammit!"

He laughed but his eyes held no humor. "Be a man? But not all of us can be a Crispin Guest. How many died in that treasonous plot, Crispin? How many brave knights plotted to put Lancaster on the throne? How many screamed as they were tortured and betrayed one another, giving name after name? Do you know I heard that you would not? No matter how they harried you, no matter how long the torture went on, you would not name any other even to save your own skin. That is the kind of man we all aspire to be. But it is not the kind of man we are all capable of being."

"It is merely a joust, Thomas. You have won many jousts and under worse conditions. Prove yourself! Defend your honor. Come back into the ranks of Lancaster's army."

"But you see, dear Crispin. That is the one thing I do not wish to do."

He rose then, leaning heavily on his sword. He picked it up, examined its fine blade, the gleam of it in the brazier's light. "I do not wish to rejoin his or any other army. I am done with that." He spoke to his sword, unwilling or unable to face Crispin. "My bosom is too weak, too frail now to cosset courage." He lowered the blade to his chair and slid the sword with the hilt side down so that the cross guard braced against the chair leg. "I wish I were you, Crispin. Yes, even after all you have suffered. I wish at least that I had your verve, your audacity. Young squire," he said, addressing Jack, "you should be proud to serve your master. He may no longer be called a knight, but it runs through his veins, it beats in his heart. Such a man must be emulated."

Crispin watched Thomas fiddle with his sword in its unusual position. What the devil was the man doing?

All at once, Thomas spun on his heel and faced the chair, placing the sword point at his gut.

It finally registered in Crispin's mind what the man intended. Time itself slowed. Crispin launched himself across the room. It seemed to take a damnably long time. He slammed into the knight at last and closed him into a tight embrace, knocking him to the floor. They rolled a few feet and Crispin landed atop him. Shocked to his core, he stared down at the man, who was weeping and struggling to cast Crispin off.

"Why did you stop me? I am good for nothing but the worms!"

Thomas struggled, but Crispin held him tight. "Thomas," he rasped in his ear. "For God's sake, man! You would take your own life?"

"Better that than the dishonor to my family when I am cut down on the lists."

"But . . . a suicide? Thomas, your soul . . ."

"What do I care of that? God will not want a coward in Heaven. He will not want me amongst his angels. Let me go, Crispin. Let me die as I will."

"No, damn you!" He pushed hard against Thomas's shoulders and ground them into the carpets. He sat up and glared. "Fight for yourself! For your mortal soul, if for nothing else."

Thomas stopped struggling and lay back. "No, not even for that. I can't go out there. I can barely stand to even look at my armor. Whatever bewitchment has enchanted me, it is as strong now as on any battlefield. Don't you see, Crispin? I am doomed."

For a long moment, Crispin stared into the eyes of his friend, willing him the courage to go on. But it was beyond his capacity. He got to his feet and offered a hand down to Thomas. He took it and reluctantly gained his own feet. He strode with leaden steps to the table holding his armor and picked up the helm, fingering the sharp, pointed nose of the visor. "I used to enjoy the tilt. You saw me. I loved it."

"I remember," said Crispin softly.

"But now . . ." He cradled the helm for a long time, until his shoulders stiffened and he whipped around to stare at Crispin. "Crispin! *You* could do it. You could joust."

He snorted. "But I am no longer a knight," he said bitterly.

Thomas reached and covered Crispin's shoulder with his hand, closing his fingers on the bone with a tightening grip. "You could joust for me, in my stead." He gestured with the polished helm in his hand. "Wear my armor and none would be the wiser!"

It was slowly dawning on him that Thomas was serious. Crispin took a step back, but Thomas's grip was strong. Crispin blinked his confusion. "You can't mean it, Thomas. I can tick off the list of ways I am not fit to be a competitor."

"But you are! You are without fear."

"I beg to disagree."

Thomas's gaze measured Crispin from head to toe. "You are hale and fit. A worthy man to take my place."

"Thomas, I am not a knight! I haven't the right to go out there. And all that aside, I haven't been in a joust in over *ten* years. Don't be a fool."

"But it could work. Crispin, as soon as I strode out there I would fall from my horse in mortal fear. But *you* could do it. No one would ever know. It would save my honor and my life. Crispin, you do want to save my miserable life, don't you?"

His blood was pumping so loudly in his ears that he could barely hear. "Thomas," he said weakly. "This is mad. Someone will discover it. And then both our lives will be forfeit."

"No, no they won't." He looked to Jack. "Your boy here will help me arm you. He'll say nothing. I trust him. I trust you."

Crispin shook his head vigorously. "Thomas, I am woefully out of practice. How can you expect me to prevail over the king's champion, the finest jouster there is? It is madness."

"But there is no choice." He released Crispin and stepped aside, the helm dangling from his hand. "There is no choice. Either I fall upon my sword as is my due, or you help me."

Crispin looked to Jack, whose face was now white as linen. To Thomas, who, even despite everything that had transpired in the last few minutes, looked as calm as he ever had. He was convinced that Crispin would not only don his armor for him but would win against the king's finest jouster.

"God's blood," he whispered. "Don't do this, Thomas. Don't ask this of me."

"But I *am* asking. Selfish as I am. You swore to me, Crispin. You told me only yesterday that you would always owe me for risking all for you nine years ago."

"But this is a cheat. It is dishonor! To you, to me, to the joust itself."

"It is my life, such as it is. Would you deny me? I will not forget this boon, Crispin. For my life and my honor, I beg of you."

"I won't do it, Thomas. I haven't the right and you haven't the right to ask me."

Thomas said nothing. He merely fastened his reddened eyes upon Crispin, his desperation flowing off of him in waves. It didn't matter. There were simply some things that Crispin could not consent to. This was to be a battle that decided Thomas's fitness to continue as a knight. If Crispin were to take his place, that would pull down great dishonor on the Saunfayl house, for what would it prove but that its master *was* a coward, unable to even stand up for his own name.

And yet. He had made Crispin swear an oath to help him in any way he saw fit. To refuse that oath was to bring dishonor upon Crispin and on the memory of what he owed Thomas.

He felt the raw bite of his predicament as it slowly nibbled at his senses. It was dishonor if he agreed to such madness but it was dishonor if he turned his back.

Which was greater?

He glanced once more at Jack, whose young face was always open like a parchment scrawled with all of his feelings and thoughts upon its surface. But he was no help at all in this matter.

Crispin was a fox in a steel trap with the hunters closing in.

There was nothing but the sound of his own panting breaths and his heart hammering in his chest. Crispin took one deep breath and expelled it through his nose. Ah, his cold was gone at last. A clear head. Clear in time to be hewn off.

He made for the tent door, the only decision possible. He even put his hand upon the flap, and stopped. He had sworn an oath. And he had never—even when his own life and comfort had been at stake—never forsworn himself.

But God help him. As much as he tried to suppress the feeling, tried to deny it, he could not. Because for all of his protestations, all the rationalizing, he *wanted* to joust. He *wanted* to be a knight again at least one last time.

He turned. Thomas wore an anxious face, pocked with sweat. Slowly, reluctantly, Crispin reached for the helm in Thomas's hand and grasped it, pulling it loose from his yielding fingers. It was a mere quarter of a stone in weight and as finely fashioned as the breastplate and the fine steel mesh of the habergeon hanging from its padded dummy.

In a low roughened voice, he said, "Arm me."

22

WITH NUMBED FINGERS, CRISPIN unbuttoned his cotehardie, and when it lay open like the skin of a butchered animal, Thomas took it from him and slipped it over his own shoulders.

Jack stood at the tent door, guarding the entrance, alternating his attention between the doorway and Crispin.

Thomas said nothing more as he helped arm Crispin. There was little left to be said. Crispin knew he should be praying, but he felt weightless, as if this was happening to another, and he couldn't come up with even the simplest of prayers. Instead, he stood like a child being dressed by his nursemaid, arms out, as Thomas slipped him into the sleeves of the aketon, pulled it taut against his chest, and laced it up.

Next, he lifted the mail shirt from its stand. Crispin bent forward and let Thomas slip the habergeon over his head, arms through the sleeves. When he straightened, he felt the weight of it resting over his shoulders as it flowed down his body to his upper thighs.

Thomas then knelt and held a sabaton for Crispin to slide his boot-clad foot into. The fit was tight—after all, it was made to fit

Sir Thomas—but the straps and spurs held it in place. It would have to do. On one knee, Thomas unstrapped the greaves from his own shins and clapped them over Crispin's, pulling the leather straps tight. He rose for only a moment and that was to retrieve the cuisses from the arming table. He soon knelt again and affixed them to Crispin's thighs, pulling the leather buckles almost pain-fully taut. Crispin didn't complain. He accepted it as he accepted all of it.

The poleyns were next, fitting just over Crispin's exposed knee-caps.

As the armor rose up his body, so did the fear at what was about to happen. His mouth felt dry. How he wished he had spent the day in the Boar's Tusk rather than coming here. His mind raced with the things he had yet to achieve. There was bringing Osbert and his ilk to justice, for one. And Anabel. She had yet to be dealt with. And then there was the Spear. Its fate was still un-known. If it did confer the power the abbot claimed it did, it was a dangerous object.

The abbot. Nicholas, his friend, dying at his estates. He would have liked to spend some time with the old man, perhaps played a last game of chess. How Nicholas would wag a finger at him now if he saw what foolery Crispin had let himself get into.

Then there was Lancaster. He would have liked to have seen Lancaster one more time. His anger at the duke for deceiving him, for putting him in the state in which he now lived, had suddenly dispersed. The fear at his impending doom appeared to have chased it into the mist.

And finally there was Jack. His gaze found his apprentice, one eye glued to the slit of the tent flap. That clever boy. Crispin did not fear for Jack Tucker now. He had skills he could use. He would have to hone them but he could do it. He could succeed Crispin.

True, he could do with a few more years in his apprenticeship, for he would stumble and get into trouble, but he was sharp. He would survive.

Crispin jerked at the suddenness of the breastplate entombing him. The heaviness of it seemed to rob him of his breath. He could not help but gasp for air even as Thomas bound him within. He put his hand to it, feeling the smooth planes of steel, the delicate carvings that made up the arms of Saunfayl. It was beautiful armor. A shame he could not fully appreciate it.

The tassets were next, articulated plates hanging over his privities and backside. Then his arms, then the gauntlets, the padded arming cap for his head, and then the mail coif over that with its wide camail that flowed across his chest and over his shoulders. He felt light-headed. Was he being choked to death by the very armor that served to protect him?

Thomas approached him with the helm and Crispin—feeling stiff and unfamiliar in the constricting armor—could only watch as the knight lifted it like a coronation crown, and lowered it over him. Time seemed to stop. Ears already padded by layers of cloth, batting, and a mesh of steel were further chambered by the helm. His vision was now relegated to trim rectangular slits. His breathing was harsh and loud within the confines of the steel encasing him and smelled of oiled metal. Thomas pushed the visor up and Crispin breathed freely again, at least as freely as the weighty breastplate would allow. It seemed heavier than he was used to, but ten years separated the last time he had worn any kind of armor, so he knew his memory was frail at best.

Thomas strapped the belt with its decorated scabbard about Crispin's metal-clad waist. He walked over to the fallen sword and took it up. Thomas did not move, looking at it for a long moment. He had meant to take his life with it. Crispin wondered what was going through Thomas's mind as he returned to Crispin and essentially surrendered it to him. His eyes met Crispin's briefly before he rested the tip at the opening of the scabbard before shoving it in.

Crispin huffed a muffled sound deep in his chest. Was it a laugh? Was it relief? Here he stood, dressed as the knight he used to be, sword at his side. He closed his eyes, savoring the moment. Dammit, if he were to die today, then he'd much rather end his life like this, dressed as he was born to be.

Eyes still closed, he rolled his shoulders experimentally. The leather squeaked. His muscles rippled under the sussurating mail. The plates of armor clacked over the others. Yes. He remembered. He moved his arms, bending and extending them. He raised each leg in turn, felt the solid metal encasing him. He reached over to the scabbard—just where it was supposed to be—and closed his gauntleted hand over the sword hilt. With a hiss of steel, he pulled it free and swung it, satisfied with the expected whistle through the air.

He couldn't resist looking at Jack. There was still terror in his eyes, but there was now something more. His mouth parted in what looked like awe. He realized that Jack was seeing him for the first time as he should have been. Walking toward his apprentice, armor clanking, he smiled at the novelty of the armor moving with him. Sheathing the sword, he rested his hand on Jack's shoulder.

"Well, Jack. Here I am at last."

The corners of the boy's mouth curled up in a fond smile and in a whispered voice he said, "You don't look no different to me, Master Crispin."

Suddenly, all that Crispin wished to say gathered as a knot in his throat. He opened his mouth but could not speak. Instead, he nodded and slowly closed the visor with a solid click.

Thomas peeked out the tent flap. "They are coming." He grabbed Crispin's hood and thrust it over his own head, pulling it low as he moved into the shadows, dressed as Crispin had been.

The squire near the entrance stopped the men from approaching, but Thomas cried loud enough for them to hear, "I'm coming out!"

He nodded to Crispin and Crispin nodded once to him. He curled a gauntlet into a fist and lightly tapped Jack's chest with the steel knuckles before he took a deep breath, grabbed the tent flap, and stepped outside.

23

THERE WAS SOMETHING ABOUT being clad in armor again that washed away all his fear. He felt more alive than he had for a long time. Even though his face was covered and his eyesight limited by the visor, he seemed attuned to everything. To the clatter of the horses trotting nearby; the people moving in the stands; even the sound of the distant flapping pennons. Every color was deeper, every sound magnified. And then, as if waking from a deep sleep, his heart warmed with the simple truth that he would be able to do it. He would win. He *knew* it with certainty.

He laughed, looking around, and brusquely strode toward the stands where King Richard sat with his quiet wife, the lady Ann.

His squire, that is, *Thomas's* squire, met him and gave him a solemn look. "Shall we, my lord?"

Crispin nodded.

"God watch over you this day, Sir Thomas," said the squire as they walked forward.

He nodded again to the young man and strode stiffly toward the stands. A page walked ahead and carried a staff with a banner rippling above it. Crispin remembered all those distant days when he strode out to the lists just like this, with his banner above him. But instead of the red dragon he expected to see of his own arms, Thomas's were a bright green and white on the fine material.

It was a wonderfully clear day. Crispin caught the deep blue of the sky out of the eye slits, inhaled a bit of the scent of sweet fresh hay through the holes in the long pointed snout of his helm. It was a good day for a victory.

Out of the corner of his vision, Crispin noted another knight approaching. *Ah, the king's champion.* His armor was similar but at this angle, Crispin could not see the blazon his page carried. Crispin wondered if he knew the man. It was a shame to have to kill him.

Another man approached, coming from the direction of the stands. He was vested in a surcote and wore a wide-brimmed roundel hat with a lengthy liripipe trailing over his shoulder. Crispin assumed this was the *Chevalier d'honneur*, the judge of the bouts. He would insist that the jousters observe the rules and make a judgment about the victor should it be called into question. Crispin wasn't certain what would be allowed, but since this was a judiciary joust, he assumed that a tilt to the death might be expected. After all, if Sir Thomas had lost, he would be hanged immediately.

But of course, this was no longer Sir Thomas's neck on the line. It was Crispin's. Yet for the life of him, Crispin could not muster the idea of any other outcome but a victorious one.

When the *Chevalier d'honneur* turned, Crispin could plainly see that it was Geoffrey Chaucer. Damn.

King Richard looked down on both of them with quiet grace. He tilted forward slightly, waiting for Chaucer to make his announcements. In a loud, clear voice, Geoffrey declared, "Your grace—" He bowed to the king, "—my lords, we are gathered here on this spot for a solemn occasion. Sir Thomas Saunfayl has been called forth to face the charges of cowardice and desertion from my Lord of Gaunt, his grace the duke of Lancaster's service." He was interrupted by the jeering of the crowd. Crispin raised his helmeted chin and faced them. After all, if he was to play the part of Sir Thomas, he would do it justice. "He denies these charges," Chaucer cried louder, hushing the masses, "and has accepted the judgment of the Wager of Battle to settle the charge against him in this unusual spectacle. Because the charge is against a knight and challenges his knightly valor, the Earl Marshall's court has determined that this judicial conflict will be decided with a joust. They will tilt until one is wounded, killed, or one or both are unhorsed. If there is no clear winner, then combat will commence on foot. The opponent is the king's champion, Sir Osbert de Troyes."

Crispin snapped his head over, encumbered by the helm. Osbert! That whoreson! Yes, there were the colors on his banner. So, the king's champion, was he? Looking back toward the stands Crispin could just see Suffolk beside the king. No doubt the choice for Sir Osbert had been de la Pole's.

But Chaucer had continued and Crispin turned his ear again. ". . . justice done this day. If the defendant is overpowered and yields the lists, he will be conveyed to the gallows and hanged. Now. The both of you must swear you are free of any sorcery or witchcraft. You must swear that neither of you have eaten, drunk, nor have upon your person neither bone, stone, feather, nor any enchantment, sorcery, or witchcraft whereby the law of God may be abased, or the law of the Devil exalted. Do you so swear?"

Osbert, in a voice Crispin clearly recognized, cried out, "I swear by Almighty God."

Crispin, disguising his voice as something coarse and roughened, declared, "I, too, so swear."

Osbert angled his helm at Crispin and seemed to stare a long time before Chaucer motioned for them to take their places.

Crispin was marched toward the horse waiting beside a groom. The horse was a destrier, chestnut brown with a glossy coat under the colorful green and white caparison. His fetlocks were adorned in long feathers, elegant as the long train on a lady's gown.

The squire bent with his hands interlaced below the stirrup to give him a boost up. Crispin stepped into the lad's hands and launched himself onto the saddle while the squire helped him fit his armored feet into the stirrups. Each little gesture jarred a memory of long ago. As dangerous as this situation was, he could not stop himself from smiling.

He settled on the saddle and shifted so that his back rested against the raised support. The armor felt good. Surprisingly so. This wedge shape to the chest for jousting, for deflecting hits, was ideal. He wished he had had something similar in his day. And yet, here he was, in sparkling new armor. He did not feel doomed. Quite the contrary. He would unhorse Osbert. Then he would take him down for the murdering coward he was.

His musings had taken his attention away from the proceedings, for Crispin finally noticed the squire standing beside his horse with his shield and lance. Suddenly aware that the lad had been waiting patiently for some time, Crispin leaned over and took the shield first, pushing his left arm through the wide leather straps. Once it was secure, he leaned again and closed his right hand around the heavy oak lance shaft. The unfamiliar weight gave him pause. But he held it straight up, securing his hand in the conical vamplate and taking a moment to balance the weight of it on his stirruped foot. It was all coming back to him, bit by bit, as if he had never been away, as if an entire decade had not separated his time on the lists from this day.

Inside the secrecy of the helm, Crispin frowned. Funny. He should be full of anxiety. For indeed, he had *not* held a lance, nor ridden on the lists, nor fought in armor for far too long. Something was amiss. He scanned the crowds uncertainly, the cheering, the jeering. He should be terrified. Any sane man would be.

The squire led his horse to the end of the lists and they waited.

A herald stood near the barrier. He raised a staff with a banner bearing the king's arms to signal that the tilt was about to begin. Crispin pressed his legs tight to the horse's belly. He grasped the reins in his left hand under the shield and steadied the lance in his right. He held his breath. Chanting in his mind was the unavoidable litany, *Ten years since I'd ridden the lists.*

But it didn't seem to matter.

The banner dropped. He dug in the spurs. The heavy horse jolted forward. He slammed back into the saddle, and his gut wrenched from the sudden clattering of his armor. His breath came in rhythmic bursts, echoed back to him in the helm, clamoring along with the cadenced gait of the horse. He aimed the stallion to ride tight to the barrier and watched through the slits as Osbert bore down on him.

Time slowed again and Crispin lowered the lance by increments, keeping it tucked tight under his right arm and close to his body. He mentally prepared for the shock though he knew full well that the body could never prepare enough. It all came back in a rush of memories. *Raise your chin. Deflect a blow if it comes toward the head. Protect the eyes. A little higher. Yes. Now faster, boy, pick up speed. Don't lower the lance too quickly. Lower. Lower. Lower. Now!* The lance tip aimed toward Osbert's head. One good blow would do it. How delightful it would be to watch that head tear loose and go spinning into the stands.

It happened more quickly than he could have anticipated. Before Crispin could blink in surprise, Osbert's lance missed the shield and crashed into Crispin's chest. He was momentarily thrown back against the saddle's high back. But the wedge design of the breast-plate slid the lance tip away. Osbert dropped the twelve-foot spear on his way to the other end of the tilt.

Crispin swayed, the breath knocked out of him. Careless. He should have been watching Osbert's lance, not his. Well, it had been a long time.

He tossed the lance down and shook out his hand. He hadn't even scored a hit. Damned careless. He had barely pulled on the reins when the horse wheeled on its own. A well-trained beast, to be sure. He swiveled his head to assess Osbert. He was rolling his shoulders, but no worse for wear. Well, *that* was unacceptable.

Crispin put his hand down for the next lance and a squire handed it up to him. He repositioned the grip several times and felt it mold better to his arm. Yes, that was it. Felt better. The horse seemed excited, too, and toed the ground. Crispin gathered him-self and held his breath, waiting impatiently for the herald to take his place again with the banner.

He gave the signal and the horse shot forward. Crispin rolled evenly with the ambling gallop, waited and watched for the best moment to bring his lance down to his target. Waited for that mo-ment when time seemed to slow again, and this time, he focused on Osbert, only him. That shiny armored body tilting toward him. His own horse's mane whipped with the wind but that, too, seemed to slow, like seaweed rippling in the waves.

His fist tightened over the lance, tighter, tighter. Lower. Then like lightning, like a thunderclap, his lance slammed Osbert's shield.

For a moment the man lifted from the saddle, head snapping back with the impact. Crispin stared at him as he passed, turning his head to watch. But though Osbert teetered precariously, he leaned forward and managed to keep his seat. He slumped, obviously in pain.

Crispin was elated. He could do this. Now he had the sense of it again. Now he was in tempo. He slapped the saddle pommel with his fisted gauntlet and expelled an excited breath. But as he moved in the stirrups, pushing on them to reseat himself, he realized the jolt of the hit had done something to his armor. He could feel it. Something had shifted within the breastplate. But . . . how could that be? It was solid steel . . .

God's blood. The armor had been unusually heavy. Heavy because there were *two* sheets of metal, making a hollow space within. He rapped on it and heard it . . . and felt something shift again.

"Good Christ," he whispered. The Spear? It had to be. It had been there all along, embedded in the armor; the unique wedge shape had allowed it a secret reliquary.

Suddenly, the overwhelming sense that he could do no wrong came crashing in on him. The Spear! But no. Crispin did not believe in the power of relics. He did not!

And yet.

Donning armor had made him feel whole again. But it could not bestow the undeserved confidence he felt. The Spear rattled around in the breast, taunting him.

Was it true? Was the explanation from Abbot Nicholas possible? Would he be the victor only because of the power of the Spear?

Osbert had recovered and was turning his horse. His squire handed him a lance.

Crispin scanned the lists desperately. It was far too late. He could not escape. He had to see it through. For the first time, he allowed the sounds of the crowd to reach his hearing. There were equal parts cheering and heckling. The king moved restlessly on his throne. Had he recalled Crispin's questioning of his faithful chancellor? Had he remembered the name Sir Osbert? He certainly looked as if he did. Discomfort was painted on his face. His wife, the queen, laid a gentle hand on his arm. He clearly doted on her, for at the merest touch, she enjoyed his full attention.

Her golden gown shimmered in the October sun. Crispin caught more glints of gold and jewels among those in Richard's box and from the stands surrounding him, the nobility of London. Perhaps even the sheriffs were there, watching, little knowing it was their favorite pet on the lists, masquerading as a sorrowful knight.

It suddenly occurred to Crispin that he was going to have a devil of a time getting out of this, even if he did win.

Didn't think it through, did you? Oh, he had protested, but in the end he was dazzled by the armor, by the chance to be a knight once more. He heard himself chuckle in the visor. "Well, whatever the outcome, it shall be spectacular."

He turned his head and noticed the herald getting impatient. He thrust out his hand for the lance and the squire placed it there. "Lord," Crispin whispered into the helm, "if this is Your relic, the Spear that pierced Your side, then let its power wash over me. For I have been lost in my own pride. And though I am unworthy to receive Your blessing . . . I beg for it nonetheless."

He rode into position, the Spear rattling within the breastplate. He held the lance high. *At least I am a knight again, if only briefly,* he told himself. *Richard can't take this from me.*

Crispin let all his worries fall away. He closed his eyes and though he felt slightly foolish, he allowed himself to feel the presence of the Spear. He splayed his hand over the breastplate, trying to feel it through the cold metal. Would there be warmth? Would he sense its power?

He waited a few heartbeats. A few more before he opened his eyes. He couldn't stall forever. And he was feeling more foolish by the moment. Except that in the back of his mind was still the thrum of his utter certainty of victory. It reminded him all too keenly of the Crown of Thorns and how it had seemingly instilled in him a feeling of invincibility. He had performed many feats that day to escape the palace. He had dodged death more times than any mortal had a right to. But to this day he did not know if he could owe his life to the miracle of the thorns or to his own dumb luck.

So why believe now?

Fear is pain arising from the anticipation of evil. Were not relics to guard against evil?

He ignored the loud cries and derision from the crowd. In the end, it wasn't for him, but for Sir Thomas, his friend who could not muster the courage to even lift a lance in his own defense. A man who had tried to cast himself upon the sword that Crispin now wore at his side.

Crispin had experienced many things in his life. He had jousted for the love of it. He had gone to war at Lancaster's side for the same reason. But for once, he felt uncertain at the outcome.

"You've truly done it this time, Crispin." The words were as hollow as they sounded, echoing back to him within the metal helm.

A hand touching his leg startled him. He jerked back. Looking down, he saw the young squire. "Sir Thomas? Are you ready, my lord?"

Looking into the young man's eyes suddenly made Crispin angry. Why had Crispin allowed himself to be a party to this deception? Shouldn't he have allowed Thomas to take his own lumps? Or his life, if he was so willing to throw it away? Crispin wanted to warn this youth to waste no more time in the service of this unworthy knight. It was the least he could do, for the boy would learn it soon enough. But Crispin's promise to his old friend stopped him. He could not go back on his oath. He had sworn to help. If he opened his mouth, he and Thomas would both die.

He nodded to the squire and raised his head, surveying the tiltyard through the helm's eye slits. Osbert waited on the other end of the lists, his horse stamping the ground as impatiently as surely the knight was himself. Crispin checked the angle of the sun. They had only tilted twice. And the combat was to go on till sunset or until there was a victor, whichever came first. How were the two of them to proceed for six more hours?

Strange, again, that Crispin wasn't the least bit tired.

He urged his horse forward. The destrier was as anxious as his comrade across the yard and trotted forth, throwing his head and snorting. Crispin encouraged the stallion by patting his neck. "You're a good fellow, though I do not know your name. If you continue to carry me well, I promise to reward you."

There he went promising again.

The herald had been standing at the barrier, almost leaning against it, when he noticed Crispin getting into position. He snapped to attention and stood, holding his banner high. With a swish of the staff, the banner came down and he ran like the Devil was after him out of the way.

The destrier didn't even need Crispin's spurs. They lurched forward, man and horse moving as one. Crispin fisted the lance. This was not just some knight facing him in a contest. This was a murderer. A man incapable of mercy, who had killed innocent apprentices just to do the bidding of his master. It was he who should be defending himself, not Crispin. No more. If fight to the bitter end this was, then it was time to end it.

He leaned forward, lance still high. Osbert's horse grimaced over his bit, head bobbing with each hard step. His hooves cast the imported soil into the air, creating a cloud of dust behind him.

Osbert seemed intent over the horse, his left hand curled over the reins.

Crispin suddenly felt so light it was as if he were flying on a winged beast. The hoofbeats became his own heart's tempo. He leaned even farther forward, urging the beast on with his own anticipation.

Osbert neared. His lance lowered. Crispin lowered his own. He let his instinct guide him, not even thinking about directing the lance.

When it hit Osbert's shield, the crack was like the gates of Hell splintering open. Osbert popped upward out of his saddle, legs wide, head thrown back. Only at the last moment did he let go of his lance. It speared forward under its own power like a deadly projectile shot from a ballista.

Right at Crispin.

He took it in the chest. He did not register the pain at first. Nor the fact that he, too, burst out of his saddle. All he saw was the horse galloping away beneath him, heard rather than felt the whoosh of air expel from his lungs as he slammed onto his back and skidded along the bridge's unforgiving span.

Only when he stopped moving did the pain explode in his breast, his back, his head. His whole body was on fire with it and for a horrifying moment he thought he might *be* on fire. Stars danced in his vision and he saw sky through the slits and nothing else. He tried to take a breath and found that he couldn't. He tried again and began to panic.

He attempted rolling upon his side. His hand scrabbled over his chest and felt the deep indentation now decorating the breastplate. It was cove in so deeply it pressed into his chest, preventing him taking a breath. Was he to die like this, like a turtle on its back?

Hands reached for him. He gasped and turned his eyes toward

the squire, kneeling over him. "Sir Knight! I must remove the breast armor."

Crispin nodded as best he could. The boy was nimble and attended to the straps quickly and efficiently. He pulled it loose and Crispin sucked in a lungful of air.

The squire sat back on his backside in relief, cradling the ruined armor. He was panting from the effort and staring into the eye slits of the helm. Between gasps, he said quietly, "I do not know who you are, but I thank you for my master's sake."

Crispin gave the youth his full attention.

"I have never seen my master fight as you did today," he said in harsh whispers. "I knew it could not have been him. You are trying to save him, and I thank you for it. No one has been able to talk to him."

There was much of Jack Tucker in that youth's eyes; the look of a young man old beyond his years. Crispin reached out and closed his hand gratefully over the boy's wrist.

"I swore an oath," said Crispin.

The squire nodded. "I thought as much."

"Take that armor to the pavilion and give it to the boy you will find there, a boy with ginger hair. His name is Jack Tucker. Tell him to guard that armor well for it contains that which we have sought. He will know the answer to that riddle."

The squire nodded again.

"Does Osbert live?"

The boy turned and looked. He nodded and turned back. "You will have to continue the battle on foot."

"I was afraid of that." And without the Spear. If it had given him an advantage it was gone now. "Help me up."

Geoffrey had moved back toward the center of the action and was making some announcement, no doubt explaining how the combat would continue. Crispin couldn't spare the energy to listen. He needed his strength to stand and to catch his breath. For it seemed that without that breastplate his vitality had fled.

His shield was broken in two and he left it where it lay. Shieldless, vulnerable, he staggered forward, feeling suddenly very weary, and drew his sword.

24

IT WAS AS IF he had forgotten everything he learned, as if the Spear had allowed his muscles to recall how to behave. For now, he was like a schoolboy all over again. Yes, he had trained with Jack Tucker only a few short days ago, but that was nothing like training with another tested knight. Nor was it anything like fighting for his life.

Osbert approached. The tautness of his body indicated his anger. Well, he wasn't the only one.

Crispin moved his hand over the grip and flexed his sword arm. They began to circle each other. They were close enough to see each other's eyes through their visors and Osbert squinted at Crispin. No doubt, he was wondering if the hit had muddled his brain enough to trick his sight into seeing gray eyes where he expected to see brown.

Osbert didn't wait. He snapped the blade forward, aiming to slash Crispin's shoulder. Crispin's instincts kicked in and he ducked out of the way, catching the blade with his own and forcing Osbert's out of the way. Sidestepping, he swung a vertical swipe up toward the man's torso but Osbert's blade was already there, deflecting Crispin's aside. This was not to be an easy defeat.

Crispin readjusted his grip and scooted to the side, one foot at a time, dragging the dirt with his sabatons. Osbert lurched forward and swung at Crispin's shins. Crispin leapt out of the way, bringing his sword around. It clanged against Osbert's on the upswing and for a moment they were helm to helm, their pointed metal snouts nearly touching. Osbert's eyes widened. "You are not Sir Thomas. Who the hell are you?" he cried through the visor.

"Your worst enemy," he replied, and with a grunt, Crispin threw him back. He had only a moment to roll his shoulders before Osbert came at him again.

I must get on the offensive, he thought between deflections. And when Osbert stepped back, he saw his chance. With a cry, Crispin charged him with furious swings over his head, aiming for shoulder, neck, head. Osbert's blade met them each time but now it was on the defensive. Even when he tried to bring up his sword, Crispin ducked under it, pushed the man's arm up and out of the way, and then bent to get his shoulder under the man's hip. Rising, he lifted him up and tossed him over his shoulder. Crispin was vaguely aware of the cheering in the background.

Osbert hit the dirt on his back but he didn't stay there long. Rolling away, he quickly righted himself before Crispin could stab at him. Osbert grabbed his own sword by the blade and used the hilt to hook Crispin's ankle. Before he knew what had happened, Crispin slammed to the ground on his backside. Through the narrow slits, he saw Osbert's sword coming at him, not with the sharp end but with the heavy pommel. Crispin rolled to one side as the heavy rouelle slammed the ground right where his head had been. He rolled again to the other side when it hit the ground again. He wasted no time in scrambling to his feet. Getting in close to Osbert, he grabbed the man's blade with his mail-clad armpit, pulling the man even closer. Osbert would not relinquish the blade and so Crispin closed his gauntlet into a fist and slammed it into Osbert's helm. He jabbed his own sword pommel up into the chin of Osbert's visor with a ringing whack, but though the man wobbled and staggered, he did not collapse. He shook his helmet-clad head and stepped back to reassess.

Crispin was panting. It had been a very long time since he had engaged in so prolonged a battle, and in armor. Though he was lighter because of a lack of a breastplate, he also felt vulnerable and had to defend his torso. It was the biggest target, and Osbert would surely take advantage of that soon. He wished he still had his shield.

Osbert seemed to be taking a break as well, and Crispin let his guard down the tiniest bit . . . and it was enough. In a heartbeat, Osbert leapt forward, sword whistling. Crispin lurched back, but not far enough to avoid the tip of the blade sliding hard across his mail-covered chest. If not for the habergeon he would have been sliced open.

The metal rings did not give way, but it was a calculated hit that Crispin had not wanted to allow. His confidence rising, Osbert pressed his advantage and began systematically slashing with big sweeping gestures, hilt rolling over his wrist. Like a grim reaper, his swipes came ever closer. Crispin deflected each blow with his sword in a ringing report. Sparks cascaded around them when steel met steel.

Angry now, Crispin struck back harder. Osbert's sword got turned aside farther and farther back until it was almost level with his shoulder, leaving his chest open to attack. Crispin shuffled in close and tried to knee him in the groin but the man's metal tassets got in the way. Crispin used his armored elbow instead to jab him in the chest near the armpit, a weak spot in the armor where Crispin had already dented it with his lance.

Osbert gasped in his helm from the harsh blow. Flipping the blade in his hand, Crispin used the pommel and swung, bashing him in the helm. The heavy rouelle folded the metal into a dent and Osbert teetered. Crispin slammed him again with his gauntlet-covered fist and this time Osbert sunk to one knee. Crispin drew back his foot and kicked him hard in the breastplate. He fell back. As soon as he hit the ground, he tried to rise but Crispin stepped on him, holding him in place. Osbert's sword arm raised but Crispin used his own blade to knock Osbert's from his hand. The crowd gasped when the sword skidded aside.

Breathing hard, Crispin stared at the sword now lying several feet away. He was just as surprised as the crowd.

But all at once hands gripped his ankle and twisted. Pain shot through his leg and Osbert rose beneath him, propelling him backward. Osbert leapt for his lost blade while Crispin struggled on the ground on his back. He rolled over and crawled after him, grabbing his foot. Osbert kicked back and managed to dislodge Crispin but Crispin reached again, grasping with metal-clad fingers toward the knight's spurs. With one long stretch of his lean frame, Osbert closed his hand over his sword and chopped behind him toward Crispin.

Crispin flung himself backward, rolling in the dirt. He knew Osbert had gained his feet and now it was a race whether Crispin could get up in time to get out of the way of the next blow.

"God's blood!" He staggered back, clutching his left bicep. Astounded that he'd righted himself, Crispin had blocked part of the blow but nevertheless took the heaviest hit to his arm.

He looked down, trying to see through the visor. The mail held but the arm in its pain was all but useless.

Osbert came at him, swinging again and again, and Crispin, wearying, blocked each strike with less and less skill. He wouldn't, couldn't think of defeat. He fended off the blows, letting his sword arm take it, but that arm, too, was tested beyond measure.

Osbert grunted as he swung each strike, and his eyes, though shadowed, glittered within the visor. Crispin did the only thing he could think to do, as weary as he was. He rushed in close and clasped the man's arms to his sides in a bear hug, squeezing tighter. With one arm wrapped around Osbert's head, he tried to work his hilt under the edge of Osbert's helm, lifting up. He knew it must have hurt like a son-of-a-bitch, hilt edge digging into the mail at his neck, helm pressing hard against the side of his head.

It was then he looked right in the eye slits of Osbert's visor, and Osbert glared at him. "You want to know who I am?" growled Crispin. "I'm Crispin Guest, and I'm going to kill you."

The eyes snapped wide and Osbert was startled enough to lose concentration. It was enough. Hooking his leg around the other's ankle, Crispin pulled it inward and Osbert collapsed onto the ground. With a shout, Crispin dug a knee into his chest and smacked his sword away.

Panting, Crispin stared into the eyes of his opponent. Fear glistened there but, unmoved, Crispin grabbed his blade and poised the sharp end at Osbert's exposed neck. With a hard thrust, the blade would easily pierce the mail and slice into his throat. It was a killing cut and Osbert couldn't do a damned thing about it.

"You killed Roger Grey," Crispin spat into his visor, "and you killed those apprentices. I will give them the justice they deserve."

He pulled the blade back.

"I didn't kill that man! I swear to you by Almighty God! Nor did I touch those boys. I have sons their age. Never would I have done."

Crispin hesitated. The tip, eager to plunge, sparkled in the sunshine.

"Roger Grey was willing to negotiate," he wheezed. "I was coming to the bridge to talk to him! He wanted to leave London. I swear! That woman kept getting in his way. He was ready to take our money, but *she* interfered."

Crispin stared, hating his own hesitancy, but hating more the thoughts running through his head with astonishing clarity. "You didn't do it."

Osbert shook his head, only his helm moving.

"Goddammit, you didn't do it. That only means . . ."

Crispin raised the blade high and plunged it down . . . into the dirt.

"I can take your life because of this contest if I so choose. If I spare it, you will tell no one who I am. You will let all believe it is Thomas Saunfayl who has defeated you. Swear it!"

"I-I so swear, on my honor and my life."

Gritting his teeth, Crispin pushed off from him and stood unsteadily, using the sword as a crutch.

He gestured toward the crowd. "*Tell* them."

Voice hoarse but as loud as he could shout, Osbert cried, "I yield!"

The stands erupted in cheers and shouts, banners waving crazily. *So now you cheer?* Disgusted, Crispin heaved the sword away from him. He turned toward the quivering stands.

Swiveling toward the king, he bowed. Richard inclined his head. Crispin couldn't help but look over at Chaucer. He gave him a curt nod as well. Chaucer startled and took a step forward, but Crispin had already turned on his heel to stalk back to the pavilion tent, whereupon he threw open the flap and instantly collapsed on the rug-laden floor.

25

CRISPIN FLUTTERED OPEN HIS eyes. He was on a cot. Gazing upward, he realized he was still in the tent but the armor had been removed and Jack and the squire from the lists leaned over him.

"Master Crispin!" whispered Jack. His voice was choked and there were tears on his face. "God be praised for your deliverance, good sir! I thought . . . I thought . . ."

"There, there, Jack. I am whole . . . I think." He looked to the squire for confirmation.

"You are indeed, my lord. No worse for wear."

"I am no one's lord, good squire." He took the arm offered and pulled himself up to a sitting position.

"And, apparently, *I* am no one's squire."

Before Crispin could ask, Jack pressed forward. "That damnable Sir Thomas! Once he reckoned what the breastplate was he snatched it from my arms and took off. Left! With you still fighting for his miserable honor out there."

Leaning back on his elbows did nothing to subdue the queasy feeling in Crispin's gut. Was there no honor left? Among knights? Among *friends*?

"Before he disappeared, he tossed me this." Jack held up a leather pouch, and by the sound of it, it was full of coins.

Crispin snorted. The price of a man's honor.

"My lord," said the squire at the tent flap. "You'd best depart. Master Chaucer is coming."

Jack scrambled to get Crispin's abandoned coat and hood—at least Thomas had left him that! Dressing quickly without time to button the cotehardie, he pushed Jack under the tent on the other side. He looked toward the squire to give him thanks, but the youth only smiled. "I see you already have a squire. A pity. I know I could have learned a great deal from you. God keep you, Master Guest."

"And you."

He hit the floor and rolled under the tent canvas, just as he heard the squire at the door address Geoffrey. He stuffed his head into the hood and kept low, running into the crowd. It was Jack who found him and grabbed his arm. Never letting it go, the boy pulled him along. Too tired to argue or to question, Crispin allowed it. Not until they were many streets away did Jack drag him into a shadowed alley and push him against the wall. He ran his hands over Crispin, looking for injuries.

"I am well, Jack. Just bruised. And tired."

"Oh Master Crispin!" The tears were smeared and dried on the boy's dirty face. "I never seen the like. You were magnificent. As if you'd never left the lists, sir. I mean, I knew that you were a lord, sir, but I never believed . . . I mean, I never could have guessed . . ."

"That I knew what I was doing?" He leaned against the wall, head thrown back, breathing in all the air he wanted. "'The proof that you know something is that you are able to teach it.'"

"I know that, Master, but to see it! Oh, you must have been a terrible sight on the battlefield."

"Enough. You say that Thomas knew what was in the breast-plate?"

"Aye, sir. The squire handed it to me and said that you had said this was what we had been seeking. When it rattled, I reckoned what it was. But so did Sir Thomas. I am ashamed to say I wrestled with him for it." And Crispin just now noticed a bruise on the side of Jack's face. He hoped the boy had inflicted at least that much on the man in return. "But he knocked me down and got away. Should we go after him, sir?"

He closed his eyes and scrubbed his face with his calloused hands. "No," he said to his fingers. "Let him go."

"But Master!"

"Let him go, I say. He will run with as much as he can carry. I doubt we shall ever see him or that miserable Spear again. God help him now."

"But what of Lancaster?"

"He had already lost a knight a while ago. But Thomas will not return to Spain to fight for his or for any other army."

"But now he's got the Spear!"

"Perhaps. If that *is* what was inside."

"Don't you want to know, sir? Don't you want to know if it helped you fight?"

"I did not have it in the end, so what does it matter?"

"But sir!"

"Leave it, Jack. Would that I could forget it all. But we still have a murderer to catch."

"Wasn't that Sir Osbert?"

He rested his hand on Jack's shoulders. Crispin shivered. Jack shook him off and divested himself of his cloak . . . and as it turned out it was Crispin's, for he had worn one over the other. He gave it to Crispin and he quickly donned it. "No, Jack. It was not Sir Osbert."

"But—"

"Osbert told me he had negotiated with Grey, offered him money. But then he told me that Anabel got in his way. She tried to insinuate herself into his scheme. He told me Grey intended to leave London."

"And you believe him?"

"Yes. How could he have known that which Anabel keeps denying? And she denied ever seeing him before. She lied, Jack, about all of it. We must now find Anabel Coterel. *She* killed him, Jack. Because he intended to leave her. And she killed Lucas Stotley, with whom she conspired to steal her father's money. There are no words to describe what she is. I will *not* let her get away."

THE TRAIL WAS COLD by some several hours. Crispin had to believe Anabel and her father would return to the bridge for the remainder of their things. But the bridge was a mass of bodies and the remnants of the joust. It might be easier and quicker to get there by boat.

Again, Jack led him through the throng of people, threading their way as unobtrusively as they could. Crispin kept thinking of the Boar's Tusk and how thoroughly appealing the idea of a jug of wine was. Wearier than he'd ever been, he pushed on, allowing Jack to make a path for them among the crowd. He heard snatches of conversation, many speaking of the combat they had just witnessed. He blushed to hear the praise of the mysterious Sir Thomas and how absurd had been the charge of cowardice, and hadn't the king more to worry over than frivolous jousts? Crispin allowed himself to wonder at the fate of his friend—*former* friend, he corrected. Sir Thomas, stealing away with a precious relic, was certainly welcome to it. He wanted nothing more than to forget it all. Except that the throbbing pain in his arm from the sword hit would not allow it. He grabbed at the bicep and kneaded it, but that ministration did little good. The arm still felt leaden at his side.

They could not seem to escape the milling people still discussing the joust. But at least more were dispersing. The king and his entourage had long ago departed, probably not long after Crispin had crept away himself.

Jack walked close to Crispin, likely to catch him if he dropped from exhaustion.

"It will be a miracle if she is still here."

"She might have been trapped with the crowd," said Crispin.

They spilled out at the edge of the throng and Crispin trotted toward the tailor shop. When he neared he slowed and edged toward the open shutter and peered around it. Dark. No sign of— Wait. He heard the rafters creak above and he wasted no time in climbing in. Turning to Jack, he put a finger to his lips and crept toward the stairs. There was no sense in going up the stairs and risking that they would squeak and give him away. So he waited below, trying to keep his breathing under control. Slowly, he drew his dagger. There would be no mistakes this time. If she didn't go quietly he was prepared to subdue her.

A step. Someone was coming down the staircase. Each tread creaked with the weight of a foot descending. Once they reached the floor, Crispin darted from beneath the stairs and grabbed her. But it was not Anabel.

He held them at arm's length. "Master Coterel! Forgive me. I thought you were . . . someone else." He sheathed his dagger.

The tailor swayed from surprise and, with a sniff, Crispin could tell it was also from drunkenness. "What . . . what . . . ?"

Crispin pulled the nervous man toward a chair and sat him

down. A flame flared behind him and Jack set the candle on the table.

"Master Crispin? What are you doing here in the dark?"

"I was looking for you. And your daughter."

"She is awaiting me. We are leaving London. She said she cannot abide the sorrows we have seen. I was just gathering the last of our things." He gestured toward the small coffer in his lap.

"Where is she, Master Coterel?"

"She's not far. We are anxious to be on our way."

"Master Coterel, I must . . . speak with her."

The tailor's yellowed eyes darted from Crispin's face to Jack's. "Why ever for?"

"The tragedy that has befallen these two houses, that of Master Grey and this one, has been great. The death of two young apprentices and of Roger Grey himself. These are foul deeds. And now Lucas Stotley. Do you not see how they tie together, Master Coterel?"

Still bewildered, the tailor looked from one to the other. He touched a quivering finger to his lips. "But how can that be?"

"I . . . some people do these deeds to . . . to help their household. I think that perhaps Roger Grey was killed for his money. To help the two of you."

Coterel shook his head, fingers still dragging against his lips. "But how can that be? He was going to marry her. He was going to—" His glossy eyes looked up. "He was going to marry her and leave London, such an evil place."

"Well, that may be so. But it does not change the fact that . . . he was killed. And others."

"What will become of my Anabel? She is so innocent."

This was damnable. The man was in his cups and unable to

comprehend what Crispin was saying. He dared not say more. He could see the bewilderment still on Coterel's face. "Can you tell me where she is? I must fetch her myself."

The door burst open and Anabel stood in the doorway. She had lost her veil and her hair was unbound, hanging in wild curls about her face and neck. Those full lips that had tasted him hung open in fear. "What are you doing?"

Crispin wasn't certain whether she was talking to him or her father, but he straightened and stood. "Anabel Coterel, you must accompany me to Newgate on the charge of murder."

She stared at him, green eyes wide, dark lashes fanning outward like an opening flower. She stared at him for a long moment. Until she laughed. Not a pleasant tinkling sound.

"You are charging *me* with murder?"

"The time for games is done. You must submit." He moved his hand over his dagger but did not draw it. She saw the movement and her eyes stayed wide and rounded.

"You would truly haul me to the sheriffs? You'd see me hang?"

Her father shot to his feet. "No, Anabel!"

"It's all right, Father." She went to him and closed her arms about him. But in a flash, she had grabbed the knife from his belt and spun, holding the blade toward Crispin. "My father and I are leaving London. We shall not return."

"I am afraid I cannot permit that."

"Will you stop me?" She reached blindly for her father's arm but he had stepped back. "You, who shared my bed?"

"Anabel." Crispin lowered his head but did not take his eyes from her. "You deceived me. No more."

She shook her head, still reaching for her father without looking. Her attention was focused solely on Crispin. "I have shared many beds and deceived many men. What is one more?"

"My daughter!" She spared her father a glance and stopped in her tracks. The tailor held a mace in his unsteady hands and had backed Jack into a wall threateningly. "You should not tell such lies to this man. He's trying to help."

"Father . . ." Her dagger lowered. Crispin swept in and grabbed her, wrestling the knife from her hand. "No!"

But now the situation was worse, for the tailor had not backed away from Jack. He seemed even more determined to hold him at bay. Jack did not seem to know what to do. Each time he reached for his own dagger, the man moved the mace toward his moving hand.

"Master Coterel," said Crispin, still holding Anabel's wrist. "Put the mace down."

"I cannot do that, young man. My daughter is an innocent maid. All these men are taking advantage of her. Roger Grey did. He said he would marry her, but I could see that he was preparing to leave the city, and he made no mention of taking us with him. He said some very bad things."

Desperately, Anabel raised a pleading hand to her father. "Father, don't. Don't say another word. I beg you!"

Coterel's face darkened. "He said some very bad things, indeed. I came to talk to him that night, to tell him to stay away from my daughter. He was not there, but his apprentices were."

"Father, be still. For the love of God!"

Crispin felt a sickening thud in his gut. He'd been wrong again. He released her wrist.

"They tried to restrain me," said the tailor. "Me! I was a tailor on this bridge long before they were ever born. I merely meant to throw them off. This was sitting on the table." He lifted the mace with a much surer hand. "But I never meant to . . . meant to truly harm them." Crispin itched to get to Jack, but he stood too many feet away. Edging closer, he tried to placate with an open hand. It wasn't at all what he had thought and Jack, too, was coming to that realization. Fear froze his face.

Coterel licked his lips. "They were good boys," he said wistfully. "I did not realize . . ." He shrugged. "When they were quite still I . . . I threw them both out the window. I had to." He turned toward the shuttered window and seemed perplexed that it was a different one. "When Grey arrived he told me to get out but I accused him of immorality and breach of promise. He lied and said he had never promised to marry my daughter."

"Oh, Father." Anabel broke down. She covered her face with her hands and wept great sobs.

"I hit him with my fist and bloodied his nose. We fought. He tried to grab me and then I hit him with this!" He lifted the mace. "That stopped him. I threw him in the Thames as well."

"And you killed Lucas Stotley," said Crispin.

Anabel gasped.

"He was a liar. He said very bad things about my daughter. It is a sin to lie. I took my scissors and stabbed him to silence his lies. It was a very good scissors."

"Master Coterel," said Crispin carefully. "Please. Give me the mace."

"And now *you* are saying lies about my daughter as well. There are very few things that a man can do to protect his daughter from false rumors and the lust of unworthy men. But I know what I can do."

He turned from Jack and took a step toward Crispin. And just as he raised the mace, Jack grabbed a stool and struck his arm. The mace clattered to the ground, and Jack tackled him. They both fell heavily and slammed against a table. Anabel screamed and Crispin moved in and yanked the man to his feet by the collar.

"There will be no more lies," said Crispin. "And no more deaths." He looked toward Anabel's face, a ruin of tears.

26

CRISPIN BROODED BEFORE HIS fire, stabbing his knife tip into the arm of his chair, pulling it out, and stabbing again in a mindless repetition of movement.

Jack stood to the side, close enough for comfort but not so close as to annoy. "So she lied to protect him," he said quietly.

"Yes. Unstable from drink, he committed these horrific murders without so much as batting an eye. He believed he was protecting her. She, of course, was using her body and her wiles to maintain a living."

"But if she told Lucas Stotley where the money was hidden so he could steal it, why'd she hire you?"

"To throw me off the scent. She never believed I would make so obscure a connection as Lucas to Lenny. Of course, she couldn't have known that I was already well acquainted with our thief. She wanted me close to make certain I followed the wrong leads, accused the wrong men, since I didn't believe Grey had killed himself."

Jack smoothed down the breast of his new coat with a hesitant hand. "He is a fine tailor, sir." He was wearing the coat made by a murderer. But he and Jack were pragmatic men. Neither could afford to dispose of it.

Crispin nodded. "But perhaps he did not work as often as he let on. His drunkenness prevented that."

"She lay with those men for money, sir?"

"A person will commit many unspeakable acts to stay alive."

They both fell silent, thinking privately of their own dark pasts.

A knock on the door broke the reverie. With a questioning look toward Crispin, Jack made to open it, but Crispin stopped him. He went instead, drawing his dagger. The hour was late and a visitor did not bode well.

He unbolted the door and pulled, letting it fall open. A figure stood on the landing and remained in the shadows until finally stepping forward.

"Geoffrey!"

Chaucer, followed by the three Spaniards, walked over the threshold. Crispin eyed them all once before he turned his back on them and returned to the fire. "Close the door on your way out," he said, and sat.

The others hung back but Geoffrey stood beside Crispin almost at the same spot Jack had stood. "I thought you might like to know that Sir Thomas has redeemed himself and all charges have been dropped."

"That is good news. Now good night."

"But it seems that after the match he has disappeared. His squires, his pages, none of his household know where he has gone."

"And neither do I. Is that what you came for? That is your answer. You can go now."

"Cris, Sir Thomas is still to return to his grace's army. But there appears to be no sign of him. Or of the Spear."

"How astute of you. He clearly has it and has made off. I am not pleased with the situation either. He owes me my fee."

"Are you not going to pursue him?"

"No. Frankly, I've had enough of this affair. And if you are wise you, too, will forget it. He is long gone. Gone from London, I should imagine. It shall be impossible to track him now."

He heard the squeak of leather and clank of armor as the others turned to one another. Clearly, this was not good news.

Chaucer took a step and grabbed the stool, placed it beside Crispin, and sat. He leaned over his thighs and warmed his hands before the meager flames. "I hear you caught your murderer," he said softly. "Well done."

"It was very *ill* done! This conversation is over. Will you leave?" He rubbed at his sore arm and Chaucer stared at it.

"How did you hurt your arm, Cris?"

"I was careless." He rubbed it harder. It was less numb than it had been but it still ached with every movement.

"Very careless. Letting the sword strike you like that."

His kneading stopped. Crispin kept his gaze steady on the hearth. "I do not know what you are talking about."

Chaucer leaned in and said quietly, "You think *I* can't recognize you? Me? How many years did we fight together, side by side? Dammit, Cris, what the hell were you doing?"

"As I said." He turned to face his friend. "I don't know what you are talking about."

Chaucer slapped his thigh and stood. "Very well. You don't know where Sir Thomas is?"

"No. And I have no intention of going after him. Good riddance."

"And the Spear?"

"He'll never use it in battle. I am satisfied."

"But Cris!"

"He said he's satisfied," said Jack, emerging from the shadows. "My lord," he added perfunctorily.

Chaucer released a long sigh. He looked at his companions, but they were silent. "Then, I must be content as well. It was good to see you again, Crispin. I'm sure we will cross paths."

"London is a big town. We might not."

"No, you are wrong. It is a very small town. Very small indeed. Take care of yourself. God keep you. I do mean it."

Crispin nodded. "I know. You, too."

Chaucer jerked his head and the others followed. They left, silently closing the door behind them.

Jack blew out a relieved breath. "S'trooth! I'm glad to see the backside of them!"

ALL WAS BACK TO normal. A murderer was brought to justice, a relic had disappeared once more, a man's honor was preserved, and Crispin was left alone again, even if his money pouch was, for once, full.

The days dragged on, cold autumn succeeding into the first signs of winter, even in the last days of October. King Richard's troubles began in earnest and he tried to escape them by retreating from Westminster to his estates at Eltham, but Parliament would not countenance it and forced his return by refusing to do any business at all. His chancellor, Michael de la Pole, earl of Suffolk, was relieved of his duties and Bishop Arundel became chancellor in his place, along with John Gilbert, bishop of Hereford, who took on the duties of treasurer.

Crispin sniffed at that. Purse strings would be kept tighter now, he supposed, but much damage had already been done. The problem was Richard himself. If he could not see to mend his ways then Crispin did not see a very rosy future for him.

It was early November when Crispin saw his way back to Westminster. Not to go to the palace, of course. No, he fully intended to steer clear of that! But he finally had time to visit Abbot Nicholas. A few small jobs had come his way after the Spear disaster and he was glad of the distraction as well as the purse.

He left Jack behind as he made his way down the Strand, holding his cloak tight against his body, protecting it from the wind boring down on him from the Thames. His eyes roved over the scaffolding erected over the abbey's façade. There was always some construction going on, some new creation enlivening the cathedral. And was it not all the abbot's doing? He stopped and watched for a time as stonemasons measured with plumb lines and pored over drawings and charts. He did not notice the horses drawing up behind him, or the sound of someone dismounting. The clack of a spur on the cobblestones finally awakened him and he spun. Henry, Earl Derby, was striding toward him with a smile on his face. Crispin dropped his head in a bow.

"Ah, Crispin! How happy I am to see you again."

"Your grace."

The younger man rested his hand on Crispin's shoulder and turned him to face Westminster Abbey again. "The work is going well."

"Yes, your grace. It will be as fine as any cathedral in Christendom. Not that it isn't now."

"Indeed. The grave of many a king. The place where heads are crowned."

Crispin measured Henry out of the corner of his eye. "Which is more infamous, I wonder; the coronation or the funeral?"

He clutched Crispin's shoulder and laughed. "You are a saucy fellow. I have truly missed you."

Crispin smiled in answer.

"Have you recovered well?"

"My cold is long gone, your grace."

"I do not mean your cold." He leaned in and said more quietly, "I mean your trials . . . on the lists?"

Crispin tried to pull away but Henry had a good grip of him. "Don't worry. Only those who knew you well could tell it was you."

"Chaucer," he hissed through his teeth.

"Yes, but he only confirmed my own suspicions. Impetuous. Foolish. You could have been discovered and my royal cousin would have had no choice but to execute you where you stood. I am glad I did not have to witness that. You should be more cautious. I realize you were most likely compelled to do it by some point of honor." He waited for a reply but Crispin kept his lips firmly shut. Henry sighed. "I only remember how kind you were to me and my siblings. I did not know the half of you. But I'm keeping watch now."

Crispin could not tell by his tone if it was meant as a compliment or as a word of warning.

"I shall try to be a model citizen henceforth."

Henry laughed, but it was more restrained this time. "Will you? I shouldn't like to see that." His smile faded as he took in the abbey again. "I hear you are friends with the abbot of Westminster. I pray you, go to visit him in all haste at La Neyte. His physicians warn he hasn't long."

"I am going there now."

"Good. Give him my best wishes and prayers for his soul."

"I will. Farewell, my lord."

"This is not 'farewell.' Merely *adieu*. We will meet again." He saluted Crispin, who gathered his presence of mind to bow.

He watched Henry mount and then turn his horse to follow the road to the palace. Crispin, on the other hand, took another road and headed on foot toward La Neyte.

HE WAS GREETED AT the door by Brother John, who looked more drawn and harried than the last time Crispin had come. Looking at Crispin with sorrowful eyes, he led him silently to the abbot's chamber.

Nicholas was abed, propped up on pillows against the bedhead. He seemed much smaller than the man of wide girth he had been. Much smaller than he had looked only a fortnight ago when Crispin visited him for the first time in his convalescence. Pale and drawn with lids papery thin, his head listed to the side, jaw hanging loose.

Fear stabbed at Crispin's chest, thinking that he was too late, but Nicholas took a sudden deep breath and expelled it through his jowled cheeks. He blinked and then opened his eyes. It took a moment, but they focused at last on Crispin.

He raised a hand feebly before letting it fall to the bed. "Crispin." The rasping voice was very different from the usual strong tones. "I am grateful you have come." Crispin moved forward and sat on the chair beside the bed. He pulled it closer.

"Of course I am here. You were a good friend to me."

"Already I am past tense," he croaked good-naturedly.

Crispin cringed. "I did not mean—"

"I know." He smiled and Crispin took his hand. "I have heard of your latest exploits."

"Oh?"

"Another murderer was brought to justice. And honor upheld." Were there no secrets at court? If all knew about the joust then what good had it done?

The abbot seemed to read Crispin's mind when he gave his hand a frail squeeze. "Only a handful of us, Crispin. Only a handful know. And the king is not among that handful."

Crispin said nothing, but a gust of breath through his nose told of his relief.

"Ah, my friend. It is clear to me that you need more counsel, but I am afraid I shan't be here to perform it."

"You have always been most valuable to me as advocate, confessor, and friend."

"And you have been my greatest challenge."

"My lord?"

"Don't feign ignorance. For that is the one thing you are not. You have been a challenge to me, for many have taken my spiritual counsel but you have always questioned it."

"I am a stubborn man," he admitted.

"Indeed you are, but it is more than that." He took longer between sentences. His breath labored.

"I am taxing you. I should go."

"No. Stay. This is my last . . . my last counsel to you." He took a deep breath but it would not seem to go as deeply as he tried to do. The rattling in his chest spoke of mortality and Crispin left the chair to kneel beside him. "Two things, Crispin." His voice was now as light as smoke and Crispin leaned in to hear him. "One, a man should marry."

He shook his head. "I have told you before, Nicholas. How could I bring a decent woman into uncertain poverty?"

" 'Better to marry than to burn,' " he said with a slow wink.

Crispin smiled. It was then he felt the tears that had reached the edges of his mouth.

"And two . . . two . . ." He paused to gasp a breath and Crispin shook his head at him.

"Hush, Nicholas. Save your breath."

"No. I must tell you. Crispin, these relics that have come to you. There is a reason. You . . . you must forget what you think you know . . . Beware of what you find . . ."

Even with his ear planted close to the abbot's dry lips he could not hear the last. Only a long exhalation of breath that seemed to go on and on.

Brother John was there in an instant, nudging Crispin aside. He brandished a goblet of wine in his hand. Kneeling beside Crispin, he took the abbot's wilted white hand out of Crispin's grasp. "Do you renounce Satan and all his works?" muttered the monk to his abbot. Nicholas nodded and took the wine that John pressed to his lips. A little dribbled out the side of his mouth in a crimson stream and then he moved no more.

The monk sank his head to the bed and wept on the hand of the dead abbot. Crispin stayed on his knees, feeling no compunction to leave.

IT WAS HALF OF the hour later that Crispin left at last, and that was only because he was warned that the king's emissaries were coming. He trudged back to the Shambles, his mind filled with mortality. When he reached the tinker shop he stopped at the bottom of the stairs and looked up the rickety wooden structure. In the winter, the stairs were icy. Inside there were drafts and the roof leaked. He owned none of the furniture and only a few of the items that inhabited the place. Nicholas was a dear man and had cared for Crispin almost as much as Gilbert and Eleanor did, but he could not know the extent of Crispin's degradation. Crispin knew that alone he was only half a man, but he could *not* bring a wife to this.

Trudging up the stairs he finally came to his door, but instead of having to dig for his key, it opened and Jack Tucker stood there, a worried look on his young face. He stepped aside and Crispin entered.

"It is done," he said to the boy. Jack becrossed himself and released a whimpered sob. Crispin had done his weeping. He stared into the fire.

"He was a good man, Master Crispin. A good soul."

He nodded, still thinking of his words. The man had tried to tell him something about the relics. Always relics coming into his hands. Why? While in that strange territory between Heaven and Earth, had Nicholas glimpsed the world's unanswered questions? Had he found reason in the chaos? *Was* there a reason these relics seemed to come to Crispin, and Crispin alone? *You must forget what you think you know. Beware of what you find.* What did that mean? It had been a tantalizing morsel that Nicholas unwittingly dangled before him.

Now it was nothing but a headache.

And the other. To marry. Before he could stop himself, he cast his eyes toward his bed, to the mattress, beneath which lay the portrait of Philippa Walcote. She had asked him, and he had refused. Partly it was because of his poverty but partly because of his pride. She wasn't fit to be the wife of a lord. *She* wasn't fit. And yet *he* wasn't a lord. He would laugh but he hadn't any jollity left in him.

Instead, he rose, and despite the presence of Jack, he knelt by his bed, reached under, and pulled the portrait out. He returned to the fire and plopped down into the chair, staring at the little picture so carefully painted. Such an unusual thing to have a small portrait of a person, not a saint, not a king. But he knew that Lancaster had such a thing. It was probably in the hands of his mistress, Katherine Swynford. She would have such a keepsake and keep it dear.

"She has a babe, you know," said Jack quietly behind him, nodding toward the portrait.

Crispin's heart lurched at the thought. "No. I didn't know."

"Aye. Married well and good. It . . . it's best to forget her, sir."

"I know." He swept his thumb across her perpetual smile, over those sleepy eyes. He thought of stuffing the image under the mattress again, but he decided to keep it in his pouch, keep it close. A constant reminder that he had once been a great fool and it had cost him.

The small fire was a comfort. Jack's silent presence beside him even more so.

Afterword

Just which lance are we talking about in this latest Crispin adventure? When we talk of the Holy Spear or the Spear of Destiny or the Spear of Longinus or the Holy Lance, there seems to be a surprising number of them to talk about.

There is possibly the most famous one, which has been used in movies and fiction before, and that is a lance that belongs to the *Reichskleinodien,* or the imperial regalia of the Holy Roman Empire. In 1796, it was moved to Vienna to keep it safe while the French revolutionary army marched near Nuremburg, where it had been stored. It was supposed to stay in Vienna only until the war was over, but by then the Holy Roman Empire had ceased to be and Vienna saw no reason to return it to Germany. Finders keepers. It is a long blade, broken in the center, and imbedded with a nail. That broken piece was bound with silver and then with an engraved gold band.

But this lance point, even though it *appeared* old enough and housed what was believed to be one of the nails from the crucifixion in its blade, was dated only to the seventh century when extensive metallurgical tests were done on it in 2003. So this clearly could not be the right spear that Crispin was involved with, even if Hitler thought it was and supposedly wanted to get his hands on it, too. (Although, it appears to have its own pre-Christian history of having belonged to, or being a copy of the one belonging to

Odin himself and hence gave credence to the German kings' claim to be descended from Odin. I'm hearing Valkyries singing in the background. Can *you* hear them?)

There was also the relic of just the point of the spear, known as the Vatican Lance. In AD 570, a pilgrim called Antoninus of Piacenza described an object he saw in Jerusalem in the Basilica of Mount Zion. In his writings, he claims to have seen the Crown of Thorns and the spear that pierced the side of Christ. Gregory of Tours also attested to the spear's location, though he was *not* an eyewitness and had *never* been to Jerusalem. He must have just read the brochure.

Such is the written record of history.

This lance, or at least its point, left the Basilica when the Persian King Khousrau II captured Jerusalem. The point got broken off of the spear and it was *this* relic that made its way to Hagia Sophia in Constantinople, where many Christian relics seem to end up. The point was later set into an icon and sold in 1244 to Louis IX of France where, along with the Crown of Thorns, it was enshrined in the Sainte Chapelle in Paris. But this is not the one we are after either.

Then there is the Holy Lance of Echmiadzin of Armenia. In 1098, crusader Peter Bartholomew claimed that he received a vision from St. Andrew showing him where the lance was buried—which happened to be in St. Peter's Cathedral in Antioch. Handy, that. He excavated, and lo and behold, found it! It gave the crusaders the oomph they needed to rout the Muslims and capture Antioch. No one really knows what happened to it after that. But many believe it is the one that fell into the hands of the Turks and is now housed in the Vatican. Is it? Or is it the one that Crispin found?

Remember that lance that was in the Mount Zion Basilica? The point broke off and was sent on to Constantinople. But what about the bigger piece left behind? This part ended up in the Church of the Holy Sepulcher in Jerusalem in AD 670. Somehow, it, too, appears to have arrived in Constantinople, because fourteenth-century pilgrims claim to have seen it in both Constantinople *and* Paris. Point and larger piece? Hard to say. (Do you see why Crispin is so skeptical?) During the French Revolution, the point was removed from Sainte Chapelle and taken to Bibliothèque Nationale, where it promptly vanished.

Whatever piece the Vatican still has, they are not necessarily claiming it as genuine. It would have to undergo scientific tests for that—to at least date it to the proper era—and the Vatican is famously reluctant to do such tests on any of its relics.

The Acta Pilati, one of many noncanonical gospels, has given us a great deal of information regarding events, people, and relics not necessarily backed up by canonical accounts. It gave us the name of the centurion who pierced Jesus's side as Longinus, but since it wasn't considered part of the canon it is hard to take it— indeed, any of the gospels—as a record of strictly historical facts. Nevertheless, it is an interesting document that throws some light on ancient events and sometimes offers more speculation than answers.

We also bid a fond farewell to Abbot Nicholas, who gave up the ghost on November 29, 1386. He was responsible for a great deal of the rebuilding and redesign of Westminster Abbey itself, and is credited with the building of the south and west sides of the great cloister, the Jerusalem Chamber, the abbot's dining hall, and the Deanery. He also seemed like a crusty bird with a lot of pluck, for among the effects in his will he left a lot of battle accoutrements to various beneficiaries, including six hauberks, eight helmets, a pair of steel gloves, some "leg-harneys", and four lance heads. He was well prepared to defend the abbey in more than just letters to Rome, or so it appeared. This is, after all, a society where anyone and everyone is armed in some way and is fully expected to defend the home turf.

As for the joust on London Bridge, there is precedent for that. Indeed, there had been jousts on the bridge and elsewhere both in and around the immediate outskirts of London. Jousts are fabulously entertaining and if you ever get a chance to see a real one I urge you to go. They stir the blood, that's for sure.

And by the way, Lancaster did indeed have a Spanish secretary, bishop of Dax, Juan Gutierrez, along with a retainer, the knight Dom Lope Perez. Though Lancaster claimed the title as King of Castile and Leon because of his marriage to Costanza, the daughter of Pedro the Cruel who was the former King of Castile, the Spanish don't bother listing Lancaster on their rolls. King Richard may have crowned him King of Spain, but the Spanish didn't. His military campaign in Spain—which was to last until 1389—was unsuccessful. Alas.

Henry, earl of Derby, also called Henry Bolingbroke for where he was born (Bolingbroke Castle in Lincolnshire), was the first-born legitimate son of John of Gaunt from his first wife Blanche. Henry, barely a year older than his cousin King Richard, would eventually lead an army against said cousin, sending him fleeing, and then seize the throne for himself, becoming Henry IV.

Because Lancaster is absent in Spain for the next few years, expect to see Henry hanging around and bedeviling Crispin.

And finally, the idea of knights suffering from post-traumatic stress disorder, or PTSD, fascinated me. I wondered if throughout history, in the days before modern artillery, combatants suffered from it. After all, it is a malady that manifests once a soldier returns home to "normal" life and many soldiers and knights were away from home for years and years. Even though there is little in the way of discussion about it in old documents because of the cultural and sociological differences between then and now, I didn't suppose it was a modern phenomenon, though we have given it fancy modern names.

In World War I, they talked of being "shell shocked" from the nature of the new style of warfare where soldiers huddled in trenches while being barraged by exploding shells. By World War II it was called "battle fatigue." General Patton famously slapped a soldier suffering from this. "Battlefield stress" is yet another term.

But in the Middle Ages it could only be recognized as a failure on the part of the soldier and labeled as cowardice. Interestingly enough, some parchment was given to the problem of cowardice. The idea, then as now, was to train the soldier so thoroughly that the "flight" part of the natural "fight or flight" response would be eliminated. Drill, discipline, and group bonding went a long way toward shaping the mind (though the medieval foot soldier wasn't drilled in the sense of practicing formations, not like their ancient ancestors in Greece or Rome. It was an impracticality. They had to rely on the discipline of the knights, those in the front lines, to form strategies for the foot soldiers to follow. However, infantry was able to save the day over the mounted knight many a time, including in the battle of Courtrai in 1302 and Bannockburn in 1314).

Instilling a greater fear in one's commander than in the enemy also proved optimal. In ancient China, for example, generals would maneuver their armies in such a way as to make retreat impossible thus making the advance the only option. Religious fervor, too, offered a standard under which one could fight while also offering ultimate rewards if death should strike.

There was a reason for rallying the troops before a battle with a stirring speech. From ancient Greece and probably before, generals and kings gave battle orations meant to bond, to encourage, and to remind the men of their reasons for fighting and for their ultimate rewards if they succeeded. Think of the St. Crispin's Day speech in Shakespeare's *Henry V.* I don't know about you, but it makes *me* want to take up arms!

Combined, this is what made up the "band of brothers," where even the general or, in some instances, the castellan of a fortress, feels close to his men in a way that defies the social classes.

Still, even with all this training and discipline, with the subsequent shame in society associated with cowardice, there were certainly soldiers and knights who succumbed to the rigors of war. A knight on a horse could flee a lot easier than a man on the ground, and there were instances where generals insisted the knights dismount in order to make fleeing more difficult. Early flight of the knights lost many a battle, including King Stephen's battle at Lincoln and Robert Curthose's battle at Tinchebrai. Are these instances of cowardice as we might understand it, or of a man cutting his losses and getting the heck out of there?

Battle stress manifests itself in running away in the face of battle, sleeplessness, irritability, irrational anger, mood swings, and thoughts of suicide. Sir Thomas in this piece suffers from these symptoms and can't understand why. All his training and discipline failed him in the face of the constant barrage of the battle royale. What's a knight to do? As he said, they can't all be Crispin Guests.

Next, the brave Sir Crispin returns in a new adventure during the turbulent years of the late 1380s. King Richard's trials have only begun and Crispin will, no doubt, be in the thick of it. But down on the mean streets of London, Crispin still has to make a living. He and his cadre of friends and acquaintances will return to hunt for a new venerated object in *Shadow of the Alchemist*.

Glossary

AKETON   padded tunic worn under armor

BALLISTA   a war machine made like a giant crossbow for shooting arrow-like projectiles

BESAGUES   disk-shaped armor to protect the armpit

BOSS   a metal convex projection in the center of a buckler. Or the central ornamental design at the conjuncture of a ribbed vault ceiling

BUCKLER   small, round shield

CAMAIL   a mail collar sometimes connected to the mail head covering (coif), or sometimes connected to the helm, that falls from the chin and spreads over the chest and shoulders

CAPARISON   a garment for one's horse, displaying the color of one's arms

COIF   mail head covering fitting the head and open at the face

CUISSES   armor for the thigh

FETLOCK FEATHERS   the long hair that grows on the fetlocks of horses (think Clydesdale)

HABERGEON   a mail shirt that falls to the upper thigh (one that falls to the knees is called a HAUBERK)

KAYLES   a game of nine pins

GREAVES   armor for the shins

PIG-FACED BASCINET   a helm with the visor shaped like a sharp snout

POLEYNS   armor for the knees

POULAINES   shoes with exaggeratedly long toes. Stylish for the fourteenth century

SABATONS   armor for the feet. Sometimes shaped like poulaines

SCRIP   a small bag used for carrying items like documents, food, or money pouch

TASSETS   plate armor hanging from the breastplate like a skirt

TRAPPER   a horse covering displaying one's colors and arms

TRIVET   a three-legged stand for a pot over a fire

VAMPLATE   conical hand protector on a lance

WATTLE   interlaced stakes or twigs used for fences, walls, or roofs